As a child, Fiona was constantly teased for two things: having her nose in a book and living in a dream world. Things haven't changed much since then, but at least she's found a career that puts her runaway imagination to use!

Fiona lives in London with her husband and two teenage daughters (oh, the *drama* in her house!), and she loves good books, good films and anything cinnamon flavoured. She also can't help herself if a good tune comes on and she's near a dance floor – you have been warned!

Fiona loves to hear from readers and you can contact her through her website fionaharper.com, her Facebook page (Fiona Harper Author) or Twitter (@FiHarper_Author).

The Other Us

FIONA HARPER

ONE PLACE. MANY STORIES

HQ
An imprint of HarperCollins*Publishers* Ltd.
1 London Bridge Street
London SE1 9GF

This edition 2017

4

First published in Great Britain by
HQ, an imprint of HarperCollins*Publishers* Ltd. 2017

978-0-00-821692-4
e-Book: 978-0-00-821693-1

Printed and bound by
CPI Group, Croydon CR0 4YY

For Andy

CHAPTER ONE

My first thought is that I am dead.

How strange, I think, as I lie very still, desperately trying not to open my eyes. Yesterday was such an ordinary day. I wasn't ill, as far as I was aware. I went to the supermarket, watched something really dull with Dan on the telly and then we argued and I went to bed alone.

Maybe that's it. Maybe I popped a blood vessel in my head while I was sleeping, from all the stress. Only that doesn't make sense. It was more of a grumpy tiff than a full-on, plate-throwing kind of row. After twenty-four years of marriage, Dan and I never do anything that involves that much energy – or passion – any more.

It vaguely occurs to me that if I'd known the previous evening was to be my last on earth that I really should have spent it doing something more interesting, something less middle-aged, like tango dancing with a brooding Latin stranger or watching the Northern Lights shimmer across the polar sky. Instead, I'd spent it in the sleepy commuter town of Swanham in Kent, watching an hour-long documentary on the life cycle of a cactus – Dan's choice.

Slightly disgusted with myself, and feeling more than a

little resentful towards my husband, I turn my thoughts back to the present.

I don't know how I know I'm dead. It's just that I had a sense as my conscious brain swam up from the murky depths of sleep of being somewhere entirely 'other'.

I heave in some much-needed oxygen, pulling it in through my nostrils. Odd. I've always thought heaven would smell nicer than this. You know, of beautiful flowers and pure, clean air, like you get on the top of a mountain.

Without meaning to, I move. There is a rustle and I freeze. Not because someone else is here and I'm suddenly aware of their presence, malevolent or otherwise, but because it sounded – and felt – suspiciously like bed sheets. For some reason this throws me.

As I remain still, listening to my pulse thudding in my ears, I start to contemplate the idea that maybe this place isn't as 'other' as I thought.

There's the sheets for one thing. And the fact that I seem to be lying on something that feels suspiciously like a mattress. As much as I get the sense that I'm not where I should be, not in my usual spot in the universe – lying next to Dan and pretending I can't hear his soft snores – there's also something familiar about this place. The smell of the air teases me, rich with memories that are just out of reach.

I really don't want to open my eyes, because that will make this real. I want this to be a dream, one of those really lucid ones. I'll tell Dan about it over breakfast and we'll laugh, last night's spat forgotten. But there's a part of me that knows this is different, that it's too real. More real than my normal life, even. I'm scared of that feeling.

It doesn't take long before I cave, though. It's just all too still, all too quiet.

I blink and try to focus on my surroundings. The first thing I experience is a wave of shock as I realise I'm right: I'm not at home in my own bed, Dan snuffling beside me. Then the second wave hits, and it's something much more scary – recognition.

I *know* this place!

I push the covers back and stand up, forgetting I don't really want to interact with this new reality, to give it any more credence than necessary.

The memories that were fuzzy and out of reach now become razor-sharp, rushing towards me, stabbing at me like a thousand tiny needles. I want to sit down, but there's nothing to catch me but a thinning and rather grubby carpet.

This is the flat I shared with Becca during my last year at university.

I stumble through the bedroom door and into the lounge. Yes. There's the faded green velour sofa and the seventies oval coffee table, which we'd thought was disgusting at the time but nowadays would fetch a pretty price at a vintage market.

Why am I here?

How am I here?

I turn into the little galley kitchen and spot the furred-up plastic kettle that produced the caffeine that fuelled Becca and me through our late-night essay-writing sessions, a kettle I had completely forgotten about but now seems as comforting and familiar as my childhood teddy bear. It's something to hang on to while I feel the rest of myself slipping away.

I press down the button at the base of the handle and when it actually clicks on I start to hiccup bursts of hysterical laughter. I have no idea why this is funny. To be honest, I'm starting to scare myself.

Breathe, Maggie, breathe.

I close my eyes and it helps. For a moment the room stops spinning. I try to pretend I'm not here, that I'm back at home. For a second I ache for my dull little life, then I force myself to think this through.

This can't be heaven, can it? My student digs? I flick that idea away and replace it with another one. My eyes open again. Maybe this isn't heaven. Maybe that's too much for a tiny human brain to handle right off the bat.

So maybe this is something else? A waiting room of sorts. Something familiar. Something pulled from my memory banks to help me feel at home.

I frown as I look at the broken chipboard cabinets. Fabulous work, Maggie. Great choice. Of all the places you've been in your life, this was the one that rose to the surface? I haven't travelled much, but what about Paris or that lovely beach in Minorca where we spent our tenth anniversary? Those had been pretty nice places. It must say something about me that I've subconsciously plumped for the grottiest place I'd ever lived. Or maybe it doesn't. Maybe I didn't choose it. Maybe the place you go to reflects what your life was like before you came here.

I can't decide which option is more depressing.

However, the decor might be dated, the windows so rotten they rattle in the slightest breeze, but, as I wander round, other memories start crowding in, stragglers that lope in late behind the initial onslaught.

It's weird experiencing a memory not only in the place it occurred but at the same *time* it occurred. The sensation takes my breath for a second, the recollection sharper and more colourful than it would be back in my little suburban semi with more than two decades insulating me from the moment.

I don't know how I can pinpoint it so precisely, but I know exactly where I am. *When* I am. It's the morning after the May Ball. Becca is out, having finally caught the eye of the one guy she's swooned over all through her drama course, and I'm in the flat all on my own. I remember waking up and just knowing that the world was full of possibilities and I was waiting at its threshold, one foot poised in the air, about to step into my future.

That's when I realise I know why I'm here, in this place, in this time.

Instead of freaking out about my surroundings, I start walking around again, looking at things, greeting them like old friends. Hello, drooping yucca that looks as if someone thought of the ugliest shape they could train you into and did just that. There is no beauty in your asymmetry, but I smile at you all the same. Hello, chunky VCR and impossibly cuboid television set that we watch *Dallas* and *Neighbours* on. Hello, mirrored Indian cushion cover that I bought from Kensington Market, which got ruined during a party when someone was sick on you. I've kind of missed you all these years, but now I realise you are really rather hideous.

I finish taking the tour and sit down on the sofa and start to wait. This is a waiting room, after all. That's when I notice what I'm wearing. A large, faded 'Choose Life' T-shirt, left over from my teenage years, which I'd kept as a nightshirt. I also notice my legs.

I start to laugh. No wonder I've come back here! Everything is tight and toned and less veiny than normal. I twist my legs this way and that to get a better look. I'd heard somewhere that people aren't old in heaven, that everyone's about thirty, but taking a good look at the bits I can see, I'd put myself closer to twenty.

I smile as I sit on the sofa, tapping my feet on the floor. But eventually the smile fades and the feet stop tapping.

OK, I think. *I'm acclimatised now. Come and get me.*

I wait for someone to appear, maybe my grandad or my cousin, who got taken out by breast cancer ten years ago. That's how this works, isn't it? But nobody comes, no one knocks on the door or floats through a wall.

I get fed up sitting on the sofa and head for the bathroom. That's the weirdest thing about being dead. I need to wee. Didn't think they'd bother with that in heaven. It's a bit of a disappointment to discover otherwise.

Anyway, I go into the bathroom and do what needs to be done, and it's only when I'm washing my hands that it occurs to me I could look in the mirror. So I do. Even though I'm half expecting to see my twenty-one-year-old self stare back at me, it's a shock when it happens.

God, that awful full fringe. I thought it made me look like Shannon what's-her-face from *Beverly Hills 90210*, but, in reality, I look more like Joan Crawford from *Mommie Dearest*.

I'm just drying my hands and wondering if I can find some celestial hair grips in this strange place, when I hear the front door bang.

'Heya!' a voice yells out. 'Only me!'

I try to answer but discover my throat has closed up.

Becca?

Oh, no. Oh, God. Becca! She's not dead too, is she? What a horrible, horrible coincidence! Both of us on the same day? We must have been in a car crash together. And both of us chose *this* as our waiting room?

That's when everything starts to slip and slide again. I hear her moving around in the lounge, dumping her stuff down, just as she'd done that morning after the ball.

'*Mags? You there?*' she shouts, and I know she's pulling her hair out of its usual ponytail and flopping down on the sofa. I nod, still unable to speak – still unable to move, actually – and stare back at myself in the mirror. I'm as white as a ghost, which would be funny under other circumstances.

Reality dashes over me like a bucket of ice water, and I know the next thought that enters my head to be the absolute and inalterable truth: *I'm not dead at all. And this definitely isn't heaven.*

CHAPTER TWO

One week earlier

I arrive at Bluewater, the huge triangular shopping centre sitting in the middle of a disused quarry just near the Dartford crossing. Becca and I have been meeting for a monthly shopping trip here for a couple of years now. We could take it in turns to go to each other's houses, I suppose, but she says, as much as she loves me, the coffee here is way better. And then there's the shopping. Becca loves shopping.

I head for our usual cafe and order a coffee. I could wait for Becca before I order, but I don't. Ever since I've known her, if we've arranged to get together, I'm always ten minutes early and she's always twenty minutes late. I know I should just adjust my arrival time and turn up late as well, but somehow I can't make myself do it.

I've just reached the silky froth at the bottom of my cup when Becca arrives – an uncharacteristic ten minutes before her usual time – and collapses into the chair opposite me. She has a collection of shopping bags with her: things she needs to return to Coast and Karen Millen that she picked up on our last shopping outing and has decided don't suit her. I also have something to return, but it's a shower curtain that needs to go back to John Lewis.

'Shall we get a table outside?' she asks, after scanning the restaurant. 'The weather's glorious.'

I sigh inwardly, reach for my bags and stand up. Becca always does this. It doesn't matter where I choose to sit, she always wants to move to a better spot. I wouldn't mind so much but I specifically chose this table because it's the one she wanted to move to last time.

Becca is practically glowing. I haven't been able to take my eyes off her since she walked through the door, and since a few male heads turn as we move tables, I guess I'm not the only one.

She's the same sort of size as me: slightly overweight, with the usual forty-something bulges and curves, but somehow she wears it better. I bought some long boots like hers in the sales last year, but every time I try them on I just end up peeling them off again. I wanted to see a stylish, mature woman staring back at me in the mirror, but all I could see was pantomime pirate. They've sat in their box at the back of my wardrobe since January.

'You look nice today,' I tell her once we've relocated. I usually greet people with a compliment, but today it isn't an automatic response pulled from my mental library at random.

Becca grins back at me. 'Thanks! I'm feeling great, too.'

I can't help smiling with her. If happiness is a disease, it's about time Becca caught it. For a long time I thought her lousy ex had inoculated her against it. 'I take it things are going well with the new man?'

'Pretty good,' she says, and orders a coffee from a passing waiter. It's very odd. Becca used to gush endlessly about her latest squeeze when we were younger, but she's being a bit cagey about this one. The only thing I can think of is that it's because this is the first proper romance since her divorce. 'We might get away for a weekend soon. If he can work out getting time away from ... I mean, getting time off.' She looks down at the table again, but I see her secret smile.

'It sounds as if it's getting serious.'

Becca flushes. 'I know. Ridiculous, really. I mean, it's early days and we've only been seeing each other a couple of months and I really should be dating and having fun, but he's just so amazing.'

I want to jump in and tell her that, while I understand how wonderful this is for her, how I'm truly pleased she's happy again, maybe she shouldn't leap into this relationship quite as hard and quite as fast as she has done all her others – but the words keep tumbling out of her in a breathless stream, as if, instead of filing up neatly behind one another to make sensible sentences, they're all racing each other to see who can get out first, and I can't get a word in edgewise.

The gushing carries on as we leave the cafe. She instinctively heads in the direction of her favourite shops and I trail along with her while my shower curtain gets heavier and heavier. I mention this after we've dropped off both her returns.

'Of course,' she responds, but then, when we've turned tail and are heading back towards John Lewis, we pass Hobbs. She gives me a sugary smile. 'You don't mind if we pop in here, do you? It'll only take a minute, and they had this gorgeous blouse that'd be perfect for work now the weather's finally turned warmer …'

I shake my head, but after Hobbs it's Laura Ashley and then it's Massimo Dutti.

I honestly don't know if she does this on purpose, or whether her memory is really goldfish-short. There are times at the end of our shopping trips where Becca has had to dash off again and I've had to stay behind to do the essential errand she promised we'd get round to an hour earlier.

This makes her sound like a horrible friend, but really she isn't. She's had a tough time in the last couple of years. Her ex, Grant, turned out to be a manipulative, controlling creep. I always worried he hit her, but she always denied it. Even so, it took her far too long to muster up the courage to leave him, which she did eighteen months ago.

He hardly let her out his sight, our shopping trips being one of the few exceptions, and the least I could do then was to let her have some power and control over what she did for a few hours. I suppose we've just fallen into a pattern now, one that's hard for me to change without bringing it up and sounding whiney.

Becca is a theatre manager now and as we shop she gives me an in-depth report on the antics of a well-known soap star who was appearing in the play that was on last week. My shoulder develops a nagging little niggle from the weight of my John Lewis carrier bag.

At first I'm nodding and smiling at her blow-by-blow account of his excessive vodka-drinking to get over his opening-night nerves but, funny as it is, after a while, I start to tune out. I mean, we've been talking about her stuff since we sat down for cappuccinos and it hasn't even occurred to her to ask if anything much is going on in my life, even if I do usually just wave the question away and say, 'Oh, just the same old same old …'

But today I do have something to say. Something big. Or at least I think I might. I really can't work out if I'm just being silly, and I could do with a friend to help me sift through the facts and sort out the truth from the muddy paranoia.

But Becca is too full of 'glow' to notice the worry in my eyes. She just barrels on. It's only after I've hauled my shower curtain onto the sales desk in John Lewis's homeware department (and almost kissed the sales lady for taking it off my hands), and completed the transaction, that she finds a new topic.

'Did you see that thing on Facebook?'

I'm tucking my returns receipt back into my purse. When I finish I look at her, frowning slightly. 'What thing?'

'The reunion. Oaklands College. Some of the guys are planning a get-together, seeing as it's twenty-five years since we graduated.'

Even though, logically, I know this is how long it's been since I left university, the fact slaps me in the face, waking me up. Twenty-five years … a rapid slideshow of my life starts to play inside my head. I'm horrified to see how many slots are filled with black and white images of my routine suburban life or – even worse – empty.

'Where is it? Who's going?' I ask, feeling slightly dazed.

'On campus, I think someone said, and only a few people have responded so far. The post only went up yesterday.'

I nod. There's not much else I've got to say on the subject.

Becca leads the way back out of the shop and turns in the direction of the food court. I'm pretty sure that's where she's heading, even though she hasn't said anything. Shopping always makes her hungry.

As we walk she turns to look at me carefully. 'Do you think you'll go?'

I shrug. 'Probably not.'

'Really? I thought it'd be fun to see the old crowd.'

Of course you would, I say in my head. You're happy. You look great. You're *glowing*. Even if I'm curious about what everyone looks like and what they are doing now, I'm not sure I want that same inquisitiveness directed back at me.

What will they see? I haven't become anything interesting or 'grown into' myself with age. If anything, I feel all that potential and passion I'd had in my twenties has been slowly diluted until I'm now a watery version of who I once was. I don't want to turn up, have to chat to people with a plastic goblet full of warm sauvignon, and see the look of vague recognition in my university mates' eyes before they smile nicely and move on to someone more interesting.

I shake my head. 'Oh, I don't know. It seems like such a lot of effort for something that was such a long time ago.'

'You're not even curious about Jude Hansen?'

At the mention of that name my pulse jumps. I make very sure it doesn't show on my face. I pretend I'm too busy navigating round a young mum dawdling with a pushchair to answer.

Becca, however, doesn't seem to want to let it go, which

is odd, as she never really liked Jude. 'Word is he's done very well for himself.'

I straighten my spine and keep looking straight ahead. 'I really wouldn't know.'

There's a part of me that wants to turn and scream at her to shut up, but there's also another contrary part that is willing her to keep talking. It's like a scab that's not quite ripe for picking. I know I should leave it alone, that it'll only sting and bleed, but part of me wants both the pain and the satisfaction of pulling it off and knowing what's really underneath.

I deliberately haven't thought of Jude Hansen for more than twenty-four years. I looked at myself in the mirror the morning of my wedding day and told myself that door was closed.

'So what do you think? Shall we go?' She nudges me as we start to peruse the chiller cabinets of the sushi place. I make a show of looking, even though I know I'm going to pick the salmon bento box. I always do.

She joins the queue, leaving me to file in behind her. 'It'll be a right laugh. You'll see ...'

I'm really irritated that she's acting as if I've already agreed, as if my role in life is just to trail around behind her and do whatever she wants. I realise that as much as I moan about having a husband who's so laid-back he just 'goes with the flow' about everything, I've chosen a best friend who is the complete opposite and I don't always like this end of the spectrum much either.

'Come on, aren't you even curious?' she asks once we've found some seats. 'You and Jude were quite a hot item at one time, if I remember rightly ...'

The penny drops then. For some reason she really wants to go to this stupid reunion and she's using Jude as leverage because she wants me to go with her.

Maybe it's because my shoulder is still twanging from carrying that shower curtain round for an hour longer than I'd wanted but I find I don't want to be nice, accommodating, doormat Maggie any more. 'Not really …' I say, feigning indifference just as well as Becca has been doing. 'It's ancient history and I honestly don't care in the slightest what Jude Hansen is doing now.'

Becca eats her chicken katsu curry sulkily after that. Normally, I'd stay silent for a couple of minutes then start to chat to her, win her round, but today I stay quiet. Let her offer the olive branch for once.

I know this spells the end of our shopping trip. When we finish we throw our rubbish away and head outside, and when we pause to say our goodbyes before heading off to our respective cars, Becca looks sheepishly at me. 'Sorry if I was being pushy … I just got a bit excited about the idea, that's all.' She looks hopefully at me. 'Are you *sure* you don't want to go?'

I shake my head.

'You won't even think about it?'

I laugh. Even when Becca is trying not to be so … Becca … she can't help herself. 'OK, OK, I'll think about it.' Usually, I employ this tactic to shut her up. I just say yes to whatever she's pushing for to keep the peace then wriggle out of it later, but I discover as I drive home back to Swanham that I was telling the truth. I can't think about anything else – any*one* else – all afternoon.

CHAPTER THREE

The house is quiet when I get back. Too quiet. I've got used to Sophie being around during the day after her A levels had finished – leaving her lunch plate on the arm of the sofa, the chart songs drifting from her bedroom upstairs, her soft laughter as she watched something on YouTube with her headphones in – but now she's off backpacking with her friends before uni. Well, when I say backpacking, I mean in the UK. They're somewhere near Fort William, exploring the Highlands at the moment. I said no to haring all over Europe for two months. She's only just turned eighteen.

I feel as if I've got too much time on my hands now she's not here. I find myself wandering round the house, looking at the empty spaces, wondering what I should be doing next.

Maybe I should ask for extra hours at work? I have a part-time job in a soft furnishings shop on the High Street. I gave up my career as a graphic designer when Sophie was born. Too many all-nighters to meet deadlines and things like that. It was nice to be here when she got home from school most days, even when she was old enough to take care of herself, and Dan's money as an English teacher isn't bad. We might not have had as many foreign holidays as some, but we've never gone short.

But when I think of doing full days at the shop my spirit sinks. I like my job, I do. It's comfortable, like a pair of shoes worn in just right, but up until now I've been telling myself it's just something to keep the money coming in while Sophie needed me. I don't want it to define me.

I realise I've wandered through the hall, into the lounge and I'm standing in front of the mantelpiece. I'm staring at a picture of Sophie taken at her school prom. She looks elegant and happy, her warm-brown hair blown back away from her face by a playful breeze.

My eyes glaze for a second then refocus, and when I do it's not Sophie I'm looking at in the picture, but myself. How I once was. Full of hope and ambition, optimism and bravado. A sense of loss engulfs me, but whether it's because of my empty nest or for something deeper and long-standing, I'm not sure.

I go and get my mobile out of my handbag and dial Sophie's number, even though I suspect she's halfway up a mountain or in a valley with no coverage.

Much to my surprise, she picks up. 'Hey, mum! What's up?'

'Oh, nothing,' I say. 'Just wanted to see if you're keeping warm and eating alright.'

Just wanted to hear your voice because I'm not sure how I'm going to survive the next three years without you.

I hide the catch in my breath and realise I should have bought flowers while I was out – white lilies. Beautiful, waxy lilies that would fill the empty spaces in this house with their pure, white scent.

Sophie, however, on the other end of the line, chuckles. 'I'm in Scotland, Mum, not the wilds of Antarctica, and it's summer! They've got shops and beds and restaurants, you know. I'm absolutely fine!'

'I know,' I say softly. A selfish part of me wishes she'd sound a little bit less carefree. Just a little.

'Anyway, gotta go! Love you, Mum!'

'Love you too,' I say back, but the line has already gone dead by the time I reach the last syllable.

I stare at the phone then decide to tuck it into my back pocket rather than putting it back in my handbag. It'll be like I'm carrying Sophie around with me. I look at the clock. It's only two. Another four hours until Dan gets home and I can tell him about the call. That's our main topic of conversation these days – Sophie and what she's up to – an oasis in the barren landscape of our communication.

I wander into the kitchen, put the kettle on, then decide I don't actually want a cup of tea. I see my laptop sitting on the kitchen table and I sit down and turn it on. On automatic I log into Facebook. I spend a lot of time on Facebook, keeping up with what other people are doing with their lives.

I pretend to myself I'm just tinkering around for a while, reading a few updates from my cousin, liking some pictures of friends who've been out on the town, but eventually I cave and search for the reunion page. I find it almost instantly. There are comments from people I know. I don't 'like' or 'join' but I do read.

One post in particular catches my attention: *Hot guys: where are they now?* I read down the comment thread. There are the predictable mentions of the college sporting gods and star drama students, but halfway down, snuggled in between the rest, I spot something:

Claire Rutt:

Anyone remember Jude Hansen?

Sam Broughton (was Stanley):

No? What subject did he do?

Claire Rutt:

Business Studies, I think …

Nadia Pike:

Ooh, yes! I remember him! Lovely dark hair and blue eyes. Not muscly, but definite eye candy! Wonder if he'll turn up?

Claire Rutt:

Sigh. Probably not. Wasn't much of a joiner, unless you had a double-barrelled name and daddy owned a yacht … I doubt he'd be interested in a poxy reunion populated with middle-class soccer mums and civil servants.

Sam Broughton (was Stanley):

Hey, watch yourself! Not only does Jack play football, but I work for the local council! Nothing poxy about me, thank you.

Claire Rutt:

:-p

Sam Broughton (was Stanley):

Anyway, pity. This Jude person was just starting to sound
interesting! I'm single again, you know, and on the lookout for
hubby no.3! ;-)

Claire Rutt:

Not the settling-down type, I'd say. I'd heard he's quite the jet-
setter now, though, so if you like a challenge …

I stop reading then. My stomach is swirling and I feel like
I'm snooping, even though this is a public conversation on an
open group. I close the browser window down and shut the
lid of my laptop. After a few seconds staring at the kitchen
cabinets, which I notice could really do with a good scrub, I
open it up again.

I don't go back to the reunion page; instead, I just type
'Jude' into the Facebook search box. A list of options turn
up, none of them him. I hold my breath and add 'Hansen'.

Nothing.

There's Joseph Hansen, but he's eighteen and living
in Montana. And a Julian Hansen who's a professor of
philosophy, with grey hair and a kind smile, but he's not my
Hansen.

No. Jude's not my Hansen. Never was, really.

I feel as if I've stepped over a line by this point, but instead
of creeping back behind it I start sprinting forward. I pull up

a search engine and enter those two names again, whispering them in my head as if they're a secret.

There are no images that relate, but I do find reference to a Jude Hansen mentioned in an article about high-end estate agents, but when I search the name of the firm I discover the website is down for temporary maintenance. In full Sherlock Holmes-mode now, I go back to the article and spot the name of a photographer connected with his – something to do with either selling or finding her a house, possibly both. I search her name and 'house', and I get another set of results. Two pages down I see a fuzzy picture, from Twitter, I think. It's a housewarming party and in the background there's someone who looks very much like the Jude I used to know, but it's difficult to tell, because it's out of focus and the photographer's finger is over the corner of the shot.

I sit back and stare at the screen, screwing my eyes up a little to see if that helps, but it just makes everything blurrier. I imagine it's him anyway.

So he did do well for himself, just as Becca said. And then I mentally whisper possibly the two most dangerous words in the English language:

What if …?

I'd never told anyone this, not even Becca, but the day Dan proposed to me – after we were back in one of our regular, college drinking holes, had shared the news and everybody was buying rounds and congratulating us – Jude had found me and asked me for a quiet word in the pub garden. Even though it was July, we'd had the place to ourselves because it had been hammering down. I still remember the scent of warm soil when I think of that moment.

He'd stared at me in the glow of the security light, more serious than I'd ever seen him. 'Don't ...' he'd said.

I'd frowned. 'Don't what?'

'Don't marry him.'

I'd stared at him then, wondering what on earth was going through his head. Didn't he remember that he'd been the one who'd pulled back and cooled off? 'What? And marry you instead?'

'Yes! I mean, no ...' He'd scrubbed his hand through his floppy dark hair and looked at me with unguarded honesty, a strange look on him, because he'd always been so careful to develop an air of knowingness.

My heart had begun to pound hard, just as it had when Dan had pulled a small velvet box from his pocket down by the river earlier the same evening.

Jude had cleared his throat and started again. 'I mean ... what I'm trying to say is that I think I made a horrible mistake.'

He'd looked at me, willing me to fill in the gaps, but I'd held my ground. Not this time. If he had something to say he was going to have to be clear about it. I had to know for sure. He'd taken in my silence and nodded.

'I think I love you,' he'd said. 'And I think it might destroy me if you marry him.' He'd screwed up his face and I'd known him well enough to know he was wrestling with whether to say something else. Finally, he'd added, 'And I think it might destroy you too.'

As fast as my pulse had been skipping, I'd raised my eyebrows, waiting for more.

He'd shaken his head. 'You're right. *Destroy* is much too dramatic. What I mean is – ' He'd broken off to capture both my hands in his. 'I don't think he's what you need, Meg.'

Meg. He was the only person who'd called me that. I pause for a moment just to run my mind over that fact, like fingers reading braille.

'And you are?' I'd asked him.

He'd given me that look again. 'I'd like to try to be.'

I'd shaken my head, more in disbelief than because I was refusing him. 'But you're supposed to be going off to France next – '

'Come with me.'

I'd frozen then, brain on overload, unable to process anything more. 'I can't,' I'd said, pulling my hands from his, and I'd backed away. It would be more romantic, I suppose, to say that I'd stumbled away from him, overcome by emotion, but I don't remember it that way at all. I remember my steps being quite precise and deliberate.

That was the last time I saw Jude Hansen. I'd left him there in the rain. I'd had to.

I close my eyes and concentrate on pausing the memory, like hitting a button on a TV remote, and then I file it away carefully again behind lock and key.

Jude had always had the potential to do well, but that had only been one side of the coin. He could also be a little bit arrogant, thinking his way was the only way, and he hadn't responded well to authority. There had been a restless energy about him. I'm glad he's harnessed it, made it work for him.

We'd got together the first year I was at uni, in the spring. I'd known Dan, too, but back then he'd been firmly in the 'friend zone', as Sophie would say.

Jude and I had a wild and romantic couple of months, where we'd hardly left each other's side, then the three-month summer break had happened. Dominic, his best mate at uni, had parents who owned a villa in the south of France but I'd come home to Swanham and spent my summer working as a barmaid. I should have known then things weren't going to work out. While Jude's family weren't too different from mine – his dad was a builder too – he'd always wanted more. The rest of his college girlfriends had been leggy and gorgeous, part of the rich crowd.

I was utterly devoted to him, and time apart only cemented those feelings. When I'd spotted him across the Student's Union the first day of autumn term, I'd had one of those moments that you see in the movies, where I'd been suddenly sure that I loved him, but it seemed the separation hadn't had the same effect on Jude. We'd continued to see each other, but it had felt … different. More casual. I wondered if there was someone else. Or several someone elses. Dominic had a rather attractive sister … But I'd never found any evidence of infidelity, so I'd continued to follow him round like an adoring puppy.

I think he'd liked the adulation. He probably should have weaned himself off it and cut me loose long before he did, but eventually he sat me down and explained he thought we were too young to tie ourselves down.

I'd agreed. We were. It was stupid to get attached, to think I'd found the person I'd be happy with for the rest of my life. I'd told myself I'd needed to grow up, be a little bit more sophisticated.

But then six months later, I'd got together with Dan. He'd liked me since Freshers' Week, he'd said. You'd have thought I'd be gun-shy after Jude, that I wouldn't have wanted to throw myself into something serious so soon, but I wasn't. Somehow I'd just known Dan was a safe bet.

Dan.

I look up at the clock on the kitchen wall. Flip! Where has the time gone? He'll be home soon. I quickly turn my laptop off and shove it on the Welsh dresser, covering it with a cookery book and some takeaway leaflets that came through the door. I start washing up, just to keep myself occupied and I don't even notice what I'm cleaning because I'm staring out of the window.

Dan, a safe bet?

After twenty-four years of marriage, I'm just starting to realise I might have been wrong about that.

CHAPTER FOUR

The door slams about half an hour later, when I'm upstairs in the bathroom, and I come down to see Dan's coat thrown in the direction of the rack and his shoes kicked off, clogging up the hallway. I've been nagging him about that for as long as we've lived together. I don't know how many times I've almost broken a bone tripping over them. I pick them up and tuck them into the Ikea unit I bought specifically for them, which is populated by lots of my shoes and none of his, and then I go into the kitchen.

'Hi,' he says and plants a kiss on my cheek.

It's a nice thing to do, I suppose, and for a long time I knew he did it because he was happy to see me at the end of the day; now I suspect it's just habit.

'You'll never guess what?' I say. 'Oaklands is having a reunion. I saw it on Facebook.' I shut my mouth quickly. I hadn't intended to say that. I was going to tell him about Sophie.

Dan raises his eyebrows in interest as he fills the kettle, and I realise that now I've opened this can of worms I'm just going to have to carry on. I reel off the names of people in the Facebook group I remember. Jude's name is on the tip of my tongue and I have to keep leapfrogging over it.

I'm usually a nice person. I try to get along with everyone, not to be bitchy or mean-spirited, but I'm aware there's a part of me that actually wants to blurt Jude's name out, just to see how Dan reacts. But I don't. I keep the words inside my head.

It's getting a bit crowded in there now with all the things I want to say but never do. I worry that one day my brain will get too full and all the things I've thought but don't want Dan to know will come tumbling out.

Thinking of things I don't want Dan to know, I feel my cheeks growing hot. I closed my laptop ages ago, but I've been thinking about Jude all afternoon. Not that last time we spoke, but other things: the way he used to kiss, how he could make me melt just by looking at me. I can't quite look my husband straight in the eye now.

He gets a pair of mugs out the cupboard then turns to face me. 'Do you want to go?'

I open my mouth and stop. I realise I have no answer. I've been so busy living in a slightly steamy fantasy all afternoon, I haven't considered it. 'Do *you*?'

He shrugs. 'Not fussed. Whatever you want to do.' And then he turns back and carries on making the tea.

I want to scream at him. I know it sounds lovely having a husband who's accommodating about everything, but sometimes I think it's just a ruse so all the decision-making is left to me. I'm tired, weighed down by the responsibility of a thousand tiny things: what to eat for dinner each night, which car we buy, what colour to paint the living room and which restaurant to visit on the odd occasion we eat out. Maybe that's why I let Becca lead me round by the nose? On some level, it's a relief.

Dan hands me a mug of tea – he always makes me one when he comes in from work – and then he heads off towards the hallway. 'Just going to go up to the study and do some … you know … marking. On the computer. What time's dinner?'

Now, this might sound like an ordinary domestic conversation, but it isn't. Dan isn't making eye contact and it all came out in a bit of a rush. I look carefully at him.

'We're having pasta … probably around seven.'

'Cool.' He turns and head upstairs with his cup of tea.

Half an hour later, I go to the box room above the hallway that we've always used as a study, seeing as that second baby never did come along. I don't knock. Dan looks startled and he quickly closes down a window on the screen. Just text, no pictures. It didn't look like a web page, I don't think, but it was definitely something he didn't want me to see.

'What you up to?' I ask breezily.

'Oh, just some marking,' Dan says, without looking round. 'By the way, I thought I'd let you know I'm getting together with Sam – you remember Sam Macmillan? We went to school together? – on Thursday evening. We're going out for a pint so I might be back a bit late.' His tone is light but there's a tension lying underneath it that stretches his words tight.

My insides go cold.

I know Sam Macmillan. I'm friends with his wife Geraldine on Facebook. And I know for a fact that they're away celebrating their twentieth wedding anniversary in Prague this week, because I've been gradually going green with envy seeing all the holiday snaps and still-so-in-love selfies.

'OK,' I say as I reach for his mug and retreat. I feel shivery inside as I head back down the stairs. I leave the mug on the kitchen table instead of putting it in the dishwasher and I stare out the French windows that lead to our small and slightly overgrown garden.

This is it, then.

Before now it's just been a feeling, a sense that something isn't right. That's what I was going to tell Becca about today. Now I have something concrete.

I pick up my mobile and open the door to the garden, dial my best friend's number. I know it's usually all about Becca when we get together, but just for ten minutes I really, really need it to be about me.

'It could be nothing,' Becca says firmly. 'It could be something really innocent.'

I take a moment to weigh her words. 'Was it innocent when Grant kept turning his phone off the moment he walked through the door so he didn't get any calls he couldn't explain, or when you discovered he had an email account you didn't know about?'

Becca sighs. 'No. I wanted to believe it was, but it wasn't.'

We're both silent as we process the implication of what I've just told her – about Dan's behaviour growing more secretive over the last couple of months. How he's spending more and more time in the study. How he often shuts down what he's doing if I enter. How he keeps meeting up with friends he hasn't seen in years, but only every other Thursday night.

I close my eyes. I don't want to go through this. I don't want to be pulled apart at the seams, like Becca was throughout the discovery of her husband's infidelity and their subsequent divorce. I don't want Sophie to come from a broken home, even though she's technically a grown-up now. She worships her father, even though she teases him about being a boring old fart. I don't want her to have to know this.

Could I? Could I just close my eyes and pretend this isn't happening?

'What are you going to do?' Becca asks, interrupting my thoughts.

My throat is suddenly swollen and I need to swallow before I can push any words out of my mouth. 'I don't know.'

I expect Becca to get all post-divorce militant on me, tell me to deck him one or go and take my best dressmaking scissors to his suits; but instead, she exhales loudly and says, 'Oh, Mags …'

That's when the tears start to fall. I wipe them away quickly with the heel of my hand. I don't want Dan to know I've been crying when I go back inside. Stupid, I know. Why does this little secret even matter when there are much bigger ones eating away at the heart of our marriage?

'You'll get through this,' Becca says, and her voice is both soft and full of confidence. 'I know you will.' We say our goodbyes, with Becca telling me to call her, day or night, if I need her.

I stand in the garden, watching the sun go down, and

imagine her faith in me to be real. I let my mind play out what surely must be coming: the inevitable tears and accusations. The confession. Dan moving out. I fast-forward over it all, just alighting briefly on the main scenarios, then imagine what it'll be like if I ever get to where Becca is now: stronger, happier, freer.

Maybe I'll find a wonderful new man too.

My mind quickly drifts back to where it's been going all afternoon: Jude.

Maybe we'll meet again at the reunion. It'll be too soon then, of course, too fresh and raw, but we'll chat. We'll keep in touch. He'll text me now and again, just when I'm feeling most down. And then one day I'll find him on my doorstep with a big bunch of flowers and I'll just know I'm finally ready to have my own 'glow'. Dan will be nothing but a distant memory.

I sigh, wishing it could be true, that I could jump forward to that moment in reality, not just in my mind, and that I wouldn't have to experience all the in-between bits.

Don't be silly, I tell myself. Things don't happen just because you wish them, and I put my phone to sleep and walk back inside the house to cook Dan's tea.

We sit eating our pasta. Neither of us has much to say. Dan keeps his focus on his plate most of the time, hoovering up the large portion I gave him – extra cheese on top – and while he eats, I look at him. I wonder who this is, who my husband has become.

You never really knew how to reach me, I tell him in my

head. *I always thought you'd figure it out some day, but now you're not even trying. You're probably too busy trying to 'reach' into some other woman's knickers.*

I chew my pasta and wish I'd cooked something that makes more of a crunch. Another thought creeps up on me, and then another and another.

What if it's not just sex?

What if he's falling in love with someone else?

What if he knows how to reach *her*, this mystery woman he must talk to on the computer?

Then I'll rip his chest open with my bare hands and kill him.

The force of my rage stops me cold. I put down my fork.

I'm shocked. I thought my love for Dan was comfortable, like a bath you're not quite ready to get out of, even though it's well on its way to lukewarm. I didn't know there was enough left to prompt such fury.

I get up and scrape my food into the composting bin, then dump my plate in the dishwasher.

'Are you OK?' Dan asks, pausing from his pasta-shovelling marathon.

My face feels so stiff I'm surprised I can answer. 'Why do you ask?'

'You didn't finish your pasta,' he says, his mouth still half full. I want to reach over and slap it closed. 'It's your favourite.'

No! I scream silently inside my head. *It's* your *favourite. Why can't you ever remember that?*

'Wasn't hungry,' I say, then I leave the room. I want to slam the door but I don't. I might as well have done, I suppose, because, a second later, Dan yells after me, 'What the bloody hell have I done now?'

CHAPTER FIVE

What if …? becomes an itch I can't stop scratching. As the days roll by, I find myself thinking about Jude all the time. In my mind he has mellowed with age, lost some of that youthful arrogance but is still ruggedly good-looking. He wears cashmere coats and Italian shoes, I imagine, as I kick Dan's muddy trainers towards the shoe tidy and hang his windbreaker on a hook.

Safe bet? Hah! I put all my chips on Dan and yet he's wasted almost a quarter of a century of my life. I think I hate him for it.

I haven't done any more digging into his secrets, although I know I should. I won't ask him if he's banging one of the perky PE teachers at school and he's not asking me if anything is wrong, even though we've hardly said more than a handful of words to each other in the last few days. I feel like I'm in a fog; everything is fuzzy and boring and grey. The only sharp thoughts in my mind are the ones I conjure up about Jude. Those are colourful and sweet and juicy. I want to live in that place, not even thinking about Dan. I am an ostrich and my head is firmly down the hole of my fantasies.

Becca comes into town on Dan's 'Thursday night with Sam

Macmillan' and we go for drinks. 'Come on …' she says, as we install ourselves at a table in the Three Compasses. 'We've talked about it, now I think we just ought to do it!'

'I told you,' I say wearily. 'I'm *not* following Dan. It would just be too … sad.'

I don't want to be that desperate woman. I want to be her even less than I want to be a slowing fading, middle-aged empty nester, and that's saying something.

'Not Dan!' she says, although she looks ready to be persuaded if I changed my mind. 'I was talking about the reunion – it's next week. Next Friday. Let's go.'

'On our own? What about Dan?'

Becca shrugs. 'Someone mentioned in the Facebook group that they'd invited Jude.'

I study my large glass of Pinot Grigio. 'Really?' I haven't told Becca about how he's hijacked my every waking thought since we last talked of the reunion. It's strange, I think. Becca tells me everything – Sophie calls her 'the Queen of TMI' – but there's a lot I don't tell Becca. I didn't tell her about Jude asking me to run away with him, not back at the time and not even now. I also didn't tell her I almost packed a bag and tried to track him down three days before my wedding.

'You never liked Jude.'

She gives me a little one-sided shrug. 'Maybe I was wrong about him. I was wrong about Grant, and we both might be wrong about Dan.' I see her eyes glaze over and her jaw harden. She's deep in thought. 'Bastard …' she mutters, shaking her head. 'Just when I was starting to think not all men were cheating lizards, as well.'

I reach over and lay my hand on hers to comfort her, which seems topsy turvy but I get it. I haven't been properly happy with Dan for five years. Maybe ten. But while Becca was stuck in her lousy marriage, she always held Dan up as the pinnacle of everything a good husband should be. She's acting as if he's let her down too. I don't know if she's ever going to forgive him for it.

'Anyway, I think we ought to go.'

I take a long sip of wine to give myself time to think. 'I really don't know … Even if he's there, he might just swan past me with his fabulous, ex-model wife. Or worse, he might not even remember me!'

'You don't know he has an ex-model for a wife,' Becca says dryly, then her eyes twinkle with mischief. 'You don't even know he has a wife!'

'You've lost your mind,' I tell her. Not because she's suggesting a bit of payback with my first love. Because she seriously thinks 'done well for himself' Jude would be even remotely interested in me these days.

'Come on, Mags. This is *you* we're talking about. You won't be doing anything wrong. It's not like you're going to drag him out of there, get a room and have your wicked way with him, is it?'

While, technically, I know it will all be tame and above board if I bump into Jude at the reunion, I'm also aware how out of control my fantasy life has become in recent days. In my head I've done just what Becca said. Every time I think of it, my heart starts to race and I catch my breath. I feel like a teenager in the grip of her first boy-band crush. It doesn't feel like 'not doing anything wrong'. It feels as if I've already crossed a line I shouldn't have done. I start to wonder if people who say that fantasises are harmless really know what they're talking about.

A voice whispers in my head, *Dan's already crossed that line. Why not?*

I don't know that for sure, I reply.

Only because you're too much of a coward to find out, the voice jeers.

I don't have an answer for that, so I tune back into Becca on the other side of the table. 'Please come with me, Mags?' she says softly. 'I really want to go.' She shakes her head. 'Stupid, really. I feel it's something I need to do to put some of these ghosts behind me.'

I feel my resolve gently slipping. 'Can't New Guy go with you?'

She shakes her head, but doesn't elaborate. 'I really don't want to walk into the room all by myself. It's just … I'm not the same since Grant. He knocked my confidence.'

I know that. I'd watched, stood by helpless, as I'd seen him rob her of it bit by bit, unable to do anything but be a listening ear until she was ready to leave him and move on. I thought she'd done just that. I thought she'd bounced back.

I suck air in through my nostrils then puff it back out again. 'OK. I'll go.'

Becca lets out a huge sigh of relief and that's when I realise this is what the constant badgering for me to go has been about all along. I feel awful I didn't realise that before.

'That's it, then,' she says, draining her glass. 'It's decided.'

When we've polished the rest of the bottle off, we book a cab to take me home and then drop Becca at the station and I give her an extra big hug.

'Love you,' she says and hugs me before I scramble out the car.

'Love you too,' I reply huskily, and then I close the door and watch the mini-cab drive away.

When I get back inside the hall light is still off. I dump my handbag on top of the shoe tidy and trudge upstairs, then I get into my pyjamas, slide between the cold sheets and try not to wonder why my husband isn't home yet.

Dan and I don't talk about it when we get up the next morning. I remember waking at 11.30pm and the bed was still empty, then again at 2am and he was there.

We waltz around each other in a practised dance as we have our breakfast – me passing him a knife from the drawer before he asks, him handing me the milk out the fridge so I can splash some in my tea. It's odd that we know each other's movements so well we can do this without thinking, while another part of me is wondering if I've ever known him at all.

We don't talk about it in the evening either. Instead, we watch *The One Show*. When it's finished Dan turns over to BBC Two. He doesn't look at me, doesn't ask if I mind, so I have to sit in silence and try to be interested in cacti for the next hour. By the time the credits roll, I never want to see another of the spiky little suckers in the whole of my life. 'That's an hour I'll never get back,' I mutter.

Dan clicks the TV off and turns his head to look at me. 'If you didn't want to watch it, you could have said.'

'You could have asked. Once upon a time, you would have. Not just assumed. Not just taken it for granted.'

He frowns. 'Bloody hell, Maggie. I told you I would have turned over.'

I shake my head. He just doesn't get it. 'You never think about what makes me happy any more.'

Dan lets out an incredulous laugh. 'How did we get from a stupid TV programme to *this*?'

I exhale and look away. Oh, for a man you didn't have to explain everything to with brightly coloured flash cards! We've been together for close to twenty-five years. He should know me by now. Suddenly, I'm very angry that he doesn't.

That was the unspoken promise on our wedding day, I'd thought. That we'd grow old together, mesh our souls so tightly that we'd finish each other's sentences, share that weird kind of telepathy I'd seen between my grandparents before they'd died. But Dan has never once completed a sentence of mine, and I seem to have to explain myself to him more than ever nowadays.

You were supposed to at least try, I wail inside my head. *That was the deal.*

I will him to understand me, but after looking at me for a few seconds, he huffs, picks up his half-empty mug and leaves the room. I slump down on my end of the sofa and cross my arms. Part of me hasn't got the energy to knock this into his thick skull; the other half wants to follow him and pick a fight.

I collect my mug, swill down the last of my cold decaf and head for the kitchen, where I let him know, at volume, just where he can put his effing muddy shoes.

CHAPTER SIX

1992

I stare at my face in the bathroom mirror. The young me.
The *wrong* me.

'Maggie!' Becca calls again. 'Are you there?'

I hear her walking into the kitchen, looking for me,
probably. If I remember rightly, she has some juicy gossip to
deliver about her night with Stevo Watts and she won't want
to wait. I screw my face up and close my eyes. No. That's
wrong. How can this be? How can I be here, now, and still
... remembering. It's not possible.

I turn the tap on and splash the cold water on my face,
hoping it'll wake me up, but all it does is cause freezing
droplets to run down my neck. I shiver.

What do I do? This can't be real. Can it?

'Margaret Alison Greene!' Becca yells, doing a passable
imitation of my mother when she's in a snit. It's not quite
perfect, though, because I can hear a smile in her voice. My
bedroom door squeaks as she continues her sweep of the flat.
I realise I can't stay here in the bathroom, hiding. Eventually
she's going to find me.

'Maggie?' she calls and this time the smile is gone. Her footsteps get faster.

Don't think about it, I tell myself. *There'll be time for answers later.*

I nod at my reflection and notice that the young girl looks tense and serious, much more like the woman I'm used to seeing in the mirror, then I dry my face, take a deep breath and walk out into the hallway. I find Becca in the kitchen, making herself a cup of tea.

'There you are!' she says, grinning at me. 'I was starting to think you'd been abducted by aliens!'

I just nod. I can't seem to find my voice.

It was weird enough seeing Young Me in the mirror, but seeing Young Becca is even more surreal. I'm caught in the grip of déjà vu so strong that it makes my stomach roll.

'God, are you alright? You look like you're about to faint. Bad night, huh?' She puts a hand on my shoulder then gives me a cheeky look. 'Or should I say a really good one?'

'Something like that …' I manage to croak.

'Well, whatever your night of debauchery was like, I doubt it could be as bad as mine!'

Wanna bet? I think.

She turns to grab two mugs off the wooden tree near the kettle. 'I'll tell you all about it, but after I've done this. I'm gasping for a cuppa!'

I watch her in silence as she begins to make the tea. Her hair is still a mousy colour with a hint of honey that I remember, the colour it was before she discovered highlights and started covering up the premature grey. That's not the only difference to the Becca I know in my real life. I'd thought present-day Becca glowed? Not compared to this. There's a sense of energy and bounce to this Becca – resilience – that's been eroded from my best friend of twenty-plus years. All the scars, all the knocks in her confidence from her crappy marriage and her horrible divorce, are gone and they're all the more glaring for their absence.

A rush of love for her hits me, for the friend she once was and for the survivor she will become. I launch myself at her and hug her hard.

'Hey!' she says, as she drops the teaspoon she's holding. It bounces on the Formica counter, but she giggles and hugs me back.

'I've missed you,' I say into her hair.

'Daft mare,' she mutters. 'I was only gone for one night!' She pulls away, shakes her head affectionately, finishes making the tea and hands me one. I keep expecting senses in this dream … this whatever it is … to be dulled, muffled, so the heat of the cheap ceramic mug against my fingers shocks me.

Becca traipses into the living room, where she collapses onto the end of the velour sofa, tucking her legs up underneath her. I follow suit, taking up my spot on the opposite end. 'So … how was it? How was *he*?' I ask, wondering if I'm a good enough actress to pull off being shocked and outraged when she tells me. I remember the details of this little escapade all too well.

Becca looks at me over the rim of her mug. 'Disappointing.'

'He was no good?'

'Never got that far,' Becca says darkly. 'His mate Dave was

throwing a party so we ended up at his flat. Ten minutes after we arrived, I went in search of a drink and when I'd got back Stevo had disappeared.'

'No!' I say with my best attempt at disbelief. Becca seems to buy it, but probably because she's so wrapped up in retelling her tale she hasn't noticed my lousy performance. 'Where did he go?'

'He skipped off to one of the bedrooms with Adrienne Palmer, that's where! All those years dreaming he was the perfect guy, and thinking, if only he'd notice me my life would be sorted!'

I don't remember much about Stevo Watts, but I do remember that as a third-year student, he'd had a reputation for prowling round the freshers. 'Fresh meat', I'd heard he'd called them.

I realise my best friend's strategy with men hasn't changed much: she finds the most good-looking, alpha jerks to swoon over, is completely bowled over if they notice her and then falls at their feet and does anything they want. That's how she'd ended up with the horrible ex. I've been crossing my fingers hard that the lovely new man back in our real life is going to break that pattern.

'You need someone who loves you for you, not just because you're their devoted follower,' I tell her. 'Someone who is ready to do as much for you as you are for them.' I have no idea if she'll listen to me, or if she'll even remember this next time she spies one of her 'guys', but at least I've got to try.

'I know.' She sighs. 'I wish I could find someone like Dan

– faithful, capable of a proper relationship. Not a total turd, in other words.'

I hold my tongue. University Dan might fit that description, but present-day Dan might be giving it a run for its money.

'That man is gold dust, Maggie. You're just lucky you nabbed him before anyone else did!' she adds, laughing.

I ignore the comment and lean forward. I've been guilty of taking present-day Becca for granted, not looking hard enough, so now I study her counterpart. 'Are you OK? Really?'

She sighs again. 'Yeah. Nothing much damaged but my pride.'

'Hey, why don't I treat you to breakfast? To cheer you up?'

Becca grins. 'At Al's?'

I stand up. 'Where else?'

How could I have forgotten Al's Cafe? He served the best greasy fry-ups in south-west London. There's no Starbucks, no Costa, here and now, I remind myself. No organic cafes where you can get porridge and compote or chia-seed smoothies. If you want to go out for breakfast, a full English or a bacon buttie it is.

Before I head off to my bedroom I run my fingers through my fringe. 'Don't suppose you've got any spare hair grips, have you?'

'What on earth for?'

I flatten the short hair of my fringe to the side of my head. 'I want to pin this back.'

Becca just laughs at me as she fetches a couple of grips she'd left on the bookshelf. 'You only had it cut like that on Saturday! Honestly, Mags, one of these days you're going to have to make your mind up and decide what you really want – none of this flip-flopping between different options until the rest of us want to smack you senseless.'

I smile at her, but I take the grips from her open hand. 'Thanks. I'll be back in two secs …'

CHAPTER SEVEN

I look down with glee at my two sausages, bacon, beans, and eggs with bursting yellow yolks. It's been almost twenty-five years since I've had one of Al's breakfasts and I can't wait. I take a bite of the bacon, a bit with crinkly brown edges, close my eyes and let out a moan of satisfaction.

'Steady on,' Becca says, with a mouthful of egg, from across the table. 'I don't want you going all Meg Ryan on me!'

'It's a distinct possibility,' I mumble as I shove another mouthful in. 'Oh, my ... It's every bit as good as I remember.'

Becca frowns. 'We were only in here on Wednesday!'

I shake my head. 'I really shouldn't eat so much junk.'

'We're young. What else are we going to do?'

I chuckle, because I realise she's right – I'm young again. No more boring forty-something life! No more ties and responsibilities! I'm free. I've got at least another ten years before my metabolism slows and I have to start worrying about piling on the pounds.

The thought floats through my mind quite benignly, but then it slams against a brick wall and I go cold all over. What am I talking about? This isn't real. I'm not *staying*. I don't even want to start thinking like that in case I jinx it and don't wake up.

Oh, God. Maybe that's it. Maybe I'm in a coma! And this is just my subconscious having a field day while my family stand around my hospital bed and cry.

'Dodgy sausage?' Becca asks, seeing the look on my face.

I shake my head, but I don't explain.

'So what's the plan for today?' she asks.

I pause. Maybe I am in a coma or having a psychotic break, but I look outside the cafe window, where the sun is shining, announcing the promise of an empty, unspoilt day; I feel Al's breakfast warming my belly, and I can't quite bring myself to believe it. It all seems so real.

Isn't this what I wanted? To wind back the years? I have no idea how long it's going to last, when I might wake up with a tube down my throat or wearing a fetching white jacket with straps and buckles, so I might as well make the most of it.

'We probably should be revising,' I say. Finals start next week. I know that much.

Becca makes a face and I laugh. Usually, I'm the sensible one and she's the one who's the bad influence, but today I sense we're going to have something of a role reversal. I'm not going to waste this glorious day stuck indoors bent over a textbook.

'I think we ought to start with shopping,' I say. 'Serious shopping.'

Her eyes twinkle. 'Kingston?' she asks hopefully.

I shake my head. 'Oxford Street.'

The twinkle in Becca's eyes reaches her mouth and she grins at me.

'And after that, whatever we want to do, whatever takes our fancy. As long as it's fun!'

'Good plan,' she says, then snaps to attention and does a Benny Hill backwards salute at me. 'Reporting for Maggie and Becca's Day of Fun!'

I smack her hand away from her head and laugh. 'Shut up.'

'Oops, don't look now.' She nods to something outside the window. 'Here comes lover boy … Just don't you go changing all our perfect plans on me now he's arrived.'

I turn and a jolt of electricity first stops then restarts my heart.

'Dan …' I whisper.

'Oh, God,' Becca mutters. 'I think I'm gonna puke.'

I can't take my eyes off him as he walks past the plate-glass window at the front of the cafe, grinning because he's spotted us, and then opens the door and walks in. He leans down to kiss me softly, lingering in a way he hasn't done in years, then sits down beside Becca so he can keep looking at me. My heart is going again, but it hasn't yet resumed a normal rhythm.

I am honestly struck dumb in his presence, part of me shocked at how young, how good-looking, how energetic this version of Dan seems to be, and part of me wanting to reach across the table and slap him hard for making me feel this way when Future Dan is quite possibly having it away with Miss Perky Gym Teacher.

Becca finishes her breakfast as mine goes cold on the plate in front of me, then she pushes back her chair and gives the pair of us an indulgent look. 'Right, I'm clearing off back to the flat to leave you two alone for a bit.' She turns a sharp eye on me. 'But I'm meeting you there after lunch to go shopping – don't blow me out!'

Things don't get any better when it's just me and Dan left alone at the table. He reaches over, takes my hand in his, then turns it over and gently kisses the back of it. I stare at him.

'What?' he says, grinning at me. 'Can't a guy get a little romantic now and then? I thought you girls liked that stuff.'

I nod. Again. And then tears fill my eyes and start to spill over my lashes. Dan immediately jumps up and comes round to my side of the table to put his arm round me. He perches on the edge of the adjacent chair and takes my hands in his, his face full of concern. 'Maggie? What is it? Tell me?'

I shake my head and swallow. I can't tell him. But this just makes me cry all the harder.

I hate this dream. I want it to stop. I want to wake up. Now.

I squeeze my eyes shut and will it to happen, but I know it hasn't worked, because I can still feel Dan's fingers wrapped around mine, hear his soft breath as he waits for me to tell him what's wrong.

But how do I tell him I'm crying because I know one day he will stop looking at me this way? That one day he will stop thinking I'm creative and wonderful and clever, and not very long after that so will I?

I haul in a breath and open my eyes. He's looking at me as if he would gladly rip his heart out of his chest and give it to me if it would make me feel better. It almost starts me off again, but I manage to hold back.

'I'm just being silly …' Just for a moment I let myself forget I'm supposed to be feeling angry and wronged and heartbroken because of him. I reach out and trace my fingertips across the fine blond stubble on his cheek – he's a bit lazy about shaving, is Dan, especially in his early twenties, when he doesn't think the grey patches make him look old and grizzled before his time. 'It's just …' My throat closes again and I have to swallow a lump down to continue. 'It's just that I really love you.'

The temporary dam on the tears gives up and they start to flow again as Dan takes my face in his hands and kisses me so sweetly that the heart I've hardened against him begins to soften. Tiny painful splits appear, like those in a dry lip that's been stretched too far.

'That's nothing to cry about,' he whispers as he pulls back and smiles at me.

I nod but the tears don't stop, even though I'm doing everything I can to make them. *It is,* I whisper silently inside my head. *Because right at this moment, I know I'm telling the truth.*

CHAPTER EIGHT

Becca and I do indeed go shopping. We wander round the giant Top Shop in Oxford Circus for at least an hour. I have no idea how much I have in my student bank account and I really don't care. I usually hate clothes shopping in my real life, but I have ten hangers full of cool stuff in my changing cubicle and I can't stop smiling.

'How's the dress?' Becca yells from the cubicle next door.

I pull the curtain back dramatically and step outside. 'See for yourself.'

She pokes her head out. 'Wow! Dan is going to have a heart attack when he sees you in that!'

It occurs to me as I admire my reflection in the full-length mirror that I hadn't even thought about how Dan might react. The dress is black, Lycra, and it hugs my bottom in an almost-indecent fashion. I would never have had the guts to wear this when I was twenty-one, believing myself fat and lumpy. Not the sort of girl who could get away with it. But compared to my forty-something self, this Maggie is svelte. Not perfect – there's a slight curve to my belly and the top of my hips look a little boxy – but good enough. I can't believe how great it looks on me.

'I'm getting it,' I tell Becca.

She makes me turn around and checks the price tag hanging down my back. 'It's over forty quid!'

I shrug. 'You're only young once, right?'

OK, maybe, in my case, twice, but I have the feeling I didn't do it right the first go around. While this strange hallucination lasts, I'm going to make up for lost time.

I buy the dress then change into it in the toilets of a pub down Argyll Street, even though it's more evening than daywear. When I walk out across the bar to where Becca is waiting for me, heads turn. The knowledge gives my walk a little extra swing.

We buy a cheap bottle of wine and head for St James's Park, where we sit in deckchairs we don't pay for. After two hours we're very giggly, slightly sunburned and more than a little squiffy. We decide to paddle in the lake to help us cool off, taking it in turns to sip the last of the wine from the neck of the bottle as we stand there, but then a portly park warden comes along and starts shouting at us and we end up grabbing our bags and running away down the path in our bare feet, shoes hooked from our fingers, until we've finally outrun him, and then we collapse under a tree and laugh until we cry.

'What next?' I ask Becca. We've been taking it turns to come up with ideas and the paddling was mine.

'I'm hungry,' Becca moans, so after we've shoved our shoes back on our slightly damp feet we head in the direction of China Town. My purse is feeling considerably lighter than it was when I left Oaklands this morning and it's the best place we can think of to stuff our faces on a budget.

We trail through Piccadilly and end up at Wong Kei's, a student favourite because of its mountainous plates of food for low prices. We have to share a table with some American tourists who obviously have stumbled in here without knowing its reputation. Instead of understanding that the rude service is what brings people to this cult tourist attraction, they're outraged. They don't understand when the waiter barks instructions at them or brings them dishes he's decided they should have instead of what they actually ordered. Becca and I just sit back, eat our chow mein full of unidentified seafood and enjoy the show.

After that we wander through Leicester Square and Covent Garden arm in arm. The wine is still having a pleasant effect (twenty-one-year-old me is such a lightweight!) and I keep telling Becca how much I love her. She's been a true partner in crime and hasn't blinked once at my mad suggestions, even though I know I'm acting totally out of character. Not many women have best friends like this, ones they can trust with their lives. I keep telling her that too, which only makes her tease me harder about my state of inebriation.

After scraping together our last pennies to share a pint of cider in an overpriced pub, we get talking to some guys who buy us more drinks and then we end up getting a cab with them to a club somewhere near Kings Cross that turns out to be an abandoned warehouse with huge rooms sprawling over multiple floors. I never went to anything like this when I was young the first time – the whole rave scene of the early nineties passed me by – and I launch myself onto the dance floor as if I'm planning to make up for that.

There's one guy who's been hanging around me ever since we got in the cab and he sidles up to me and tries to grind his hips against mine. I attempt to back away but he just keeps coming at me.

Becca leans in and shouts in my ear. 'Ladies! Now!'

I nod, totally trusting her to be my wingman … woman … whatever. Creepy Guy tries to follow, but we slip away too fast and instead of heading for the loos, we sprint up a flight of stairs and lose ourselves in yet another room full of heaving, slick bodies. We dance most of the night away and when our feet are burning so hard we can't stand to groove any longer, we catch a string of night buses that eventually deposit us on Putney High Street and stagger back to our flat, arm in arm and propping each other up, feet bare on the rough concrete paving stones as the sky turns from grey to pale-pink. Becca keeps starting to belt out 'Rhythm is a Dancer' and I have to keep shushing her, so by the time we reach the front door to the house where our flat is, we're almost giggling as loud as the singing would have been.

I fall into bed without taking my make-up off and smile at the ceiling as my eyelids drift closed. Now *that* is the way to do twenty-one!

CHAPTER NINE

I've been avoiding Dan as much as possible. Mainly because I just don't know how to deal with him. However, there's only so much 'pretending to be revising' a girl can do before she can't put her boyfriend off any longer, and I end up going to a party with him on campus the following weekend.

Derwent Hall is the old-fashioned kind of student accommodation. None of these 'flats' with en-suite showers and homey little kitchens you get at universities these days. Instead, it has corridor upon corridor of single bedrooms painted in a colour Becca calls 'anti-suicide green', a tiny shared kitchen with only a Baby Belling and a juddering fridge to its name, and a communal bathroom with shower cubicles and sinks, and one bath in its own stall that takes twenty minutes to fill.

However, Derwent's one advantage over those smart student flats we looked over with Sophie is that it has a common room. Not huge, but large enough to fit forty or so students in if they don't mind squishing a bit, which they don't.

The music is already pumping when we get there, the sparse furniture pushed back against the walls or shoved outside on the grass, and people are dancing, cans of warm lager in their hands. I'm tempted to join them but Dan has hold of my hand, and when I lean in to tell him I'm off to strut my stuff, he takes the opportunity to steal a kiss.

I plan to end it quickly, but I get kind of sidetracked. I'd forgotten Dan could kiss like this. His dad is a pastor and is a little old-fashioned about things, so Dan hasn't had a lot of experience. The upside of that is that what he does do, he does *very* well. By the time he's finished with me, I'm thrumming.

Oh, why couldn't you stay this way? I ask him silently. *You're so sweet and loyal and full of devotion.* But then I remember the betrayal that is to come. I can't let myself feel anything for him. I just can't.

So I push away from Dan and head for the dance floor, playing memories in my head to stop me going back, pinning him against the wall and continuing that kiss: the guilty look on his face when I go into the study unannounced, the fib he told about meeting Sam Macmillan, the way he's been lying to me about where he's going once a fortnight for months and months. I use those mental images to keep me angry, because as long as I'm angry I'm safe.

I channel my anger-fuelled adrenalin spike by dancing to the twelve-inch version of 'Love Shack'. Paul Ferrini comes over, Derwent's resident stud, and joins the group of girls I'm dancing with. He offers me his bottle of vodka and I take a sip. We dance together after that. Nothing inappropriate, nothing too flirty, I reason to myself, as I feel Dan's laser-like glare from the other side of the room, even though there's a glint in Paul's eyes that tells me it could be more than innocent fun if I wanted it to be. There's a part of me that enjoys this tiny moment of payback.

When I'm finally so thirsty I can't keep dancing any more, I return to my boyfriend. 'Just having fun,' I tell him as I slump against the wall and neck the paper cup of flat Lambrusco he hands me.

Dan harrumphs. He's upset with me. But he's not going to say anything. He's not going to do anything about it. How very *Dan* of him. 'Got a problem with that?' I ask, unable to stand his passive-aggressive grunts a moment longer.

He fixes his stare on Paul, who is now half draped over Mandy Gomez. 'You didn't have to have quite so much fun!'

I've had enough of his hypocrisy, maybe not in this life but definitely in the other one, and the mixture of wine and spirits is spurring me on. I push myself off the wall. 'Fine!' I shout back at him over the music. 'If I'm not supposed to be having any fun, then maybe I'll leave. You'll be happy then, because I won't be having any fun at all!' And then I stare straight ahead and start walking down the corridor to the exit.

'Maggie? Mags!' I hear him start to run after me but then the footsteps stop and he shouts something I don't catch. The cool night air hits me as I open the door and march across the courtyard in the direction of the main gate. There's no sound behind me but the dying breath of today's summer breeze in the trees. I exhale with them, loud and long. I can no longer hear him loping along behind me.

Finally.

I don't want him to follow me. I don't want to have to deal with my real-life problems, most of which centre around him, while I'm having this weird trance or dream or whatever it is. All I want to be able to do is enjoy it while it lasts.

Oaklands College, a satellite of a larger university, has a beautiful campus. I don't think I really appreciated it when I went there. Oaklands House, where the administration offices are, is a lovely, white Georgian mansion, surrounded by statues and tended gardens, complete with fountain. Beyond that is a large lawn, always covered in toxic-green goose poop, that leads down to a small man-made lake.

Rather than heading straight back to the flat I share with Becca, I decide to take a walk. I head down towards the black water, trying not to think about what might be sticking to the underneath of my DMs. I stand by the reeds and watch the moon, reflecting on the water, breaking apart and rejoining itself, only to be disassembled again by the ripples of the next goose that swims by on the other side of the pond.

The moment of stillness after my week of frenetic activity allows thoughts and feelings I've been keeping firmly at bay to come flooding back in.

I miss Sophie.

I wonder if she's missing me, if she even knows I'm gone? Until I work out what strange trick my brain is playing on me, I don't know if she's quietly grieving, Dan's solid arm around her shoulder, or whether she's living it up in Oban or Ullapool while I sleep soundly in my bed. I know she doesn't need me as much as she once did, but that doesn't mean she doesn't need me at all. I don't want to be dead. I don't want her to have to go through that.

I close my eyes.

No.

I can't think like that.

My stay here is just temporary. It has to be.

When I open my eyes again I'm aware of another presence on the lawn. I can hear squelching footsteps behind me, someone tracking their way from the ugly student union building towards the rose garden.

I feel very safe here, maybe because it still doesn't feel real to me, but I suddenly remember that one year a girl was assaulted on campus when she walking between the spread-out halls of residence, and I turn.

The figure jumps and then a hand flies to his chest. I don't think he'd seen me standing there near the reeds.

'God Almighty, you gave me a fright!' he says, and I instantly recognise the voice, even after all these years.

'*Jude?*' It's just as well his name is only one syllable, because I'm not sure I can manage anything more.

The figure walks towards me, his edges becoming less blurry as he gets closer, and when he is ten feet away, I see that it is indeed Jude, the subject of all my recent fantasies, living and breathing right in front of me and smiling that smile that always turned my knees to custard.

'Meg?'

I inhale. There's something about hearing him say my name that way that makes me do that. 'Hi.'

He frowns. 'What are you doing out here?'

I shrug. I'm not about to tell him I just had a fight with Dan.

He smiles again and I almost start to feel dizzy. 'Long

time no see,' he says in that lazy, posh-boy drawl he's still in the process of cultivating, copied from his upmarket circle of friends.

I nod. And then, because I really need to say something else, I croak out, 'How are you?'

The smile becomes lopsided and I know he's quietly laughing at me, that he knows he's got me all off kilter and he likes it. It would have made the other twenty-one-year-old me angry, because I would have thought he was mocking me, but the real me knows that he's actually pleased to see me. The real me knows that in just under a week he's going to ask me to run away with him, and he's going to mean every word. That's not disdain I see glinting in his eyes but honest-to-goodness pleasure at seeing me again.

He reaches out his hand. 'Let me walk you home. You know Catriona Webb was attacked out here a couple of months ago?' He points to a spot only a couple of hundred feet away past the rose garden.

I hesitate. Something inside, some strange kind of instinct, tells me he's dangerous. Oh, I don't think he'd ever hurt me, not physically, anyway, but it suddenly occurs to me that this meeting never happened in my old life.

What if I should have been more careful up until now? What if, by not sticking to the same script, I've been changing things, causing the repercussions to ripple out like the waves from the swimming goose, until the life I once knew is pulled out of shape and made into something different? While I'd love some things to change, what if I never get home back to Sophie? What if Sophie never even exits?

But even after thinking all of this, I reach out and place my hand in Jude's. He's right. With a sexual predator on the loose – maybe someone from outside the college who slipped past the lax security, maybe someone lurking in our midst – I really shouldn't be wandering around in the dark on my own.

We start walking towards the front gate in silence, but after a couple of minutes he says, 'So where's Dave?'

'Dan,' I reply, even though I suspect he got the name wrong on purpose.

'Dan, then,' he adds, and I hear the smile in his voice.

'Party in Derwent. I got tired.'

'And he let you wander out here alone? That's not very gallant.'

No, it wasn't, I think, for a moment conveniently forgetting that I'd made it my mission to push ever-affable Dan to his limit. 'Where were you coming from?' I ask Jude, so I don't have to answer his question.

'Went to hang out with a friend, then we headed down to the bar for a drink.'

I nod. Without any more details I know this 'friend' was a girl. I change the subject. 'So what are you up to after exams?'

He chuckles. 'You know me … I haven't got a plan. Dom and I are going to bum around the South of France for a bit and then, well … we'll just see what crops up.'

I sigh. Seeing as I know 'bumming around' leads Jude into a successful career somehow along the way, I feel jealous. I worked hard, but I never amounted to anything more than 'ordinary'.

'What about you?'

I sigh again. The twenty-one-year-old me might not have known what the future holds, but I do. In just a few short days my life will be set on a course to suburban mediocrity and simmering discontentment. 'I'm going to run away with the circus,' I say wearily.

Jude laughs. Not one of his slightly cynical huffs, but a proper loud one, as if what I said tickles him. 'Never really thought of you as the running-away type,' he says and there's an added edge of velvet to his tone. In an instant, the air around us changes.

I stop, turn and look at him. I know I'm being stupid. I know I could be endangering everything by just being with him, let alone feeling … this … with him, but it's like having an itch I've been trying not to scratch and on a reflex I'm reaching for it, taking my satisfaction in shredding what's left of my resolve to pieces with my fingernails.

'Sometimes a girl's gotta do what a girl's gotta do.'

He answers me with a smile. A wicked one. 'You've changed.'

I stare him straight in the eyes. 'Yes, I have.'

He glances towards Derwent Hall and then back to me again. The sounds of the party are drifting through the open common-room windows and across the lake. The geese pay no attention. It's nothing they haven't heard before. 'Then Dave's a very lucky man.'

I hold my breath and stare back at him. I feel as if my life is teetering on a fulcrum, that if I make one false movement it'll tip. I know this moment is crucial but I don't know what to say. I don't know what to do.

All I know is that Dan is going to propose to me in four days and not even the tiniest part of me wants to say yes.

Becca finds me the next day in the canteen, while I'm buying a sad-looking tuna-and-sweetcorn baguette. I deliberately pretended to be asleep this morning, because I didn't want to talk to her about last night. However, it appears that may not have been the best call, because my boyfriend clearly got to her first. 'What's wrong with you?' she asks. 'Dan told me you were a total bitch to him last night.'

I raise my eyebrows and turn to look at her. 'He said that?'

'Those weren't his exact words. But I can read between the lines.'

She picks up a bottle of Appletiser and joins the queue. 'You need to apologise to him.'

Part of me wants to remind her what she said on the phone the night I told her Dan might be cheating on me, but I know that I can't. She'll think I'm crazy. I also know she's right. This Dan has done nothing. If I filter out all the things he will do and will say, and look at the situation objectively, I can only come to one conclusion: I *was* a total bitch to him last night.

'I know,' I reply with a sigh.

After lunch I go in search of Dan. I find him at Al's, nursing a cup of half-cold tea. I sit down opposite him. 'Sorry,' I say and he looks at me warily. 'Put it down to hormones and the stress of looming exams.'

His jaw remains tight, but there's a softening in his eyes. 'We're alright, then?'

I nod. As alright as we can be in this version of our life,
I suppose.

He surprises me by half-standing, leaning across the table
and planting a lingering kiss on my lips, right in front of
Al and the rest of his motley customers, then he pulls away
and looks at me seriously. 'You're the best thing that ever
happened to me,' he says. 'I can hardly believe I'm the lucky
man you picked. Always remember that. Always make *me*
remember that.'

A lump forms in my throat and my eyes grow moist. All
morning I've been imagining what it would be like to say yes
to Jude, but now I don't know what I want. Could I make
Dan remember how he feels about me in this moment, even
years from now when he really doesn't want to? Our whole
lives could be different if I could.

CHAPTER TEN

Three days. Two days. One.

My brain is counting down to the inevitable. I know it's coming. Dan's proposal. Even my fit of extreme bitchiness last week hasn't seemed to have put him off. If anything, he's trying harder than ever because of the seed of doubt I've planted in his mind.

When I'm with him it really is like the old days and I don't have to fake the affection in my smile, but when we part … well, that's when the old memories – the 'forward' memories – start creeping in.

What do I do?

Up until now I've been doing my best to just go with the flow, do what feels good. It was easy when I thought I'd wake up and realise this has all been a vivid dream, but it's been over two weeks now. I'm also pretty sure this is no waiting room for heaven.

Which leaves only one possibility: this is real. Somehow I've jumped backwards in time, fully conscious of the life I've already lived and I've got to do it all over again. I've always thought the opportunity to go back and change the things you regret would be a blessing. Now the prospect of it frightens me.

If I'm staying here I can't keep messing around. If I've really got to do it all again I've got to start thinking about the choices I'm making. Making the wrong one tonight could ruin everything.

I shake my head as I look in the mirror. I'm supposed to be getting ready for a meal out with Dan, but all this mental wrangling is making it a heck of a job to do my mascara. I keep poking myself in the eyeball or blinking before it's dry and being rewarded with a row of black dots under my lashes and then having to wipe it off and start again. I take a deep breath and will my hand to stay steady.

Dan's done a good job of being nonchalant about this date, but I know he's booked a posh Italian restaurant in Putney and afterwards he'll suggest a walk along the river and then he'll take my hands, look me in the eye and my future will be sealed.

Last time I was so sure what I wanted.

They say hindsight is twenty-twenty. What they don't tell you is that it's crystal sharp and painful.

My heart is telling me to run, to veer off course and to do the things I'd always wished I'd done: to travel, love furiously and have wild affairs, to find a job I love and excel at it, but my head is urging caution. I wish I could dismiss those doubts, but unfortunately I keep coming up with very good points.

What about Sophie?

Could I stand a future without her in it?

Because if I don't choose Dan, she might never exist. Or even if I do, there might not be any guarantees. What if we have sex ten minutes later that night of conception? Will I end up with a different little girl? Or was Sophie always meant to be? What if she's more than the sum of two joined sets of chromosomes?

I put my mascara brush down and stare at myself in the mirror. There are clumps on my upper left lashes and a smudge on my right eyelid but I really can't face another attempt. I'm too tired.

There's a knock on the door as I'm putting my lipstick on. Red. The sort of colour I never wear any more. The sort of colour I didn't really opt for much when I was this age the first time around.

Becca answers the door and when I walk into the living room, she and Dan are standing there, laughing at a joke I've not been privy to. He turns to look at me and hands me a bunch of red roses. There's hope in his eyes, but also nervousness.

Becca makes the same sort of noise Sophie used to make when watching cute cat videos on YouTube. 'Awww ... aren't you sweet,' she tells Dan and then she gently prises the roses from my hand. 'Why don't you two get off? I'll put these in water.'

I want to snatch them back. I want to tell Becca I'd rather do it myself, to delay the moment when I have to walk out that front door with Dan and be on my own with him, but I don't. I don't know how to say it without seeming rude. Or slightly insane.

Becca practically shoves us out the front door and into the hallway. 'I won't wait up!' she jokes and, as the door closes behind us, I wonder if she knows, if Dan has confided in her, and two things strike me – one, that I wonder why I hadn't twigged that he was going to propose this night the first time around, because I had a suspicion at the time he was working up to it and, two, that I'm jealous. I don't like the fact that my husband-to-be and my best friend have shared a secret and left me out of it. Hypocritical, really, when I'm seriously considering breaking his heart this evening. Until I came back here I hadn't realised how selfish I can be, how wrapped up in my own stuff that I don't see what's going on under my nose.

'Shall we?' Dan says, and offers me his arm. I smile at him, a smile that's warm and bright and about as substantial as candy floss.

Dinner is a blur. I eat, I drink, I nod and laugh in the right places, but the only sensation I can really remember when it's over is a growing sense of panic. As Dan takes my hand and heads towards the river my heart starts to pound. I can hear the echo of it rushing in my ears.

We walk past the crowded pubs with drinkers spilling out across the narrow street and onto the embankment. We keep going until their laughter and chatter is more distant, until we reach the rowing club. There's a break in the railings and we walk down to the far edge of the shallow concrete slope the rowers use to put their boats in the river. As we stand there, staring across at the tree-lined bank on the other side, I can hear the music of the water slapping against the hulls of the little motor boats moored close by.

Dan seems paralysed. I keep shooting glances in his direction, wondering when he's going to make his move, but he just keeps staring at the darkness in front of him. Was he like this before? I wonder. If he was, I didn't notice it. I remember the night being balmy and warm, the lapping of the gentle river waves romantic.

Just when I think he's chickened out, he sucks in a breath and turns to me. We've been still for so long it makes me jump, and that makes him smile. The serious look he's been wearing for the last ten minutes vanishes.

He reaches for my hands and I swallow.

'You know how I feel about you …' he says softly.

My heart can't help cracking a little at his words. How can you love and hate a person at the same time? I want to slap him across the face, hard enough to make my fingers sting, but I also want to kiss him.

'… and I know that we're young and everyone is going to say this is a bad idea, but I can't imagine my life without you in it.'

I still don't say anything. Partly because I have no response, but partly because I'm realising I really can imagine my life without Dan in it. It's been something I'd been doing even before this strange experience happened to me, after all. I just hadn't expected my wishing to make it real or, at least, the possibility of it real. Dan, however, takes my silence for agreement and he carries on.

My heart stops. Just for a beat. Because as he draws his next breath I know exactly what words are about to come out of his mouth, and I still don't know what my answer will be.

'Maggie,' he says, and his voice catches on the last syllable, 'will you marry me?'

CHAPTER ELEVEN

I stare back at Dan. His face is full of hope. Hope, I realise, that neither of us have left for our marriage back in our other life. A hole rips open inside me, deep and long. How can this man – the man who looks at me with such tenderness and worship – have turned into the one who's sneaking around behind my back, who's let slide all the promises he's been holding so faithfully for the last twenty-four years?

I don't have an answer for him. Not the one he wants, anyway. Not the one I gave him last time. 'I don't know,' I finally stammer, and then I watch all that hope melt away and turn to confusion.

'Don't you love me?'

I nod. 'Yes … no … I don't know.' And then I begin to cry.

He scoops me into his arms and holds me tight. I can tell he's staring over my shoulder, asking the night sky what went wrong. I know he's hurting and confused, that his instinct was to back off and protect himself, but the fact he's chosen not to do that, to comfort me instead, just makes me cling on to him all the harder.

'What's wrong?' he whispers. 'You haven't been right, not for the last couple of weeks.'

I let myself mould against him, just for a moment, and then I lift my eyes and look at him. I shake my head as the tears fall. 'I'm sorry,' I say, and then I find I can't stop. I say it over and over and over.

'No,' he replies and silences my litany with a kiss. 'I got ahead of myself. It's too soon.'

I shake my head, because I know in another version of our lives it wouldn't be too soon. The problem is, I'm not sure I want that reality any more, even though the thought of losing him suddenly seems much bigger and more final than I ever realised.

It'll be like him dying.

Because I won't just grieve him the way I would if we'd split up when I was twenty-one. I'll grieve for all the extra years we've had that he'll never know about – the way he looked when Sophie was born, as if he could burst with pride and love for the both of us. How nervous he was on our wedding night. Even silly little things like that cup of tea he always brings me when he gets home from work.

That Dan won't ever exist in this world, and I feel the loss of him like a physical pain in my chest.

He hasn't got a hanky, so he uses the cuff of his shirt sleeve to dry my tears.

It's not you, it's me, I want to say, but I'm aware it sounds over-used, even in this decade, so I don't. *Or maybe it's us. The us we will become. I'm setting us free from that, from the boredom and the simmering resentment. From the disappointment of knowing that even though we once thought we could be everything to each other, we clearly can't.*

By silent agreement we walk back towards the High Street, heading for the bus stop. When we reach my flat, I open the front door that leads into the communal hallway of our converted Victorian house, but Dan doesn't cross the threshold with me.

'Aren't you coming in?'

He shakes his head.

'This doesn't mean I'm breaking up with you,' I say. 'Just that I need time to think. You're right – we are both so young, we need to be sure this is the right thing. For both of us.' I stop then, because I know that I'm lying, that as much as I'm pretending nothing's changed, there's been a seismic shift in our relationship.

He shrugs and looks at his shoes. 'I know that. It's just that … I need time alone. I need time to think too.'

I would have accepted that without a doubt once upon a time. After all, it's a perfectly natural response for someone whose proposal of marriage has not been as enthusiastically received as it was delivered – especially for a man like Dan, who likes to lick his wounds in private.

'Where are you going to go?'

Another pause. I can almost hear him thinking his response over.

'I dunno. Just for a walk, I expect.'

Totally understandable. And I would have believed him, I really would, if when he looked at me he hadn't worn that same expression he always used in our future life, the one that accompanies his oh-so-innocent declaration that he's off down the pub with a long-lost mate who is actually having a second honeymoon in Prague.

CHAPTER TWELVE

The flat is empty and I sit down on the sofa in the dark. The ugly sunburst clock above the electric fire ticks.

I did it. But I don't know whether to feel sorry or relieved.

I don't know what to do now. This is the first time since I've been living this crazy … whatever it is … that I've veered completely off script. I was still friends with Becca, still doing my uni course, still with Dan. But now I haven't just amended a bit of dialogue, skipped a scene or fudged a bit of stage direction; I've completely changed the ending.

I think about that night – the *other* night like this. The two realities couldn't be more different. In that one I was laughing, happy, full of hope. In this one I'm just … numb. And wondering why my almost-fiancé is lying to me about where he's going.

I shiver as I recall the look on Dan's face.

I thought the fibs, the sneaking around, had been a new thing. What if it isn't? What if he's been doing this the whole time and it's just taken me this long to catch on?

I screw up my face and squeeze my eyes shut, as if by doing so I can stop the spinning in my head. I can't believe that's true. It doesn't fit with the steady, reliable, slightly boring

Dan I know. But then I think of women who find out their husbands have had a secret family on the side for years, or whose husbands have committed rapes or awful sex offences and they truly have no idea.

Maybe I made the right call after all.

The numbness fades a little and just the tiniest smidge of peace seeps in. I breathe out. I haven't burned my bridges yet, I suppose. I've just told Dan I need time, which is just as well, as I need at least a week to work out what I'm going to do.

A thought flashes through my head: *Jude*.

Dan's proposal wasn't the only surprise on this night. My heart skips into a higher gear.

I need to see him, I realise. I need to hear him say those words again. Not just because I'm keeping my options open, but I need to know I haven't romanticised that scene after all those Facebook-prompted fantasies. If I'm really going to change my future, I need to be sure.

I stand up, grab my handbag from where I dumped it near the door and head out again. It only takes me ten minutes to make the usual fifteen minute stroll to the Queen's Head. When I push through the heavy oak door with the etched glass panel, I stop in my tracks, confronted by two colliding realities. I look over at the corner where Dan and our friends had gathered that night, laughing and celebrating, and there seems to be an emptiness, even though all the tables are filled.

I order a lager and black, take a quick sip and then head out to the pub garden. It's started to rain now. Hard, like it had been that night. A heavy shower after a sunny day had sent all the drinkers scurrying back inside. Not bothering to cover my head or put up the umbrella I have in my bag, I look around, and then I look again. My stomach goes cold.

He's not here.

Of course he's not.

He has no reason to be. I'm not thinking this through clearly.

Jude only came to the pub because he'd heard Dan and I were there. If I don't say yes to Dan, word won't have got round the college grapevine. The tiny flame of hope I've been carrying inside since I walked out my flat door falters and flickers. I sit down on the end of an empty picnic bench, deflated. It had all seemed so easy in my head.

I could look for him, I think, as rain splashes into my hair and runs down my scalp.

I could, but I go back into the pub, find a wall to prop myself against and drink my lager and black, ignoring the chattering people around me. But maybe that won't be the same either. Jude doesn't know he might lose me forever. Without that very specific kick up the backside, he probably won't come looking for me at all.

I drain the last of my half pint and stand up. I have to try. I can't just let this life drift by without fighting for it. I did that with the original one, and look how happy I was.

I plant my empty glass down firmly on the bar, then walk through the crowds and out back onto the main road. I turn and head in the direction of the college, the Student's Union bar, to be more exact. Jude is a bit of a regular.

I shake my head as I walk, not only to clear the rain from it but to clear my mind. I was so stupid. Complacent. Letting so many chances slip by me. They say youth is wasted on the young, but not this twenty-one year old. Not this time.

I trudge out of the Student Union. I'd been in there for about an hour, nursing a warm and rather sweet white wine. Thank goodness student prices and minus-twenty-four years of inflation meant I only paid about a pound for it. I'd have been miffed otherwise. I really can't understand how I stomached the stuff.

No Jude.

The rain has stopped, but the pavements are slick and shiny. I frown as I start to walk, not really caring which direction I go. I thought this would be easy: pick a man and that would be it. Heads or tails. Jude or Dan. I hadn't really considered I might end up with neither.

When I look up I find myself at the edge of the lake, just short of where the reeds provide a natural barrier to prevent inebriated students from tumbling into the water. The rain has stopped now, the dark clouds pressing on towards central London, leaving the lake still and the grass sparkling clean. I spot a smear of sludgy green poop on the edge of my shoe and I start to try to use the damp lawn to wipe it off, but it's been freshly mowed and all I succeed at doing is adding grass clippings into the mix. I'm so busy doing this I don't notice someone walking up beside me. I'm precariously balanced on one leg, and when he speaks it surprises me so much I almost topple right into the lake.

'Meg?'

It's only his hand shooting out to grab my arm that stops

me. As it is, my shoe – a rather old and ill-fitting suede ballet pump – flies off my foot and into the reeds. Seconds later, I hear a distinct *plop*. We both stare at where my shoe has just sunk below the surface of the dank water and then I turn to find Jude smiling at me.

I don't smile back, not yet. I'm too nervous. There was me, hoping I'd dazzle him so much that he'd suggest running off to the South of France for the summer without the news of my impending marriage to spur him on, but any hopes of being poised and elegant and desirable have just disappeared into the duckweed with my shoe.

'Hi,' I say softly.

'We must stop meeting like this,' he says, the smile growing ever more mischievous.

My lips curve a little too. *No, we really shouldn't.*

'How are you?' I ask, and I'm aware I sound a little breathless. I'm hoping he'll think it's because of the shoe incident.

'Good.' He looks me over. 'That Dave isn't doing a very good job of being your knight in shining armour.'

I turn to face Jude, still hanging on to him, because I'm balancing on one foot. 'Actually,' I say, looking him straight in the eye, 'he's applied for the position permanently. He asked me to marry him tonight.'

That wipes the smile off Jude's face. He stares at me, and then it's as if someone's flicked a switch. I see the charm he turns on so easily for others beaming bright in my direction. 'Well … congratulations.' His perfect teeth are showing, but there's no warmth in his eyes.

I take a breath. This is it. My moment. I can either let it drift past me again or I can grab it. 'I didn't say yes.'

Jude's eyes widen. 'You turned him down? Mr Perfect?'

I frown. Mr Perfect? Is that who he thinks Dan is? I almost laugh. Hasn't Jude ever tried looking in the mirror? Or taken a really good look at Dan?

'I told him I didn't know, that I had to think about it.'

I'm wobbling harder now, as my leg muscles are starting to tire. Jude's arm comes round me more firmly. 'Come on, Cinderella,' he mutters and, before I know it, he's picked me up and he's striding across the lawn towards the main house. He deposits me on a flagstone path under a portico. A dull-eyed statue of a half-naked woman eavesdrops on us.

Jude hasn't let go of my hand, even though he could. He's lost his don't-care-about-anything sheen. Suddenly, he looks as if he cares very much. 'And why would you say that to him?'

I swallow as my heart flings itself against my ribcage. It's one thing to cheerlead yourself into 'seizing the day', another thing entirely to actually do it. 'Because of you,' I finally whisper.

'I was hoping you'd say that.'

My heart starts to float like a helium balloon. 'Really?' I start to feel that giddy, heady sensation I should have felt earlier in the evening, after saying 'yes' to Dan.

'I think I made a horrible mistake …' he begins, and suddenly everything is back on track again, and he's saying the words he said to me last time, only we've changed the scenery to somewhere way more romantic. He ends with, 'I don't think he's what you need, Meg.'

'And you are?' I say, remembering my line well.

'I'd like to try to be.'

I keep going with the script, and while I'm thrilled it's all turned out the way it should, a little nagging feeling tells me it's only because I engineered it, that there may be a price to pay for that. I swot that nasty little thought away. 'But you're supposed to be going off to France next month …'

He reaches out and grabs both my hands, and I get a sudden flashback to a couple of hours ago when I was standing with Dan by the river. The memory is so strong it almost wipes over the present moment and I have to fight to keep it in focus. 'Come with me,' he says.

I sway and then I stare into Jude's eyes to anchor myself to him. Inside I feel as if something is pulling apart, like a piece of cloth being roughly torn, all jagged edges and loose threads. I feel my future unravelling.

'OK,' I say.

CHAPTER THIRTEEN

I knock on the door of Dan's shared student house and my knees are literally shaking. His mate Rick opens the door. Instead of giving me a hug, as he usually would, he just eyes me warily and leads me silently to the sitting room. I find Dan there, in just a T-shirt and boxers, staring at a *This Morning* segment on how to turn grunge into a wearable look for summer.

'Hi,' I say.

He stares at the TV for a full five seconds before turning to look at me. 'Hi.'

'Are you OK?' I ask. I can detect the faint whiff of stale lager and Dan's eyes look bleary, which is odd, because he's not much of a drinker.

He shrugs.

'What did you end up doing last night?'

He looks away quickly. 'Not much.'

I see that look again, the same one he wore last night, the same one that knelled the bells of doom for our future marriage and is doing a pretty good job of messing up the possibility of this one too. Any pity I'm feeling for him evaporates.

He's lying to me, and this just confirms it wasn't a heat-of-the-moment, one-off incident last night because he was hurting. 'You must have done *something*,' I say, maybe a tad more shrilly than a girl about to break up with her boyfriend ought to, but his cowardice incenses me.

He talks to Judy Finnigan on the telly, not to me. 'Rick and I had a few beers.'

Judy chatters on, not the slightest bit interested in Dan's lacklustre social life.

I stare at him as he stares at her. This is already a habit, I realise – lying to me – and it started much, much earlier than I'd thought. I feel as if hot air is being puffed into my face as I consider how many other women there may have been, because that's what he must be lying about. What else would he need to hide?

But then something clicks inside my head and I realise this is what I want. This makes everything so much easier, because I know I'm making … that I've made … the right choice.

'I know I said we weren't breaking up last night, but maybe we should.'

Dan's head snaps round. *That* got his attention. 'What?' he says, although I'm pretty certain he heard every syllable.

'I want to end it.' Even though I'm trying to steel myself against it, I flinch inwardly as my words hit home and Dan's face falls. All the righteous, disgruntled anger he's been wearing as a shield melts away, leaving only confusion.

He stands up. 'What are you saying?'

'It's over, Dan. You and me. It's just not working.'

He shakes his head. 'Last week it was working … A month before that it was working … What's changed?'

I start to answer but the way his eyes have filled up arrests me. The backs of my eyeballs start to sting too and I will them to stop. *You did this,* I try to tell him silently as I look at him. *Not yet, maybe. But you will. You have no one but yourself to blame.*

He swallows. 'Are you sure? Can't we work on this?'

'No,' I say firmly. 'Sorry.'

I can tell, in the midst of his confusion, Dan is finding my certainty off-putting. He scowls as he tries to compute my response, looking at the patterned carpet, complete with greasy kebab stain, for help. After maybe thirty seconds, he looks at me again, and there's something different in his eyes. Something glittering. 'Is there someone else?' His tone makes goosebumps break out on my arms.

I nod. 'Sort of.'

He lunges towards me, but stops just short of making any kind of physical contact. The look in his eyes is pure fury. 'You're sleeping with him?'

That's when I take the shock and twist it into rage. *Hypocrite!* I want to yell at him. *What you think is the moral high ground is actually stinking, boggy quicksand!* And if Dan has one fault it's that he occupies a whole mountain of moral high ground, probably learned it from his dad. When he said he wanted to wait until marriage, I thought it was sweet and old-fashioned, if a bit frustrating. I thought it signalled up what an upright and honourable guy he must be. Now I start to wonder if the premature marriage proposal has more to do with the fact he's panting for it rather than everlasting love. His sex drive clearly overrode his morals in our future life.

I pull myself up straighter. 'No. It's nothing like that,' I say, and I try not to blush when I remember the night before with Jude, when it almost had been very much like that, until I'd come to my senses and remembered I hadn't actually broken up with Dan yet. Even the fact I'd kissed him made me feel horribly disloyal this morning.

'Then what are you flipping well talking about?'

Even now he can't quite bring himself to say the F-word. Even when I'm prising his heart from his chest and crushing it in my fingers. A part of me despises him for it.

'I'm saying that I have feelings for someone else. Feelings I haven't acted upon – ' Dan snorts but I carry on undaunted. 'Feelings that I shouldn't be having if I'm ready to marry you.'

'Jude?' he whispers and his long frame crumples into the armchair nearby.

'Yes,' I say, and my voice is hoarse.

Dan shakes his head. 'I always knew that guy was trouble …'

'It wasn't him. It was me … or at least it was that I found myself thinking about him all the time, even when I knew I shouldn't.'

This is the most honest thing I've said to my husband in about five years. I also realise that maybe if I'd told him this in the future, maybe if he'd had the guts to tell me the same when his eye had started to wander, that we wouldn't have ended up in the horrible situation we did, lying to each other every day by omission, pretending we were happy when really we were just coasting.

We talk then. Properly. Honestly. It's not comfortable and I'm not sure it makes either of us feel any better, but when he walks me to the front door, I feel as if we've reached a shaky kind of resolution. Only time will tell if it holds or not.

And then I walk out of Dan's house, out of his life, and into my new one, full of the hope only a future full of blank pages can bring.

CHAPTER FOURTEEN

I spend the rest of the day with Jude. Even though he should be revising and I should be putting the finishing touches to my final art piece. We catch the Tube into central London, wander through Portobello market hand in hand and then through Kensington Gardens. It's odd, expecting to see the Princess Diana memorial fountain there then realising it isn't because she's still alive somewhere, miserable in her fabulous life.

As we amble past the spot it will one day occupy, Jude stops, turns and kisses me. I have the sudden urge to write to Diana, to tell her she only has one life to live and she might as well grab happiness while she can. No one knows how many days they have left. I also consider telling her to wear a seatbelt at all times, but as quickly as the idea comes into my head, I dismiss it. Even if I sent it, the letter would be intercepted and rammed into a shredder.

'Come back to mine ...' Jude whispers in my ear. I pull away and smile at him. I feel like a different person today, someone to whom yesterday's rules don't apply. For the first time in years I feel free to do what I want instead of what I should. Number one on that list is Jude. I'm tired of being the good girl.

So that's what I do. I spent a lazy, warm summer afternoon in bed with Jude, and as the sun starts to set I kiss him at his door and leave him. I've promised I'll go and see Becca's drama performance tonight.

She's already left the flat when I get back. I've forgotten exactly what time she needed to leave for the studio theatre to get ready and I must have missed her. Since we hadn't planned to go together but meet up after the show, I potter round the flat, changing into the dress I bought in Oxford Street and grabbing a cropped denim jacket.

Becca is too busy to come out from backstage before the performance, so I find a seat with a few of her drama friends that I remember being on a nodding basis with and I watch *A Midsummer Night's Dream*. Becca is playing Titania.

Afterwards, I go and wait outside the main entrance. The small studio theatre is used by both the drama and the dance department and doesn't have anything as posh as a stage door. Most of the rest of the cast have appeared, been told in megaphone-loud voices how wonderful they were by their friends and have drifted off to the bar by the time Becca appears.

She marches out, looking a little strange in her stonewashed jeans and hot-pink T-shirt but with her green-and-silver-glittery stage make-up still streaked across her face. She nods at me then sets off at a blistering pace down the narrow path that leads back towards the main buildings of the campus.

'What's up?' I ask, trotting after her. 'You were amazing! Best I've ever seen you do it! Don't worry about that fluffed line in your first scene.'

Becca stops, turns and looks at me. 'You think I'm worried about missing a line?' she asks, placing her hands on her hips. The stage make-up has the effect of making her look even more ticked off.

'Aren't you?'

She shakes her head.

'Unbelievable … So wrapped up in yourself you just don't ever see!'

'What?' I say and my volume increases to match my level of confusion. 'What don't I see?'

Becca pokes me in the hollow between the top of my right boob and my shoulder with an acid-green fingernail. 'You don't know what I'm talking about? What planet are you on?'

I step back and rub the spot. It usually wouldn't have been so bad, because Becca is a bit of a nail-biter, but she's been adorned with long green plastic talons by the costume department. 'Um … this one?' I say tentatively. I'm getting that same reality's-gone-screwy feeling I got when I first woke up here.

'You broke up with Dan!' she screams at me. 'After he proposed, as well! What the hell's wrong with you?'

I blink.

Oh.

I didn't know she knew. I also didn't know she'd take it so personally. It's not her who's broken up with him, after all! I stiffen and stand up straighter. 'Nothing's wrong with me, actually. Nothing at all.'

She throws her hands wide, shakes her head. My answer seems to have thrown her.

'We're not right for each other,' I tell her, trying to keep my voice calm.

She gives me another one of those looks that tells me she thinks I've had an aneurysm or something. 'Don't be ridiculous! I've never seen two people more right for each other.'

'Who told you?'

She inhales deeply through her nose as she stares at me. 'Dan. He's a mess.'

I feel a little kick of guilt down in my stomach, but I push it away. I'm being cruel to be kind, but I'm the only one who knows that. 'He'll thank me in the long run.'

Becca laughs, but it's not her usual bubbly giggle. 'What? For breaking his heart?'

I turn and start walking. 'You're just being dramatic now.'

I'm halted by Becca grabbing my arm, wrenching my shoulder in my socket. 'What's wrong with you, Mags? You've been acting really weird the last couple of weeks! You've changed.'

I pull my arm away from her and scowl. 'How?'

'You're … you're …' She looks desperately at me, as if she really doesn't want to let the next couple of words out of her mouth. 'You've just started being really selfish.'

I blink again. Selfish?

Well, maybe it seems that way because I'm not being my usual doormat self – I'm not going along with what everybody else wants, letting life happen to me instead of taking it by the horns. I suppose if she wants to call that selfish then maybe I should let her. 'You don't understand.'

'Then explain it to me.'

For a moment, I actually consider this. Could I tell her? Could I tell her everything? But then I imagine the words coming out of my mouth and what her reaction will be. For all her wafting around like an unearthly being this evening, Becca is probably one of the most grounded people I know. She'll just get even angrier with me, thinking I'm making fun of the situation. 'I can't.'

Her expression hardens again. 'Or won't.'

A sudden drop in my stomach alerts me to the fact that this is a crucial moment, that I have to handle it right. Dan and Becca are my anchors in this world, my only connections to the life I've left behind. I've cut one loose and I really don't want to lose the other.

'Remember that time we went to that gig at the Hammersmith Apollo,' I say, 'and we were a little bit tipsy, and we got on the bus and dozed off on each other?'

Becca looks warily at me. 'Yes?'

'How we woke up and realised we were going the wrong way, that we needed to get off and change buses, or we'd end up in Islington instead of Putney?'

She nods.

'Well, that's what I felt my life was life. The destination was fine and all that, but I had that same sudden shock in the pit of my stomach – I wasn't going the way I was supposed to be going. I know it seems drastic and all, but I had to do something before it was too late.'

I look at her, begging her to understand. She sighs and then we fall into step beside each other, making an unspoken decision to change direction and head for the bar. I know she's confused and angry but I also know she'll stand by me. She's only being like this because she's trying to protect me, trying to steer me down the path she thinks leads to happiness for me. Somehow, I'm just going to have to convince her that path doesn't always lead to Dan.

CHAPTER FIFTEEN

I creep into the flat. It's gone eleven and the lights are off in the hallway. I start to tiptoe past the living-room door when I hear a voice.

'So who is he, then?'

I press my hand to my chest to stop my heart galloping right out of it. As I walk towards the slightly open door, I see blue light flickering on the walls. I push it open and find Becca inside, watching *The Word* with the sound turned right down, which, in my mind, is the only way to cope with it. I sit down beside Becca on the sofa and watch Terry Christian interview a scruffy-looking rocker whose name I can't remember. 'Who's who?'

I can feel her looking at me. 'You know who. The guy … the new guy.'

I keep my mouth closed and continue to stare at the TV. Maybe I should have sneaked around more with Jude. Maybe I should have waited a little longer after ditching Dan to dive straight into a new relationship. I can't even use the excuse that I'm young and impulsive. On the outside, maybe, but not on the inside. It's just that I spent a whole lifetime waiting to feel like this, a whole life of waiting, full stop. Waiting to feel important. Waiting to feel special. I can't wait any more. I just can't.

While most people have no idea I'm seeing anyone, I should have known it wouldn't take Becca long. It's been two weeks now since I split with Dan and I'm spending a lot of my free time at Jude's. Partly because he lives with Dom, whose parents pay for his rent and it's a heck of a lot nicer than this dump, and partly because I've been avoiding having exactly this conversation with Becca.

'Maggie?' she prompts softly when I don't answer.

I breathe in deeply. I'm not sure if I'm ready for this. I was only just feeling we've been getting back to normal after I turned Dan down. She seems to have become very protective of him all of a sudden.

'Take a wild guess,' I mutter, keeping my eyes trained on the singer on the television, who is now yelling at the audience. He makes a few choice hand gestures and then throws his drink over the people in the front row.

Even though the TV's turned down, the air seems to become even more still, more quiet, all of a sudden. 'Please tell me you're joking,' Becca finally says.

I shake my head and risk looking her direction.

'No,' she says, her voice firm and low, as if she can change the truth by being determined enough about it. 'You are *not* seeing Jude the Jerk again!'

'I am,' I reply, just as firm and determined. 'And he's not a jerk.'

She lets out a dry laugh. 'That was *your* name for him, remember? Not mine!'

'This time it's different, Becs.'

She shakes her head wearily. 'You chose *him* – the guy that broke your heart then used it to mop the floor – over Dan? I really don't get it.'

'I know,' is all I can say back. I know she doesn't get it. I also know if I try to tell her the truth, she'll have me locked up in a mental asylum. Becca's a really down-to-earth sort. She doesn't believe in ghosts or God or even horoscopes. She won't even watch *Quantum Leap*, for goodness' sake!

'Poor Dan,' she says, shaking her head.

That's another reason I've been avoiding the flat recently. Every time she looks at me, I get the sense I'm guilty of something. And I'm not. I realised Dan wasn't the one for me and I broke it off. Even without the whole insane time-hopping thing, it was the right thing to do.

I know I won't be happy with him.

Not properly. It'll look that way for a time, but then it'll die. Not quickly and cleanly in a nuclear bust-up but slowly, almost imperceptibly, until we're drowning in our own stagnation and we don't know it. 'I don't expect you to understand,' I say calmly, 'but I would like you to respect my choice.'

Becca closes her mouth and her jaw tenses. 'He's going to break your heart again, I hope you know that. Once a selfish womaniser, always a selfish womaniser ...'

I stand up and glance at the TV screen. The scruffy rocker is gone, replaced by a group of desperate wannabes who are trying to prove they'll do anything to be on TV by having a full body wax on camera. 'I'm sorry if you don't understand, Becs, but he makes me happy.'

She stares at the unfolding horror on the TV as long as she can, before wincing and then looking away. 'It's up to you if you decide to flush your life down the toilet, I suppose.'

'I'm not,' I say softly, but I know she doesn't believe me. To be honest, I can't blame her. If you'd talked to the real twenty-one-year-old me back then, she'd have said exactly the same as Becca.

She turns and looks at me full on. Really looks at me. I start to feel uncomfortable under her scrutiny, as if she can see past the youthful varnish to the real, older me underneath, but then she turns away. 'Lately, I feel as if I just don't know you any more,' she says as I stand up and head for my bedroom.

CHAPTER SIXTEEN

The next morning, even before I open my eyes, I feel my stomach rolling slightly. It feels as if the room is moving around me. I bury my head under the pillow and try to go back to sleep.

Ugh. Hangovers.

But as I lie here I think back to the night before. Jude and I had gone out to dinner and I'd had a couple of glasses of wine, but nothing more, and I remember being fairly lucid when Becca and I had our argument about him. Surely I didn't drink enough to –

There's a loud noise above my head. My eyes pop open. The roof is low, only a couple of feet away, and I can hear someone walking around on it. I try and focus on the ceiling as I hear someone calling my name.

It's Jude. Jude is calling my name.

He sounds happy, which is nice, but what's he doing here in my flat with Becca? I'm not sure she's ready to face him yet; her loyalty to Dan is still so strong. And how has my bed become a top bunk overnight, my face so close to the ceiling? I also don't remember that skylight.

'Meg?' I hear him yell. He's no longer above me now, but

further away. I can hear a door banging, other noises I can't identify. 'We've brought breakfast!'

Breakfast. Now there's something I *can* get a handle on, I think, as I stare up through the rectangular skylight with the rounded edges. The sky beyond is blue and crystal clear and I suddenly notice there's a silver handle at the bottom. I reach for it and push it open with my fingertips.

Instantly, the smell of river water hits me, which is weird, because the Thames is at least half a mile away from the flat I share with Becca, and even so, this water smells fresh and blue, not muddy and eel-grey. Without thinking about it, I put my feet on my mattress and stand up, pushing the skylight open with my head as I do so. What I see outside causes my legs to lose all co-ordination and I crumple not only back down onto the mattress but off the bed and I end up in a tangled heap on a hard wooden floor. I seem to be jammed into a tiny triangular space I don't recognise.

There's the sound of footsteps rushing towards me, echoing as if we're in a large box, and then the door opens and I see three faces peering down at me. One of them is Jude's.

'Are you OK?' he says as he offers me a hand.

I latch onto his upside-down face. It's the only thing that's made sense since I woke up. 'I think so,' I mutter. 'Don't know what happened …'

'You fell out of bed, you muppet,' the girl behind Jude says. Her long, wavy, blonde hair is hanging past her face as she smiles at me, slightly bent over.

I grab Jude's hand and he pulls me up. As I find some

balance on my wobbly legs, I hear the other person – a guy – say, 'Well, it was quite a heavy session last night …'

Jude chuckles. 'And we now have empirical evidence Meg can't hold her G&Ts.'

I frown at him as I pull my 'Choose Life' nightshirt further down my thighs with my free hand. I hate gin and tonic. And I certainly didn't have any last night. And who are these people, anyway, grinning at me like loons, like we're all part of some in-joke?

But then I think about what I saw outside.

Instead of chimney pots and TV aerials, low-hanging grey cloud and leafy beech trees, there is blue sky – lots of it – streaked with wispy clouds. And there are mountains. There aren't supposed to be any mountains in Putney.

I look down at my bare thighs again and that's when it hits me.

I've done it again.

Moved. Jumped. Shifted. Whatever you want to call it …

My knees get a strange crunchy feeling, like fresh cotton wool balls out the packet, and I head floorwards a second time. It's only Jude's grip on my arm that saves me.

'Come on, you …' he says and plants a kiss on top of my head before hauling me through a narrow door. I stub my toe on the raised threshold and yelp. Jude and the onlookers just laugh again. 'We've got cheese and rolls and meat. And Cameron is going to make his famous espresso if we can get the galley stove to light.'

I sit on a bench with a padded cushion and all the pieces of information that have been hurtling at me since I opened my eyes suddenly snap together to form a complete picture: I'm on a boat. A sailboat. And the room I was in is the cabin at the front, hence the strange shape, and the skylight is actually a hatch. I feel myself relax a little and I breathe out.

Are we in the South of France? That's where Jude said he was going after the end of term. I think about the mountain I saw, towering over the marina so high it seemed as if it might topple down on us at any moment. I think about the shape of the buildings on the shore, their square towers and terracotta-tiled roofs.

No, not France. Italy, maybe. Although how we ended up here is anyone's guess.

And how long since I last remember anything? One month? Two?

I'm obviously supposed to know these other two people. From the state of the main cabin – clothes littered around the floor and beer cans and full ashtrays on any available flat surface – I get the sense we've been living together on this boat for more than a day or two.

'Here.' The girl plonks a mug of water down in front of me. 'You look like you could do with this.'

She reminds me of Amanda de Cadanet, all swooshy blonde hair and private-school accent, and I consider for a second that I might just be having a rather intense nightmare brought on by watching the *The Word* while I talked with Becca last night, but then the boat lurches as the wake of a passing ferry slaps against the hull, sending my hand shooting for the table in front of me to steady myself, and I dismiss the idea.

No. This is real. At least, as real as the last 'jump' was, anyway.

I sip the water and it seems to help. 'Thanks …' I croak, trailing off because I realise I don't know the girl's name.

Jude offers me a round, crusty roll and I tear it open with my hands and stuff a healthy helping of ham and slices of pale-yellow cheese inside. The biting, the chewing, the swallowing that follows helps anchor me to this day, this time, more firmly. By the time I finish breakfast I almost feel normal again.

'So what's the plan for today?' I ask and look round, hopefully. Maybe I can play detective and piece the rest of what I want to know together if I'm clever about it.

They all look at me, then look at each other, then burst out laughing again. I feel my hackles rise.

'It was your idea!' the nameless guy says. 'Wow. Those G&Ts really did their job, didn't they?'

'Humour me,' I say, not sounding very humorous at all.

'We were going to sail down to the island. You know, the one with the palazzo? See if we can moor off one of the beaches.'

I nod as if I know what he's talking about. 'Of course we were,' I say, as if everything is completely normal. 'When are we setting sail?'

'Soon as we're all ready,' he replies.

I nod again and stand up. 'Better get dressed then.' I've decided that short sentences and concrete facts are my best friends right now.

As I throw on a stripy T-shirt and some shorts, find some

blue-and-white plimsolls I don't recognise but assume are mine, because my socks, which I do recognise, are stuffed into them, I let the questions come.

Why? I think to myself. Why did it happen again? Was it something I did, something I said? Something I wished really hard in my heart? Part of me hoped it was, because then at least there'd be some rhyme or reason to this … whatever it is. At least I'd have some control, even if I have to work out what the trigger is. The thought it might just all be random doesn't sit well with me.

And I've missed so much! Saying goodbye to all my uni friends – for the second time, anyway, but I'd been looking forward to that bit – the summer ball, graduation … Those were some of my best memories of my time at Oaklands, yet I've skipped straight over them.

I peer at myself in the little mirror attached to the inside of the cupboard door. The awful fringe is longer, but not quite long enough to tuck behind my ears, which leaves me looking like an old English sheepdog. I think about the blonde's effortless honey waves and wonder I can learn enough Italian to get myself a haircut.

We cast off less than half an hour later. By perusing some navigational maps left on a tiny desk to the side of the stairs that lead up to the cockpit, I manage to work out we're on Lake Garda. I have a vague idea of this being somewhere in the north of Italy, but I'm not exactly sure where. When I get up into the cockpit and sit down on the moulded bench next to Jude, who is confidently manning the tiller, I check out the position of the sun and decide we're heading south. I refer to the mental snapshot I made of the map and decide we must have been moored somewhere near either Riva or Torbole and are now heading down to where the lake broadens and the mountains become less rugged.

It takes longer than I expect to travel the distance. Hours. But then the only experience I have of boats is the kind with pedals that you can rent by the half hour on a pond in the middle of a park. The sun is right overhead by the time we spot the tiny island Cameron was talking about.

Cameron Lombard, that's right. I've worked out who he is now, and this is indeed his boat. Well, his dad's boat, to be more precise. Cam is the son of a sporting-goods tycoon and, from what I gather, he's enjoying an extended gap year after finishing uni two summers ago and has spent most of it bumming round Europe. If I have to admit it, I'm slightly intimidated by Cameron. He's got that kind of confidence that makes him seem invincible, makes every decision seem like the best plan ever rather than a whim of the moment.

Thankfully, his girlfriend, Isabelle, or Issie – I'm not sure of her surname yet – is much less terrifying, if no less confident. She's laid back and friendly and talks to me as if we've known each other for years.

From the conversation that ensues between barking sailing instructions and having to run around the boat pulling ropes and tying things to kleats (in which I am, yet again, the butt of the communal joke: 'Watch the boom, Meg! After your dunking last week, I'd have thought you'd learned that lesson!'), I glean that Jude and I bumped into the other couple in Cannes about three weeks earlier, and after a week full of lounging around on pine-fringed beaches and bar crawling, we – well, let's face it, it was probably 'they' – decided it would be a jolly good jape to nip over the alps into Italy and pick up Cam's daddy's boat, *Vita Perfetta*, from Malcesine.

They seem a nice enough couple, I suppose, but I find it awkward trying to relate to them as if I know them, as if we've shared close quarters for more than a fortnight now. So, as we sail the last part of our journey, I sit in the cockpit with them, cradling an open bottle of beer, but not actually drinking it, and I let the conversation flow around me like I'm a rock in a stream. I am in the middle of it but I am not part of it.

I try to dip my toe in when the facts are safe and neutral, to capture any bits of relevant information, but when they all start talking about the street entertainer in Riva's town square the night before, or the amazing *moules* they had in that little cafe near San Malo, I have to shut up and the river of words rushes around me again, making me feel separate. Apart.

To be honest, it's not just the missing chunk of time that's the problem. It's them. The life they lead. I should count Jude in with me, because we come from very similar backgrounds, but somehow he seems more like Cam and Issie. He talks like them, knows what to wear and what to say to seem effortlessly sophisticated. He fits right in. That, and the fact that I can't remember the last six weeks of my life, means I can't help feeling as if I'm an alien that's been teleported in.

As we near the island, Cam and Jude drop the sails and tie them up – the big one at the back against the big swingy thing, which I now know is the boom, and the front one onto the railings and posts at the front of the boat. The motor putt-putts away as we drift across water that's the colour of a cloudy emerald. I stand on the deck, one arm wrapped around the mast for stability, and shield my eyes from the sun with my hand. As we get closer to the long strip of rock in the middle of the lake, I let out only one word: 'Wow!'

Jude comes to stand beside me. He doesn't need to hold on to anything, just relies on his natural grace and balance. 'It's pretty amazing, huh? I can see why you wanted to get a closer look.'

The boat moves past the rounded tip of the island where the palazzo stands. It takes my breath away. It's all pink and white, like one of the fondant fancies my nan used to serve up when we went round for tea, but there is nothing frou-frou about its architecture. There are bold arches that remind me of Venetian palaces on the Grand Canal, and the house stands majestically amongst the manicured gardens that cover the small lump of rock, proudly facing the lake to catch the rays of the midday sun.

None of us say anything as we motor past a small private dock, to where another boat has dropped anchor off a gently curving beach no more than a few metres wide. 'Bloody great idea, Meg,' Issie says from the cockpit. 'Well done, you.'

For the first time since I jumped into this time, this place, I feel as if I have managed to get something right. Even if it was the 'other' me that did it.

And how exactly does that work, by the way? I feel like me, if you know what I mean? The me that jumps from time to time. Is there another me that inhabits the spaces, the gaps? And, if there is, what happens to her when I arrive? Does she just disappear? And if she doesn't exist, if it's just me, why can't I remember things? It's all very confusing.

I'm mulling this all over when I feel an arm snake around my waist and feel a warm pair of lips against the back of my neck. My ears start tingling. I smile as I look at the beautiful scene laid before us.

'Are you OK?' Jude whispers.

'Why do you ask?'

He holds me tighter, just a little. 'You've just been really quiet today.'

I twist to look at him. 'Have I?'

He nods. 'I was starting to get worried about you.'

The urge to tell him everything balloons up within me but I swallow it down again. 'I'm OK,' I say, looking into his eyes. 'But if anyone had told me a couple of months ago that I'd be here with you, now, I'd have told them they were crazy.' I don't have to lie, because this is all true, just not in the way he understands it to be.

'I know,' he says softly and teases my lips with his before kissing me properly. 'I feel the same way too. It was a moment of madness on my part when I asked you to dump Dan for me. I really hadn't been intending to say all that.'

His words make my stomach wobble a little. 'Do you regret it?' I ask.

He laughs at me, but this time it is soft and warm and I

don't feel the sting of humiliation. 'God, no, Meg! It may have been the sanest thing I ever did. It scares me to think we might have missed out on this, that we might just have gone our separate ways after Oaklands and never seen each other again.'

I hug him tighter, mainly because I know how awful it was to actually experience that. Even though we've only been together again a short time, I can't imagine my life without him.

Jude turns me so I'm facing him and looks into my eyes. 'What I'm trying to say – very badly, as it happens – is that I'm glad I have you, that I ...' He hesitates for a moment and the force field of confidence that usually surrounds him shimmers and becomes patchy, just for a second. He swallows, as if his mouth is dry. 'That I love you,' he finishes. A piece of dark hair flops over his forehead, making him look all Hugh Grant in *Four Weddings,* and totally adorable.

The wobbling in my stomach stops and I look him back in the eyes without wavering. 'Good,' I say firmly. 'Because I love you too. In fact, I may not have ever stopped.'

He pulls me to him roughly and hugs me to him maybe a little too tightly but I don't mind. I can feel him shaking a little while I remain rocksteady and firm, even without my grip on the mast. 'I was such a fool not to do everything I could to keep you the first time,' he whispers, 'and I'm so sorry for it. I promise, I won't ever do that again.'

I close my eyes and feel the warm, slightly salty breeze on my face, and then I smile, because that is all I have ever wanted him to say to me. That's all I've ever wanted anyone to say to me. I kiss him softly on the lips then playfully push him away.

'Sure about that?' I ask, laughing, as I start running towards the cockpit where I've left my bikini. 'Because last one in the water is a loser!'

CHAPTER SEVENTEEN

We swim in the clear waters of Lake Garda as the noonday sun beats down on the tops of our heads, and then, because the other boat has motored away and there's nobody here to see us, we row ashore in the inflatable dinghy and lie on the beach that's been unfurled by the lake's receding tide. We bring a picnic over and drink more beers and eat more rolls with speck and rubbery cheese slices and eat juicy cherry tomatoes and plump, fat olives.

And when a short irate man appears at the edge of the woodland that borders the strip of sand and starts yelling at us in a tidal wave of Italian, we squeal and rush around collecting up our belongings, throwing them into the dinghy. In their haste to get away, Cam and Issie just start rowing and Jude and I have to dive in and swim to catch up to them. I'm laughing so hard I swallow at least a gallon of lake water before I haul myself over the edge of the dinghy, but I really don't care.

This is it, I think. This is the life I've always wanted, and it's mine now. In my hands.

Back on the boat I sneak a glance at Jude, who's deep in conversation with Cam about which is the best town to moor at tonight and an ache – not horrible, but pleasant and warm – begins to pulse in my chest.

I can't spoil this, I say in my head, praying to no one in particular but praying all the same. I can't mess it up a second time. Once was just careless. Twice and I'd deserve the dull life I've managed to escape.

I want to believe I can do it, but I realise I still don't exactly know how I'd ended up so miserable, because miserable I was. I can see that now. What if I just make the same mistakes all over again? What if I'm fated be boring old Maggie, no matter what I do?

I take a deep breath and calm myself. I can't think like that. I'm just going to have to do what everyone else does: the best they can. At least I've had this chance, this wake-up call, to help me.

We end up motoring to the nearest cluster of buildings on the shore, which turns out to be the small town of Salo. It lies just south of the headland which marks the end to the really steep parts to the lake's shore, where the mountains seem to plunge downwards into the water and tiny villages cling so fiercely to the cliffs above I often expect to see one lose its grip and start sliding down into the water. In comparison, the lakeside area of Salo is flatter and the hills roll gently upward behind it.

It's siesta time and a lot of the shops are closed, so we wander through the cobbled streets, window shopping, spying out a decent restaurant for dinner later that evening. Our collective cooking skills extend to shoving things in rolls and frying things, so it makes sense to eat out in the evenings. We don't go to the classy restaurants in the hotels but tend to stick to little family-run places, to get the authentic feel of Italy, Cam says, and that's fine by me. Even the shabbiest-looking place with plastic garden tables and paper tablecloths serves amazing food.

I stop outside a tourist shop and gaze through the window at the rack of postcards inside: over-bright pictures of the lake and mountains, the little fishing boats almost painful in their painted-on neon colours. It seems ridiculous that someone has done that. Why would anyone need to try and add beauty to a scene that's already perfect?

'Thinking about writing home?' Jude asks, coming up beside me.

'I really ought to,' I say, realising that my parents might not even know I'm in Italy.

There are no Internet cafes yet, as far as I know, and brick-like mobile phones aren't the sort of thing an unemployed, just-graduated student like me can afford. I look at Jude's reflection in the window as I say my next words, 'I probably ought to send one to Becca, too.'

The face he pulls while he thinks I can't see him tells me all I need to know. I turn round and look at him. 'Are you OK with that?'

He shrugs. 'You know she thinks I'm the devil incarnate …'

'She doesn't! She just was really invested in me marrying Dan – I think she thought it was this wonderful fairy tale, and it gave her hope she could have a happy ever after of her own too. She'll come round, you'll see … you just have to give her a chance to get to know you.'

'After what she screamed at me that last night, do you really think that's going to happen?'

Ah. So things hadn't gone well before I'd left for Europe with Jude. Good to know. I still needed to try to piece the rest of the last month or two together in my head. I was finding recent history much easier to uncover, as it was more likely to be part of the conversation on board *Vita Perfetta*. Jude hasn't said much about what happened between us getting together and leaving England and it's hard to introduce it into the conversation naturally.

'She's my best friend,' I say quietly. 'I have to at least try to mend fences.'

Jude kisses me on the forehead. 'Whatever you want, lovely Meg. Whatever makes you happy.'

I lean against him and feel his warmth, sure again for the thousandth time today that I've made the right choice. Jude is so understanding and caring, much more so than I'd given him credit for all that time I'd hated him, and when I look into his eyes I believe what he told me earlier on today: that he loves me the way I love him. I couldn't be any happier.

'We'll see,' I say as I turn away from the shop. 'I can't buy one now anyway. Maybe later, after dinner.'

We wander back to the boat and I end up falling asleep in our cabin. The sun and the fresh lake air seems to have that effect on me. When I wake up the sun is much lower in the sky and the rest of them are bustling around getting ready for our evening onshore.

I wander into the main cabin in my T-shirt and shorts.

My fringe has decided to launch a rebellion and one side is sticking up no matter how many times I try to run my fingers through it. My sleep-fuzzy eyes come into focus and I notice that the boys have linen trousers and nice shirts on and Issie has swapped her wardrobe of various cut-off denim shorts for a dress. I stop and stare at them. 'What's the occasion?' I ask as I rub my face, still feeling like a large truck has reversed over me.

'Bumped into one of my father's business associates when we were exploring the town earlier,' Cam explains.

I rub my face again. 'Does he live here?'

'She,' Cam replies, correcting me, 'and, no, but I think my father's love of *Lago di Garda* can be infectious. He's always preaching about it to his friends, telling them to visit. He even recommended the villa they've rented.'

I look the three of them up and down. While this is all very nice, I don't understand what it has to do with getting all dressed up.

'She's invited us to eat with her there,' Jude explains.

I attempt to flatten my fringe once more. 'I suppose I'd better get changed then.' And I slink back into the cabin, pull every piece of clothing I've brought with me out of my bag and out of the cupboard and lay it on the bed and stare at it. I've only got two dresses with me. One is made of jersey and is more suitable for throwing on over the top of a bikini than anything else and the other …

Well, I thought it looked like one Julia Roberts wore in *The Pelican Brief* when I bought it, with its tiny white flowers on a dark background and A-line maxi skirt that buttons to just below my knees, but now I take another look at it, it doesn't look flowy and classy to me at all, just very … High Street.

There's a knock on the cabin door and Jude sticks his head in. 'Ready? We need to shuffle off in about ten minutes.'

I look down at the dress on the bed. 'Do you think this will be OK?'

Jude frowns. 'Is it all you've got?'

'Well, apart from the cherry-red one that only just about covers my bum.'

He grins. 'Well, you know I like that one … but maybe stick with this one for now.'

He disappears back into the main cabin and I hear him and the others talking. I hope it isn't about me, about my lack of suitable wardrobe.

Cam's dad's business associate is called Priscilla and her villa has a terrace that sweeps down to the lake's edge, where a pair of wrought-iron gates give access to a private dock. The gardens are all sculpted box hedges and geometric shapes, but, somehow, given the wildness of the backdrop, they are charming rather than overly formal, as if the two things balance each other out.

The house itself is huge. Just the entrance hall is the size of my mum and dad's Victorian terrace. I keep expecting hotel staff to pop out from somewhere but they never do. If Cam and Issie and Jude think the same, they don't show it. In fact, they lounge as effortlessly on the cream sofas on the terrace – *Cream? Think of the dirt!* my mum would say – as they do on rickety wooden chairs in a lakeside bar.

They sip Prosecco and eat the caviar canapés without staring suspiciously at them.

I look down at the shiny black roe on the blini in between my fingers. I'm not much of a fish eater, really, but I don't want to appear rude.

Looks like slimy shotgun pellets to me ...

I hear Dan's voice in my head and it makes me smile. And then, almost as quickly, I frown. I shouldn't be thinking of what Dan had said the first time he was offered it his cousin's wedding. I've left that life behind.

But as the conversation drifts on around me – about people and places I don't know – I can't help thinking about my husband. Or the man who would have been my husband. I wonder what he's doing now.

In our old life we'd have been knee-deep in wedding plans. Neither of us had wanted a long engagement, so we'd tied the knot three months after leaving university. Is he happy? I wonder. Moving on? I hope so.

I don't say much as the dinner progresses, but I start to feel more comfortable. These are nice people, Priscilla and her husband, Bruce. They might have different tastes and budgets to my family but they want the same things out of life that my parents do: security, and success. Happiness for their children.

Later, we amble back down through the town on our way to the marina, not quite ready for the evening to end yet. Jude and I stop to kiss every ten paces. I can still taste the limoncello that was served after dinner on his lips.

Coming up for air from one of these little intervals, I realise that we are standing outside the tourist shop we'd stared through the window of earlier in the afternoon.

'Do you want to go in?'

I look at the rack of postcards for a few moments and then shake my head.

'But I thought you wanted to send a postcard to Becca?'

'I do. It's just …' It's just I'm still not sure how things stand between me and Becca, and despite his suggestion to the contrary, I could tell Jude would rather I didn't. I shake my head. 'I think maybe what needs to be said should be said face to face. I'll talk to her when we get back to London.'

He smiles at me softly. 'Whatever you want, Meg.'

Whatever I want.

And what I want now – more than patching things up with Becca, because I know she'll come round – is to make this future work with Jude.

I turn and walk away, back in the direction of the marina, leaving my good wishes and love from the Italian lakes unwritten and unsaid.

CHAPTER EIGHTEEN

I'm on the train from Waterloo to Wimbledon early on a Thursday evening. It's September and I'm back in London, with Jude. Our carefree summer came to a sudden end when he phoned home and discovered his father had had a heart attack. He's OK, but the doctor said he needs to take it easy, cut back on work. That's where Jude comes in, apparently.

Jude says the reason he went to uni is because he didn't want to join the family firm, but now he feels he can't say no. He feels trapped and miserable, facing a future of leaky roofs and plastic conservatories. Having been stuck in a life I hated, I sympathise completely. But what else can he do?

So we're renting a flat in Lewisham, to be near his parents in Hither Green, and I'm looking for design work. Freelance or with a big firm, I don't care. I just need a job. However, while I still have some free time, there's something I need to do …

I stare at a small shell bracelet I'm holding between my fingers, then put it in my pocket as the train pulls into the station and I get off. It's high time I gave Becca her present from Italy. I've heard from mutual friends she's working at the bar in Wimbledon Theatre. I haven't called ahead. I'm telling myself it's because I want it to be a surprise, but really

I'm scared that she wouldn't speak to me if she knew I was coming.

Two and a half weeks. I really should have summed up the nerve before now. But I know exactly what went down that last night I saw her. Jude tells me she got hysterical, shouting at the pair of us, telling me I'd gone insane, throwing all sorts of wild accusations about, although I haven't been able to discover exactly what those were. I'd been in tears, trying to explain, but eventually he'd pulled me away and taken me home, scared she'd go for him. Or me. That had just made Becca even angrier.

My hand moves to my pocket and I move the bracelet round between my thumb and forefinger a shell at a time, feeling each one's knobbly perfection. I haven't 'jumped' again since that morning I woke up on the boat in Lake Garda. I remember everything, have lived every second, both exciting and tedious, and I've enjoyed every one of them. Hopefully, it was just a hiccup. An aftershock.

The theatre bar is virtually empty when I arrive there. The performance has already started and there's at least forty-five minutes until the interval. I'm praying that'll be long enough for Becca and I to catch up before it gets busy.

A lone man with a stomach that overhangs his jeans by quite a bit is on a bar stool, sipping his beer with reverence. Guess he's not into musicals, then, as the overture from *Annie* drifts in from the adjacent auditorium. Probably just came in for a quiet pint while everyone else is watching the show.

I choose an empty stool and look for movement through the double doors behind the bar. I can hear someone bustling around back there. Seconds later Becca emerges carrying a plastic crate full of mixers.

'I'll be with you in just a – oh.'

'Hi,' I say. My voice sounds weak and insipid.

She puts the crate down and stares at me, hands on hips. 'So, you're back, then?'

I nod. The only thing I can hear in the silence is the big-bellied man slurping at his beer. 'It's good to see you.'

Becca makes a noise that is half sniff, half snort. 'Is it?' she says, turning to stack the bottles of bitter lemon and ginger ale onto a shelf under the counter. ''Cos I thought you'd forgotten all about us.'

Us? I almost say, and then I realise she's talking about Dan – that while I've been away they've become a unit of two. United in their disappointment with me, I suspect.

Becca stands up and looks at me. 'It's been almost three months. No card, no phone call …'

'I was going to send a card, but … but they were all so ghastly and fake-looking, and my Italian never really did get good enough to handle a trip to the post office …'

I regret the lame excuse as soon as it's out of my mouth. But I couldn't tell her that while my boyfriend would smile and tell me to do what made me happy, there was always an undercurrent that he would be disappointed with me if I did. That would just be throwing unnecessary ammunition her way.

I pull the bracelet from my pocket and slide it across the mahogany bar. 'I got you this …'

Becca stares at it, then picks it up. For a moment, I think

she's going to soften, but then she puts it back down on the bar and pushes it back to me. 'Sorry, don't take gifts from strangers.' And then she turns and marches off through the swing doors, which bang satisfyingly behind her.

I sit there, stunned, for a second. Big Belly Man glances in my direction and just shrugs. When I realise that Becca isn't going to come out again, I slide off the stool, the melody of 'It's A Hard-Knock Life' mocking me as I slink from the theatre.

CHAPTER NINETEEN

My eyes are closed but I'm aware I'm awake, although I haven't been for long. I shift in the bed and let out a comfortable sigh. Everything feels so homely and familiar. It even smells familiar. Every morning I'm glad of that feeling, glad I'm not waking into a new reality where I have to find my bearings and play detective.

I stretch and reach out a hand for Jude, but where I expect to find him there is only fresh air. And not just the space where he'd been lying moments before. My searching hand finds no sheet, no bed.

I open my eyes and sit bolt upright.

No!

Not again.

I'm back in my childhood bedroom with the stripy wallpaper and the ugly brown shaggy carpet. I just didn't realise at first because a part of me knows it better than my current home.

I quickly throw back the duvet – a grass-green one with strawberries and sprigs of white flowers on it – and check myself over, then I flop back down on the pillow and let out a juddering breath. Oh, thank God for that. For a second,

I thought I might have gone even farther backwards, to my teenage years, but I seem to be roughly the same age as I was when I went to bed next to Jude the night before.

So why am I here? Did Jude and I break up? My chest cramps at the thought.

I let the sadness, the anger, come. Not just for whatever might have happened between me and Jude, but because I've skipped time again. How much have I missed? Who am I now? All of this is making me feel rather disconnected from myself, as if I'm an actor in a play of my own life, swapping scenes and parts at random.

Just as I'm starting to properly wallow, there's a soft knock and my mum puts her head round the door. 'You up, love? Big day ahead!' Without waiting for an answer, she nudges it open and enters. She's balancing a cup of tea and a plate of Mother's Pride toast cut into triangles, and she places them carefully on the bedside table.

'I suppose so …' I say, then take a sip of the tea. After my last 'jump', I learned that short and non-committal answers are the safest.

Mum lets out a surprised laugh. 'I'd say!' she adds, still chuckling, and her gaze falls on a garment covered in dry-cleaning plastic hanging from the front of the wardrobe door. For a moment, what I'm seeing doesn't compute, but then my heart skips into overdrive.

It's a wedding dress.

I push the duvet back and climb out of bed, feel the thin slippery plastic of the covering between my fingers then lift it slightly to look at the bottom of the skirt. It's plain. Pure white taffeta. Not dissimilar from my wedding dress the first time around. Obviously, my tastes haven't changed much.

I look at my mum, an expression of wonder on my face. *I'm marrying Jude?*

I let out a little hiccup of a laugh, just because I can't help it, but then I stop. How far have I jumped forward? There hadn't even been a hint of that between us in the time and place I've just come from.

'Drink up,' Mum says, glancing at my mug of tea. 'Becca will be here in half an hour.'

'Becca's coming?' My heart catches again. Oh, thank goodness for that. We must have made up. Relief washes through me.

'Of course she is. She's your maid of honour!' Mum shakes her head. 'You're in a strange mood this morning, but I suppose if a person is going to be in a strange mood, it might as well be on their wedding day.'

I launch myself at her and hug her hard. 'I love you, Mum!'

She laughs again, kisses the top of my head and extricates herself from my grasp. 'Like I said … strange mood. You'd better watch it, or you'll be in a buckle-up-at-the-back white jacket by the end of the day, not a white dress.'

I grin at her, then peel back the flimsy covering from over the top of the wedding dress to get a good look at it. It's almost identical to the one I wore when I got married to Dan, except for the puffy sleeves. I'd loved them at the time, but years after the wedding I'd never been entirely sure about them. I'm really glad I saw sense this time around.

Mum comes and stands next to me, and we both stand

and smile at the dress. 'I love it,' I whisper. I can't wait to put it on and walk down the aisle to the man of my dreams.

'It is beautiful,' Mum says wistfully, and then she turns and gives me a wink. I always loved it when she did that. Mum always seemed a bit older than my other friends' mothers, a little more buttoned-up and fixated on manners, but when she winked you could see her mischievous side sparkling underneath.

She takes one last look at the dress and heads for the door. 'Dan is going to think he's the luckiest man alive when he sees you in it.'

I spit out my tea at that point, only just managing to avoid spewing brown spots all over the skirt of my perfect white wedding dress.

CHAPTER TWENTY

Dan? My mum didn't really say that, did she? She meant Jude. She must have meant Jude. It was probably just a slip of the tongue.

My heart rate evens out.

That must be it. Stressful day and all that. Easily done when she and Dad had been willing Dan to propose for months before he actually did. They'd been pretty invested in that outcome.

I sit down on the edge of the bed, rest my elbows on my knees and support my head with my palms.

Phew. OK ... you can calm down now, Maggie.

I'm still sitting there, breathing in through my nose and out through my mouth, when Becca bursts in, laden with a garment bag and two plastic carriers stuffed full of make-up, curling tongs and hair products. She drops the bags on the floor, throws the other one over the chair in the corner, then pulls me into a bear hug. 'I am so happy for you!' she breathes into my ear.

I squeeze her back. Oh, I've missed her so much. 'I'm so glad we were able to get over the whole Jude thing ...' I say. Obviously, she supports me now, otherwise she wouldn't have agreed to be my maid of honour. I knew her unswerving loyalty would have to kick in at some point. 'I know he's going to make me really happy.'

Becca pulls back and the top of her nose wrinkles. 'Why on earth are you talking about The Jerk on a day like today?'

'I ... I ...'

'I mean, talk about making a girl want to lose her cornflakes or something!' Becca says, laughing, and starts pulling cosmetics out of her plastic bags. 'Now ... do you want to do barely there make-up, or are you going to go for something a bit stronger? I think your features can take it, if you do, and I've got a really nice shade of berry lipstick that'll – '

'Becca?'

She stops and turns her head. 'What?'

'Who am I marrying today?'

She looks confused at first, then beams back at me. 'The most wonderful man in the world, of course.' She thinks this is banter, but instead of making me smile her answer makes me feel queasy.

'And that would be ...?'

'Your mum said you were being a bit weird. Wedding-day jitters, she reckons.' Becca stops smiling and studies my face carefully. 'It is just that, isn't it, because I really don't think – '

I hold up my hand to stop her. '*Who*, Becca?'

Her expression says, 'I don't really want to play this game', but she humours me: 'Dan, of course.'

My stomach goes cold and my skin prickles all over. The floor seems to rush towards me. I wobble, and I'm surprised when I look around and find that my legs are still supporting me. I put a palm on the edge of my bed and ease myself down onto it.

Becca rushes over. 'Are you going to be sick? You look like you're going to be sick.' She tips everything out of my wastepaper basket onto the floor and holds it under my face.

I push it away and gulp. 'No ... I'm fine, really I am. It's just ... like my mum said ... wedding-day jitters. I'll be OK in a moment.'

Becca stands there looking at me suspiciously. She doesn't put the wastepaper basket down.

'Actually,' I say, as an idea pops into my head. 'I could really do with a glass of water.' I look at her hopefully. She takes the hint, places the bin carefully near my feet, and goes to fetch one, giving me the space and silence I need to process what she's just told me.

Dan?

I'm marrying *Dan*?

How can that be? I changed things ...

I stand up, feeling the sudden urge to move, although I don't really know why.

I can't marry Dan today. I can't. It would be ... wrong. I'm with Jude. It would be like cheating on him.

Only ... hadn't I felt that way when I was first with him too? And that hadn't been real, had it? I mean, you can't be unfaithful to someone you're not actually with, can you? I close my eyes, knowing that, logically, this makes sense. I just wish I could get my emotions to believe it.

I don't love Dan. Not any more. I love Jude.

And I really don't want to marry Dan. Ever. Not in the other reality and not even in this one.

That thought slices through my confusion and it falls away.

OK, then. That's all I need to know. I'm not marrying Dan today.

I walk over and cover the wedding dress back up with its filmy plastic sheath. I put Becca's blusher and berry lipstick back in her Miss Selfridge carrier bag, and then I pull on my dressing gown and prepare to go downstairs and break the news to my parents.

I'm still holding the bag when Becca bustles back in with a glass of water. She sets it down on the dressing table, takes the carrier bag from my hand without commenting – I don't think she's even noticed anything is amiss – and starts gathering everything she needs to tame my mind-of-their-own waves into regimented ringlets.

I'm sitting staring at myself in the dressing-table mirror and Becca's on her second corkscrew when I put my hand up and push the curling tongs away. 'I can't do this,' I say.

'It'll be fine,' Becca says and picks up the next strand of hair. 'I can work wonders with these things, I promise you.' And she brandishes the tongs, grinning at me in the dressing-table mirror.

'No. I mean, I can't do … *this*.' I wave in the general direction of the wedding dress hanging off to my left, refusing to actually make eye contact with it.

'Don't be stupid,' she says lightly, and returns her attention to my hair.

I pull away so the strand she's feeding round the tongs slips off. 'It's not just nerves, Becs. I know this is a huge mistake!' I stare at her in the mirror, willing her to understand. The look of slight annoyance she's been wearing since I unravelled the last ringlet disappears and she puts the tongs down on the dressing table then sits on the edge of the bed. I turn to face her.

'What's going on?' she asks gently.

'It's not supposed to be like this!'

'Then what's it supposed to be like?'

I lift my hands and drop them again. 'I don't know … more. It's supposed to be *more*.'

A flicker of irritation passes across her features. 'You're living in fairy-tale land. What you're thinking about is for story books and chick flicks. It doesn't happen in real life.'

But it does! I want to yell back at her. I have it with Jude. In my other life. 'It should,' I say. 'I'm tired of settling. I want to go big, live big.'

She ponders my words and then she sighs. 'You know what your problem is?'

I shake my head.

'You've always thought you were a little bit better than Dan.'

I blink, sit back a bit on my stool. 'I have not.'

Becca cocks her head and raises an eyebrow, as if saying, *really?*

'I don't,' I say, but it's more a reflex than an actual considered opinion. We fall into silence as I do just that – consider her words. Her judgement.

She softens her voice. 'You take him for granted, you know,

and you really shouldn't. He's your biggest fan, he clearly adores you and sometimes I even get jealous because I feel as if he's muscling in on the "best friend" part too.'

I look at her. 'Really?'

She nods. 'Really. I don't know how you can even think of saying no to all that.'

I slump into myself and let out a heavy breath. Becca's words make sense, but I can't help how I feel about Jude, and I can't just marry Dan because he's a nice guy, even if he is going to be the one waiting for me in the church today. I don't love him. Not any more. And even if I did, I know how that story ends.

'And what are you going to do, anyway? Are you really going to leave Dan standing there at the altar?' She stands up and picks up another strand of my hair, winds it around the curling tongs. It steams softly as she holds it there for a few seconds.

I stare straight ahead. Becca knows me too well. She knows I have a thing about movies where someone leaves someone else standing at the front of the church while they run off with the person they really want.

I don't understand why people think those scenes are so romantic. As the music swells and the lovers run off out of the church, laughing, I can't help feeling angry on behalf of the poor chump left behind. How humiliating, to be abandoned to deal with the fallout on your own, publicly rejected in front of all your friends and family. And the truth is that the jilted party often isn't evil; they don't deserve their sentence. Mostly, their only crime is not being The One.

And maybe Dan isn't my 'One'. That still doesn't mean I can do this to him.

As Becca works her way round my head, creating thick twirling ringlets that will probably drop out in half an hour, I start to think about how I'd been intending to take control of my life, to make decisions rather than letting circumstances dictate my destiny.

So maybe I should *choose* to marry Dan today, instead of just letting it happen to me. I can do this because I'm not going to be here forever. I have a feeling this isn't the end of my jumping around. Somehow I know I'm going to find my way back to Jude again soon.

I'll just have to *last*.

It'll be like marking through a dance. I'll be doing all the right movements at the right times but my soul won't be in it. That way it won't be real. That way I can do this without betraying anyone, not even myself.

The rest of the morning disappears in a blur. It's like when you're waiting for something – a bus or a hospital appointment – and the first half-hour seems to crawl by but after that you hit your groove and time just starts to slide past you. Even the people become blurry: Becca, my mum and dad, my cousin Francesca, who is the other bridesmaid. Before I know it I'm stepping out of a vintage Rolls-Royce Silver Shadow in front of our local Baptist Church. I can hear the organ playing inside. The September day is fresh and clean and warm beneath a deep-blue sky and a slight breeze ruffles my veil. It's a perfect day to get married.

I only get through it because my body knows what to do

and goes through the motions, like a robot. That version of Maggie smiles shyly at the gathered guests as she walks down the aisle, says her vows without a single trip or stutter; but all the while, the inside Maggie, the *real* Maggie, is looking away slyly, crossing her fingers behind her back.

CHAPTER TWENTY-ONE

Dan closes the door behind him. 'Thank the Lord that's all over!' He smiles at me. We are completely alone for the first time today and the crust of numbness that's been clinging to me since I put my wedding dress on this morning starts to crumble.

It was easy to stay detached in a church hall crammed with people, all the cheers and smiles and toasts blurring together. I'd even managed to remain remote, in that weird floating-above-yourself way, during our first dance, when we were supposed to be locked in a bubble with eyes for no one but each other.

But now it's just the two of us in a tiny little country hotel. There are beams on the low ceiling, a Persian rug on the floor and a hefty-looking four-poster in the middle of the room, quietly confident that, despite its age, it will be able to withstand any amount of wedding-night gymnastics.

And smiling at me from the other side of the mattress is a hopeful-looking man with a tell-tale look in his eyes. My stomach bottoms out but, more surprisingly, once the feeling of standing on fresh air while a trap door has opened up underneath me subsides, I discover there's a humming warmth low in my abdomen too.

Oh, heck.

Why, oh, why had I agreed to Dan's old-fashioned idea of saving ourselves until this day? Until this very moment? It would have been so much easier to keep that floating-above-myself feeling going if this was just another night in the sack, despite our attempt at grand surroundings on our shoestring budget.

My gaze fixes on the panelled door that leads to the en-suite bathroom. I gather up my overnight case and scuttle off inside, closing the door behind me as I say something about needing to get ready.

Once inside, I slide the bolt across quietly so Dan doesn't hear me, and then I sit down on the closed toilet lid and rest my head in my hands. I can hear him moving around in the room, turning down the bed, maybe, and it only makes my stomach twinge harder.

After a couple of minutes, though, I realise I can't just sit here. What am I going to do? Lock myself in the bathroom for the entirety of my wedding night? So I stand up, place my holdall on the closed toilet and carefully unzip it. The first thing I pull out is a white satin nightdress, ankle-length but with pretty spaghetti straps and lace at the top. I swallow, and my stomach plummets again.

I turn away from the mirror and strip off, refusing to look at myself as I put it on. My pulse is racing and I feel sick. I rummage in my holdall for my wash bag. There's something about brushing my teeth that always seems to settle my stomach. I don't know why. And I suppose minty-fresh breath isn't a bad idea considering what's coming next.

When I've rinsed out the last of the toothpaste, I move my bag and sit down on the toilet again. My heart is trying to escape my ribcage, like a bird desperately throwing itself against a window. This is ridiculous. I've done this hundreds of time with this man in the last quarter of a century. Why am I so scared? I should be able to check out emotionally and do it on automatic. That's certainly how I'd approached the whole issue of sex back in my 'real' life for the last few years.

I breathe slowly for a minute or so, trying to stop my head churning, and, as I start to calm down, images of Jude as I last saw him float through my mind.

Jude. My chest squeezes tight. He's the love of my life, I think. The kind of love people sing about in songs. The kind I've always hoped was real but was scared was just a fantasy. How can I let anyone else touch me the way he's touched me? It seems wrong.

Even though everything is back-to-front and it's Dan's ring on my finger and not Jude's and it feels like being unfaithful, it's not just that. I don't want to dilute what I've got with Jude. If he's really the love of my life it should be impossible to feel something for anybody else, shouldn't it? I shouldn't feel this pull towards the man on the other side of the locked bathroom door.

My thoughts are disturbed by a gentle knocking. 'Maggie? Are you almost finished?' I'm glad he doesn't try the handle.

'Why?' I snap back, and my voice bounces off the tiled walls. 'Do you need a wee?'

There's a pause, as if he's taken aback by my rather unromantic comment. 'No,' he says softly. 'It's just … You know what? Never mind.' And I hear him walk away from the door. I can picture the look of confusion on his face as he tries to work out if he's just imagining the bite in my tone, which he isn't, but what bride starts sniping at her beloved groom on their wedding night? I can tell he's convincing himself he heard it wrong.

I feel a pang of sympathy for him and that just makes me angry. I turn and glower at myself in the mirror. I don't want to care about how Dan is feeling. I don't want to feel anything for him at all. I close my eyes and wish with everything I've got that I'll just 'jump' again, that I'll open my eyes and I'll be standing in the flat I share with Jude in SE13, but it doesn't work. When I open my eyes I'm still staring at the champagne-coloured corner bath, complete with Jacuzzi, that fills half the tiny room.

I move around then, turning taps on, zipping and unzipping my make-up bag loudly. I even flush the toilet. Anything to explain why I'm stuck frozen in here like a zombie while my expectant groom paces around outside. Eventually, I run out of audible excuses and I just go still. I walk over to the bathroom door and place a palm on it.

Dan surprises me by trying the handle and I jump backwards. 'Maggie?' He tries again, just to check, and I know he must be wondering why his new wife has barricaded herself on the other side of the door. 'Are you OK? Is everything alright?'

No, I want to shout back, *everything is not alright! And flipping well stop being so understanding! It's making it very hard to keep pretending you're a cardboard cut-out in this little scene, a two-dimensional prop with no feelings.*

I turn and lean against the bathroom door, glad for its solid bulk, and then my knees soften and I start to slide, my back in contact with the wood, until my bottom hits the black-and-white-tiled floor.

I hear another noise, a shuffling, and I realise that Dan is on the other side, just as close as I am, and that he's sitting down too. How he knows I ended up on the down here and matched his pose to mine is a mystery to me.

'It's OK,' he says, and I hear his voice drift through the old-fashioned keyhole, twisting its way round through the levers and mortices. 'I'm nervous too.' He's filling in the blanks I've left with my inability to explain, I realise, and he's doing a pretty good job of it.

I hear him haul in a deep breath, as if he's just made a big decision, and then he continues. 'We don't have to do anything tonight if you don't want to. We can just kiss. Or cuddle.'

He pauses and I'm overtaken by the idea of just cuddling. It shocks me how much I want that.

His voice is quieter when he speaks again, but less hesitant. 'We've got a whole lifetime. There's no need to rush.'

A tear escapes from beneath my lashes, one I didn't even know was brewing. I know how much he's been looking forward to this. I know how much I was first time around, even if it did turn out to be slightly disastrous and we'd ended up in hysterical laughter before trying again. It hadn't seemed to matter, though. Dan was right. We knew it was just the start of a journey we were taking together and by the end of our honeymoon we'd certainly worked out a good number of the kinks.

I close my eyes. It would be so much easier if I was just flipping from life to life without having lived one of them first. I might be able to switch off at this point if that was the case, but despite the state of our marriage in the future, I've loved this man for more than two decades. I can't seem to forget that, not when he's being so thoughtful and understanding of my needs. Not when he's being the Dan I've always wanted him to be.

The truth is I'm here in this moment and I don't know when I'll jump back and be with Jude. Maybe it'll never happen again. And what am I going to do if it doesn't? Cross my legs for the next twenty-five years? Invent a headache every night until Dan becomes convinced I've got a brain tumour and takes me to see a specialist?

I stand up slowly and face the door. My fingers hover over the tiny brass bolt but I don't draw it back because Dan starts to talk again. He sounds weary. 'Talk to me? Open the door? We can sort this out together.'

More tears fall, but I'm frozen, unable to move.

'I know it was my idea to wait, and maybe that was stupid, because now it's become this huge thing, but I can't help believing what I believe. I don't know what the problem is, not if you won't talk to me. If anything, I should be the one locked in the bathroom, because at least you've done this before …'

I open my mouth to object but he carries on before I find the words.

'But I don't care about that, Maggie. I don't care if you're my first but I'm not yours. All I care about is here and now, and making sure you're OK, because I love you.'

My fingers, which have been sitting loosely on the little knob screwed into the door bolt, now grip it more tightly.

'And I know you have trouble opening up to people, that you're scared people will disappoint you or let you down, but I promise I won't. That was what today was all about, wasn't it? Promising we'll always take care of each other, no matter what. And I promise I'll always do that for you, Maggie. I really promise.'

My nose is running now. What a beautiful, glowing bride I must look! But I never knew he understood those things about me. I pull back the bolt and open the door. I don't even care that Future Dan will break every one of these promises, because here and now I know he means them with all his heart.

Dan scrambles to his feet and looks at me, searching my face for an answer. I don't have one to give him, not verbally, anyway.

'I know I'm the luckiest idiot alive,' he says, looking very earnest. 'I know you're too good for me, but I'll spend every day of my life …' He breaks off, unable to say any more.

I step forward and press the tips of my fingers to his lips as I shake my head. I remember what Becca said in that other reality, the one where I broke Dan's heart, about thinking I was better than him. 'No,' I say, 'that's not true.' Because I don't know if I've ever been as selfless with Dan as he's being with me right now.

He takes my hand and kisses it. There's a chain reaction of tiny fireworks up my arm. Dan's gaze drifts downwards to what I'm wearing and he smiles softly. 'You look beautiful.' I can't help blushing, smiling back. And then we're kissing and it all feels so right, so natural.

It goes better this time than it did on our first wedding night, probably because one of us knows just what works between us, there's more give and take and I'm braver; I say what I want.

Afterwards, I curl into him and close my eyes. His warmth is familiar and comforting. Just as I'm drifting off to sleep, Dan murmurs, 'And to think I almost lost you, that you almost didn't become Mrs Lewis.'

My eyes open. 'What do you mean? I said "yes" straight away, didn't I?'

Dan nuzzles into me. 'Classic Maggie … always rewriting history from your own perspective.' He doesn't sound annoyed, though. Just indulgent. 'Do you really not remember you strung it out for almost a week? I never said this at the time, but at one point I was really scared you were going to break it all off.'

I turn and prop myself up on one elbow so I can see his face, see whether he's joking, even though every bit of knowledge I have about this man tells me he isn't. He cranks one eye open.

'What are you looking at?' He waves a hand, indicating his naked body. 'Can't believe you almost turned this down, huh?'

I laugh, punch him softly in the chest, then lie back down again. 'Bighead.'

I can hear his breathing becoming more even as I lie there, warm and comfortable, staring at the jacquard canopy over the bed.

I haven't considered this. I thought this reality was a carbon copy of the one I'd left behind, but it must be a new version. In this one I didn't accept Dan's proposal straight away, but I obviously did accept it in the end. Was it still Jude that made me wobble? And if it was, why didn't I choose him again?

I lie there, running the bits of the life I can remember as a slideshow in my head. Because of all my jumping around the memories don't bleed into each other as they would have done if time had marched steadily on, instead each is its own little nugget, complete but separate from those around it. I thread these moments together, like beads on a string, piecing together the history of this version of my life. As I add the memory of the night Dan proposed and then the one of the morning after something occurs to me. Dan is seventy-five per cent asleep now, but I speak anyway: 'Where did you go that night?'

The night he lied about the next morning.

He doesn't move, but I'm painfully aware he's now fully awake. 'I went for a walk to clear my head,' he says lightly.

And just like that, the intimacy that's gently woven itself around us as we've been loving and laughing and talking hardens into a spiny, brittle thing. I feel like pushing my way out of the bed, getting away from this feeling that, once again, his niceness has lulled me into a false sense of security and that I should have been more watchful, more wary. I don't move and I deliberately control my voice. 'You told me you went out with Rick.'

His breathing becomes more shallow and he runs his hand through his hair.

Busted, I think, and I wait.

'You'll laugh if I tell you,' he finally says.

That was not what I'd been expecting him to say. I roll over and turn to face him. Even though it's dark, I need to be able to see what I can of his expression. I know I can catch the lie if I'm looking for it. It was only because I'd stopped watching, stopped caring, that I missed in the future.

'You can tell me,' I say, mimicking the same open tone he used on me earlier. I'm lying, though, because I will not accept any answer he gives me, the way he was ready to accept mine.

This is different, though. I don't want to hear about a horrible mistake because he was upset, a drunken shag in the back of Rick's borrowed-for-the-purpose Mini. Because when those words fall out of his mouth it will make everything that has happened this evening a lie.

'You promise you won't laugh?'

'Yes,' I say, entirely confident I won't find whatever he has to say the tiniest bit funny.

He moves to lie on his back so he doesn't have to look me in the face. 'I wrote a song.'

I blink. And then I blink again. It's so not what I'm expecting him to say that I let out a small giggle.

I see his brow lower as he glares at the canopy of the four-poster. 'You promised you wouldn't laugh.'

'I'm not … I'm not … at least, not like that. You just took me by surprise.'

He drags his arm from underneath my neck and puts both hands behind his head. No part of us is touching the other any more.

'I'm sorry,' I say and I reach out to lay my hand on his bare chest. 'You wrote a song? What about?'

He grunts. 'About that night. About the possibility of losing you. I do that sometimes … It helps.'

Much to my utter astonishment, I know he's telling the truth. Dan has always been one to internalise his emotions. I just didn't know he ever needed, or indeed had found, an outlet. 'Will you sing it to me? Just a bit?'

His frown deepens.

'What? It all worked out in the end, didn't it? Don't be embarrassed.'

Because that's exactly how he looks right now: embarrassed. And the feeling only gets stronger as he clears his throat. 'I can't.'

'Why not?'

He stops looking at the canopy and turns his head just a little bit away from me so I can't see his eyes. 'Because it was more of a poem than an actual song.'

'A poem?' I want to laugh again, but I don't know why. It's not funny but sweet. And surprising.

Dan keeps staring upwards. 'Yeah.'

I literally don't know what to say to that for a good minute or so. I can't quite marry up the idea of good old dependable Dan, who likes a pint of proper ale and pottering about in the garden, with someone who writes poetry. I don't know why I'm so surprised. He did end up as an English teacher, after all.

'Can you tell me a bit?'

He sighs. 'Not sure I can remember it properly now …'

Yes, he can, I think. He just doesn't want to say the words out loud, and it's OK because I understand that.

'I can show it to you when we get home, though.'

'Really? You don't mind?'

He waits a moment before he answers. 'We should share everything, shouldn't we? Not keep things hidden away.'

'We should,' I say as I lie down again and place my head on his chest. But we failed to do that last time. Quite spectacularly. And I'm just not sure, despite all our good intentions, we'll succeed this time either.

CHAPTER TWENTY-TWO

'Come on, slowcoach! We're almost there!'

I hear Dan's voice above me on the trail and I can tell he's smiling, possibly even laughing, at me. I'm doubled over with my hands on my bent knees, hauling in oxygen as fast as my lungs will allow. My calf muscles are awash with lactic acid. I'm supposed to be young again. Why the heck am I so unfit?

'Sadist!' I try to yell but only manage to puff before I straighten and start walking again. Gentle stroll, the lady in the B&B said. She probably thinks Ben Nevis is a minor pimple too.

We're in Scotland on our honeymoon. Nothing as fancy as a holiday to Spain or Greece for these two cash-strapped newly-weds. We spent all our money on the wedding and we've both still got overdrafts in our student bank accounts. However, my mum and dad chipped in to help us with a week in the Highlands. Last time it was Wales.

We've been in Inveraray for three days, and this is the first that's been drizzle-free enough to attempt a walk up to *Dun na Cuaiche*, which sits on the so-called 'hill' above the town. Dan's been eyeing up the small, square watchtower ever since we got here and as soon as the sun came out this morning he pounced on his chance.

The last section is a steep and windy path and I'm puffing and red-faced by the time I reach level ground. Dan doesn't let me look at the view, but pulls my baseball cap down over my eyes and leads me silently towards the rough stone folly, giving me a leg up to get into the high entrance and almost causing me to land flat on my face in the process. When we've stopped laughing and he's finished dusting me off, he positions me just where he wants me, at one of the tall stone arches, then he lifts my hat up and lets me see.

'Wow!'

'I know,' Dan says, his voice close to my right ear. Below us Loch Fyne lays stretched out like a long sheet of brushed steel, curling round the rocky headland where the town sits. Inveraray looks even more neat and orderly up here than it does from the ground, with its uniform white buildings and their stark, black windows. The castle sits majestic in its gardens, its four conical turrets making the whole scene look like something from a fairy tale.

'Told you it would be worth it.'

Without taking my eyes off the view, I reach back to punch him with a loose fist and I'm rewarded with an ear-tingling kiss on the side of my neck. It's the most natural thing in the world to turn and kiss him back.

We've been married for almost a week now. I was dreading this at first – being on my own with Dan for a fortnight – but I'm actually rather enjoying myself. I'm discovering that being with him is easy. Our relationship is new and clean, unpolluted by the million little disappointments of our future life. I don't love him the way I love Jude, but I had forgotten we could be friends. Friends with benefits, it seems, lots of enthusiastic newly-wed benefits.

And I reckon that's OK. I've managed to shelve away the part of me that feels guilty about Jude. After all, I didn't choose this, and I certainly don't seem to have any control over it. I may as well try to live whatever life I find myself in as well as I can. There's no point in sulking and making both of us miserable.

Dan sighs. 'Back to reality in six days.'

Which one? I think silently. I could be here, or I could wake up tomorrow and find myself back with Jude in London. It's making it very hard to care too hard about what's in my immediate future, because as soon as I get invested in what's going on I jump again. However, I know that attitude is dangerous. I've been given this second chance and I need to get in the driving seat of my life, not take the easy path of being the perpetual passenger.

I kiss Dan's cheek. 'We can't stay on honeymoon forever.'

He lets out a heavy breath and we both turn to look at the amazing vista in front of us. Clouds are queueing up to roll across the sun, grey and vengeful, and the landscape below is carved into uneven chunks of bright sunshine and dark shadow.

'I know,' he says. 'We're grown-ups now. No more mooching off our parents. No more getting someone else to do our washing. We'll have rent and bills to pay – flipping Poll Tax, for goodness' sake!'

Dan's sudden melancholy is starting to affect me too. 'Ugh.' I'm thinking of the amount of laundry I've done between leaving college and my forty-sixth birthday. Now I've got to do it all over again. 'Being grown up is overrated,' I mutter.

Dan slides his hand under the hem of my T-shirt and his fingers start an upward journey. 'Really?'

I roll my eyes. 'OK, maybe there are some perks …'

He kisses me but breaks off after a short while and his hands leave the bare skin of my torso. He pulls them away to put them on my shoulders as he looks into my eyes, suddenly very solemn. 'Are you scared?'

'Of being a grown-up?'

He nods. 'Of our future. It starts now. No more putting it off with endless education.'

He stares so seriously off into the distance that I almost let him get away with that, but then I start laughing. 'What do you mean? You're going back to college to do your PGCE, aren't you? What's that if it's not more education?'

He shrugs. 'Somehow this feels different. I'll be working too. Cementing myself into a choice of career. Everything feels so set in stone.'

'I thought this is what you wanted.'

'It is …' Dan shakes his head and smiles. 'Don't mind me. I'm just being silly. Pipe dreams …'

I realise I'd have quite happily taken Dan at his word first time around. I'd have put that little sigh he just made out of my mind and wouldn't have given it another thought. This time I find I want to excavate.

'What dreams?'

He smiles again, more sheepishly this time. 'You'll think I'm silly.'

'You've got to stop saying that,' I reply, half scolding him. 'Did I laugh last time? I mean, properly laugh?'

He shakes his head.

'Then tell me?'

He stares out at the changing landscape for a few moments, watching the strong wind push the clouds out of the way of the sun so we're bathed in golden warmth again and the threat of rain is something only the people of nearby Loch Gilphead need to worry about. 'I don't want to just teach. I want to *do*.'

I start to wonder how Dan is going to 'do' English, and then I think of what he told me on our wedding night. 'You want to write?'

He nods. 'Don't worry. I know it's a stupid idea, that we won't be able to pay the bills if I hole myself up in the spare bedroom with a typewriter. Mum and Dad drilled that into me endlessly from about the age of thirteen. But I can't help feeling it's the safe option, that I'm not just settling down but settling.'

I wish I could tell him to go for it, and part of me really wants to, but I know how hard it was financially for us in the early days, how we became experts at turning soya mince, padded out with lots of cheap vegetables, into any type of cuisine, just by varying the spices we flung into it. How my entire clothing budget for the first year of our marriage was a tenner and how I once had to scrape together pennies and halfpennies just to buy a bottle of shampoo in Superdrug. I remember being so embarrassed handing it over to the cashier.

'OK, you're right,' I say. 'It's definitely the practical option. I mean, no one's going to pay you to sit at home and write but that doesn't mean you can't sit at home and write in the evenings after someone's paid you to do something else.'

Dan doesn't say anything but he picks me up and swings me round then kisses me with an intensity that steals my breath away. 'I love you so much,' he whispers into my ear before kissing me again.

And, as much as I'm telling myself this life, this reality, is all about putting right past wrongs, about friendship and closure, my mind whispers *I love you too* before I can stop it. This Dan is different, more open, more dynamic, and I have a feeling it's because I'm letting him be that way. I try to think of Jude as I kiss Dan back, try to keep him in focus in my heart, but new Dan is making it unexpectedly hard to do.

CHAPTER TWENTY-THREE

I can hear fire engines. They're coming this way. Louder … louder … they're almost deafening now. Oh, my God! The house must be on fire. My house is on fire. But I can't seem to move. I can't seem to run …

I sit up and open my eyes, dragging in breath. The room is light, quiet, except for the police siren disappearing down the road outside. I am clammy with sweat and I push the duvet off myself and relish the sensation of cold air hitting my damp skin. It wakes me up properly, and my heart, which had just started to slow a little after the nightmare, starts to speed up again.

I don't know where I am.

Last thing I knew I was preparing for my first Christmas with Dan, but I can tell just by the quality of light behind the white roller blinds that this isn't December in Swanham. The light is too warm, too yellow.

Where am I? I don't recognise this place. It isn't the Lewisham flat and it isn't my parents' house in Bournemouth. I push the duvet back and stand up. Wherever it is, it's very stylish. None of the dado rails and *Changing Rooms* garish colours of the early nineties. It's all white walls and bluish-grey carpet. The armchair in the corner is soft grey too, and the lampshades on the bedside tables are the same colour as the carpet, with large stylised dragonflies on them.

I spot an old-fashioned alarm clock on the bedside table. It tells me it's 2pm. Two in the afternoon? Why aren't I up at two in the afternoon? Am I ill?

After taking a quick physical inventory, where everything seems to be working fine, and nose and throat are snot and cough-free, I walk out of the bedroom, down a short corridor and into a spacious living room. There's a bay window that looks out onto a leafy street. The walls are white here too and there's a sectional couch. In the corner is one of those modernist chairs that's all chrome tubes and black leather straps, the kind that look great but are horrendously uncomfortable to sit in.

I start to shiver. I look down and realise that I'm wearing my 'Choose Life' T-shirt and relief and affection for it swell in my chest. At least I have that one thing to hang onto.

There's no Dan in this place. No Jude. Is this somewhere else? Some new reality with a man I don't even know yet? The thought makes me want to crawl back under the covers and hide.

But then I spot a photo frame on a bookshelf. Black and white. Me and Jude. I start to laugh. I'm back! I'm really back! I spin around with my arms stretched out, needing to do something to release the joy surging up from within me, but it isn't long before I slow again and then I stop.

How much time has passed? I swallow as I realise it might be more than a year. Our lease on the other flat was that long and we'd been there less than a month when I jumped.

I explore further, looking for clues. The more I can work out before I see Jude again, the less crazy I will seem as I try to stumble my way through this time, this future. I find toiletries in the brands I use in the bathroom and the vase my grandmother gave me is in the kitchen, filled with white daisies, my favourite flowers. I open the wardrobe in the bedroom and find my clothes hanging there – well, at least a few I recognise, anyway, and plenty more I don't.

As I'm assimilating the fact I really do live here the phone rings, making me jump. It's one of those corded ones with the little oval buttons and a clear plastic insert covering a square of card where you can write your favourite numbers. I stare at it for a few seconds, almost fearful of touching it, and then I make myself reach out and pick it up.

'Hey, sleepyhead. I didn't wake you up, did I? You were out for the count when I left.' The voice is soft and warm and full of love.

'Jude …' I start to say, but then I choke back a sob.

He starts to sound worried. 'Meg? Are you OK?'

I smile through the tears. 'I'm wonderful,' I say. Just stupidly happy to hear his voice. I've missed him so much. 'Just need to blow my nose …' Which is true, despite my earlier snot-free status. 'Hang on a sec,' I say and put the phone down so I can run to the bathroom, grab a wad of toilet paper and tidy myself up. When I return, I take a breath and steady myself before picking the receiver up again. 'I'm back.'

'Don't you want to know why I'm ringing?'

'Of course I do!'

'It's finished.' He pauses for a moment. I can tell he's smiling.

Grinning, even. His voice is full of pride and accomplishment. The only problem is I have no idea what he's talking about.

'That's wonderful!' I say.

'Do you want to see it?'

Even though I have no idea what I'm agreeing to I say yes. It's Jude, after all. Of course anything he's done is going to be wonderful.

'Then you'll need to get a move on,' he says, sounding a tad more serious. 'I've got a viewing at four, but you can sneak a look before then.' I hear him sigh deeply, as if he's looking at something that has him awestruck. 'Meg …? It's pretty impressive, even if I do say so myself.'

'I always knew you could do it,' I tell him. I don't know what it is, or exactly how impressive it is, but I do know that I always knew Jude was going to go places, do things that other people only dream about doing. That's why I picked him.

'Well, my dad didn't,' he says, and I can hear the resentment in his tone. 'When I told him I wanted to bid for this project he told me I was getting above myself. I think he sees it as a personal insult that I wanted to do this. Thank God Cam's old man felt differently and stumped up the cash.' He lets out a gruff laugh. 'I don't think Dad's going to argue about the bank balance once this one is sold, though. If that doesn't convince him I shouldn't start concentrating my efforts on this instead of the regular building work, I don't know what will.'

'Give your dad a break, won't you?' I ask softly. 'Underneath all that gruff bluster, he really loves you. I just think he had these grand ideas of retiring and seeing you carry on Hansen and Son the way he always had.'

Jude goes quiet and then he says, 'It should only take you about half an hour to get here if you catch the trains right.' I can hear in his voice that his attention has been caught by something in the room with him, that he's moving onto the next thing. 'So I'll see you around two-thirty?'

'I've only just stumbled out of bed! Give a girl time to get dressed, will you?'

He gives an indulgent chuckle. 'OK. Two forty-five. I'll see you then. Gotta go. Love you.'

'I can't wait,' I whisper into the phone, but I'm talking to the dial tone. I don't mind, though – Jude's drive, his passion for what he does, is why I love him. I run into the bedroom, throw open the wardrobe and wonder what to wear. I end up picking navy trousers and a cute little cream blouse. Not too dressy, not too casual. Hopefully, it'll do, seeing as I have no idea where I'm going.

I have no idea where I'm going.

Oh, hell. And I've told Jude I'll be there in under an hour, wherever 'there' is. I run into the living room and start searching for clues.

CHAPTER TWENTY-FOUR

I blink as I run out of Notting Hill Gate Tube station into the glaring sunshine. I'm too tired to run, but I do it anyway. I race off again down Holland Park Avenue. It took me a good half hour to work out where I was supposed to be going. I eventually found some papers in a neat stack on a desk in a tiny second bedroom I hadn't realised was there, one we're obviously using as a home office.

I also found a computer on a second desk full of clutter that bears the hallmark of my disorganisation when I'm working on a project. By the row of coffee cups places strategically amongst the sketches and notes, I'd say the reason I was asleep at two in the afternoon is because I'd just pulled an all-nighter to get a job in on time.

The letterhead on the correspondence found on Jude's desk told me he was still working for his dad's firm, but it seemed he's branched out into buying wrecks cheap, doing them up and then selling them on.

I've also discovered that we live in a garden flat in Nunhead, on a hill populated by orderly rows of red-brick Victorian houses with white-painted masonry and large sash windows. It's certainly a step up from the Lewisham digs. This flat makes a statement. I am no longer living like a student, it says, happy to have pizza boxes stacked up near the kitchen bin, a collection of empty beer cans on the mantelpiece and Ikea flatpack furniture that has been assembled so badly it's barely standing. I have grown up, it says. I am on my way. Even though, in my head, I'm in my forties, I'm still not sure I feel grown up enough for it.

As I turn into Campden Hill Square, I belatedly realise Holland Park Tube might have been closer. However, without the benefit of a handy London travel app – I don't think 1990s Maggie even owns a mobile phone yet – I had to do my best the old-fashioned way with an A–Z clutched in my hand. As I stride down the road I read the house numbers on the three-storey Georgian buildings, mentally ticking them off until I reach the right one.

It's not quite as grand as the houses with the pillared porches on Ladbroke Square, but it's still impressive. It sits one house away from the corner and it has a bright-blue door and stairs leading down to a basement kitchen. I sigh out loud. I always wanted a basement kitchen.

And then I see Jude swing open the heavy front door in an expensive-looking grey suit, not the usual builders' attire I'd expect, and I can't help it. I rush towards him and nearly knock him over as I wrap my arms round his neck and hold him tight.

He laughs. 'That's one of the things I love about you, Meg. You don't hold back.'

I close my eyes and try to absorb the feel, the smell of him, through my pores and into my skin. I've missed him so much. I'm not ready to let him go when he pulls away, eager to show me his finished work, but I do.

He takes me by the hand and I can't stop smiling as he points out the beautiful original mahogany staircase, with polished turned rails and glossy white balusters. I'm not taking any of the information in that he's spouting at me, but I don't care. I can feel his hand warm in mine. I'm back. That's all that matters.

As the tour continues, though, I can't help but pay attention. This house is gorgeous. Even though it's obvious it's been recently decorated, it looks dated to me. Victorian flourishes and too much terracotta make it seem a bit fuddy-duddy compared to the sleek minimalist look it would have been given in the twenty-first century, but it's still a stunning home. The orangery Jude has built to extend the kitchen is a work of art.

We wander upstairs and take in the high ceilings of the drawing room with its fold-away wooden shutters that sink into the wood panelling like secrets, and then he shows me the balcony of the master bedroom that overlooks the garden in the centre of the square. I place my hands flat on the stone balustrade, close my eyes and feel the sun on my face.

'Imagine being able to drink your morning coffee out here,' I say without opening my eyes. 'I can't think of anything more perfect.'

Jude slides in behind me and snakes his arms round my waist, just as I knew he would. He kisses the tingly spot just below my right ear. 'Then one day I will make sure you have a house of your own, just like this one, with a balcony outside every window if you like!'

I turn and look at him. Laugh. 'If only in our dreams …'

But Jude's not laughing. 'I'm serious, Meg. I want to give this to you. I don't want to just renovate houses like this – I want to live in one. And one day I'm going to do it.'

I look back at him, looping my arms around his neck. 'I know you will,' I say, because this man has a strange ability to bend his future to his wishes. He has a gift for that, and I'm so glad I'm with him, that my life is meshed with his and he's talking about owning property with me years from now, that I kiss him the way I've wanted to since the moment I saw him opening that blue front door.

We stumble back into the bedroom. The rooms are all sparsely decorated, only a few pieces of furniture in each. I'm not really paying attention to them at the moment, though, because all I can think of is Jude, wishing I knew how to make this reality stick for good.

At first I think he's going to laugh and disentangle himself from me – after all, this is hardly the time or the place – but then his hands slide around my waist, under my blouse, and his fingers start to explore. He glances towards the bed, it's blue-and-white floral duvet cover crisp and inviting, and I know what he's thinking.

Old me, boring me, would laugh it off, say that we couldn't, we shouldn't, and save the fun and games for later. Present me is so tired of putting off the pleasure of the moment to do what's expected of me. 'Thank God for the bed,' I say as we lurch in that direction and crash down on it.

Jude smiles wickedly at me as he starts to unbutton my blouse. 'Thank you, darling Meg, for suggesting we went with this new idea of "staging" the home to help it sell.' He nuzzles into the side of my neck as I struggle with his shirt buttons, my fingers too shaky to do any good, but, before he gets very far, he freezes.

'What was that?'

I push my rumpled hair away from my face. We both stay still.

'Yoo-hoo!' we hear in a shrill voice from the flight below. 'Mr Hansen?'

Jude and I look at each other in panic. He swears. 'They're early!' he mouths at me as he tucks his shirt back in and runs a hand through my hair.

I don't have time to ask who because I'm trying to do my shirt up with roughly the same amount of success as I had taking Jude's off him. He ends up having to help me as I try to smooth my hair down and locate my left shoe, which flew off when we landed on the bed.

We hear footsteps on the newly varnished floorboards downstairs and muffled voices. 'The Whitleys,' Jude whispers as we give ourselves one last check. I spot my shoe in the corner of the room and run over to fetch it as Jude opens the bedroom door. 'I must have forgotten to lock the front door. Hardly surprising, since you had me a little … distracted.'

We share a conspiratorial smile as I fetch my shoe and he opens the door, and heads towards the landing. One moment he's my Jude – the ordinary boy made good – and then something happens: he seems to get taller and straighter and his walk is less swagger and more confident grace. He even talks a little differently, not so much the accent but in his choice of words, slight tweaks in his intonation. I'd seen him pull the same trick many times in our uni days when he was around his high-flying friends.

'Mrs Whitley,' he says as a middle-aged lady in a coral suit appears from the double doors that lead into the drawing room. Jude glides down the last few stairs and takes her hand. I half think he's going to kiss it, but he doesn't. 'How lovely to see you again! And Mr Whitley … nice to meet you finally.' A man appears behind her, hands in pockets, and looks questioningly at his wife. It's obvious who wears the trousers in this relationship.

'We found the front door open,' Mrs Whitley says, not taking her eyes off Jude, who's radiating charm and charisma, 'so we stepped inside. I hope you don't mind we're a tad early.'

'Not at all,' Jude says smoothly, as if he hadn't just groaned with frustration when we'd heard her foghorn voice travelling up the stairwell.

'And who is this young lady?' I've just slipped down the stairs and I'm trying to hide myself behind him. She leans to get a better look at me and at the same time, Jude steps away, leaving me exposed. I smile and fervently hope my blouse buttons are all done back up the right way.

'This is Meg Greene,' Jude replies, not missing a beat. 'My interior designer.'

It takes every ounce of effort I have to not let my eyes pop open wide at his lie. Instead I follow his lead and smile back warmly, faking a confidence I don't feel, and I shake her hand. I grip her round fingers firmly. 'Nice to meet you,' I say as I release them again.

Part of me is expecting her to narrow her eyes, look me up and down, then tell Jude he must have made some mistake, that this scrap of a girl couldn't possibly be that important, but she nods and turns back to Jude, both dismissing me and swallowing his untruth in the same moment.

I trail behind them as Jude shows them the house. It seems the Whitleys have been looking for property in this area and spotted the scaffolding. They're so excited about it they've jumped the gun and haven't waited for it to go on the market, but sought Jude out directly. I almost lose my composure when he mentions the asking price. Mrs Whitley, however, doesn't bat an eyelid and just nods.

We arrive at the master bedroom and she glances around. 'This is a lovely room, but I can't seem to imagine what to do with those windows,' Mrs Hamilton says. There are three sets of paned floor-to-ceiling windows that lead out onto the small balcony, the centre pair being a set of French doors. 'Pinch pleat or a pelmet? What do you think, dear?' And she turns and looks at me.

In a moment of stage fright, I'm tempted to turn tail and sprint away, but I'm aware Jude must have poured a lot of money into this. He probably needs this sale desperately. So I take a deep breath, frown and stare at the windows, pretend I'm using my professional expertise to size them up when really my mind is a blank.

But then it hits me. I can see it. 'You know, I wouldn't bother with curtains,' I say. 'There'd be so much material you'd lose a lot of that wonderful natural light when they're opened, even if they were fastened with tie-backs, and that's what makes this room. I'd suggest white venetian blinds with voile curtains at the sides. Although the blinds would be enough on their own to allow both light and privacy, the sheer panels would soften the look.'

Mrs Whitley blinks and looks at the windows again. At first she frowns, but then her features soften and she turns to look at me. 'It's very different,' she says. 'Not many people have those sort of blinds these days.'

I hold her gaze, even though I'm aware my legs feel shaky. Blagging has never been my strong suit, but Jude must be rubbing off on me, because I say, 'I hope you don't mind me saying, Mrs Whitley, but you don't strike me as the sort of woman who likes to follow the herd.'

She gives a tiny laugh and she turns to Jude. 'The girl's a genius, Mr Hansen. If we seal the deal, I insist she oversees the rest of the interiors.'

I'm glad she's facing the other way and can't see the look of terror on my face. Jude just smiles and nods, giving nothing away, promising nothing, and leads the couple back downstairs and efficiently dispatches them out the front door.

I slump against the newel post at the bottom of the stairs when it's fully closed. We both start laughing. 'Oh, my goodness! Why on earth did you tell them I was an interior designer?'

Jude smiles back at me. 'Well, it sounded more professional than saying I'd brought my girlfriend round to have a nose. I know I'm young to be doing this kind of thing, so impression is everything.'

I sit down on the second step. 'I honestly don't know how

you manage to keep a straight face telling such huge fibs!' I start laughing again at the ridiculousness of it.

Jude comes to sit beside me. He leans his elbows on his knees then twists his head to look at me. 'Is it so absurd?'

I'm still smiling, but my brow creases. 'Of course it is. I'm a graphic designer – at least I'm trying to be. It's what I trained for.'

He kisses me on the side of my head. 'One thing I love about you is your clarity, the way you see a goal and fix on it, but it does mean you don't always see alternative possibilities when they crop up.'

If Dan had said that to me in our old life, I would have taken it as criticism, but the upside of getting to live this life again is that I'm aware I need someone to point out the flaws in my thinking, my personality, so I don't get stuck in the same rut again. So instead of getting in a huff with Jude, I wait for him to continue.

'You *could* be an interior designer if you wanted to be.'

My eyes widen. It's as if Jude has just told me I could win an Oscar or walk on the moon. 'But – '

He grabs my hands. 'I mean it, Meg.'

'Really?'

He smiles at me. 'Of course,' he adds softly. 'After all, it was you who suggested we do this new thing of staging the house, of not having it empty when we showed it to prospective buyers, and it worked, didn't it? The Whitleys were sold.'

'But it was only a few basic pieces, some cheap cushions and a couple of candlesticks!' I'd paid attention as we'd taken the tour, curious about my input.

He shakes his head. 'But look what you did with it. There might not be much here, but the house feels almost fully furnished.'

I look again, let my imagination loose and in an instant I can picture this living room with off-white walls, big white sofas and dark wood furniture with splashes of crimson all around in the form of cushions and vases, lampshades and modern art.

However, while that is all crystal clear in my head, I can't visualise myself in the middle of that scene, flipping through swatch books, pointing at walls and explaining to decorators where I want what. Someone else, maybe. Some faceless woman in a flawlessly cut suit. But not me.

But then I look back at Jude, and I see the excitement, the belief in his eyes. 'Maybe,' I whisper. 'I'll think about it.'

CHAPTER TWENTY-FIVE

I'm sitting alone, looking at the clock in a cute little Italian restaurant only ten minutes' walk from Waterloo station, where the 11.58 from Wimbledon pulled in over forty minutes ago. Becca's train. She should have been here by now if she'd actually managed to catch that one. Some things never change.

According to the black-leather Filofax I found in my handbag, I jumped more than a whole year. Sixteen months, to be exact, and Becca is listed as having an address in Merton. She must have moved closer to work.

I try not to think about it too hard, because it scares me to feel time rush past me like this. The sensation is similar to one of those rides at a theme park that spins you in three different directions at once then spits you out onto solid ground, leaving you queasy and disoriented.

There aren't many entries in my smart new Filofax – a gift from Jude our first Christmas, I discovered – that are meet-ups with Becca. I went back through this year and last year but I've only found one mention of her name. What's happened? Why have we drifted apart so much?

I'm starting to get irritated with the other Maggie, the one that inhabits this place when I'm in my other life. She's been making choices I don't approve of in my absence. Anyway, I'm here now, and it's time to set things right.

Becca arrives ten minutes later, looking flushed but not particularly apologetic. I decide to let it slide.

'Went the wrong way out of Waterloo and got lost,' she says breathlessly.

I smile, but I know it looks bright and plastic. 'I thought this might be easier for you than crossing south London on tubes and buses to get to my flat.'

''Spose so,' she says, casting a wary eye over our surroundings. 'This is a bit posh, though, isn't it?'

I shrug. 'Jude has a business associate who brought us here a while ago. He's raved about it ever since.' Now, *that* had been noted in my Filofax in great detail. In fact, one favour 'other' Maggie has done me is to record what's been going on in my life religiously, not just times and dates, either. I've found mini-journal entries on some of the lined pages too. Sadly, nothing much about Becca.

However, I see her reaction to Jude's name. Her upper lip curls slightly and she looks away. Her mouth doesn't move, but I hear her words as if she'd spoken them out loud. 'Oh, *him*.' I have the answer to my question.

I bristle but part of me is relieved to be able to turn the sense of irritation outwards, to stop blaming just myself for our lack of contact. I search around for something to say, but I struggle. I want to be able to tell her about the wonderful house Jude showed me last month, the fact he's already accepted an offer from the Whitleys and is looking for more property like it. I want to tell her I'm seriously considering juggling a new career alongside my graphic design but I can't, because all these bits of news are tainted by a man she hates.

'How are things?' I finally say.

She shrugs. 'Much the same.'

Thanks, I think. *For giving me so much to go on.*

'What about your love life?'

'Oh, I've met a new guy,' she says, her eyes sparkling. 'He's amazing.'

My stomach sinks. She always said that about her 'guys' and not one of them ever turns out to be amazing. 'Oh, really?' I say, trying to sound as keen as she is. 'What's his name?'

'Grant,' she says, and I almost spit out my Perrier.

'Grant what?' I reply, my voice hoarse, my mind trying to buoy itself up with the vague hope this is another man, another Grant.

'Grant Buchanan,' she says, sighing wistfully.

I nod. On the outside I am calm and composed. On the inside I am screaming.

Already?

In my original life she didn't meet him until she was nearly thirty, didn't marry him until she was thirty-one. How can it be so soon? We're only twenty-three!

As I listen to her drone on about him, how handsome he is, how he's so 'in charge' and exciting, I start to feel sick. What if this is something *I* did? What if the current state of our friendship has drawn him to her, as if he sensed she was without back-up, that she was vulnerable? After all, it was during that low patch I had when Sophie was about five and I realised the dream of a second baby might never happen that he had swooped in on her the first time. My heart starts to kick a little harder.

But as we order our meals I see that glow in her eyes, how happy she is. I don't know how to say what I've got to say. How do I tell her this guy is bad news? I have no proof but memories from another life. In this one I haven't even had the displeasure of meeting him.

We order, and she continues to gush about a guy that will one day shred her self-confidence so entirely she'll believe she's lucky to have him treat her like dirt, a guy who's going to tie her brain in knots with his mind games. 'Aren't you jumping in a little quickly?' I ask, as she outlines her plans to move in with him, even though they've only known each other three months and have been romantically involved for one.

She gives me a look. 'You're one to talk.'

Ah. I suppose she's right there. In this life, my choice to be with Jude must have seemed rather sudden and dramatic. She doesn't understand it was twenty-plus years in the coming.

'I know.' I take a breath, not content to leave difficult conversations in the place of surrender, as I usually do with Becca. 'But I'd known Jude for a couple of years before things finally fell into place. You don't even know this guy. Not really.' I try to smile, try to let her know that I'm not lecturing, just concerned, but it doesn't want to sit right on my face.

Becca's mouth pinches. 'And during most of those many years you knew Jude – ' she pauses, as if she's slightly disgusted with herself at having had to say his name ' – he either ignored you completely or treated you like crap. At least Grant has always been good to me.'

'I'm sorry,' I say, even though her words have stung. 'I just care about you. I want to make sure you're with someone who's going to treat you the right way.'

Becca gives me a long look. 'Sometimes we just have to accept our friends' choices.'

Hah! I want to shout back. *Like you've accepted Jude?* Is that really what she thinks she's done?

'Why don't you come over for dinner and meet him?' she says, and I see her waiting to weigh up my answer. 'Judge for yourself?'

My eyes open wide. 'You want me – and Jude – to come over for dinner?' For a moment, hope floats like a balloon inside my chest. There's nothing more I'd like than to mend these burned bridges that separate me from my best friend, all petty irritations aside. And maybe this is my opportunity. I can work on her about ditching Grant later. But then I see Becca's uncomfortable expression and my balloon of hope is popped.

Not Jude and me.

Just me.

Hypocrite.

The word cycles in my head until I have no other option but to spit it out of my mouth. I see Becca wince as it hits home, but I can't find it within myself to feel any pity. How can she ask this of me when she's not prepared to give even an inch herself?

'Sorry,' I say, as I stand up and sling my handbag over my shoulder. 'I don't think I can stay and do this. If you want me to meet and rave about this *wonderful* Grant, then at least you could try with Jude.'

'That's different! And don't be silly. You can't leave …
not over this.'

'You can't ask one thing of me then refuse to do it yourself.'

Becca looks back at me, shocked. I don't know whether
it's because I'm about to leave or because she's finally got an
inkling of her own unreasonable stubbornness. I'm too furious
to care. Even though the food hasn't arrived yet, I throw
down enough cash to cover both our meals, which feels like
another tiny victory, and then I turn around and walk away.

I wonder if she'll try to stop me. If, for once, she'll be the
one to offer the olive branch, but, as I stride towards the door,
she yells out after me: 'You don't know him as well as you
think you do! There are things you don't know …'

I let the sound of my clacking heels drown her out as I
leave the restaurant and head back out onto the busy street.

CHAPTER TWENTY-SIX

'Push, Maggie! *Push!*'

Maggie? Why is Jude calling me Maggie? He hasn't done that for years. And push *what,* for goodness' sake?

And then the squeezing begins. Deep down in my abdomen. It feels as if I'm trying to turn myself inside out. My body takes over while my mind races to catch up. Dan's face comes into blurry focus above me. He looks dishevelled but there's a glow behind the tiredness.

How? Why? I start to think but then the squeezing starts again and I can't concentrate on anything else for a few moments.

Dan grins at me. 'Thought you dozed off between contractions there for a minute,' he says chirpily, and I determine that as soon as I'm done here I'm going to smack that grin off his face and into next Tuesday.

But then the realisation hits me. I'm only moments away from having a baby. *My* baby. And I'm filled with a strange energising joy that causes me to curl myself up further, push harder. I don't care about the pain when the next contraction hits and I bear down for all I'm worth. Instead of screaming or grunting, I laugh, a stream of pure joy bubbling out of me.

The midwife at the end of the bed gives me a weird look. This must be a new one on her.

I don't even want to moan about exactly when I 'jumped', about why couldn't it have happened afterwards, when I was nodding off, exhausted, the baby nestled in my arms, instead of right at the most intense moment.

I talked to Jude about having babies a couple of months ago and he smiled that smile at me, his 'whatever you want, Meg' smile, and then he explained quite carefully how he thought it would be better to wait. We're both so busy, you see. He's been 'flipping' houses as fast as he can, each one bigger and more luxurious than the last, and I landed a layout job with a magazine. I've still been helping with the staging of Jude's houses, getting steadily more confident and ambitious, but the extra work fills up my evenings and weekends.

It wouldn't be fair to the child, Jude hinted, as if it was just a dog I wanted for Christmas. Maybe we should wait until we were better established? And then he'd kissed me on the nose. Whatever I wanted, of course, though …

I'd nodded, put those yearnings away. Because he was right. Of course he was. Maybe I was just being selfish. We're both so young. Not even twenty-five. We have years of possible childbearing ahead of us.

But now it's actually happening! It almost makes up for being catapulted back into this life with Dan against my will. I give one last massive push and the midwife tells me to pant. I know it's only moments away. I want to laugh. I want to cry. If I could I'd get up and dance a jig around the room.

That would certainly be another first for the midwife! But they don't understand …

Sophie is going to be here in a minute! And I've missed her so much.

I've bemoaned the things I've had to repeat in this redo of a life – shaving my legs, commuting, toilet-cleaning and washing up – but this is one experience I will relish every moment of the second time around.

The next few minutes are spent entirely in the present. Dan, Jude and my strange two-pronged life melt away and I pant, push, listen to the midwife, following her clear instructions to the letter, and I'm rewarded with the sound of a reedy, warbling wail.

After a few moments she hands me a tightly wrapped bundle – this is too soon for the fashion of skin-to-skin contact for mum and baby straight after birth. 'Here you are, Mrs Lewis. You have a beautiful baby boy!'

I almost drop the bundle. 'Are you sure?' I ask.

I look at Dan for confirmation and he nods. 'I know the scan said it was going to be a girl, but they did say it was only seventy-five per cent accurate and, taking a look at him, it's kind of obvious he's a boy, if you know what I mean!' he says, grinning even wider now. He'd adored Sophie, but I knew he'd always wanted a son too.

Sophie is a *boy*?

That seems impossible. I try to transplant my memories of her almost-translucent white-blonde hair, the little curls that used to collect at the sweet curve where the back of her head met her neck, her love for all things pink and frilly until her ninth birthday, onto a boy and find the picture doesn't fit.

Will it change her, I wonder? The fact she has one different chromosome? The different levels of hormones in her blood? Or will she still be my Sophie, just a little more rough and tumble?

I look down at the baby in my arms and that's when the biggest surprise comes. There's no blonde peach fuzz, just a shock of dark, straight hair. Sophie's pointed little chin that used to stick down below her chubby cheeks is missing too and her nose is the wrong shape.

I try to lift the baby to hand him back, but find I'm too exhausted to do it, so I stare at the changeling in my arms, waiting to see if this is just some post-birth hallucination and if I'm patient everything will shift back into what it should be.

Dan and the midwife were smiling at me to start off with but over the next few minutes their expressions change. I know I must be behaving oddly to them, but I can't help myself. 'Can you take him?' I ask Dan, without fully making eye contact. When he lifts the baby out of my arms, clumsily trying to get the head right into the crook of his elbow, all I feel is relief.

And then we get on with the business of the third stage of labour, and stitches. Joy, oh, joy. When it's all over, I close my eyes, blocking out as much of this reality as I can, and the midwife talks to Dan in a low voice: 'The hormones can do strange things to new mums after delivery. Give her a moment. It was a long labour, even for a first one.' And then I hear her walking away, off to check something, probably, and the door opens and closes. I keep my eyes closed, even though I know Dan is tearing his eyes from his son periodically to look at me.

'What are we going to call him?' he eventually says. 'We can't call him "Sophie" – '

An icy coldness slices through me at his words.

' – and we never could agree on a boy's name …'

I turn my head away, not even bothering to feign exhaustion. 'I don't care,' I say. 'You choose.'

And I really don't.

Sophie is gone. I've lost her.

And now I don't feel anything. I don't want to.

I roll over, turning my back on my husband and brand-new son, and will sleep to claim me so I can be free of it all.

CHAPTER TWENTY-SEVEN

Dan peers over the clear, plastic, hospital crib and frowns. 'I think he's hungry.' He looks at me, waiting for a response. 'I've changed him and burped him, so that's the only thing left to try.'

'Check his nappy again,' I say. I'm looking at the wall, painted apple-green, like the rest of the maternity ward, apart from the delivery suite, which is gardenia. I've been staring at a lot of walls lately, so I've started to notice these things. 'Babies love a clean nappy to poo into.'

I can feel Dan's eyes on me as he coos to the baby, who is doing that grunting and snuffling that usually precedes a full-on wail. I hear the snap of poppers and the rip of plastic tabs. A few moments later the sounds repeat themselves, but in reverse. 'Nope. Clean and dry.'

I nod. The high-pitched, scratchy moaning starts and I have to stop myself from closing my eyes to shut it out. Dan walks across the room and presents the pink and crumpled bundle to me. I look at it, but I don't reach out and take it. 'I think we should re-consider formula,' I say, and go back to studying the wall.

I don't have to look at Dan to know the expression on his

face. It's a mixture of confusion, frustration and sympathy, with an ever-diminishing smidgen of hope mixed in.

'The midwife says breastfeeding will help with the bonding process,' he says, 'and we always said we'd breastfeed.'

I let out a snort of a laugh. '*We* did, did we? Well, you get your knockers out and get on with it then, because mine are red raw and in need of a good rest.'

'You know what I mean.' There's more irritation in his tone now. For some reason I'm pleased. 'You were adamant about breastfeeding beforehand, almost evangelical.'

That was before I knew my nipples were going to drop off, I think caustically. I hold out my arms. 'OK, then. Give it here …'

'His name is Billy,' he reminds me quietly.

I know that. William, after my grandad, because Dan thought I might like it.

I open the front of my nightdress and my son latches on straight away. Pain shoots from my nipple and right under my armpit, causing me to grip the armrests of the hospital chair. Sophie never was this enthusiastic, this … greedy. Quite the opposite. We had to call up the NCT breastfeeding counsellor to come and give me some tips, because she couldn't quite get the hang of it, and, when she did, feeding her was lovely – soft, relaxed, gentle – not like this, so forceful and hungry that I'm sometimes scared he's sucking more than milk out of me, that the bit of me that makes me feel alive is slowly being pulled out and separated from me too.

'Still sore?' Dan asks and I realise he's hovering again. He's not sounding irritated any more, just sickeningly sympathetic. 'I can get you more of that cream, if you like …?'

Oh, God, I think. Stop being such a wimp and man up, will you? I close my eyes and wish Jude was here. Why are the things I want split between two realities? The love of my life in one and the child I long for in the other. Only, this isn't quite the child I expected. Someone delivered the wrong package. Dan probably, seeing it was his sperm that made the final race to the finish line. Bloody typical. He had one job to do in this 'getting pregnant and giving birth' malarky and he couldn't even get that right!

Jude wouldn't be over there, messing around with the nappy bag, trying to find the Kamillosan. He'd have made me look him in the eye, and he'd have told me, not nastily but firmly, that I needed to snap out of it. The baby comes first now. He'll do everything he can to support me, but I have to at least try.

And then I would have done. I'd have tried for him. Because he wouldn't have been faffing around with tubes of cream and worrying if he'd bought the wrong size paper knickers from Mothercare. He'd have taken charge.

I realise the intense sucking has lessened to an intermittent tug. I look down to see his eyes have closed. One tiny hand rests on the top of my breast, fingers splayed, and I feel a rush of something from deep inside. 'He's finished,' I say and hand him back to Dan, before the feeling grows.

I hear a noise in the corridor outside. It's visiting time. I sigh and prepare myself for another round from my parents, or Dan's parents, whichever set has won the fight to be the 'two per bed' for this session. They will try to lift me out of my 'baby blues' by the force of their will, the sheer brightness of their smiles. It's completely exhausting.

And completely pointless. Because this isn't just the baby blues, is it?

Dan goes to the door of my room – they gave me one on my own. All the rooms here are either doubles or singles – and I hear him talking to someone in a low voice. I stop looking at the wall and turn my head so I can hear better.

Becca. It's Becca. Even though I can't make out her hushed words, I recognise the tone, the earthy softness of her voice.

'Maybe you can do something, say something?' Dan says. I note that he's careful not to sound quite that desperate when he's in the room with me.

A moment later, Becca and Dan enter. They're both wearing the masks everyone puts on outside the door to my hospital room. Not the surgical kind, but the happy kind. False and plastic and scarily smiling, reminding me of ventriloquists' dummies. It's as if the whole world has turned into performers and I am the lone member of the audience. Unfortunately, the show's been running for days now and the bill never changes: cheer Maggie up.

I mentally beg Becca to be her usual blunt and inappropriate self. I want her to tell me my hair looks a mess and I've got bags under my eyes, that finally I've got the boobs I've always yearned for, but she's too busy navigating the eggshells everyone has been crushing into the linoleum floor.

She sits down on the edge of the bed, looks at me installed

in the high-backed armchair beside it and leans forward a little, taking her weight on her palms. 'How are you?'

'OK,' I say. We both know I'm lying. An awkward silence follows. Where has our easy chatter gone? I search for something normal to say but realise I don't know what that is anymore.

Eventually, Becca walks over to where Dan has placed Billy in the plastic cot and leans over. 'Just as good-looking as yesterday,' she says, smiling up at me. 'He definitely got your genes instead of Dan's!'

Dan is hovering again, outside, it seems, because he says, 'Oi!', and pops his head round the doorway. 'I heard that!' He's smiling at Becca and she's smiling back at him. For a split-second I feel jealous, that they're sharing something I'm excluded from, that they still remember how to pull the right facial muscles to form that signal of joy.

'You're so lucky,' Becca says as she sits back down. There is meaning behind her stare.

'I know,' I say. Logically, I do know that. There are women who would kill to have a lovely healthy baby like mine. I can see the truth of it when I run it through my brain, but when I try to send the message to my heart, it just doesn't want to plug in. Wrong lead. Wrong connector or something. Computer says no. And I don't know how to reboot it. I'm not even sure I want to. I don't want to wipe the memory of Sophie away.

Becca comes back to the bed and sits down. 'It's OK to feel like this,' she tells me softly. 'Lots of women do.'

It's only the fact that I know, ten years from now, that

Becca's sister will have a severe form of post-natal depression, that Becca will have to take the baby in for a month, that she knows what she's talking about – or she will one day – that stops me from yelling at her.

'The hospital might have someone you can talk to ...'

I suspect Dan told her that during their hushed conversation in the corridor, about how I refused to see the woman. I shrug.

'It might help?'

I turn to the wall again. I'm beginning to think about painting my bedroom apple-green. It's not that bad as colours go.

'Maggie?'

'Maybe,' I say. And maybe I will, just to stop everyone bothering me. It won't help, though. I haven't got the 'baby blues', not in the sense anyone else means. It's not hormones. I'm grieving. Grieving for a daughter I'll never have, and if I try to tell a counsellor that, she'll probably have me sectioned. Fat lot of good that would do.

I turn to look at Becca. I'm fed up thinking about myself. She's got that look, that glow, I remember from the cafe in Bluewater, even though the shopping centre is probably still a dank old chalk pit at this point in time.

'You're seeing someone,' I say.

She replies with a grin and the blanket of concern is shooed away like the sun coming out from behind the clouds. She leans forward and begins to talk, her normal self again. I breathe a sigh of relief. 'How did you know?' she almost squeaks. 'You're always so intuitive.'

Not really, I think. Because if I was that clever I'd have

known this whole weird experience was going to happen. I wouldn't have had a life that would have bored a corpse in the first place. But I don't want to go into that. I'm happy to be distracted by Becca's news. Delighted, in fact.

I smile back at her and see a rush of hope and delight in her features at my response. She glances over her shoulder, as if she wants to call Dan in so he can see it, but then the urge to spill her secret takes over and she turns back to me. 'Oh, God, Maggie … he's amazing. Not like any of those other losers I've been seeing. He's kind and thoughtful and romantic, and he's already said he thinks he might be falling in love with me.'

I take a breath, let it wash through my lungs. It's the first one I've taken recently that hasn't had to fight against the tightness of my ribs, the muscles pulled taut, as if I'm literally trying to hold myself together. 'I'm so pleased,' I say. 'Tell me more.'

And I sit there in a half-daze as Becca chatters on. He's training to be a barrister, she says, but they're the perfect pairing. He loves that she's creative and expressive, even though he's more cerebral, and he doesn't mind at all that she works front of house in a theatre. He just loves her for who she is. I smile again. Maybe this is it, the guy she's been waiting for. Thank goodness. A part of me feared she was going to say Grant's name, but it can't be him – he's a banker. Although, after the divorce, Becca would often swap that first letter for another one.

So I listen, letting Becca's story of their first date, which started off badly. The restaurant in Covent Garden they'd been planning to go to was closed when they got there, with an exterminator van parked outside, but they broke the ice by having a good laugh about it and it ended up with them walking through the city hand in hand, talking into the wee hours.

'It sounds wonderful,' I say.

Dan sidles into the room again. He picks up the baby, who's now in the kind of deep sleep that only a stomach full of milk can bring. At least I'll have a few hours' reprieve now. I'm supposed to be going home tomorrow and I can't wait. At least Dan will be there at night. I don't like being on my own with it.

'Five minutes before kicking-out time,' he says, smiling at Becca. Not-so-secret communication flashes between them again, and this time it does make me feel sad. I'm tired of being in this thick, grey bubble that dulls everything and keeps me separate from everyone else. I think I need to pop the skin and climb out, but I know I'm scared of that too. What if all the feelings I'm holding back rush in and drown me?

Becca stands up. 'I'd better go.'

I push my way out of the chair, the first time I've done so in hours, I realise, as my hip joints complain, and give her a hug. She squeezes back gently. 'I'm glad you're happy,' I say. 'When we're back home and settled, you'll have to bring him over so we can make sure he's good enough for you.'

She pulls back and slips her handbag straps over her shoulder. 'It's a date!' she says brightly. 'And I'm sure you'll love Grant. Everybody does.'

The warmth that's slowly been building inside me since

Becca walked in the room drops through a trap door deep inside me, leaving nothing but cold air behind. 'Who?' I ask as my heart begins to beat painfully inside my chest.

'Grant,' she says, frowning slightly. 'My new boyfriend. Didn't I mention his name before?'

I shake my head. 'Grant what?' I ask, hoping against hope this is just a horrible coincidence. My tone is shrill, angry.

Becca frowns. I know she's confused by my reaction, but she doesn't understand. I have to know. When she tells me his name that trap door inside opens again, but this time I fall through it. I collapse into the chair and start to cry.

'Oh, Mags,' Becca says and kneels down beside the chair and hugs me hard. I can hear that she's crying too. 'This won't last forever. You'll be OK, I promise.' And that just makes me cry all the harder, because I can't promise her the same. Not in this life. Not in any life, and I wish so hard that I could.

CHAPTER TWENTY-EIGHT

'It's your turn!' I yell up the stairs to my husband. 'He's done another one.'

'He can't have!' Dan yells back down. 'I thought you'd only just changed him!'

I turn to look at Billy, who is wide-eyed and innocent in his Moses basket, but a sweet, fetid smell is filling the room. 'Like father, like son ...' I mutter as I walk over to him, but I pick him up and cradle him. We've been home three weeks now and as much as I wanted to pretend he didn't exist immediately after the birth, he's definitely growing on me. I can't blame him for not being his sister ... or his almost sister ... or his alternative self ... or whatever this weird reality would make him, can I?

I still don't love him the way I loved Sophie, though. I think that part of me might have switched off. I love him like you'd love a cute puppy or a kitten. I don't feel any more connected to him than that.

I realise I haven't heard Dan's heavy feet on the stairs, so I wander out into the hall and look up towards the landing. 'Dan!'

Silence, and then, 'I'm just coming. For goodness' sake!'

And then he appears, scowling at the top of the stairs and thumps down them. He hardly looks at me as he takes Billy from me and heads over to where the changing mat is laid in the corner of the living room, nappy bag spilling its contents beside it. We don't bother putting it away, because it's in constant use. I never knew a baby could produce so much poo. It's like the milk runs straight through him.

I don't know what's got Dan's knickers in a twist. After all, I let him sleep while Billy snuffled and fed and pooped his way through the night, getting up four times, even though I think looking after a newborn all day is every bit as draining as dealing with Year Elevens and their mock exams. I was trying to be supportive, but now I want a little bit of traffic coming back my way, I get nothing. Typical. I mime strangling Dan behind his back as he lays Billy on the changing mat, despite the fact my son, even he could focus that far, is far too young to be in on the joke.

'You might want to get the wipes ready,' I say, peering over Dan's shoulder. 'And the cream.'

I can see Dan's shoulders tense beneath his rugby shirt. 'Who's changing this nappy, you or me?'

'You, but – '

'Well, just let me bloody well change it, then. I don't need a backseat nappy changer. I'm perfectly capable of doing it on my – oh, hell!'

I close my eyes and shake my head. I don't know how many times I've warned him that Billy likes to get one last squirt in after the fresh air hits his bottom. And now baby poop is everywhere: all over the changing mat, all over Billy – and

I'd just changed him into that Babygro half an hour ago – all over Dan's sleeves. 'That's why I – '

'Don't,' Dan says through gritted teeth. 'Just don't.'

'Fine.' I cross my arms and walk off. 'I was only trying to help.'

'No,' replies Dan, as he finishes cleaning the poop up with a few deft wipes and installs a brand-new nappy on our son, 'you were just taking another chance to pick away at me. I know I'm supposed to be supportive because of the hormones and everything, but since Billy was born I haven't been able to do anything right!'

Billy must pick up on Dan's tone because instead of staring at him in fascination, as he usually does to the person who changes his nappy, his little face crumples and his bottom lip hooks over. Seconds later he starts to wail.

'Now look what you've done,' I say.

Dan stands up and hauls Billy against his chest. 'What *I've* done? It was you who …' And then he shakes his head and walks towards me. 'You know what? Never mind. It's not worth it.' And then he holds Billy out to me. 'I've got to finish that marking.'

I keep my arms folded, wondering when I'm supposed to get a chance to rest. I'm dead on my feet and I'm not a hundred per cent sure Dan's still going through those exam papers. It doesn't usually take him this long and I suspect it's just an excuse to hide away in his study and mess around on the computer. He's got a new game on there – *Lemmings* or something – and he's obsessed with it. But instead of saying anything, instead of letting him see me crumble and cry, I straighten my back and accept Billy, resting him in the crook of my elbow. It's no good, though. He starts to cry harder. Must be able to smell the milk.

Dan turns and trudges up the stairs.

'Just as long as you know I won't be able to cook tea while I'm minding our son,' I say to his retreating back.

'Whatever.'

I want to scream and stamp and shout, but I can't. It'd upset Billy, and now he's got the idea of milk in his head he's not going to shut up until he's had another feed. Muttering under my breath, I head for the corner of the sofa where I have my 'V' cushion, comfy pillows and muslins waiting for me and as Billy feeds I decide that if I don't get out of this house soon I'm going to go crazy.

All Dan and I do is snipe at each other. It's like we're in a competition to see who had the lousiest night's sleep so we can claim an hour off while the other one looks after the baby and feel justified in doing it. Or who had the worst nappy. Or who bounced him up and down the most when he had one of his colicky episodes.

It wasn't like this with Sophie. Not this bad, anyway. I mean, we fought, we moaned, but it wasn't like this. I don't know why but everything Dan does and says irritates me. I end up snapping at him and then he accuses me of picking and retreats even more into himself, which just makes me even more angry. It's a vicious cycle. One we've been in before, not even this bad, and we still hadn't managed to jump start ourselves out of it almost twenty years later. The fact that it's not only happening again, but that it's worse this time, makes me want to lie down and cry.

But I can't. I've got to look after Billy, so I decide to get the pram out and get some fresh air. There's no telling how long his self-absorbed father is going to be 'marking', even if it is a Saturday afternoon.

I decide to give Becca a quick call before I leave. She's popped in a few times since I've been home, full of the joys of her new romance, but I really need to talk to her properly. I've got to find a way to make her see sense.

Thankfully, Grant is away this weekend, so Becca is more than ready to make the forty-minute drive to Swanham. I arrange to meet her at a cafe on the High Street. It'll only take me ten minutes to walk there, but I wander round the busy streets with Billy in his pram and eventually he drops off into one of those sleeps I pray for, the kind where you could drive a freight train past his head and he wouldn't wake up.

I go in and order a pot of tea and a brownie and for once Becca turns up right on the dot. She gets herself a coffee and a large slice of carrot cake and we sit at a table in the corner, where there's room to park Billy's pram.

'How are you doing?' she asks, sympathy weighing down her words. Lots of people seem to speak to me that way at the moment.

'Actually,' I say, 'I'm doing much better.' And I am. I'm starting to cope with being stuck in this unwanted life. Knowing that I won't be here forever keeps me putting one foot in front of another in the mornings.

'You look it,' Becca says, and I don't miss the tiny sigh of relief. 'Now you're feeling more up to it, perhaps we can have that dinner we talked about? Rather than me and Grant foisting ourselves on you, maybe you can come round to mine? I'll cook and you can get to know him a bit better.'

I busy myself checking on Billy, who is sleeping so soundly he hasn't moved, not even twitched an eyelid, in the last five minutes. I need time to think. When I look back up again I say, 'That's a lovely idea, but I'm really not sure about taking Billy out for a whole evening.'

Becca glances over at the pram. 'Seems like he'd be good as gold.'

'He's not always like this, you know. Sometimes he just screams his lungs out for no reason.'

'But that won't matter, will it? I mean, we know you've got a new baby, that things don't always go smoothly. We'll just work round it.'

I avoid Becca's gaze and tuck Billy's blanket more snugly round his middle. 'I just don't want you to go to a lot of trouble cooking a meal and then us ruin it by not being able to sit down and eat it, because we've got to walk around burping his highness here – '

'Maggie?'

'What?'

Becca purses her lips together. 'Is there some other reason you don't want to come to dinner?'

I try to look innocent. 'What other reason could there be?'

'Grant.'

'What about him?'

Becca takes a sip of her coffee then looks me in the eye. 'I saw the way you looked at him when we popped in last weekend. You hardly said a word to him.'

'I said "hello" and "how are you?". I asked how his work was going. Sorry if I wasn't full of sparkling wit and repartee, but I'd only had three hours sleep the night before.' I'm getting cross now, but mostly because Becca has caught me out. I'd tried to be nice to Grant, tried to remind myself that things could change, that he could be different in this life – he certainly had a different job – but all I could think about was those times when Becca had appeared on my doorstep in tears, or worse, the times she'd gone silent on me, not answering her phone for days, because he'd been so awful she couldn't even bring herself to tell me about it. 'I didn't mean to be rude to him.'

Becca's expression softens. 'Good,' she says. 'Then next Saturday evening you can come round and have another go.'

I open my mouth, brain frantically searching for another excuse, but she knows me too well. 'Don't be like that,' she says, cutting through the waffle I haven't even spouted yet. 'I've never been that way with Dan. I've always loved him because you loved him. That's what friends are supposed to do, isn't it?'

I have no answer for that. Yes, she always has been wonderful with Dan. They're kind of like brother and sister now, teasing each other, bickering over silly things, but underneath there's a deeply-held affection. But it's different. Dan's a good guy.

What confuses me most is how Grant and Becca keep ending up together. Does that mean it's fate? Does that mean the universe keeps trying different patterns, different variations, until the right one works and they're happy together? And if it is, doesn't what seem a really cruel way to go about it? What about all the other Beccas who are miserable and hurting? I don't get it.

'I just want you to give him a chance,' Becca says, her eyes pleading. 'That's not too much to ask, is it?'

I sigh. Maybe it isn't. Because in this reality, this world, Becca is in love and all of the bad stuff hasn't happened yet. It's not lost on me that in my 'other' life, she's doing exactly the same to me – rejecting the man I love for no good reason – and I suppose I could make it tit for tat, but where does that get me? Our friendship is disintegrating in that life, and I don't want that to happen here too. Besides, if Grant really does turn out to be a sadistic prat again, she'll need me more than ever. I have to stand by her, stand by her choice. I can't see any other way.

CHAPTER TWENTY-NINE

I open my eyes and instantly realise there's something wrong. Billy isn't crying. I check the bed next to me and find Dan gone. Light is seeping through the curtains and the digital alarm clock blinks a time of 8:03.

I leap out of bed. I last fed Billy at twelve-thirty. He normally wakes every three hours on the dot screaming for more milk.

I scramble across the bedroom, dodging a stack of Dan's school stuff and a pile of clean washing that I don't remember putting there, but I can't see Billy. His Moses basket is full of more clean washing – Dan's socks and pants – and I start digging, flinging them behind me as my heart thuds in my ears. I keep going until I find … sheet.

Nothing else.

No Billy.

That's when I really start to panic.

'Billy!' I scream into the air. '*Billy!*'

I'm rewarded with a gurgle, but it's not coming from our room. Oh, thank God!

I scramble out onto the landing, which is filled with its usual mountains of crap – why did I marry a man whose idea of cleaning up is just to create a fresh pile of his stuff somewhere new in the house? – and race in the direction of the raspberry-blowing noise I can hear.

It's coming from the spare room. I fling open the door and spot Billy's pink skin behind the bars of the cot bed we'd got for when he's older. What on earth was Dan thinking, putting him in that? He's far too small.

But when I lean over the railing I discover Billy is *huge*. He's lost that scrawny translucent newborn look and now has fleshy, dimpled wrists and elbows. His hair is twice as thick and twice as dark as it was yesterday. I mean, I mean … he looks like a four-month-old!

That's when my brain catches up with my panic.

I've jumped again.

Not back to Jude. Not back to the man I love and the life I want, but just further along in this one, like I did that time in Italy. I feel as if something hard and blunt is piercing my heart. What if I never go back? What if I'm stuck here now? Perhaps I've subconsciously made my choice and this is where I'll stay. Because I have a feeling, you know, that one day one of these realities will stick, and it'll have something to do with me. I just haven't worked out the hows and whys of it yet.

But then Billy looks up at me, waggles his legs up and down and gives me a gummy grin. A rush of warmth pours from that hole in my newly skewered heart and I reach down and pick him up, hug him to me and stroke his downy soft hair with my chin. He clutches onto me with his chubby fists and I start to cry.

'Where did you learn to smile like that, my beautiful boy?'

I ask him and I'm rewarded with another showing of his dimples, his complete and unguarded joy at seeing me. I kiss his fat little cheeks over and over and when he starts to giggle I can hardly stand it.

I've missed so many precious moments: his first smile, his first laugh. Possibly even his first taste of solids. I want to scream out to God or heaven or the universe – whatever is pulling me this way and that through time like this – and tell them to hand over the remote. I want to rewind, to catch up with what I've missed.

I wander downstairs and check the kitchen calendar, Billy tucked between my armpit and my hip. I've been making sure to keep it up to date, marking off each day with a tiny dot in the corner of each square. The last dot is on the sixteenth of November.

Wow. Three and half months. That means Billy is almost eighteen weeks old and, for me, autumn has frosted into early March overnight.

I spend the day with my son, getting to know him again, finding out the new things he can do. I discover he's incredibly vocal, babbling away to both me, himself and any passing toy, with great gusto, that his favourite hobby after exercising his own voice is sucking his toes and that he's desperately trying to work out how to roll over onto his front, but can't quite get that last arm out the way and it makes him very cross when he finally topples back down onto his back again.

I feel different, I realise, as I walk Billy through the park in his pram, trying to get him off to sleep for a good chunk of the afternoon. I'm not exactly happy, but I don't feel that sense of heaviness I did just after I gave birth. Maybe it was something to do with hormones after all. Or maybe jumping is like dreaming and my brain has processed the shock of having Billy instead of Sophie while I've been unaware of time marching on around me.

I always wanted a second child, so maybe my wish has come true. Just not in the way I expected it to. I've got to try to find some joy in this life if I'm going to be spending time here, and since my marriage is clearly not going to provide that, maybe Billy is it.

I also feel differently about Dan. I've noticed that after a jump I often feel as if I have a bit more perspective. Maybe it's because I'm no longer in the middle of whatever I was feeling and doing. It gives me a sense of distance. I start to remember that it wasn't so long ago that things were good between Dan and I.

So, when I'm back at home and I hear the door go around six, I wait for Dan to make his usual trip to the kitchen to peck me on the cheek and put the kettle on. After the inevitable *thud-thump* of his shoes hitting the hall carpet, one after the other, I hear him go upstairs. I wait to hear the loo flush or something, but there's nothing. Moments later the study door shuts. It doesn't exactly slam, but he didn't just nudge it closed either.

OK, I think. This is new. So I decide to take the initiative and I make the tea myself and take Dan's upstairs. He's on his computer again. No pixelated lemmings in sight, thank goodness, only a Word document that he seems to be annotating. Doing marking after all. 'Here,' I say, as I put the mug of tea on the desk. And because there's an atmosphere, because we always seem to be at each other's throats these days, I add, 'Peace offering.'

My gesture does not have the desired effect. Instead, Dan turns to me, his expression at once both scoffing and incredulous. 'You really think a cup of tea is going to wipe out what you said to me last night?'

I stutter. It's times like these when I really hate my stupid kangaroo life. I have no idea what I said, whether it was justified or not, whether Dan has just decided to take my words in the worst possible light, which tends to be his default position these days. There's only one way out. 'I'm sorry.' I say.

He doesn't respond at first. Too surprised at hearing those words leave my mouth, probably. I realise that I don't often apologise without a good deal of justification and putting my side of the story out there first. In this instance, however, I have no choice, because I have no story. I have no justification.

'Are you OK?' I ask, and Dan runs a hand through his hair, which is shaggier than it's ever been. He doesn't speak, just shakes his head and that makes me worried. 'What is it? Are you ill?'

He shakes his head. 'It's work.'

'What about it?'

'You know I've been Acting Head of Department for the last half-term?'

I nod. I didn't know, and I'm really pleased for him. I'd been hoping they'd offer him the post when I heard the current Head of Department was going on maternity leave.

'Well, Mrs Shroffield let them know she's not coming back. They're looking for someone to take on the role permanently.'

I look at Dan, his dejected expression. This can only mean one thing. 'They told you they don't want you to apply for it?'

'No, that's just it! They've offered me the job.'

'But, Dan! That's great!'

He looks at me as if to say, *Really? Is it?*

'But – '

'More paperwork, more hours at the school? I'm not sure if that's what I really want.'

I'm trying not to let my frustration grow, but I don't get it. When Dan got this job at Swanham High School, all he could talk about was his dreams of being the youngest Head of Department they'd ever had. 'Then what do you want?' I ask. That would be a step forward, at least, from the Dan I knew. Some kind of goal.

He nods, more to himself than to me. 'That's what I've been thinking about. Them offering me the post just made me realise how much I didn't want it, and since then I've been piecing together what I do want.'

'Hang on … "since then"? How long have you known about this?'

Dan has the grace to bow his head and look sheepish. 'Two weeks.'

My mouth drops open. 'And you didn't think to tell me? To discuss it with me?'

He looks up at me from under his shaggy hair. 'I needed to get it straight in my own head, first. You know what I'm like.'

I sigh. Unfortunately, I do. And this is classic Dan. 'So have you now?'

He nods.

'Feel like clueing me in?'

'What I really want is to write. I need to find more hours in the week to do that because I never have time for it any more. Taking the Head of Department post would erase any chance of that.'

I feel tears welling up against my lashes. I don't know why I'm getting so emotional. Maybe it's because I'm just so tired all the time. I don't know if Billy sleeps better now he's four months, but, even if he does, I was still on the newborn sleep schedule last night. 'But if you take more time to write every week – don't get me wrong, I don't want to stop you – I'll have to pick up your slack, and I'm exhausted enough as it is!'

He looks me in the eye. His gaze is steady. He's made up his mind about something. Finally. 'That's why I'm thinking of handing in my notice and doing supply work. It pays well and it'll give me more free time.'

'Yes, but it's not regular, is it? It's not guaranteed. How are we supposed to last through the school holidays, or when the jobs don't come in?'

His mouth thins into a grim line.

I don't care. There's another reason too. Something I'm better off not saying: in the long run, this won't help Dan at all. It won't help *us*. Future Dan lacked ambition, direction. Just doing supply work, tinkering with his poems and stories on the side, isn't going to give him that. He'll just be bumming around aimlessly, no career path, no nothing.

'I not happy, Maggie. Neither of us are. And I don't know if it's the sleepless nights or we've got ourselves in a rut, but I feel like I've got to do something to change that. Can you understand? Can you at least try?'

I look back at him, helplessly. I do understand. It's just that he's going about it totally the wrong way. 'Do you think I want to be stuck at home cleaning up poo and sick all day? We don't always get what we want! Now is not the time to be selfish, Dan. We need to work as a team!'

Dan grunts. 'Some team …'

'What does that mean?'

He gives me a scathing look. 'It means it's not really a team if there's always the same leader and always the same follower, and I know which role you cast yourself in!'

'Only because of your chronic lack of motivation! If I didn't take charge, no one would. It's so unfair you're blaming this all on me!'

Dan stands up. 'I'm going out,' he says.

'Where to?'

'Dunno. Just out.'

And before I can ask him if he's going to be back for tea, he jogs downstairs, throws his coat and shoes on and stomps out the door, slamming it behind him, which wakes Billy up and he starts to wail.

Once I've soothed Billy, I order a takeaway. I honestly can't be bothered to cook after this. It takes ages to get Billy down for the night and when I check the clock and see it's past nine, there's still no sign of Dan. I'm tempted to scrape the rest of the Chinese into the bin, but I resolve to be the bigger person and grudgingly shove it in the fridge and then I go in search of the phone so I can call Becca to vent.

I dial her number and wait. It rings six times and goes to the answerphone. I leave a message – nothing too ranty – and then I place the phone back in its cradle. It's one of those massive cordless things we all thought was the height of technology at the time but is five times the size of my home phone in my future life. I stare at the handset. Not just because of its historical interest – ha! – but because I'm thinking. I'm trying not to read anything into Becca not answering.

She could just be out.

She could have stayed late at work. She could be out having fancy dinner with Mr Scum. She could be in the bath, up to her earholes in Fenjal.

But I'm worried it's none of those things. I recognise this behaviour, you see; this cutting herself off and hiding away. This is what she does in the aftermath of one of Grant's rages.

CHAPTER THIRTY

I think this is where I'm going to stay. I've been here with Dan and Billy almost a year now. I've jumped a couple more times, but always in this timeline and only skipping weeks, mostly. Once, I just missed a few hours and woke up later the same afternoon.

Dan and I have just had another row. The same old things. He didn't take the head of department job, but he didn't leave his job to do supply work, either. A compromise, we both said. Somehow I know he's blaming me for it. I see the resentment in his eyes every time he's home extra late because he's been blackmailed into helping with a school function or supervising a trip.

I'm upstairs and I hear rustling down near the front door. He's putting his coat on. He always seems to be putting his coat on these days, escaping the house – escaping me – whenever possible.

It's soul destroying. Not just because of the sting of rejection, but because I really have tried in this life. I've tried to help him, tried to encourage him to grab life by the horns, but every suggestion is an accusation. Every helpful idea, judgement.

We've proved it, I think to myself. We never should have got married. We've tried it in two lifetimes now and it hasn't worked. We were obviously never meant to be more than college sweethearts. I should have had the guts to walk away on our wedding day.

'You're going out?' I ask, appearing at the top of the landing.

He nods as he winds his scarf round his neck. 'I fancy watching the match, but thought I'd go down the pub, leave the telly free for that thing you like that's on tonight.'

I frown. I wasn't aware there was a match on, but I have little interest in football. 'Which match?'

'Oh, it's the … the Sunderland versus, you know … um … City … one.' He shuffles about putting his coat on.

I nod. 'OK.'

'Won't be too late,' he says, not quite meeting my eyes before he heads out the door.

I slump down and sit on the step I've been standing on. So that's it, then. It's started again.

I sit there, staring at the plain white back of the front door. And when I get up I don't run after Dan and demand to know where he's going and who he's going with – I go and check on my sleeping baby.

I pass the study on the way back downstairs to put the dishwasher on and I stop. I wait a few moments and then I nudge the door open. I stare at the pile of papers on the desk, the vague mess created by someone who's not particularly untidy but never cleans the clutter either, so it ends up slowly eroding the free space, like a coastline losing centimetres each year as it's nibbled away by the waves.

I step inside the door and close it behind me, holding my breath. I've done it now. I've committed. I know I'm going to snoop. Something inside feels dirty and unclean, but another part of me feels strangely exhilarated.

I start with random bits of paper on the desk, things that were put down last so might be current. Nothing. Not unless you count marking, run-of-the-mill work stuff and bills Dan said he'd pay and obviously hasn't got round to. So I open the top drawer of the desk. It's filled with stationery and other junk: batteries, rubber bands and film canisters from our holiday last summer that haven't been developed yet.

The bottom drawer is just filing by the looks of it. School stuff. I have better luck with the middle drawer. Underneath all the letters and scraps of paper is a narrow box file, the sort of thing you'd keep important stuff in, special stuff.

I lay the rest of the paperwork carefully on the desk, ready to put it all back in so it looks like nothing's been disturbed. Then, after staying completely still for a few moments to make sure I can't hear Dan's key in the door, I carefully lift the file out, release the elastic keeping it together at the corners and look inside.

I don't know if I'm disappointed or relieved not to find love letters or receipts from hotel stays inside. That's bad, isn't it? If your marriage is really going well, the reaction to finding out your husband *isn't* cheating on you should pretty much be a slam dunk.

It's just the usual keepsakes in the file – his degree certificate, some old school reports, birth certificate and passport. But under that I find something of interest. Something unexpected.

Tucked away inside a huge Valentine's card I sent him our first year together, I find both one of our wedding invitations and a matching order of service. I turn to the order of service, curious to know what's inside. I honestly don't remember much about that day.

I liked the reading his dad suggested both times we got married. It outlined everything I thought love should be, even if I'm not sure about the existence of the God it represents. One Corinthians thirteen, verses four to seven:

Love is patient, love is kind. It does not envy, it does not boast, it is not proud. It does not dishonour others, it is not self-seeking, it is not easily angered, it keeps no record of wrongs. Love does not delight in evil but rejoices with the truth. It always protects, always trusts, always hopes, always perseveres.

While the promises we made to each other that day were all about sickness and health, riches and poverty – practical things – these words were the silent promise I thought we were making, but just look at where we are now. Are we capable of doing any of these things for each other? Dan isn't patient with me. He isn't kind. When I open my mouth, he always expects the worst to come out of it and, like a self-fulfilling prophecy, I've started to oblige him more often than not.

I sigh as I fold the order of service and put it carefully back in the folder, replace everything else in the drawer. We had so much potential, Dan and I. At least I thought we had. How do we manage to keep getting it so wrong?

And now I worry that not only having welched on this part of the bargain, Dan might be on the road to dismantling the other promises we made too. Specifically, the one about keeping himself only unto me.

Suddenly, I can't face just my own company any more. I need to talk to someone. I put Dan's office back the way I found it and tread lightly downstairs and pick up the phone. I need my best friend. At least in this life she's actually talking to me.

But the phone rings and rings. I stare at the handset. It's really unlike her not to be in on a Thursday evening, all set up to watch *ER*. We usually talk about the episode the following day, deconstruct it and argue about which doctor is the sexiest – she's for George and I'm Team Noah.

I wonder if she's OK. I decide to phone her at work tomorrow – that is, if I can co-ordinate Billy's nap with Becca's lunch break. She's got a new job as Assistant Front of House at the Orchard in Dartford and has more regular hours now.

I'd be worried that it's something else, but since that time after I last jumped when she just didn't pick up for three days, everything's been fine with her. She and Grant had a row, but he apologised and he's been on his best behaviour ever since. They're all loved up still and I'm starting to eat humble pie, albeit secretly and silently, about him. Compared to the Grant I knew in my other life, this one is attentive and courteous to his girlfriend. A complete turn-around.

I put the phone back in the cradle, walk over to the kettle and turn it on. More for something to do than because I really want a cup of coffee. And that's when it hits me. Becca is forgotten and Dan comes sharply back into focus.

ER.

It's Thursday night.

My husband, once again, is lying about Thursday night.

CHAPTER THIRTY-ONE

Dan comes in before eleven, a very respectable hour, given the fact he was lying to me about where he was. I checked the TV guide and couldn't find a hint of a Big Match anywhere, unless he was talking about Swanham Town playing Outer Mongolia. Not.

I know I need to make some decisions about this life. I can't spend the next twenty years in this purgatory. I don't want to do it to Billy, but maybe Dan and I would be better apart? I need a man who can fulfil me emotionally, not a husband who grunts and hides away in his study, who makes me feel as if I'm invisible.

The next day, I phone Becca at work, only to be told that she isn't in today. She's off sick. OK, I think. If she's ill, she probably just went to bed early last night. I ring her house but there's still no answer there, either.

By four o'clock, I'm imagining Becca collapsed on the kitchen floor, what she thought was a bit of a sniffle having turned into something life-threatening. By four-fifteen, I'm strapping Billy into his car seat and we're making the drive from Swanham to Sidcup, where she's taken advantage of the current slump in property prices and bought a three-bedroomed house.

I arrive at her deceptively spacious 1960s townhouse just before five. I park my car behind hers in the drive, leaving Billy strapped in the back seat, and ring the doorbell. I think I can hear a television murmuring away to itself but then it goes quiet.

'Becca?' I call from outside, loud enough to be heard, but not so loud the neighbouring net curtains will twitch. There's no answer. Just in case the doorbell's not working, I knock. Loudly. And then I ring again, just to make sure.

I glance back at Billy in the car. I've left the door open and I can hear him chattering away to himself, which means he's happy at the moment but that might change at any minute. You don't get much of a build-up with Billy. One moment he's all sunshine and the next the world is ending.

And then I realise … Becca's got to be in. Her car's here.

I knock again and then, when there's no answer, I bend down and push the letter box up with my finger. I'm relieved I can't see any legs, any limp form sprawled in the hallway. 'Becca? It's Maggie. Are you OK? I'm getting really worried about you!'

The house seems to hold its breath along with me for the next few seconds and then I see movement. Moments later, Becca opens the door. She's wearing tracksuit bottoms, a T-shirt with a stain down the front and her long hair is messy, hanging down over one side of her face. 'You'd better come in,' she says grimly.

I nod. 'I've got Billy in the car. I'll just …' I run off as she leaves the front door open and slopes back to the living room.

Hangover? I think, as I lift Billy from his car seat and sling the nappy bag over my shoulder. I can't think of anything else to explain it. But Becca's usually sheepishly funny if she's had a bit too much to drink the night before, or moaning loudly about being in pain and never touching a drop of tequila again.

I close the door behind me and walk down the hall into the living room, which spans the back of the house. The curtains are drawn and *Countdown* is playing on the TV at low volume. Becca is slumped in an armchair. I take one end of the sofa, with Billy on my lap, and I let him play with my keys, a rare treat since he threw my last set down the toilet.

I feel a tremble in my throat but I manage to keep it out of my words. 'Work said you were ill. Are you?'

And by ill, I mean, *really* ill. Not the kind of ill that lays you out in bed with the curtains closed, but the kind of ill that makes you sit in a room with the curtains drawn, looking as if the world is about to end, because it is. For you, anyway.

'No,' she replies hoarsely. 'It's …' She trails off, unable to speak, and that's when I see it. Her hair moves as she silently shakes her head, revealing a bruise the size of a closed fist on her temple.

I pop Billy down on the sofa beside me and I'm up and across the room. 'My God! What happened?'

She looks at me, her eyes full of knowledge, and the truth sinks through me like a lead weight. I hug her hard, holding her to me, as if, by the sheer strength of my love for her, I can suck the colour out of that bruise and make it disappear. 'No, no, no, no no …' I chant into her ear. She begins to cry softly.

I lead her to the sofa and we both sit down. Billy has forgotten my keys and is now staring, wide-eyed, at the TV, transfixed by a youthful-looking Carol Vorderman as she does her sums. I think it might be love at first sight.

'What happened?' I ask.

Becca takes a deep breath. 'We had a fight. He didn't want me going out with the girls from work. But it was Shanna's birthday do.'

I nod. I met Shanna at Christmas. She's the stage manager at the theatre. Loud, brassy, incorrigible. Just the sort of woman control-freak Grant would hate his girlfriend to be around. Becca loves her, though. I find her a bit over the top, but I've got nothing against her in small doses.

'Anyway, one thing led to another, and before I knew it we were shouting at each other.' Becca looks at me, her eyes huge. 'Oh, Maggie, I said some awful things to him! You know how I can get when I really lose it.'

'I know, but it doesn't – '

'I pushed him too far!' Becca wails, covering her face with her hands. 'You're always telling me I'll go too far one day, and now I have!'

I peel her hands away from her face and make her look at me. 'Becca,' I say sternly, 'this is not your fault.' I wait for my words to sink in but her attention is fractured, all over the place.

'I know' she says weakly, but she doesn't sound very convincing. 'But if I hadn't – '

'If you hadn't nothing,' I say. 'There's no excuse.'

I think of Dan, of how he just backs off from every

confrontation now, and I silently thank him for it. There are worse things, I remind myself. There are definitely worse things.

The TV cuts to adverts and Billy loses interest. He turns round, and when he sees Becca, he beams. It just makes Becca cry again, even though she smiles back at him. She scoops him up and hugs him tight, doesn't even mind when he grabs fistfuls of her hair, and breathes him in, closing her eyes.

He's magic, this kid, I think. A charmer, in the real sense of the word. He has the ability to bring people back from the brink. He did it for me and now he's doing it for Becca, too. I see her shoulders relax.

As if he knows his job is done, Billy stops being adorable and begins to grizzle. 'Promise you'll always be sweet and lovely like this,' she whispers to him. 'Promise you'll never grow up.' It's past his tea time. I break out the emergency pot of raisins from the nappy bag and make him sit on the floor to eat them.

'What happens now?' I ask, while Billy is absorbed in mastering the pincer movement of chubby thumb and forefinger that will make catching raisins easier.

'I don't know. I mean, I haven't even seen him since Wednesday night. I haven't answered the door, haven't answered the phone. But I'm going to have to talk to him eventually, aren't I?'

I nod. While I think the best thing she could do is call the police – and I'm going to bring that up later – the first thing she needs to do is to get Grant out of her life, and she's going to have to communicate with him somehow if she's going to do that. 'Do you want me to be there?'

Becca looks confused. 'Be where?'

'With you. When you tell him it's over.'

She looks away.

'Please tell me you're not going to stay with him?'

She speaks to the rich, patterned curtains. The ones Grant bought her. They were far too expensive, Becca told him, but he ordered them anyway. Anything for *his* girl. 'I have to at least hear him out. I have to give him a chance to explain.'

'Fine. But after that you're telling him to sling his hook, right?'

'Right,' she replies, but she's still staring at the curtains and there's no determination in her voice, no determination at all.

'Becca?' I raise my voice, make her look at me. 'But then you're telling him to get lost, right?' I stare at her as she looks back at me, her eyes hollow. 'Promise me?' I say, and everything I feel for her is packed into those two tiny words. 'Promise me!'

CHAPTER THIRTY-TWO

Becca doesn't give me a clear answer, and the next morning I open my eyes to high white ceilings with Victorian mouldings and the smell of Jude's aftershave lingering in the dent in his pillow. I bury my face in it and cry.

I'm back. In my real life. The other one is just a shadow, a cautionary tale.

But I can't quite settle into the joy of being back where I belong. Firstly, because of that conversation with Becca. I left her nodding and agreeing she'd be strong, but I could see the yearning in her eyes. I could hear her murmuring to herself in her head, 'But I love him …' as I'd laid out all my sensible advice. It's like reaching the final episode in a season of your favourite TV series and being left on a bombshell of cliffhanger. Except it's not just scripts and sets and actors; it's real life, and that version of Grant is way, way worse than the other one. At least the original kept his hands to himself.

And then there's the feeling as I wander round our stylish flat that something is missing, and I don't mean Jude, who must have risen early to get to some building site somewhere. My 'mummy radar' is still switched on. I keep wanting to go and check the cot. Every now and then I find myself glancing at the clock, calculating how long it is until the next nap or the next meal.

It's only the knowledge that I will go back – I have a gut sense I'm not done with this yet – that I will see Billy again, that stops me bursting into tears a second time.

I always feel a bit strange after a jump. Not disoriented, but more like when you come back from holiday and your house still looks like your house, but feels strange and not-quite-right for the first twenty-four hours, so I take my time wandering round the flat, reacquainting myself with my life, the way I slot into it. I search for diaries and calendars, anything to give me a clue to where and when I am, to work out if I've moved seamlessly from one reality to another, or if I've missed a huge chunk of time in the transition. It's weird these things are becoming normal for me, isn't it?

A quick look out the windows, to the grey skies and large, plopping rain, leads me to suspect it's still early 1997, but when I turn on the TV to catch the morning news I discover it's November and almost two years have gone by. It feels as if the madness is accelerating. I don't like it. In 'Maggie time' – the time I feel I've actually experienced – I haven't seen the man I love for a year, which is far too long, but by the calendar it's even worse. Close to four years! I'll be twenty-eight soon.

I can't possibly pretend this is a dream any more. As bonkers as it sounds, it's time to call a spade a spade, or to be more exact, a time-travelling housewife a time-travelling housewife.

I laugh softly to myself. Even inside my own head it sounds insane.

I decide to go and get dressed, do something completely normal, to stop myself losing it altogether. It's weird, though. I don't recognise many of the clothes in my wardrobe. They're two sizes smaller than post-baby Maggie wears. I look down and check out my flat stomach, my toned thighs. I wonder if I've started going to the gym.

As much as I'm pleased to be in such good shape, I can't help feeling a bit thrown too. I look in the mirror. This Maggie hasn't got split ends and she has her eyebrows done. She's had time to shave her armpits and even her legs, and her uterus is pristine and unused.

If I'm not careful, I'll start to think I'm dividing into two people. I'm going to have to hang on to who I think I am quite tightly, which might not be as easy as it sounds. With all these different versions of myself wandering around, I feel it would be quite easy for one of them to get lost. Maybe it's just a matter of deciding who I want to be and choosing that. And maybe that's the key to all of this – that when I work out which one I'm really supposed to be, I'll naturally slot into the right life and stop all this jumping around.

Anyway … enough philosophising. I have to dig new hooks into this life. I might as well work out what I'm supposed to be doing today.

I turn my computer on and wait for it to boot up, then search my graphic-design folder for any current files. There's nothing. The last folder is dated more than two years ago. I try looking in other places on my hard drive but I can't find anything else. Maybe I had a virus?

I rummage in my handbag. Actually, I rummage in three

handbags until I find an unfamiliar one that is obviously the one I'm using at the moment and pull my trusty black Filofax out of it. I hug this anchor to my chest, hoping that this other Maggie, this 'Meg', never stops filing it in in her small, neat handwriting. I flick to the current week and find an address and an appointment time.

OK. So maybe I'm meeting with a new client?

I check the clock and realise I need to get a move on if I'm going to make it. The address is in Dulwich. A cute little outfit catches my eye on the rails, a cornflour-blue dress with a short, flared skirt and matching jacket. Very Ally McBeal. I pull it on, along with some chunky-heeled shoes from my wardrobe, grab my handbag and head for the door. It's only as I catch my reflection in the mirror that I realise I've got so out of the habit of wearing make-up I've forgotten to put any on. I backtrack to the bedroom and rectify that before setting off.

I arrive in Dulwich forty-five minutes later. The address is not what I expected. It's a large Victorian house with soft sandstone bricks and bright white masonry and windows. There's a tall flight of stone steps leading up to the front door, so I make my way carefully up them and press the doorbell. That's odd again. If there's an office here, a design company I'm freelancing for or something, then I'd expect there to be multiple bells with labels or an entry system. Instead, there's just one large white button set in its original circular casing.

I can hear heels on the hallways and a girl in her twenties with a pencil behind her ear and a clipboard clutched to her chest answers. She's wearing a delicate gold necklace above her cropped mohair jumper that declares her name is Holly, but she's the spitting image of Britney Spears, complete with bared midriff. The mother in me wants to ask her if she isn't a bit chilly dressed like that at this time of year, but I know it's none of my business.

'Oh, thank God you're here!' she exclaims and grabs me by the arm and drags me inside. 'The chandeliers arrived early and I have no idea how low we should hang them.'

'OK …' I say calmly. Going with the flow is the easiest way to tackle 'jump day' scenarios.

'How are you not a wreck?' Holly asks as she trots past the staircase into the back of the house. 'I'm always a wreck on install day!' She leads me into a spacious dining room. It has the original cast-iron, arched fireplace, cornices to die for and large French windows leading onto what looks like a brand-new conservatory. The decor is amazing. The space is big and light enough to cope with walls painted in a colour somewhere between crimson and burgundy, the floor is dark mahogany and there's a long dining table flanked with antique chairs.

There are a couple of workmen in paint-spattered trousers hanging around and when they see me they jump to attention. One climbs up a step ladder, and another one hands him a stupendous Venetian crystal chandelier. I marvel at the delicate beauty of the curls of blown glass, quite mesmerised by them.

'Here alright?' he asks, puffing.

'Down a bit,' I say, just going with the scenario. I have no idea how high or low to hang a chandelier, so I just follow my gut. He does as requested and I tell him it's perfect before he drops it. The other man rushes in to ease it gently from his hands and then a whole team of them go to work hanging both that one and an identical one at the other end of the room.

Holly looks at me nervously. 'It's just like the sketches, right? The team's been working really hard to bring your vision to life.'

My vision? I stare at Holly.

'Do you want to do a final walkthrough of the top floors?' she asks. 'I know you let me oversee the install of the bedrooms, and I followed your checklist to the letter, but I wondered if you want to add any final touches?'

I nod dumbly. As we walk up the large turning staircase with its gently scrolling banister, I piece it all together. Jude had suggested interior design, hadn't he, last time I was with him? I must have followed his lead, even though I wasn't sure I had the eye for it; but as I walk round this house, which has slightly more of the twenty-first-century mix of minimalism and good-quality traditional features than is right for the late nineties, I recognise myself. Not in an obvious way, but in the choice of colour of a vase or the eclectic mix of photo frames in a wall display.

I did this?

For the first time in my life – any of my lives – I'm astounded by my own abilities. I sigh as I look round the gorgeous master bedroom, with its large picture window overlooking the landscaped back garden. This is who I am, I think. This is the me I've been searching for. I close my eyes for a moment.

'Any last things you want done?' Holly asks.

I open my eyes again, walk around the bed, and stare at

the room from another angle. Can I do this? I know the other Maggie, Meg, has excelled herself, but I feel like an imposter standing in her cute little designer suit. I look round the room again, inspecting it more critically this time.

I sense an empty space on the bed. The bedding is an exercise in complementing neutrals – oatmeal, hessian and taupe. 'More pillows,' I say, without almost deciding to. 'In aubergine …'

Holly stares at the bed. 'You're right. It needs a lift of colour.' She frowns. I can tell she's disappointed at not having thought of it herself. 'How about those darling Chinese silk ones with the birds embroidered onto them that we found in Paris? I can hop in a cab and fetch them from the office?'

I nod. 'Do it,' I say, hoping my assistant's eye – because that's who I'm guessing Holly is – is as good as mine. She grins at me and rushes out the door. I hear her clumpy shoes thumping down the stairs. 'You might want to take a – ' the door slams, cutting me off ' – coat.'

I wander through the house then, looking at everything a second time, trying to take it all in. I'm an interior designer, I think to myself, and I'm flipping good! A warm glow follows me through the rest of the day.

When Jude comes home that evening, I make my way to meet him. I find him standing in the hallway, a bottle of champagne in one hand and a huge smile on his face.

'What?' I ask, unable to help smiling back.

'I did it!' he says, putting the bottle on the console table against the wall and shrugging his coat off. 'I sold the Mayfair house – my first million-pound property – and you know what that means?'

I nod and laugh, even though I have no idea what I'm agreeing with; I'm just so happy to see him. He picks me up and spins me round, plants a kiss on my lips and then breaks away to laugh out loud.

'The final offer was for a million and five! The commission means we've finally got what we need for the house! No more squishing into this pokey little flat.'

Our flat is hardly pokey, I think. The square footage equals that of the three-bed semi I share with Dan in my other life, but I'm too thrilled to be back again to argue. We open the champagne and order food in because neither of us can be bothered to cook, and over dinner I manage to piece together most of what has happened since I was last here.

Jude is no longer working for his father. He bought the business out so his dad could retire and started focusing almost exclusively on high-end renovations, doing for other people what he'd been doing for himself when he was flipping houses. However, that wasn't enough for him. Capitalising on his charm and sales patter, he's started his own luxury estate agency, figuring there was much more money to made in buying and selling of property rather than the assembling of bricks and mortar. And that's where I come in too, because when his clients decide they need to rip everything out and put their own stamp on their new seven-bedroomed, five-bathroomed property, he knows somebody *fabulous* who can help them do just that.

'This is our way *in*, Meg,' he says, his eyes shining. 'It's our way to the top rung, where we belong.'

He's so unshakeable in his confidence, and just so flipping handsome when he smiles like that, I don't even think to question whether that's really where I fit too, or whether I'm just hitching a ride on his coat-tails. We're a team, aren't we? We come as a package.

However, I know that's how *I* feel about our relationship, but I've noticed my ring finger is still naked, and I start to wonder if Jude feels the same way? I don't *think* I'm kidding myself about him, about our relationship, but then Becca didn't think she was kidding herself about Grant. I smile to hide the butterflies fluttering weakly in my stomach as I ask, 'Together?'

Jude leans over and gives me a lingering kiss. 'Always.'

I kiss him back, the warmth spreading inside lifting those butterflies, letting them flit free. I smile against his lips, feeling braver. 'Are we going to do something about it?'

I feel rather than see him frown. He pulls back and looks at me. 'What sort of thing?'

Ah, he hasn't been thinking along these lines at all. However, the look on his face crystallises everything I've been thinking and feeling today into one hard truth: if this is the life I'm going to pick, the one I'm going to stay in, I want more. I want to be married, totally Jude's. And I want to have children. I want to have my chance at bringing Billy or Sophie into this life – maybe both, if I'm lucky – to make it complete.

'How long have we been together now?' I ask him.

'Five years? Six?'

I nod and then I take a large breath. 'Don't you think it's time to do something to, you know, show our commitment to each other?'

'Like what? You mean get married?'

'Would that be so bad?'

He smiles at me. At first I think he's going to drop down on one knee, but he reaches out and touches my face, strokes the baby hairs at my temple with the tips of his fingers. 'You know I love you, right?'

I nod.

'Do we really need a piece of paper to cement what we have? It's real enough anyway, isn't it?'

He does have a point. I have that piece of paper with Dan and it hasn't bestowed any magical properties on our relationship. 'No, I suppose not … Are you saying you don't ever want to get married?'

He looks up at the ceiling, considers my question. 'No … and I understand you girls like to have the big day, the dress, the cake and everything. I'm just saying that there's no rush, that's all.'

I breathe out, relieved. 'It's just that the practical side of it is so much easier when children come along – '

I stop. His eyes are wide, his expression hovering between shock and laughter. 'I never knew you were this much of a planner, Meg,' he says, giving me a playful nudge.

'Well, I think I am. At least, I'm starting to be.' Which is good, I tell myself. I can't moan about my life not being what I want if I'm not prepared to do something about it.

I take a deep breath. It feels as if my next words will send me diving head first off a cliff. 'I want babies one day, I've always said that.'

He kisses me softly. 'I know … and any babies you make will be adorable. But it's not the right time right now, is it?' He waves a hand to encompass our current celebrations. 'What with the business expanding and your career really starting to take off. You know that once Carnegie has moved into that house he's going to brag about it to all his television-producer friends, don't you? You'll be rushed off your feet with hot new clients.'

'I know,' I say. When Jude puts it that way, I can see he's right, but it doesn't stop that ache deep down in my soul, that painful hole that just won't close. I'll just have to be patient, I suppose, but I can do that. At least I know time skips by faster for me than for other people. For all I know I might be pregnant tomorrow, even if that tomorrow is hundreds of tomorrows away in real time.

'But I get it,' he says. 'You're … you … and you want the kind of things you want. And what you want from me right now is something tangible, something to show how much you mean to me.'

I feel a rush of gratitude, of love, at his words, so glad I don't have to explain, like I do with Dan, only for it to fall on deaf ears. He kisses me again, at that tender spot at the base of my neck where he knows I like it. 'Then we'll just have to work something out … I've always said it: whatever you want, Meg.'

CHAPTER THIRTY-THREE

I miss Becca. Apart from my children, she's the person I miss most when I'm in this life, when I'm this person. It's hard to switch our friendship off and on every time I shift paths. In my other life I've got used to calling her nearly every day. I want to tell her about my fantastic new career as the owner and founder of Meg Greene Designs. I want to tell her about the totally amazing house that Jude has found for us in the heart of Notting Hill – our dream house. It's a total dump at the moment, a four-storey Georgian terrace that was turned into bedsits, but if anyone can return it to its former glory, Jude can.

I've pored over my Filofaxes from the last couple of years, searching for any hint of her name that might suggest a meeting or even a call, but there's nothing. It's as if I've cut her out of my life.

I'm not surprised, really. We were both really angry that day we met up in the Italian restaurant. But the me that travels through time has had other experiences with Becca since then. We've laughed and cried, bickered and made up countless time. Emotionally, I moved on from that angry place a long time ago.

All I can think about is that she might still be with that psycho Grant in this life too. And what if he's not better but worse in this world? What if Becca's tragic story could be featuring on *Crimewatch* five years from now?

I pick up the phone and dial her number. I don't even know if it's the right one. She might have moved. Someone else could pick up the phone …

But after four rings the answerphone kicks in and I hear her voice. I know what to do after the beep, her tinny voice informs me, then she laughs that soft, throaty laugh of hers before the recorded message cuts out. I'm so relieved I almost want to cry. She sounds happy.

But my joy is short-lived, because suddenly I realise this isn't just about hearing Becca's voice; I've got to leave a message. I've got to say something sensible, something that'll convince her to give our friendship another chance after years of silence.

I get stage fright.

'Hey,' I say, and my voice sounds Mini Mouse-high in my ears. 'It's me … Meg. I mean, Maggie …' My brain empties. 'Anyway … I just, I just …' Oh, God. This is going worse than I thought. What can I say? What excuse can I give?

And then it hits me. Maybe excuses aren't what's needed. I clear my throat. 'I'm sorry,' I say, 'about the way we left things. I know it's been a long time, but I don't want to lose our friendship. Call me?' I recite the home phone number written in my Filofax, then I think I'd better add something: 'I'm still with Jude. I just thought you should know that. But we have a nice life, Becs. He's doing really well and so am I …' I trail off, realising that my attempt at convincing her Jude isn't still a jerk might sound like bragging instead. 'Anyway … I miss you. Please think about giving me a call. Bye.'

And then I hang up. It's stupid; I almost expect the phone to jump to life the moment I put the receiver down, but it stays calm and silent in its cradle. I sigh. Well, I've made the first move. Now all I can do is wait.

CHAPTER THIRTY-FOUR

Christmas comes and goes, and then New Year. I begin to think Jude's forgotten our conversation about taking things to the next level, until one day I come home to find a message on the answerphone. He wants me to meet him at Green Park Underground Station at seven because he's taking me out to dinner. Somewhere nice. I start to get excited.

Jude has a mobile, but I don't yet. I've been holding out. Partly because I've got used not to being tied down to one, partly because as soon as I make that step I feel I'll have crossed a threshold. I'll no longer be firmly in the past – young, part of my own history. Life will be more similar to the one I left behind and that's going to make me feel older.

I phone him to try and worm some more details out of him, but he's surprisingly tight-lipped about our destination. He refuses to say any more, and I can hear the smile in his voice as he fends off my questions. He's enjoying this, which means he's up to something he thinks I'll like. I wonder if Cam and Issie are over from their home in Provence, and that's what the surprise is?

Jude's definitely a man who likes to surprise me. His Christmas gift was a weekend in Paris. I thought we were going to spend a couple of nights with his parents until he had a cab deliver us at Waterloo, where he produced my passport from his inside pocket and we stepped onto Eurostar. I really can't moan, can I? What woman doesn't like big romantic gestures? It's just … well, it's just I'd like to be part of the decision-making process sometimes.

Without much else to go on, I choose a DVF wrap dress in petrol-blue from my wardrobe and get ready. I feel like a million dollars when I step from the flat. The dress hugs my curves but it doesn't cling mercilessly. Even so, it's the sort of thing I wouldn't even have dreamt of wearing in my former life.

I don't bother with a cab. There's something about the buzz of London as it morphs from serious workday into night time that gives me a buzz. By the time I'm climbing the steps onto the south side of Piccadilly, I feel almost giddy.

Jude is standing there waiting for me, with a huge bunch of perfect red roses. He hands them to me, then he takes my arm and leads me down the street and to the Wolseley.

I love this building, with its grand stone arches and wrought iron outside and the elegant deco-inspired cream, gold and black interior. We've eaten here once before when Jude was entertaining clients, but when we are shown to our table I'm pleased to find that it's set for two.

The flowers are whisked away to be kept hydrated, with the promise they will be returned to me when they leave. We order, we eat our appetisers, and Jude is infuriatingly silent on the reason for this dinner, enough to make me wonder if there's any reason at all, but when our entrees finished, he clears his throat and looks at me in that hypnotising way he has when he's got something big to say, the way he did on the lawn of Oaklands when he asked me to run away with him. I catch my breath and hold it.

'I have something for you …' He slides a plain but elegant black box across the table, topped with a large, gold, satin ribbon.

It's too large for a ring, I tell myself, but my pulse begins to gallop anyway.

I prise the lid off, and buried in mounds of gold tissue paper I pull out … a phone. A mobile phone. Top of the range for the time. I shoot Jude a questioning look.

'I know you've been thinking about it,' he says, that smile still hiding behind his eyes. 'So I thought I'd get you one.'

'Thank you,' I stammer, and I try to smile back. My confusion gets the better of me. 'I don't understand …'

He looks down at the tablecloth for a moment. Hang on, I think. Is Jude … *nervous?* My heart pounds even harder.

'I want you to know that I haven't forgotten the conversation we had before Christmas,' he says, raising his gaze to meet mine. I see honesty in his eyes, and love. 'I've been thinking very hard about what to do about it.'

I nod, unable to say anything in case I break the spell. This wouldn't be beyond Jude when it comes to surprises, to double bluff me, making me think one thing is the gift, when he's actually got another up his sleeve. I watch his hands to see if he's reaching for anything else, something like a small velvet box, but he doesn't move.

'That's a company mobile,' he says softly.

I stare at the phone in my hands. It's not a ring and he didn't even buy it with his own money? I look back up at him, confused. 'You want me to work for you?'

'No … I want us to work together.'

I see him willing me to understand, but I'm just not getting it. I shake my head from side to side, tiny little movements that don't even make my hair bounce. 'I'm not doing a very good job of this, am I?' he says. 'Maybe because I'm scared you're going to say no …'

'No, to what?' I whisper.

He pushes the box and phone aside, takes my hands. 'I want us to be partners …'

I nod. That, I get. The phone, not so much.

'Business partners,' he continues. 'Meg, I want you to join me at the helm of Hansen International. We'll change it to Hansen and Greene, if you like. It's got a nice ring to it, sounds really upmarket.'

'But I don't know anything about selling houses,' I say. 'Only what I've picked up from you.'

'You've worked on so many of the houses we sell anyway …' He's right about that. I've discovered his rich clients would much rather tell their high-end estate agent to 'get someone in' when they want things done than bother with organising it themselves. 'It makes sense to bring Meg Greene Designs in-house, don't you think? Staging houses, offering a bespoke design service to every client? I think we'll make a killing!'

I think we will too. It's a fabulous idea.

'So, will you?' His eyes search mine. I have a feeling he'll be crushed if I say no.

Maybe it's my crappy other life I have to blame, but I can't help looking for the catch. I know how much this means to Jude, that his firm means everything to him. In his eyes this is probably more significant than giving me an engagement ring. Yet I can't seem to quell the little voice in my head that's asking if he'd be quite so keen if my little company was just limping along instead of being the hot new thing in town.

Is this what I want for my fledgling business? I don't know. But I do know that I love Jude completely, that I'd do anything to connect more fully with him. I imagine us ten years from now – a power couple, running our successful business that's a byword for style and quality. We'll have moved to a pretty commuter village, somewhere like Shoreham or Eynsford, where we'll convert an old chapel and fill it with kids.

'Yes,' I say, my face breaking into a smile. 'I'd love to be your partner.'

He grins back at me, overjoyed. Then, in lieu of sliding a ring on my finger, he shows me how to use my new phone.

CHAPTER THIRTY-FIVE

Things move swiftly after that. I become a director of Hansen & Greene. It's not lost on me that we wouldn't have needed to change the name if Jude had given me a ring instead of something that *has* a ring, but I'm trying not to focus on that.

I wanted a dynamic man, didn't I? And that's what I've got. I can't really complain, can't ask him to be something he's not, and he's never said 'never'. I really need to learn to enjoy what I have. I'm starting to realise that's a flaw of mine.

A month ticks by, and then another. Before I know it we're in January again and I'm another year older. I flip back to my life with Dan, just once, and only for one day. Billy was walking ... talking ... I hadn't even had enough time to work out all the new things he could do before I was snatched back again. I feel the roots holding me to this life with Jude are stronger, not so elastic any more.

However, twenty-four precious hours with my son awakens the yearning I'd wrapped up in gold tissue paper, packed away in the box that stupid mobile phone came in. I'm getting close to thirty now. I try not to think about it, but sometimes I wonder if I can actually feel my eggs slowly deteriorating.

Jude has never mentioned that conversation again. Not

that I think he's avoiding it. I just don't think it's on his radar. I'm kind of scared of asking in case he buys me something else, like a briefcase.

We're showing a house to new client today. Jude asked me to come along because he says I'm good at painting a picture of how a property *could* be. The richer our clients get, the poorer their imaginations. Probably because they just don't need to use them any more. You don't need to dream when you've already got more than you could ever want, do you?

We dress smartly and, even if I do say so myself, we do scrub up pretty well. I'm not a great beauty. I'd always considered myself quite ordinary, but I've discovered how having the time and the budget to really look after myself makes the most of what nature gave me. I'm feeling pretty confident as we turn up at a three-story townhouse in West Brompton.

This house is a bit like the one we've just finished renovating for ourselves, in that it's a bit of a disaster. The previous owner was elderly, had inherited it in her youth and had lived there on her own, slowly letting it deteriorate. When she moved into a nursing home it had stood empty for a good few years and in that time there was considerable damage from not only a leaky roof but also a small fire. It could be amazing, though. And through my secret knowledge of the future, I know it'll be a fantastic investment. You could spend a million or two now and get ten times that back in a couple of decades.

We meet the prospective buyer, Jasmine, outside and she's not quite what I expected. She's maybe five years older than Jude and me but instead of Armani, she's wearing cargo trousers, a vest top and a biker jacket. She looks like a slightly older and slightly more weathered member of All Saints. Ethnic beads are wound round both wrists and an Indian scarf is twisted around her tousled, dirty-blonde hair as a headband. She isn't wearing a trace of make-up.

'Hi,' Jude says, smiling his most charming smile, which he always uses on clients. I jokingly call it his 'money' smile. He reaches out and shakes hands with Jasmine, who seems slightly perturbed at the gesture, as if she's not used to it, but she joins in enthusiastically all the same. When she's finished with Jude, she turns to me and does the same, grinning all the time.

'So happy to meet you two,' she says, looking from one to the other of us. 'I've heard great things about you from my chum Caroline.'

'Caroline Palmerston?' I ask. We sold her a flat round the corner in Drayton Gardens last year, a crash pad for her family to use when they were up in town. She was very insistent I filled it with acres of lilac damask and very expensive French antiques. I can't imagine her being 'chums' with Jasmine.

Jasmine, however, nods. 'We were at Benenden together. Top girl.'

'Well, we're very glad to have Caroline's recommendation,' Jude says smoothly. I can tell he's about to steer her inside the house. He's not really one for chit-chat when it comes to business. 'Shall we take a look?' he says and leads the way.

The house does not look good at the moment. While the rooms have gorgeous high ceilings, it smells mouldy and damp and the entire kitchen has been ripped out and all that is left is the soot stains. We're horrified to discover that a three-foot section of the top-floor bathroom ceiling has fallen in since we were last here and the claw-footed tub – the room's one redeeming feature – is now filled with bits of wood, plaster dust and insulation. To make up for this I chatter on about the amazing potential. Jasmine doesn't say much, just nods occasionally. I have no idea what she's thinking.

It transpires she's a photographer, the kind that has exhibitions in galleries, the kind that wins awards. I get the impression from her sparse conversation there is family money that has allowed her to follow her passion around the world and that still supplements her current income. She's a relaxed, earthy sort, who doesn't give a flying fart what other people think about her. I find I rather like her. She's a breath of fresh air. Even though she travels eleven months of the year, she wants a home in London, because she's ready to settle down. Jude and I exchange a look when she says this, confident Jasmine's definition of settling down might just as be as unique as her dress sense.

From a design perspective, too, I'm starting to get excited. Because we go after a certain type of clientele, I'm discovering they mostly want one of two looks: 'uber bling' or 'faux aristocracy'. My own terms, I hasten to add. I'd never describe it that way to the clients.

The first set want everything mirrored, shiny and covered in anything that looks like diamonds and crystals. They like modern, edgy and very, very expensive, even if it is hideously ugly. The faux aristocrats want their houses to look as they've been born to English nobility, no matter what their original nationality. To be honest, after a year or two of doing this, I'm finding it all a bit samey, but Jasmine doesn't want any of that, so I'm starting to get just as excited as Jude about the prospect of selling her this house.

I hang behind Jude and Jasmine, stuck looking at the most stupendous ceiling rose hanging over the top of the three-storey staircase. It's giving me all sorts of ideas. The shapes, both abstract and floral, bound within its geometric confines, are speaking to me.

I don't know how long I'm up there, scribbling in my big notebook, but when I return downstairs I find Jude and Jasmine in the remnant of the kitchen and he's telling her how he can arrange for an architect to draw up plans for extending back into the garden, maybe even adding a basement. They don't notice me enter. I stand just inside the doorway and watch them.

Jude has dropped the professional manner he always, always uses with clients, and he laughs at something she says. And it's not just a polite, that's-so-amusing laugh, but one that erupts right up from his belly. My eyes widen and I feel the tiniest pin-prick of jealousy.

When was the last time I made him laugh like that?

I shake the feeling off. It's stupid, I know. It's just that ever since that first life, when I suspected Jude let me go because of another woman, I've been weak in this area. I can't erase the memory. Or maybe it's just Becca I can hear whispering inside my head?

I tell myself there's nothing to worry about. Jasmine isn't flirting with him; the body language is all wrong for that.

Besides, she's not Jude's type. Too earthy. Ambitious for her art and not for success.

Or maybe it's just a slick manoeuvre on Jude's part, because we leave the address with firm instructions from Jasmine to put in an offer on her behalf, and she's excited about our ideas for both building work and interiors too. He's happy and smiling as we leave, and I'm relieved he doesn't mention Jasmine once on the way back to the office.

CHAPTER THIRTY-SIX

'That's just typical!' I look down at the massive ladder in my tights. It starts just above my ankle bone and runs up the side of my leg before disappearing under the hem of my knee-length skirt. I'm heading for Oxford Circus, just having just finished a meeting with prospective clients – a video production company based in Soho who want something more quirky and artsy for their new offices.

I've just had my second visit, the one where I show them my vision for their space. When I mentioned reclaimed, velvet-covered, theatre seats for the waiting area, I knew they were sold. I was flying inside as they gave me a guided tour, asking me for ideas for some of the other spaces they hadn't mentioned before, but somehow in the midst of negotiating cables and big black boxes with metal edges and big clips on the side, I must have snagged my tights.

I look around. I'm approaching the entrance to Oxford Circus tube station now. It's nearing five o'clock and a relentless tide of commuters is making its reverse journey out of the city centre. It threatens to sweep me along with it if I don't conform and join the flow, but I manage to slip around it.

I thought I would have time to go home and change before meeting Jude for a dinner date at six-thirty but I don't think I have time now. I'm staring down the street, wondering what to do, when I spot the reassuring concrete bulk of John Lewis a short walk away, and I cross the road and head in that direction.

I stride down the street, smiling to myself. I feel buoyant, confident. We're in the new millennium now and, despite the ladder in my tights, I love my life. I love being someone who other people listen to, who they think is an expert on something. I love being someone with talent instead of regrets.

I smile at a lady coming the other way as I head into John Lewis and hold the door open for her, and after she's thanked me and the door has closed behind me, cutting out the chilly autumn evening, I realise that what I love most about this life is that now I am a perfect fit. I'm no longer an imposter in my own shoes.

I browse the selection of hosiery on offer. How odd, I think, I hardly ever made it out of jeans and tracksuit bottoms in my other life. In this one tights have become part of my daily uniform. I can't remember the last time I wore trousers.

I'm heading for the till with a pair of black fifteen denier when something makes me stop. It takes a moment to work out what it is and then I spot it. A familiar dark head browsing the lingerie.

'Becca?' I say, even though I'm sure it's not her. Ever since I hopped back into this version of my life, I keep seeing Beccas everywhere. Maybe it's because I never did hear anything back from her. I think the not knowing keeps me searching.

She turns round and I'm already forming the words, 'Sorry, I thought you were someone else', but they dry on my tongue.

'*Maggie?*' Her mouth drops open. I wait for her widened eyes to narrow, for the moment of surprise to wear off and her to tell me to get lost, but she just stammers, 'Hi.'

We both start talking at once.

'How have you – '

'I'm so glad we – '

We stop and smile awkwardly and then I jump in. I've been waiting to speak to her for so long and I've got to grab my chance while I have it. 'I'm sorry,' I say. 'So sorry for walking out on you last time we met.'

Becca looks at me. I can tell my outburst has surprised her, maybe because the Maggie she's used to is queen of letting things simmer unspoken under the surface. 'Me too,' she finally says and then glances in the direction of the grinding escalators that fill the centre of the building, transporting people up and down as if they're unwitting participants in a giant game of snakes and ladders. 'Have you got time for a coffee?' she asks, as I remember the cafeteria on the top floor.

'They'll be closing soon,' I say. 'How about a proper drink instead? There's a decent pub just near New Bond Street.'

She smiles. 'Sounds like a plan.'

I brandish the pack of tights at her. 'I just need to pay for these. Don't want security chasing me down Oxford Street!'

She laughs. I'm not sure if it's because she actually finds it funny or because she doesn't want to make things any more awkward. 'OK. I'll wait outside. I'm supposed to be meeting – ' she stops, considers her words and starts again

' – meeting my boyfriend in a couple of minutes. I'll just send him a text, let him know he can take his time at his … thing, and where he can meet me.'

A shiver ripples through me. It didn't escape me the way she caught herself, changed tack, and that can only mean one thing: she doesn't want to mention his name. And that, too, can only mean one thing: Grant. I don't react, though, too scared of fracturing our fragile truce.

By five-forty five, we're sitting at the bar of the Duke of York. It's a little shabby, with flock wallpaper and over-stained wood, but it's comfortable enough and we find a couple of stools at the bar.

I decide to straight to the point. We've wasted too many years already. 'Can we just wipe the slate clean, start again?'

'I'd like that.'

We both smile at each other, not sure what to say next.

'So …' I eventually say, 'what's new?'

I've decided it's better to let her talk first. That way, by the time the conversation comes around to me, and the inevitable subject of Jude, the ice will have been broken. I'm relieved when, instead of telling me all about how wonderful things are with Grant, she starts on a long story about how she's got a front of house manager position at a new theatre on the fringes of the West End. As she's nearing the end of her story, explaining how she nearly blew her interview, she gets more passionate, more animated, and that's when I spot a flash of something sparkly as she waves her hands around.

She catches me looking, hides the ring by putting both hands in her lap.

'You're engaged?' I whisper, and all the while my stomach feels as if it's being churned by a meat grinder. I don't care if he's flipping Prince Charming in this world, I'm never going to be able to believe that Grant is anything but a manipulative, sadistic pig underneath.

She nods, but she doesn't say anything, which just confirms my fears.

I force out my congratulations, but I know I'm not ready to hear all the details yet, so I steer the subject round to me, telling her about my career change. I produce my portfolio from my bag and let her flick through it.

'Oh, my God! These are amazing, Maggie! You're really talented!' Her praise warms me, but I feel a shiver too. It doesn't take her long to spot the company logo. She looks up at me. 'Still with him?'

'Yes. Almost eight years now. And he hasn't left me, hasn't cheated on me.' I sigh. 'I really wish you'd give him the benefit of the doubt now, Becca.'

She doesn't say anything at first, just stares at me, and then her head makes one curt bobbing motion. 'OK.'

I'm surprised how relieved I am at her words. I find myself exhaling my thanks on a hushed breath. She smiles weakly back at me.

We exchange addresses, me filing hers away in my trusty Filofax, her scribbling mine down on the back of a receipt she dug out of her handbag, and then, because something has now broken, swept the shards of the last few years away, we dive headlong into one of those chats we always used to have, laughing, sighing, talking about anything and everything, although we're careful to tread lightly round the subject of the men in our lives. I'm shocked when I look down at my watch and discover it's twenty to seven. Jude will be waiting for me. I start to gather my belongings back into my briefcase. 'I'm so sorry! I'm really going to have to go,' I say. Becca looks at her watch and her eyes widen.

'Me too! I'm supposed to be meeting – '

Her words are cut short as a masculine hand clamps down on her shoulder. 'Thought I'd better come and drag you out of here, you lush!' he says with a laugh and bends to kiss her on the cheek.

He might not have done that if he'd seen me, if he'd realised who she's with. Because it's not Grant's well-manicured, long fingers that are resting on my best friend's shoulder, declaring ownership, declaring intimacy. They're Dan's.

CHAPTER THIRTY-SEVEN

I'm stuck looking at Dan, can't tear my eyes away, yet all the time inside my head I'm re-computing, trying to add up the elements of our conversation, the events of the last couple of years, trying to reconfigure everything so the answer I come up with is … *this*.

I can't seem to do it.

'Hi,' he says now awkwardly. He and Becca exchange a look, the kind that only people who have been together long enough to half-read each other's minds can trade. My stomach rolls.

'Hi,' I croak back. It's odd. This Dan is only a year older than the one in the life I left behind, but he looks different. Younger. Dare I say it, more handsome.

'I'm sorry,' Becca says quickly, breaking the weird, time-slowing spell that has woven itself around us. 'I should have said. I just didn't know how you'd … you know … take it.'

I blink. 'I'm taking it fine,' I say. After all, why shouldn't I? I've just been telling Becca how happy I am with Jude. 'I'm just a bit … surprised. I suppose I never really thought …'

I trail off as a myriad memories, some from this life, some from the others, hurry through my brain like the pages of one of those flick books. The image I end up on is one of Becca the morning after the May ball. Her mouth is moving. I can hear her saying my man is gold dust, that I'm lucky to have him.

She always did have a soft spot for him, didn't she? I just hadn't ever thought it went anything beyond being mates. Well, that's not true, really. I don't think I'd ever even thought about it at all. I'd just accepted that as truth. Because Dan had been mine.

'How …?' I begin, but I don't manage to get the rest of my sentence out, mainly because I don't think I have one. It's just a general expression of bewilderment.

'We've always kept in touch, haven't we?' Becca says, glancing at Dan. There's that look again. That sense of them being a unit I'm not part of. 'Always stayed friends … And then, well, about eighteen months ago, it just became something more.' She looks at me, asking me to understand, asking me for my blessing.

'Well, that's wonderful,' I say, smiling at each in turn, but, the truth is, I don't know how I feel about it. I still haven't even begun to process it. I slide down off my bar stool and offer it to Dan. 'It really is …' I pick up my briefcase. 'I can't think of two nicer people …'

I look at my watch, even though I already know what time it is, because there's a clock with oversized Roman numerals behind the bar. 'But I've got to shoot off. I was supposed to meet Jude almost fifteen minutes ago.'

This time, I observe Dan's jaw harden at the mention of his name. Still doesn't like him, eh? For some reason, I feel as if I've scored a point, but then I keep seeing the way Dan's hand slid easily around Becca's waist as he leaned in for that kiss. It plays over and over again in my head on a loop.

'It's been lovely to see you,' I say smiling brightly as I give them both a peck on the cheek. Dan's aftershave is different. Nicer. I direct the last line to Becca. 'And we'll have to keep in touch …'

She nods enthusiastically. I can see the doubt in her eyes, though. She knows this has been a shock for me. I suspect she thinks it might be years before we see each other again. I've tried to contact her a number of times since that first phone call and it occurs to me that maybe this is the reason she hasn't responded to any of my messages. Maybe she thought it would be awkward.

I hear a harsh, barking laugh inside my head.

And then I glide gracefully from the bar, suddenly glad of my well-cut clothes, my expensive shoes, the fact I know I look business-like and competent. Together. But inside I'm not together at all. I'm all spaghetti and tangled knots, because as I emerge from the smoky haze of the pub into the fresh air of the street, all I can think about is my original life, about Dan's Thursday nights, the woman he was seeing behind my back.

And Becca's mystery man.

CHAPTER THIRTY-EIGHT

I meet up with Becca one afternoon in the West End before she starts an evening shift at Her Majesty's Theatre, her new place of work. I drag her to a newly opened Starbucks. They're starting to pop up all over the capital, and I have a weird feeling of reverse déjà vu when I spy the familiar green sign and dark-wood decor.

I can't stop looking at her as we chat about our lives, our news, because I have the strangest feeling this is someone who looks like Becca but isn't Becca. I've felt that way ever since I learned about her and Dan.

She can't have been Dan's Thursday-night woman. I can't believe that. There's no way that Becca, in any of the three lives I've known her, would do that to me.

But then there's a niggling little memory of how wounded and broken she was after Grant had finished with her that first time, how she'd hung around at our house a lot, how patient and sympathetic Dan had been with her.

I'd always seen them as surrogate brother and sister for each other, but …

No. I can't go down that route. I won't. I don't want to

believe it. So we chat as if none of these thoughts are going through my head. 'When's the wedding?'

Becca blushes, actually blushes, and looks down at the rim of her coffee cup. 'July. We were just getting ready to send out the invitations.' She looks up again. 'I really like it if you'd come, Maggie, but I totally understand if you'd rather give it a miss.'

'Don't be silly. Of course I'll come.'

'Really?'

I nod.

'Then I have something else to ask … I don't know if this will be too weird, but …'

Oh, hell, I think. I know what's coming. And there's no escape.

'Well, it's just that we always said we'd be each other's maid of honour.' Her voice gets quieter towards the end of the sentence, as if she's ashamed of bringing it up. 'Would you consider …?' Her eyes plead with me.

'I think I need to think about it,' I tell her, and she nods. I guess that is good enough for now. For both of us.

'Anyway,' I say, moving the conversation swiftly on, 'tell me more about your plans. Are you going to live in Sidcup or Swanham?'

'Swanham,' Becca says firmly. 'I can commute just as easily from there, and Dan has a new job lined up there for next term. He's switching to a different school, going part-time. He wants to write.' She looks at me questioningly. 'Did you know he likes to write? He kept that light under a bushel for quite a long time …'

'Yes, I know all about his writing,' I say wearily. Poor Becca. 'Timing was never his strong suit,' I add. 'It's going to be tough for you with a wedding to pay for, too. You didn't manage to talk him out of it?'

Becca blinks. She puts her mug down and frowns. 'Why would I want to do that?'

'Because it's … because you …' The look of confusion on her face stops me. She really hasn't considered that at all.

'He's good, Mags,' she says, leaning forward. 'But you must know that if you've read his stuff?'

I nod, even though it's a lie. Aside from that one poem – and that was in another life – I realise Dan has never once let me see anything he'd written. He's guarded it closely from me.

'And he's going to St Saviour's. You know, the private school? Same money for not as many hours.'

'And you're OK with this?' I say, searching her face. I try to work out if she's just being brave, but she grins back at me.

'God, yes. I mean, you only get one life to live, right? And if you can't go after your dreams when you're young and stupid, when can you?'

I shake my head gently and then realise I should be nodding. 'Dan doesn't mind you being the breadwinner?'

She laughs. 'Are you kidding? He thinks I'm a goddess!' And then she gets more serious. 'He's happy, Mags … and I like to see him happy. I hope you don't mind me saying this, but after you left him he wasn't happy for a very long time.'

Becca's words are a like a cold dash of water. I can't have my cake and eat it, can I? And if I deserve the dream life I want with Jude, why should I begrudge Dan his? I should be happy for him.

When we part, we hug outside the coffee shop. 'You'll think it over, won't you?' she asks as she pulls away. 'The maid-of-honour thing?'

'I just need to know it's the right thing. For all of us.'

She nods.

'My treat next time,' I say. Becca insisted stumping up for the lattes – and the inevitable brownies that followed. 'I insist.' And then an idea floats across my brain. 'In fact … Jude and I are throwing a dinner party in a fortnight, a kind of housewarming thing now the house is finally finished. Why don't you and Dan come?'

I can see the hesitation in Becca's eyes, but the fact I've been so understanding about her and Dan has kind of painted her into a corner. 'That sounds lovely. I'll just check with Dan that he's free …'

I hug her again. 'I'll ring you with the details.'

As I watch her walk away, I'm not sure whether my bright idea is a great way to put the past behind us, or the most stupid thing I've ever done.

'I've got a confession to make.'

Jude rolls over in bed and looks at me. It's Sunday morning, two days after I met up with Becca. I haven't told him about it yet. I don't know why. 'Have you been naughty?' he says, with a definite Sunday morning glint in his eye.

'Only a little,' I reply as I laugh and slap away the hand

that's travelling up my thigh under the sheet. 'You know that dinner party for six we've been planning?'

'Yup?'

'Well, it might be for eight now. I kind of bumped into some old friends and invited them.'

Jude raises his eyebrows. 'Anyone I know?'

I swallow. 'Yes, actually … you remember my roommate from uni, Becca? I invited her and her fiancé.'

Jude flops back on his pillow and stares at the ceiling. 'That woman thinks I'm the devil incarnate.'

I snuggle up to him, press a soft kiss to the side of his neck. He makes a grudging moan deep in his throat. 'I know … but it's been a long time since Oaklands. And she didn't mime being sick or make gagging noises when I mentioned your name, so that has to be an improvement.'

He turns to look at me. 'You really want her to come?'

'Yes.'

He sighs. 'OK … And she's found someone who wants to marry that mouth, has she? He must be either the biggest loser in the universe or a total saint.'

I look down at my fingers, which are gently stroking his chest. 'Well, that's the thing … you know him too. He was at uni with us.' I can hear Jude waiting. I carry on but I don't look at him. 'It's Dan, you know, my – '

'Your jilted bridegroom? Bloody hell, Meg!'

I look at him from under my lashes. 'I can't help who she's ended up with, can I? I certainly wouldn't have invited him on his own, but they kind of come as a package deal. Besides, it's you I chose.' I look him in the eye, even though he doesn't know the multi-layered meaning in my words I say them anyway. 'It's you I will always choose.'

That does the trick. He leans in and kisses me. 'OK,' he murmurs, 'they can come, but here's the deal …'

I laugh. With Jude, there's always a deal. I should have known.

'… I get to invite a couple of people I choose too. Let's make this a real party!'

'OK,' I say, 'but if we're feeding ten, I don't think my famous roast chicken is going to go far enough. If you really want to do this, I might need help. Like, cooking help.'

'Well, then, if we're going to do this thing, we might as well do it right. Really celebrate in style! I'm talking caterers, plenty of champagne, even someone to man a bar. All you will have to do is turn up and look beautiful. Deal?'

That's the best deal I could ever have imagined so I almost cut his last word off by kissing him. 'Who are you going to invite?' I ask when I pull back.

'I was thinking maybe Andrew, you know that architect I've been working with a lot recently, and we might as well make the other one a girl … how about Jasmine?'

'Jasmine?' I say, propping myself up on one elbow so I can look at him better. 'She's a client. We haven't really seen her since I finished the decoration of her house.'

'I know,' Jude says, and he finds that spot on the ceiling to stare at again. 'But if you're going to bring Mr Dull and his soon-to-be Mrs Dull, we might as well add a little colour and flavour into the mix.' He turns his head to look at me. 'She'll be an interesting dinner-party guest, you have to admit that.'

Unfortunately, I do have to admit that. I'm just not sure why it makes me feel so uncomfortable. And I can hardly veto his choice, not when he's said yes to Becca and Dan.

'Let's do it,' I reply. 'What the hell could go wrong?'

CHAPTER THIRTY-NINE

I check my make-up one last time and feed my earrings through my ears. Not bad, I think, as I take one last look in the mirror. I'm still a size twelve and I look good in this little black dress. I will miss this waistline when Jude and I finally have kids.

I make my way to the kitchen, where Jude is busy giving everybody orders. I see the chef rolling her eyes, but it makes me smile. It'll be my job to go and soothe a few ruffled feathers once he's marched off to micromanage the bar staff, but I don't mind. This is just Jude. This is how he gets things done, and we're a team.

The menu is something I'd dream about eating in my other life, let alone having prepared for me in my own home by a team of professionals. We're having a quail's-egg salad to start. I'm not that mad on eggs, but Jude wanted it and they're so tiny I'm sure they'll slide down easily. It's filet mignon for the main course and we're finishing up with lemon tart. While that doesn't sound impressive for a dessert, the actual tart will end up looking like something from *Bake-Off* – not that any of my guests know what that is yet – with sugar cages and smears of coulis.

The house is finally finished and fully decorated and I have to pinch myself to believe I actually live here. Jude even got me what he promised me – a balcony of my own to drink my morning coffee on. I painted the house white and I've been filling it with beautiful things, sourcing them at auction houses and 'secret' little shops dotted across London that all the good decorators know about.

Overall, I hope the effect is elegant but homely. I didn't want a show home, as many of my obscenely rich clients do. I wanted something beautiful that looks as if it could actually be lived in. We're going to show the house off to its best tonight, serving drinks and appetisers in the drawing room with its vast marble fireplace and parquet flooring and then leading everyone through to the *pièce de résistance*, the dining room, which is the one exception to my clean, light style. The room is huge, the chandelier impressive, but it feels warm and intimate because of the rich wood panelling and dark green walls.

Cam and Issie are the first to arrive, bearing champagne. I hug both of them hard. We haven't seen as much of them since they moved to France. I feel we need reinforcements this evening, and we've stayed close with this couple since that summer-long holiday on Cam's dad's boat, so they definitely fill the role.

Andrew arrives next, the architect who was one of Jude's wildcard choices. I wonder if he's chosen him to set him up with Jasmine, but that doesn't seem very likely. Andrew's creative and imaginative like Jasmine, but that's where the similarity ends. He doesn't travel much outside of Europe because he hates flying and he's very particular about his appearance. For a man who spends a great deal of time on construction sites he has a rather healthy dislike of mud and dust. He can also waffle on for England about fine wines if you let him.

Hot on his heels are Patrick, who heads up the construction arm of our firm, and Flora, once his very efficient PA but now also his wife. They're a lovely couple and we seem to socialise with them a lot.

We stand in the drawing room, sipping champagne cocktails out of delicately thin flutes, laughing and talking. I dreamed about moments like this, I realise, as I slide my arm round Jude's waist and lean into him.

I want to take a moment to absorb it all, savour it. *This is what I was always reaching for,* I think to myself, *when I was old, sad Maggie, who hated her life, who wished she'd done it differently. I just didn't know what it looked like until I was here, in this moment.*

And in the centre of it all is Jude – the man I love, bold, dashing and clever. I smile up at him as he tells a story about being invited to go on one of his client's yachts and say a silent prayer of gratitude. I know I've made the right choice.

I wait for a feeling inside, maybe a sense of something clicking into place or coming to rest, but it doesn't come. Maybe it's because I'm distracted by Dan and Becca's arrival. They bustle in with a waft of cold air, apologising about trains. Their coats are whisked away and introductions made.

While the other men are wearing suit trousers and nice shirts, open at the neck, all beautifully cut and tailored, Dan has his 'best' pair of jeans on — obviously, they're not the same ones he owned in his life with me, but I know how the man dresses – and a shirt that looks as if it was ironed by someone wearing boxing gloves. Issie, Flora and I are all in shift dresses in various dark colours and styles, but Becca is wearing black trousers and the kind of sparkly top she likes to go clubbing in.

I'm not snobby about it. It doesn't bother me in the slightest what they wear. I'm just glad they're here. It's just that I'd never noticed this kind of difference between my two lives before and now it's presented to me it's jarring.

Even more jarring is the sight of Dan stiffly shaking Jude's hand. Jude is all charm and smiles, but I see him sizing Dan up, like a prize fighter weighing up his opponent. I hug Becca, kiss Dan quickly on the cheek, someone hands them a glass of champagne and we all smile at each other as the conversation stalls.

'How are you, old boy?' Jude says, leaning on the fireplace and looking for all the world like Jay Gatsby. 'Still living in Essex?'

Dan looks steadily back at him. 'Kent, actually. Swanham.'

'Oh, too bad!' Jude says, still smiling. 'Property prices have crashed a bit there in the last year. You should get out while you can – although Tunbridge Wells isn't a bad bet if you want to stay in that area.'

Dan smiles tightly. 'Bit beyond my price range, I'm afraid.'

This leads to a discussion about the best places to live in both Kent and nearby East Sussex. I think it's meant to be helpful, but Jude and Patrick end up just talking to each other about luxury property, effectively cutting Dan out.

I feel bad. I know what Jude is doing. But he's just that kind of man who's very territorial and, if I'm honest, there's a tiny part of me that loves the fact he's still territorial about me, even after all these years.

Jasmine is the last to arrive. She also doesn't fit in, wearing a creased linen skirt and a top that look as if they've just been pulled out of a backpack; an ornate Indian silver necklace finishes the look. Somehow, it doesn't seem to matter. Unlike Becca and Dan, who are trying hard and haven't quite got it right, Jasmine is wholly 'other'. She's like that bright pop of colour in a monochrome decorating scheme. I realise Dan – I mean, *Jude* – was exactly right to invite her. She's already entertaining us with a story about almost getting arrested because she wanted to climb the Brooklyn Bridge in order to get just the right shot of the mesmerising pattern made by its suspension wires.

We sit down to dinner and when the servers have made sure our glasses are filled, Cam stands up. 'Can't start a good dinner without a toast,' he says, grinning. 'So, cheers to Jude and Meg, the most annoyingly stylish couple I know!' There's a murmur of *hear, hear* and everyone downs a sip, but Cam doesn't sit down, instead he turns and looks down at Issie. 'I hope you don't mind,' he says, sneaking a look at Jude and me, 'but I want to make a toast to this lovely lady too …'

The women at the table go all soppy, apart from Jasmine, who looks on with the same kind of interest one reserves for a riveting documentary.

'To Issie … who's finally decided to make an honest man of me!'

Issie blushes and flashes the absolutely massive diamond gracing her left hand. Dinner is delayed while hugs and congratulations are exchanged and when we're finally back in our seats, Jude lifts his glass and says, 'If you're going to find yourself a ball and chain, Issie is certainly one of the sweetest, loveliest ones imaginable.'

Cam was looking fit to burst with joy, anyway, but now his smile reaches maximum wattage. 'Had to really … she's preggers, you see.'

I hadn't been expecting that. And while everyone else fusses round Issie, congratulating her gently then slapping Cam heartily on the back, I'm frozen to the spot. Frozen inside. At first I make it look as if I'm hanging back to give her some room, but then I realise I can't behave like that. I force myself to move and kiss her on the cheek, whisper how happy I am for her.

But then Flora chimes in and says, 'What a coincidence! I was going to tell everyone tonight that I'm expecting too …'

I find I have an urgent need to leave the room and check on something in the kitchen.

Get a grip of yourself, Maggie, I tell myself as I brace my hands against the counter and take a few deep breaths, aware the catering staff are doing their best not to watch me. I heave what feels like a whole pint of air in through my nostrils and stand up tall.

When I get back to the table, they're talking about due dates – only five days apart! Isn't that amazing? – and NCT classes. I slide into my seat, keeping my gaze lowered, and I feel Jude's eyes on me. He squeezes my hand under the table. 'OK?' he asks, only loud enough for me to hear. His expression is questioning, but not the I-know-what's-up-and-just-checking-you're-OK sort, more the I-haven't-got-the-foggiest-what's-got-into-her variety. I give him a look that says it'll save for later, then flash him my best smile and turn my attention to my guests.

'What about you, Jasmine?' Patrick asks as we dig into our quails' eggs. 'Got any children?'

Jasmine looks up, genuinely surprised he has asked her this question, even given that pregnancy and babies has been the sole topic of conversation for the last five minutes. 'No,' she says, after cutting into tiny, shiny white egg so the sunflower-yellow yolk bleeds out, 'never saw the point.'

The pregnant mums in the room stare at her. The men stroke their backs gently, as if the state of not having any babies could be infectious and they need to guard them against it. Jude's hand stays on his cutlery.

Jasmine's not stupid. She knows the effect her statement has made, but she seeks to qualify its bluntness. 'It's my work, you see? Wouldn't be fair on the sprogs. I'd want them with me, not tucked away in some ghastly boarding school. Would have been OK when they're tiny, I suppose, but I visit some pretty desolate places. Not much in the way of healthcare or education.'

Both Flora and Issie relax visibly. Becca nods her understanding.

'There you go,' Cam the joker says, 'talking about New York again ...'

It's not actually that funny, but everyone jumps on the chance to laugh, to lighten the celebratory atmosphere that Jasmine shot down with her statement. I got the strange impression she rather enjoyed that.

'Anyway,' she says, picking up the thread of the conversation again and taking ownership of it, 'I made a choice. When it came to children or career, I chose career. For me, at least, children would have been a compromise. I needed to follow my passion.'

The logical bit of me and the feminist side of me applaud her honesty and her sacrifice, respect her choice. The side of me that sees Jude nodding along and smiling at her words wants to shout and scream, but this is my fancy dinner party so I do neither.

No one else has anything to say on the subject after that, so they get to the business of finding out more about each other. Andrew gets quizzed on his work and there's a great deal of interest when he reveals someone has asked him to install a panic room. Most of the rest of them don't know what this is, but I do. I saw the film with Jodie Foster. Two years in the future.

Jasmine holds court about her precious photography for at least half an hour. Am I being a cow if I say she's starting to irritate me? There's something so ... entitled ... about her. Anyway, she hogs centre stage until the main course is cleared and while she pops to the loo, Patrick turns to Dan.

'So what do you do?'

Dan isn't fazed by the question, even though we've just been listening to Andrew talk about the celebrity pads he's built or Jasmine's tales of trekking through forgotten mountain ranges to meet isolated tribes. 'I'm an English teacher.'

'Good for you,' Patrick says. I don't know if he's trying to be patronising but it certainly comes out that way.

Becca bristles. 'He's writing a book too,' she says loudly. 'He's very good.'

Jude smiles magnanimously at her. 'Everybody's mum and their girlfriend always thinks – '

'I'm his fiancée.'

Jude pauses, sends a knowing look towards Patrick. 'I do apologise,' he says smoothly. 'What I was trying to say is that the people around you always think what you do is wonderful, don't they? I was wondering if you've had any success with someone in the profession, someone who knows what they're talking about?'

'It doesn't matter if you haven't yet,' I cut in, earning myself a look from Jude. 'I mean, everyone's got to start somewhere.'

'Actually, there's an agent who's interested in seeing the book once it's finished,' Becca chimes in, her smile more than a little triumphant.

'How wonderful,' Flora says, managing to sound much more genuine than her husband. 'What sort of book is it?'

Dan turns his attention to her, ignoring the men at the table. 'It's an adventure story for eight- to eleven-year-olds. Aimed at boys, really. I've always been saddened by how many lads don't read regularly by the time they get into my class, and this one here – ' he jerks a thumb at Becca and gives her an affectionate smile ' – told me I should stop moaning and do something about it.'

'We weren't together, then,' Becca adds, smiling back at him. 'Just good friends.'

'Anyway, I listened. I've always liked writing, but I'd never thought of writing anything for kids, but the more I chewed over what Becca had said, the more the idea grew on me.'

'And what sort of adventure story is it?' Flora asks, clearly much more enthralled with all this creative genius than she had been the talk of load-bearing walls and foundations we had all through the first course. 'Does it have treasure in it? I do love a good treasure-hunting story.'

'Sort of,' Dan says. It's about a group of kids who accidentally fall through a rip in the fabric of time, and then they get catapulted from place to place, time to time, searching for the magical item that'll send them back home. This one mainly deals with World War Two and Victorian times, but I'm thinking it could be a series ...'

Dan carried on talking but the words melt together around me. I can stop staring at him. How did he pick that storyline? Could he know something? About me? About my ... situation?

Jude's voice cuts through my questions. 'Isn't time travel a bit old hat nowadays, a bit too *Doctor Who* or something?'

I realise he has no way of knowing that in a few short years 'the Doctor' will be all nine-year-old boys want to talk about.

He laughs and looks round the table, subtly asking his

friends to back him up. Patrick and Andrew join in, but Cam, bless his dear little heart, just smiles awkwardly and looks uncomfortable.

Dan isn't cowed and I'm suddenly very proud of him. The Dan I live with would have sulked or got defensive; this one is more confident. He used to be this way, I realise. Before I married him.

'Dinosaurs were completely out of fashion until *Jurassic Park* hit,' he says. 'Like Jasmine says, sometimes you've just got to follow your passion, go where your heart and muse take you.'

'Bravo!' Jasmine says, and then the conversation shifts and turns to favourite books people read as kids, and whether anyone else has ever heard of *The Tree That Sat Down* or read Enid Blyton's Adventure Series, which nobody remembers because they were all too busy talking about the Famous Five.

I realise I'm feeling very clammy, that I suddenly need some air, so I excuse myself and head for the bathroom. I decide to go upstairs to my en-suite, where it's quieter and more insulated from the action, and when I get there I stare at myself in the mirror.

It's just coincidence, I tell myself. Time travel, aliens and dinosaurs, they're all staples of boys' adventures. The fact Dan picked that doesn't mean anything. Still, his speech has left me with an idea. Is there something, some object or incantation or guru who could get me home again? I'd given up hope but maybe I shouldn't have. But if there is some magical object that could help me get home, there's one more question I need to answer: would I really want to go back to that original life?

OK, Jude has gone all alpha this evening and really isn't on top form, but would I really want to swap him for the 'other' Dan, who'd given up on me so much he'd found someone else?

No. I think firmly inside my head. Definitely not. I breathe out.

I feel better now. More sorted in my head. More tethered to this reality. It's just been strange having the two men in my life in the same space. I should probably avoid it from now on.

I'm just about to make my way back downstairs when I hear voices. Someone has just flushed the downstairs loo and they've opened the door and met someone in the hall. A man and a woman.

For a horrible second I think it might be Jude and Jasmine, although I don't know why that's where my brain went first, but then I realise it's Dan and Becca.

'You doing OK?' I hear Dan ask. 'It's a rough crowd.'

Becca sighs then chuckles. 'Yeah … I could do with less of the male posturing.'

'Sorry,' he mutters. 'Jude always used to try and make me feel small at uni, especially after I started seeing Maggie. I mean, Meg. Can't get used to that …' I imagine him shaking his head. 'Anyway, I used to let him get away with it back then but there's no way I'm going to let him do it now.'

'Not *you*!' Becca says, laughing. 'I meant Mr Peacock. He might as well just pee round the perimeter of the dining table.' She sighs. 'I don't like him, never have. There's things about him she doesn't know … but he's her choice. I don't want to lose her friendship again, so that means I've got to support it.'

I smile, hidden away on the top landing, standing just far back enough that they can't hear me. I know I should probably make a noise, warn them I'm there and come down the stairs, but I'm too busy feeling warm all over from Becca's words. I'm not sure she'd ever say that to me out loud but I'm glad I heard it. I'm just about to lean back and close the bedroom door deliberately loudly when Dan speaks again.

'You know it's not about her, don't you?' he says softly. 'He won. A long time ago. I've moved on.' They stop talking, but I can hear a faint rustle of clothing. I suspect they're kissing.

It makes me feel strange. Not because I want Dan in this reality, no matter how much more he's like the man I always wanted him to be, but because for fifty per cent of my crazy life he *is* mine. I can't just seem to switch that off.

'It's you I love,' Dan says.

'I know.'

'She never believed in me the way you do and I'm not angry with her any more, or hurt. I really ought to thank her, although I probably never will. To be honest, I think I dodged a bullet there.'

His words spear me, even though he's not the one I really want. I wonder why I bother trying in my other life, if we're both so toxic for each other. Maybe, even taking Billy into account, we'd be better off apart in that one too.

'I hate to say this,' Becca begins, and I really wish I'd taken the opportunity to sneak off when I'd had the chance, 'and it's not because I hold anything against her. She was right about Grant, after all. God, I dodged a bullet there too … thank goodness you came along to pick up the broken pieces and mend my heart.'

I've never heard Becca be so gushy about a guy. Even though I know they've been together a long while, that Dan's ring is on her finger, this is when it becomes real to me. They really *are* in love.

'I don't think Jude is good for her,' Becca continues. 'I never did. He's got all this strength and energy she admires, but she's not his equal.'

Not his equal! Is that what my best friend really thinks about me? But then she carries on …

'She doesn't stand up for herself with him, and I think he likes it that way. To be honest, I'm sad. I think she deserves better.'

Dan makes a soft snorting sound. 'I might be over her, but I'm not feeling that generous. She made her choice, now she's got to live with it. After all, she had "better" and she threw it away.'

Becca laughs softly. 'For which I am eternally grateful …'

It's at that point I decide I can't listen any more. I also can't 'fake' coming down the stairs. I don't want to see them. I don't want to see them looking at me after what they've just been saying. I creep back to the bedroom, close the door softly behind me and sit on the end of the bed.

After ten minutes, I rejoin the party. Jude raises his

eyebrows as I slide into my seat, asking if everything is OK and I make an imperceptible nod. I've decided I'm not doing this now. I'm blocking it out.

The rest of the dinner goes well, I think. The guests rave about dessert, just as I thought they would, and the vino flows. I was feeling so great, so at home in my life, before I heard that conversation between Dan and Becca, but now I'm second-guessing everything and it's paralysing me. Thankfully, with nine other people at the table, and three or four of them big personalities, no one notices I'm quieter than before and when Jasmine launches into one of her long stories of artistic endeavour, I'm actually grateful.

I notice that she argues with Jude when he says something facetious, that she stands her ground. But he's not dismissive with her, the way he often is with me when I voice an alternative opinion – charmingly dismissive, to be sure, but dismissive all the same. When Jasmine challenges him, he seems to enjoy it.

Why don't I do that? I think. And the only answer I can come up with is that she doesn't love Jude, which means the stakes are low. If they fall out, they fall out, and they don't have to see each other again. It's not the same for me. I don't want to lose him.

But seeing the way he is with Jasmine, more animated than I've seen him in months, because he's always so tired from working every hour God sends to build the business, make it bigger, better, stronger, more profitable, I realise that we've lost a bit of that. He's not flirting with Jasmine, just bantering, but I see the spark of interest there. I don't believe he's going to do anything about it, I don't think he's going to stray with her or anyone, but if I want to make sure of that in the coming years, maybe I need to up my game. Maybe I need to do what Becca said and become his equal.

Unsurprisingly, she and Dan are the first to leave, citing their need to catch the last train. Most of the others follow within the half-hour, but Patrick and Flora linger on. The boys drink too much whisky and get louder and more arrogant. I chat with Flora in the now-deserted kitchen, pretending to tidy what has already been tidied and tiptoeing around the subject of babies.

When they go home Jude and I go to bed. I'm not really in the mood for sex, to be honest, but maybe I'm more like him than I realise because I feel a need to stamp my presence on him in the most primal way, just so I'm sure I've erased any thoughts of how clever and interesting Jasmine was tonight, because in my book that makes her very, very sexy.

I lie there afterwards, staring at the crease of orange light slicing through the gap in the curtains and creating a luminous gash on the opposite wall. My thoughts turn to Dan.

Why are the two versions of him so different? One sure of himself, ready to reach out and pursue his dreams, and the other one lacklustre and apathetic?

I start to wonder if it has anything to do with finding the right person. I mean, my relationship with Jude isn't perfect, but it is a heck of a lot better than my marriage to Dan, no matter Becca's opinion on it, and it makes sense that even if you find that perfect person that a lifelong relationship is going to involve some work, some challenges. So maybe Becca is Dan's right person. His soul mate.

Those words echo inside my head and I roll over and close my eyes, happy to go to sleep now I've wrapped all my doubts about my first life and tied them in a neat bow.

CHAPTER FORTY

The phone wakes me up. I roll over to reach for the handset on the bedside table, but somehow I end up tumbling onto the floor. I land smack on the carpet and, as I open my eyes and try to work out what the heck happened, I notice it's daytime, and then I realise I'm lying on an Ikea rug, not a hardwood floor. A moment later, a little boy runs into the room holding a toy car in one hand and a plastic wheel in the other. 'It fell off, Mummy!' he says shoving them towards me.

My mouth drops open. *Billy?*

I can hardly believe it. He's so tall! He must be three now, maybe even four.

I'm so stunned I just do what he's asked and take both car and wheel from him and click them back together. He goes to grab for them, but I hold fast, my wits starting to kick in. 'Give mummy a kiss first,' I say.

'No,' he says, stubbornly, pointing at the car. 'I *need* my car.'

I grin back at him. He's talking in whole sentences. My son is a freaking genius! I'm so overjoyed at his prodigy that I haven't got time to be sad about all the things I've missed. 'No,' I say, hiding it behind my back. 'Not until mummy gets a kiss, and if I don't get a kiss I'm going to … tickle you!'

For a moment he looks worried, but then a glint of mischief appears in his eyes. That's all the encouragement I need. I drop the car and start crawling towards him. He screams and runs out the room, giggling, shouting, 'Urgh! No kissing, Mummy! No kissing!' However, if I get too far behind, he slows down and waits for me, still making sure he's just out of grabbing distance.

I finally capture him at the bottom of the stairs. I tickle and kiss him at the same time until he's almost sick with laughter, and then we go back into the living room to retrieve the car. It's only then I notice the red light flashing on the answerphone and remember it was the phone that woke me up in the first place.

Since Billy is now engrossed with his car, running it along the arms of the armchair and down onto the floor, I pick the handset up. This isn't the house phone I remember, so it takes a little bit of guesswork to find how to listen to messages, but I manage to work it out in the end. I use speed dial to call Becca back.

'Hey!' she says when she picks up. 'I was just trying to call you!'

The familiarity of her voice is just what I need right now. 'Sorry,' I say. 'Must have dozed off on the sofa. What's up?'

She chuckles. 'What a fabulously exciting life you live!'

I look at Billy, his dark head bent over in concentration as he drives his car up the side of the TV cabinet. I've lived an exciting life. I own a fabulous house in Notting Hill, had luxury holidays in the best resorts in Europe and I'm no stranger to Michelin-starred restaurants, but I'm glad

I've swapped every single one of those experiences for this moment. 'Too right,' I say.

'I'm inviting myself round to dinner tonight,' Becca informs me.

I laugh. 'Oh, you are, are you?'

'Yep. I've got something I need to talk to you about. You provide the chilli con carne and I'll provide the booze.'

I frown. 'How do you know we're having chilli tonight?'

Now it's her turn to laugh. 'You always do chilli on a Monday!'

I'm stunned into silence. Have I really become my mother, rotating dishes on a weekly basis until Tuesday seems wrong without bangers and mash and Sunday without a roast? The thought makes me feel slightly queasy.

'I'll make sure I bring a nice red!' Becca adds, taking my silence as acceptance. 'See you later!' And she rings off before I can say anything else.

After a quick trip to the supermarket, I don't do anything all day but play with Billy. I intend to go and make myself a cup of tea and then get some housework done while he's quietly absorbed in kids' TV, but I end up taking my mug back to the living room and watching him sing and dance along to *The Tweenies*. I get this feeling, that's both wonderful and horrible at the same time, that I'm only visiting. I don't want to miss a second.

When Dan comes home, he finds Billy and me crawling round and round the living room, in and out of his pop-up tunnel. Dan stands at the door, with his coat still on and his messenger bag clutched to his chest and watches us. When I've finished one more circuit, I sit back on my haunches and smile at him. 'Hi. How did your day go?'

'Hi,' he says back but he doesn't smile. In fact, he looks rather confused, as if this is an unusual question for me to ask.

Billy races to him and grabs his trousers. It's only when Dan's scooped his son up and has held him upside down until he's giggling so much I think he's going to choke that the wary expression melts off of his features and he smiles.

'Becca's coming for dinner,' I tell him.

'She might as well move in and pay us rent for the amount of time she eats here!' he says as he heads off to the kitchen to put the kettle on, but there's no trace of irritation in his tone. I follow him in there a few minutes later and find him frowning as he stirs his usual two sugars into his tea. 'No chilli tonight?' he asks.

'Nope,' I say. 'Thought we'd have a change: Thai Green Curry.' And as I walk past him to the fridge to get the ingredients, I give him a kiss on the cheek.

'You're acting weird,' he says, not taking his eyes off me. He's acting as if it's a complete stranger making herself at home in his kitchen and he's not quite sure what to do about it.

And maybe he should do something about it, because I'm not entirely sure he's wrong. I don't feel like the Maggie who left here when she had her last jump. I don't feel like her at all.

CHAPTER FORTY-ONE

Becca arrives just as I'm dishing up. I've been so obsessed with Billy today that I've forgotten that last time I saw her I was begging her to kick scumbag Grant to the curb. The fact I've seen her so happy in my other life only makes me want to see that happen in this one too. I'm going to have to do some careful digging to find out how the land lies.

It seems like a normal night with the three of us, how it used to be. With Becca as a buffer, Dan has finally unclenched and is actually laughing and joking. I try to look beneath the surface, beneath what I always assume I see when them together. Is there a spark between them?

There's laughter, yes, and the odd bit of physical contact – Dan's elbow nudges Becca gently in the ribs when she takes a joke too far, Becca ruffles Dan's hair – but nothing that seems out of place. It's as if, in this life, they don't know if they're supposed to be together.

What is clear, though, is that he's obviously more comfortable and relaxed with Becca than he is with me. Maybe we had a big bust up before I arrived this time?

I mull that thought over and reject it. I don't think so. Dan just seems to have got into the habit of expecting me to be on the offensive with him, and habits aren't born overnight. Have things really deteriorated that far between us while I've been gone?

Once we've finished eating, Dan retires into the living room to watch a quiz show and Becca and I stay at the kitchen table, drinking the red wine she brought with her to go with the chilli. It didn't really work with the Thai food so we decided to wait until after.

I've had a chance to consult my calendar in this life, and I've seen a couple of entries with 'B'. No mention of a 'G' alongside it, so I'm carefully optimistic. She also hasn't mentioned him all through dinner either, so I'm starting to feel hopeful.

I have no idea what's been going in in the life I've just landed in, so I pull one of my standard openers from my memory banks. Having to plug myself back into in each life when I arrive is making me a really great listener. 'How are things?' I ask.

'Good,' Becca says, nodding, but she looks slightly uncomfortable.

'What?' I say.

She looks down into her wine glass. 'About this news …'

'It's good news, I hope?'

She nods. 'At least I think so.' She takes a deep breath. 'Grant's asked me to move in with him.'

I'm so stunned my mouth refuses to work. The fact she's still with him would be a hard enough pill to swallow, but the fact she's thinking about shacking up with him? Is the woman crazy?

My thoughts must be spilling out and painting themselves all over my face because she says, 'I know you don't like him, but be happy for me, will you, Mags? Please?'

'I don't like him because he *hurt* you! I don't know how to forget that happened. I don't know how to forgive him. You can understand that, can't you? What would you say if Dan ever did that to me?'

'Dan would *never* do that kind of thing.'

I nod. 'I know.' Whatever our problems, at least I have that.

We're both silent for a moment, but I can't keep it up. I can't let it happen again. I can't let it lead to marriage a second time. 'Please, think about this, Becs. Please!'

'He hasn't done it again, not in years.' There are tears in her eyes now. 'And he's so sorry. He was horrified with himself.'

I shake my head. 'But there are so many better men out there!'

'That's easy for you to say! You've got one.'

I'm tempted to say, *Here … I'll step back and you can have him. I think you're better for him than I am anyway,* but I know it doesn't work that way.

'Why?' I ask. I need an answer.

'I love him,' Becca says weakly. 'And that's what you do when you love someone, isn't it? You give them the benefit of the doubt, you believe in them, even if no one else does. Real love is giving yourself to someone. Completely.'

I want to tell her she's talking utter rubbish, but I can't. I keep remembering that reading from my wedding. On the face of it, Becca's words hold the truth, but I can't accept them. That can't be what it means, can it? To lose yourself so completely in someone else that you let them treat you like dirt?

'I don't know what to say …'

Becca nods. At least she understands where I'm coming from. At least we haven't had another huge blow up with one of us storming out.

'You know I'm saying this because I love you, right? I just want to see you happy.'

'Yes.'

'OK,' I say. I can't change her mind. All I can do is be there for her. 'But if he hurts you again, I'm coming after him.' Because I totally would have no problem ripping off Grant's tender bits and making them into a chilli con carne any night of the flipping week. No problem at all.

While I'm saying goodbye to Becca at the front door, I hear Billy grizzling in his bed. I go up to see what the matter is. He isn't hot, isn't clammy. There's no reason I should take him into bed with us, especially the age he is now, but I do anyway, hugging him to me and smelling his clean, kiddie shampoo smell.

'Great,' Dan says as he rolls into bed and turns off the light. 'He'll be kicking us all night.'

I don't care. I also don't care that I've given Dan another reason to be annoyed with me. I don't belong in this world any more. I know I won't stay here permanently, and I have the craziest idea that if I'm hugging Billy in my sleep, that next time I jump, maybe I can take him with me.

I do wake up the next morning with Billy in my arms, but it's because I'm still in my little three-bed semi in Swanham.

Although I have a constant feeling of waiting for the other shoe to drop, I stay here. For now, anyway.

One evening after dinner, I take Dan up a cup of coffee. I knock gently on the study door, hear a grunt and take it as permission to enter.

There's a document of text up on the computer when I walk in, but I'm not quite at the right angle to see what it is.

'Thanks,' he mutters and starts shuffling bits of paper, putting them into piles. Then, as if he's just noticed it sitting up there, he closes down the file I glimpsed on his computer screen.

'What was that?'

'Nothing really.'

'Anything I might be interested in?'

He doesn't look shady when he answers, just really, really tired. 'I doubt it.'

I try not to feel hurt but I do. This man, who on our wedding night was so open, so giving, now won't share anything with me. He doesn't trust me with even the smallest details of his life. They're all locked away inside his head, held captive by his smouldering resentment.

The memory of lines of Times New Roman on the computer screen gives me an idea. I remember how he looked sitting next to Becca at my dinner table, talking about his children's books. He needs a passion to follow, like Jasmine said. I was wrong to go down the route of pushing about his teaching career, I can see that now.

'Was it something you'd written?' I ask him, keeping my voice light and interested. 'A poem or something?'

'No. It wasn't.' Dan's gaze back at me is pure granite. If he was any more annoyed he'd been baring his teeth and snarling, the way next door's dog does when it sees the milkman.

'Oh,' I say, trying not to let the urge to lash back take over. 'You ought to start doing that again. You were really good.'

'Just back off, Maggie.'

'What?' I ask. 'I'm just trying to be supportive.' I'm not managing to hide the irritation now. I'm just about at the end of my rope with this surly, grumpy man. He never *ever* gives me the benefit of the doubt.

'You're just trying to make me do what you want again,' he says, scowling at me. 'Although, I have no idea why you've picked writing this time. You've always been dead set against it before!'

'That's not fair.'

'Isn't it?' He's standing now, glaring at me.

Suddenly, I can't take any more. I don't know how to get through to him. I turn and leave him to his nice coffee, to the secrets he keeps on his computer, and I go back downstairs and cry silently, watching *EastEnders* through my tears.

For some reason that reading I found on our order of service floats through my mind, only this time the words have changed:

Love is angry, love is rude. It thinks of itself first, rather than anyone else. It thinks the worst rather than believing the best. It keeps a record of every tiny transgression...

If that is what our marriage has become, how far removed from what we believed it would be when we looked at each other and said our vows, then maybe what Dan and I have isn't love any more. I'm shocked to realise that, if this is true, that even if I try really, really hard, maybe we shouldn't be married any more.

And the more I think about it, the more I realise I'm right. I need to set him free. All I do is make him miserable. It's me. I'm the variant between this life and the other one, aren't I? I'm the one who's made him like this.

CHAPTER FORTY-TWO

I wake up with a gasp. I felt something. I'm sure I felt something. A sensation of …

Falling.

I felt like I was falling. It must have been a nightmare.

I can hear Dan breathing and even though I know he might shrug me away if he's awake, I reach out for him. My fingers meet warm flesh and I gasp again and start to roll over, the sheet falling off me.

It's Jude. I'm touching Jude.

I don't know how I can tell just by the feel of him, but I can. My heart is beating hard in my chest. I gulp in air trying to calm it. I think I woke up right after the very moment of the jump. Maybe right in the middle of it. Was that important?

Jude grunts and shifts. He flings his arm over his eyes and then his breathing softens again.

I'm back already? Six days? I was only there six days?

For the first time since I've begun this crazy journey, the first thing I feel at finding myself back with Jude is not relief but irritation. Not that I'm unhappy to be back with him. It's just that I wasn't there long enough. I didn't accomplish anything. It's going to take a lot longer than six days to burrow through Dan's deep defences. And Becca? I'm scared for her. I feel as if I've abandoned her.

I flip over and roll out of bed, stand up and head for the door. It's only when I'm halfway across the room I realise I'm acting out of instinct. I was going to check on Billy. When I remember that there's nothing in the bedroom next to ours but a rather lovely cast-iron Victorian bed, I want to cry. I walk across the landing anyway, open the door just to make sure. It's horrible in its stylish perfection.

I press a palm to my chest. It gets worse each time, the sense of loss. The gaping, tearing feeling right in the centre of me. I hoped I'd get accustomed to it, that it would get better.

Without a sense of anything else to do, I trudge back to the master suite and collapse back down on the mattress. Jude rolls over and opens his eyes. 'Hey, you,' he says and kisses me on the nose. 'Good morning.'

'Morning,' I say.

He frowns and reaches for my face, touches my cheek. 'Are you OK?'

I shrug. There are too many words to pick from and none of them form an explanation that will make sense to him. Once again, I'm stuck by how lonely this life-swapping lifestyle makes me feel. I'm the only one in on a secret I really never wanted to be part of. How can I tell Jude I'm missing a child that has never existed in his world?

'Don't think I slept that well,' I say and I push my way out of bed again. 'Want a cup of tea?' Before he answers, I grab my robe from the back of the door and head downstairs.

The kitchen is beautiful, all gleaming white cupboards

and artfully placed bowls of lemons, but I can't help wishing for the MFI kitchen back in my home with Dan. This whole house, stunning as it is, feels like a shell, a skeleton.

Pull it together, I tell myself as I make a cup of tea. You're back with Jude. That's the important thing, isn't it? You're back where you're supposed to be.

When I turn on Breakfast TV, I discover I've arrived back with Jude the morning after I'd gone to sleep next to Dan's silent back. Is it all slowing down? I don't know. Part of me is relatively relieved I'm not hurtling through two lives at break-neck speed. Being away for only a short time should make this life much easier to slip back into.

Or it should. Over the next week, I try to get back into the swing of this life, but it's no good. It's like a shoe that has, for no reason at all, begun to pinch or rub. I just can't seem to get comfortable in it.

After two weeks, I crack. I wait for Jude to come home from work one night. He has a dinner with a prospective client, a friend of Jasmine's: someone big on the New York art scene who's looking for a London pad for his son while he goes to university here. Instead of changing into my usual pyjamas to watch TV, I put on something comfy but a little more elegant. I choose a long grey jersey dress with deep leg splits in the skirt and tiny thin straps, and I drape a cashmere cardigan around my shoulders. Jude likes me best in power suits – or should I say he likes me *out* of power suits? – but I think that would look too formal, like we're conducting a business meeting. I also don't want to put him on the back foot by noticing something is different, so I've chosen something soft to the touch, his second favourite. I pour a glass of nice red wine and wait for him in the kitchen, pretending to read *Elle Decoration*.

When he comes in I don't hover round him instantly; I give him a good half hour. He slumps on the sofa in the corner of the kitchen and I listen to a blow-by-blow account of the dinner as I dish up some olives to snack on. It turns out Jasmine attended as well at the last minute, seeing as she was back from Guadalajara early. I wonder why Jude didn't ring me up and ask me to join them, make up a foursome, but I bat the thought away. I have more important things on my mind this evening.

When he finally kicks off his shoes and loosens his tie, I know he's ready. Or as ready as he'll ever be.

'Jude?' I say lightly, as I potter from one side of the kitchen to the other, putting the glasses that are still gently warm from the dishwasher away.

'Hmm?' he says. His lids are looking heavy. I need to get in now before he flatlines. When Jude's brain switches off, it really goes. After that the only thing he's good for is grunting and single-word sentences. And sex, of course. He never seems to be too tired for that. My body thrums at the thought. A way to kill two birds with one stone, I think, if this all goes my way.

I walk over to him. 'We're in a good place now, aren't we? I mean, financially?'

He nods, looking ever-so-slightly pleased with himself. 'Sure are.'

'So what would you think about me taking some time off?'

The sleepy look melts from his expression. He sits up a little straighter on the sofa, props himself up with an arm along the back. 'How much time off? You've really built up some momentum at the moment, and you don't want to lose – '

'About a year.' I hold my breath, waiting for his response.

'A year? Bloody hell, Meg!'

I smile, the kind of barely there smile you do when you've got a lovely secret to share. I'm inviting him to join me in it. 'Not right away,' I say, 'but if everything works out well, maybe I'll need to in about nine months …'

He's fully alert now, all that wine-induced fuzziness gone. I see his eyes widen as the penny drops. 'You're pregnant?' he whispers.

I swallow. I'd like it if he sounded slightly less horrified. After all, he's already turned thirty and I'm only weeks away from doing the same. All our friends are having babies.

'Not yet,' I say, 'but I'd like to be.'

His shoulders relax and he takes a huge glug of wine, draining his glass, then he looks back at me. 'This is all about the other day, isn't it? The dinner party?'

'No,' I say, and I'm telling the truth. Even though it was only last weekend, it feels like it was years ago. 'You've always known I wanted children. You said you did too someday.'

'I do,' he says carefully. 'But just – '

'Not yet,' I finish for him. We sit in silence for a minute or so. He looks as if he's about the change the subject. Usually, I'd let him. Save the battle for another day. This evening I don't attack, but I do press on. 'It's OK for you, you know. You can father a child at any age, but there's a time limit for me. I want to be able to do it while I'm still young and healthy.'

'Jesus, Meg!' he says laughing softly. 'You're making it sound as if we're about to start drawing our old-age pension. Anyway, people are having babies later and later these days. We've got plenty of time.'

He stands up, walks across to put his wine glass on the counter above the dishwasher and starts heading for the door. Subject closed. Or at least postponed. I go and get his glass, upturn it and place it *in* the dishwasher. I'm standing there, staring at it, when I realise this is one of those moments. I can give in, drop the subject as Jude wants, or I can be bold and unafraid, like Jasmine is, and say what I'm feeling.

Is that being selfish, though? Neither of us are wrong to want what we want. We just don't want the same thing right at this very moment. I thought I was being patient, but maybe I'm pushing Jude the way I push Dan.

I think about Becca. Both versions of her: the one who will do anything for the man she loves, who will capitulate on any point as long as he loves her, and the one who is cross because she thinks Jude doesn't treat me as an equal. How can one person hold completely opposite views? And which one is right?

I want to love Jude that way, but that doesn't mean this longing for a child will go away. I don't know what to do.

I close the dishwasher and then I follow Jude into his office, the smaller reception room at the back of the ground floor, because I know that's where he's gone. He's sitting there at his desk, the log-in screen waiting for a password, yet he's staring into space.

'I know we've got time to have babies,' I say, 'that we don't need to rush. I suppose what I want to know is that we're at least on the same page, that it's somewhere in our future.'

He nods. 'It's not that I don't want kids, it's just … I don't know.'

I do. He's scared they'll slow him down. That part of him that drives him, I always thought it was a good, helpful thing. A strength. Now I see it might have a darker side, that it maybe chases as much as it energises.

I may not have made wedding vows out loud to Jude. I know we haven't stood in front of God and our family and friends and made promises about our life together, but in my heart I have. If I love this bit of him, the bit that drew me to him in the first place, then I have to love all of it, don't I? I suddenly understand where Becca was coming from, even if I can't quite accept this kind of love applies to a monster like Grant.

I walk behind him and drape my arms around his shoulders, put my face next to his. 'It's OK,' I say. 'I get it. I get all of it. You can't stop being who you are …'

But neither can I, I add silently. *Can you understand that too?*

Jude swings the swivel chair round unexpectedly and it catches me off balance. I fall neatly into his lap – just, I suspect, as he planned – and he buries his face in my neck, kisses it. 'What would I do without you, Meg?'

'I don't know …' I try to imagine it. Life without Jude. I

think I'd be devastated. I try to picture how he'd handle our break up, but I can't see him crumbling like I would. I can just see him taking the pain and using it to push himself forward, even higher, even harder. 'Just promise me we'll talk about it.'

He looks up at me and every doubt I've ever felt about him is erased from my mind. It's all there, everything I've ever wanted to see. I know he loves me the way I've always wanted to be loved. 'You know I want whatever you want,' he says. 'But I'll tell you what …'

Here it comes. The deal.

I'm not cross, though. I was secretly hoping he'd do this, because then we'll come to terms. I'll have something concrete to pin him down with.

'This year is going to be crazy. I've got sell those ten apartments in the Knightsbridge development and you've got that house, your first million-pound budget … Once they're all wrapped up … later in the year. How about that?'

'In the summer?'

He nods.

'We start trying then?' I ask. 'Or we talk then?'

Jude's lip twitches. He knows I'm messing with him. 'We talk,' he says as he drops a gentle kiss on my collarbone, slips my cardigan off my shoulder and then the spaghetti strap of the dress underneath, 'but we can do as much practising as you like until then …' I laugh and then, as his mouth continues its downward journey, I stop laughing and let my head drop back.

*

The next morning I'm feeling more philosophical about it, less like everything has to happen right this very second. I'm sure if I just give Jude the space to come round to the idea, he will.

I remember how freaked out I was when I found out I was pregnant with Sophie. Although I was over the moon, I was scared out of my wits by the feeling everything had changed forever. I have to remember that Jude's never done this before. For him, it's still as nerve-wracking as the first rollercoaster ride of the day at a theme park.

When I get downstairs and fetch the milk from the front step, I find a thick, cream envelope on the mat. After putting the milk away, I stand in the kitchen and slide my nail under the flap, then ease out the thick card with embossed gold lettering tucked inside:

Dan and Becca's wedding invitation.

Together with the envelope, I press it to my chest, smiling. Hopefully, by the time it comes around, I'll have some happy news of my own to share.

CHAPTER FORTY-THREE

On a sunny July afternoon, we gather outside Swanham
Baptist Church for Dan and Becca's wedding. I stand beside
the bride in a floor-length lilac dress with thin straps and
a cowl neckline. My stomach is depressingly flat. I know
logically, of course, that even if I was expecting it probably
wouldn't be affecting my waistline yet, but the fact it definitely
isn't has put a dampener on my mood. Or it could be the fact
that I'm just about to watch my other husband marry my best
friend. That'd do it too.

I'm trying not to be let anything show, though, trying to
smile and be happy and ignore the weird knotting sense in my
stomach of too many lives twisted up and tangled together. I
fuss around Becca with the other bridesmaids, making sure
her veil is hanging right, that she's not holding her flowers
wonky. One thing at a time. That's the way to handle this.

As we stand there in formation at the top of the aisle,
listening to the beginning of Handel's 'The Arrival of the
Queen of Sheba', I can't help thinking about a conversation
I had with Jude a couple of weeks ago, the one he'd promised
we'd have. The one I'd been waiting for. He'd taken me out to

a really nice restaurant for our 'chat' about babies. Afterwards, I wondered if that was an exercise in containment.

He asked for another year. Just to get the business really established, he'd said, then he wouldn't have to work so hard, he'd have more free time, be able to be around at weekends and evenings more. He'd taken my hand and looked into my eyes and said he didn't want me feeling like a single parent. His mum had always complained about that with his dad. I agreed, of course. What else could I do? It's supposed to be give and take, this thing, and he's listened, he's willing to compromise.

As we start walking down the aisle, I realise tonight would be the perfect opportunity to take advantage of the flowing booze and the fact Jude's laptop is back in London while we're here. I'm ovulating. I've been learning how to keep track of these things recently. In readiness.

I start imagining how I'm going to find Jude with his tie undone, looking weary but happy at the end of the reception, how I'm going to sit on his lap and kiss him slowly and how, after the bride and groom have driven off and all my maid-of-honour duties have been dispensed with, I can drag him back to the hotel and see if we can't jumpstart the baby-making process a little.

Not that I'm intending to be backhanded and avoid contraception or anything like that, but you never know what might happen in the heat of the moment, even if we're sensible. No form of protection is one hundred per cent effective, is it?

By the time I've finished thinking all this I'm shocked to

discover we're at the front of the church. Becca practically has to shove her bouquet at me and I realise it's time to step aside, to slide away from Dan so she can stand beside him instead of me.

I feel as if I'm watching myself watch the ceremony as it progresses. It's weird. On one hand I feel disconnected, as if it's someone else standing here holding Becca's bouquet, but on the other hand it all seems too close. Like that feeling you get when someone holds something too near to your face and you just can't focus on it. I have to keep stopping myself taking a step back.

I turn to look at the happy couple when it's time for the vows. As Dan begins to speak the first bit, his voice low and deliberate, I see tiny flurries of movement in the congregation. Husbands and wives squeezing each other's hands, signalling they're cementing those same promises they made to each other, repeating them in their heads. Yet-to-be-marrieds darting glances at each other and sharing shy smiles. I look towards the back, where Jude has positioned himself – on Dan's side. The lesser of two evils – but he's staring at the ceiling, so I turn my attention back to the bride and groom.

I'm pleased to see the glow on Becca's face, one I recognise from a life I've almost forgotten was once mine. I find it easier to concentrate on her than focus on Dan. Seeing him look at her the way he once looked at me makes me feel as if I'm paper thin, as if I might vanish from this reality and appear in the other one, right while I'm standing here.

I breathe out when it's all over and Becca and Dan head back down the aisle.

I need to get used to this, I tell myself, as I check we've got the full quota of 'little' bridesmaids and herd them off behind the bride and groom, like a troupe of lilac-clad ducklings. They're married now. Joined in the eyes of God and everyone else, and I have a sense that if I can get it to stop feeling weird that I'll sever the last ties I have to that other life. I'll be able to loosen the ropes, cast off and drift free from it. That way, I'll stay in this life, where everyone is happy: me with Jude, and Becca with Dan, not Grant.

Billy.

I inhale sharply.

Yes, I know. Billy.

But I could be pregnant this time next year. Billy could be on his way back to me. Or even Sophie. Maybe, if I do everything right, play this game fate has set me by the rules, I'll be rewarded with both. I have to hang onto that, or at least the hope I'll be reunited with one of my children in this life.

Jude isn't in a very good mood during the reception. Hardly surprising, really, seeing as he doesn't much like Dan or Becca, and I'm at the top table while he's been stashed away somewhere at the back of the room next to somebody's aunt, who insists on taking her false teeth out to eat each course and then putting them back in again so she can talk his ear off in between.

I discover that watching your best friend marry the man you once loved, are supposed still to love, is a great clarifier. I look at Becca and I think to myself, *I was never that much in love with Dan*. I wanted to be, but I never was. I was too busy counting all the things about him that weren't quite perfect to let myself.

I have to stop being so nitpicky and dissatisfied, I decide. I have to make sure I don't start secretly resenting Jude for not being ready for babies *right now*. I have to believe that he'll make good on his word, that within the next couple of years we'll be a family, maybe even get married.

Love is patient ...

So I suppose I will just have to be too.

CHAPTER FORTY-FOUR

Nine months later, when I jump back into my life with Dan again, I'm prepared. Maybe it's because I've been watching re-runs of *Quantum Leap,* but I've come up with a plan to take control of my crazy life. I've decided that, just like Dr Sam Beckett, there must be something I have to fix and I think the thing I need to fix is Dan. He's the loose end I need to tie up. If I can make *this* version of Maggie and Dan happy then my work will be done and I can move on and leave them to it.

I'm also ready to go all guns blazing to get Becca away from Grant, even if it means she doesn't talk to me for a decade. Keeping her safe is more important than keeping her to myself. I phone her straight away, ready to put my plan into action, and discover that, much to my relief, they're no longer an item. Not only that, but there's a lovely little restraining order in force. That means I can focus all my attention on Dan.

When I hear his key in the door that evening I try not to be nervous, but I am. He comes into the kitchen and dumps his keys on the side. I'm surprised by the rush of warmth I feel when I see him and realise that maybe all that jitteriness was really anticipation. Dan, however, doesn't seem to be feeling much of anything for me. There's no kiss on the cheek and he makes me my obligatory cup of tea without hardly making eye contact, then slopes off into the living room to watch *The Weakest Link*.

As soon as I exit the kitchen door I see Dan's shoes thrown across the hallway, one right at the bottom of the stairs in prime tripping position. *Oh, for goodness' sake!* I think, feeling the familiar crawling sense of irritation across my skin. I turn and yell, 'Dan!' but before I get any further, I stop myself.

'What?' comes the distracted reply from the lounge.

I stand there and stare at the shoes for a second. 'Nothing,' I call back, and then I gingerly hook the heels with my fingers – they've just been kicked off and they're still ... fresh ... if you know what I mean – and then I pop them into the shoe tidy. They look weird in there, I decide. Foreign.

Now, don't think I'm going to be doing this for Dan every day. At some point he's going to have to learn to pick up after himself. All I know is that if I want things to be different, then I'm going to have to do things differently, and the best idea I've got is to think of what I'd usually do, which always seemed to make things worse, and do the opposite.

Project 'loose ends' has officially begun.

It takes a couple of weeks but, gradually, I see Dan smile more and more. Sometimes he even comes into the kitchen and, instead of bypassing me for Anne Robinson, actually sits and chats about his day with me while he drinks his cup of tea. Once or twice we've even laughed together. But I can't shake the idea that we're more like flatmates than husband and wife. I don't know how to change that.

What did we do to ourselves? I often ask myself silently. Unlike Grant the Scumbag, who did something dramatically wrong to end his relationship with Becca, Dan and I managed to bludgeon our marriage to death with a thousand tiny blows, so slowly, so carelessly, that we hardly even noticed it happening. It's only by living it the second time that I've even become aware of it.

'Dan?' I ask absentmindedly one evening, as he's doing a stir-fry for dinner.

He thinks he's Gordon Ramsay, or Nigel Slater, or whoever's popular at the moment, when he's cooking. 'Mm-hmm?' he mumbles as he's carefully cutting peppers into strips of exactly four millimetres. Dan's a bit OCD about stir-fry.

'Do you want to go out tomorrow? As a family, I mean? The weather's supposed to be lovely.'

He stops chopping and looks round.

'I thought it would be fun,' I add.

He looks slightly bemused, but he nods. 'OK. What did you have in mind?'

'Oh, just a stroll in the grounds of Elmhurst Hall, maybe? I thought we could take a picnic. Billy would love running up and down some of those hills ...'

'Yeah,' he says, and I see a new light appear in his eyes. I suspect he's thinking about bringing a football along. 'Let's do that.'

So the following morning, I make a picnic up and we put it in the cool bag-slash-rucksack-thing Becca gave us for a

Christmas present that we've never used, and we head off to Elmhurst Hall.

We eat first; it's noon anyway and it means we won't have to lug the picnic bag around. I put a blanket down on the grass and we eat cheese and ham sandwiches, bags of salt and vinegar crisps, a few sausage rolls I found left over from last Christmas in the back of the freezer and a selection of fruit. Not the most stylish picnic I've ever had – I don't think anything would beat the champagne and oysters I ate with Jude on the beach on Lido island in Venice – but there's something about the simple pleasures of the fresh summer breeze, the rolling hills, that makes it the best thing I've eaten in a long time.

Dan and I don't chat, but there's a companionable silence as we work our way through the food, taking turns to encourage Billy to eat something other than endless packets of POM-BEAR.

After lunch Dan's eyes light up. 'Let's build a camp!' he says to Billy.

I'm not sure Billy knows what a camp is, but he'd do anything if it meant doing it with his dad, whom he adores. So for the next hour or two, I am demoted to wood carrier and leaf picker as the two boys construct a lean-to in the woods from which they can spy any bandits or pirates without being detected.

I have to do a bit of fast talking when we're finished, because Billy initially insists it's only for boys, but eventually we all clamber inside and sit there, eyes peeled, eating the last of the chocolate buttons from the picnic. Billy's not very good at sitting still and lasts about five minutes before he decides, actually, it would be much more fun to be a baddie and runs around outside, doing his best one-legged pirate impressions until Dan and I are helpless with laughter.

When we finally manage to breathe properly again, Dan turns to me. 'You're right,' he says. 'This is fun. I think we needed this.'

I nod, too full of everything I want to say to say anything. I lean forward and rub his arm. 'I do love you, you know,' I say, making sure my eyes don't leave his. 'I know we don't say that much anymore, but I really do.' My voice catches embarrassingly on the last few words, because I realise it's true. As much as I've chosen the life with Jude, it doesn't mean I don't have feelings for him. I think on some level I always will.

'I know,' he says softly. 'And I love you too. It's just …' He shakes his head, unable to articulate what he wants to say.

I exhale softly, thankful he's finally ready to hear this. 'I'm sorry I'm such a crabby wife sometimes, that I always want to do things my way …' I trail off, having an odd moment of déjà vu, although I don't really know if you can call it that, about my other life. I'm thinking about Jude, how my role with him is reversed, and suddenly I understand how deeply frustrated Dan must get with me sometimes. It strikes me, even though I haven't felt very much that he loves me recently, that maybe he gives in to me for the same reason I do to Jude: because he loves me. Maybe he hasn't given up on me – on us – yet.

'I think it started to get bad when Billy was small,' I say.

'I know I wasn't in a good place and it can't have been easy for you.'

He gives me a look filled with gratitude and I know I've hit the nail on the head. 'I really tried to be there for you, Maggie, but you just kept pushing me away.'

I nod. 'I know. It wasn't your fault. I'm not even sure it was fully mine, either. It was just … hard.'

'So how do we make it better?'

I think for a moment. 'You know those two-person rowing boats we used to see on the Thames when we were at college?'

He gives me a quizzical look. 'Rowing boats? You think we need to get one?'

I laugh and shake my head. I could never quite get my head round the fact Dan is both a storyteller who's imaginative and creative and a husband who always takes everything so literally. It still fascinates me how those two parts of his personality sit so comfortably side by side. 'Do you remember that time we stopped and watched those two who just couldn't row in a straight line?'

'Oh, yes! They were awful! Couldn't manage to row in sync with each other at all, let alone the same direction!'

'Well, I think maybe that's us,' I say. 'We've been pulling in opposite directions for too long and all that happens is that nobody gets where they want to go and everyone gets frustrated.'

He ponders this for a moment. 'I think I get what you mean. Do you think we can learn to do it the other way?'

'We'll just have to figure it out. I'd rather make some

mistakes while we try and be happier at the end than not
bothering and being miserable.'

Dan reaches out and holds my hand. His thumb strokes
my skin softly. It brings a lump to my throat. But before either
of us can say anything further Billy comes charging towards
us with pretend cutlass raised and we have to do some fancy
invisible sword fighting to avoid being robbed of our last
remaining chocolate buttons.

That night, Billy is almost asleep before his head hits the
pillow, worn out by all the running and the fresh air and
sunshine. When I'm sure he's snoring softly, I slip off and have
a shower. When I come out I'm so tired I just crash onto the
bed, my towel wrapped round me, not really caring that my
hair is making the pillow wet. I close my eyes, but I don't go to
sleep. I just exist in a dozy hinterland where reality is limited
to sound and the vague sense of light beyond my eyelids.

The mattress dips and creaks beside me.

'I'm all finished,' I say without opening my eyes. 'The
shower's yours if you want it.'

A hand brushes up my thigh, nudging under the corner of
the towel. 'What if it's not the shower I want?' Dan's tone is
playful, but I can hear a hint of a question in it too. I open
my eyes and look at him.

This feels weird. Partly because I've got used to thinking of
him as belonging to Becca and partly because when I've been
back in this life sex really hasn't been on the menu much. At
first it was because I was too down but later it was because
we were constantly fighting. And not the kind of fighting

where you blow it all out of your system then have explosive make-up sex afterwards, either.

However, as I look into his eyes, I realise the Maggie and Dan in this life need it. It would be taking a step backwards to push him away now. So I don't answer his question, I just reach up and curl my hand around his jaw, sliding it round the back of his neck as he dips in for a kiss.

CHAPTER FORTY-FIVE

The moment before I open my eyes the following morning, I have a tiny moment of panic. Not yet, I whisper in my head. I don't want to go yet. I'm relieved when I have the courage to look and spot curtains that have seen better days rather than cream roman blinds, all folded in perfect lines. It's not that I've changed my mind. Just that I'm tired of being weighed down by all sorts of unfinished business in both my lives. I want to make sure that everything is neat and tidy when I leave this one for good.

I stretch slowly and a smile creeps over my lips. My body feels good this morning. Relaxed. I smile harder as I remember why and turn to look at Dan.

'Hello,' he says then laughs when I almost jump a foot off the mattress. I didn't realise he was awake too.

'Don't do that!' I say, starting to laugh myself. 'I almost had a stroke!' I notice he's propped up on one elbow but I don't remember him moving. 'What are you doing? You weren't watching me sleep, were you? Because that's creepy, you know.'

He grins at me. 'Might have been. Just for a moment or too.'

'Crazy stalker,' I mutter, but he's pulling me into his arms and his day-old stubble is grazing my cheek, and we go for a re-match of the night before. It's even better this time. Although I'd wanted to last night, I'd still been nervous. I felt a little rusty, as if I'd forgotten how it could be between us. But this morning it's easy. Right.

We've not long finished when Billy bursts into the room, informing us at the top of his voice that it's been breakfast time for *ages* and mummy and daddy are being really lazy this morning. He's full of the camp we built the day before so we end up making another one under the duvet, me and Dan taking it in turn to use our legs for tent poles, but after a while Billy decides it's much more fun to tickle us and have the camp collapse on top of him.

'We'd better feed him before all this laughter turns to tears,' I tell Dan and make a move to throw the duvet off and get up.

'You stay there,' he tells me. 'I'm thinking of going to church this morning, anyway, so I'll give him breakfast and you can have a slow start.'

'You're going to church?' I say. 'I thought you'd ... Well, you just haven't been much lately.' Not as far as I could tell from my family calendar, anyway.

'Just feeling like I've got reasons to be thankful today.' And then he's gone, counting the stairs with Billy as they jump down each one on the way to the kitchen.

When he comes home we have roast chicken and then we take Billy to the play park. Dan and I take turns to push him on the big swings, and as we're standing there, keeping our eyes on Billy's retreating and advancing form, he says, 'I'm going out on Tuesday. I'll be in for dinner, but back about eleven.'

'Oh,' I say lightly. 'Where are you going?'

'Just meeting up with friends,' he says.

I watch Billy swing back and forth for a moment. 'Hey, I've got an idea,' I say, glancing sideways to catch his reaction before it happens. 'How about we see if Gwen next door can babysit and I'll come with you. We haven't been out together in the evening for ages.'

Dan's face becomes suddenly expressionless. 'It's just the lads, mainly,' he says. 'We'll probably talk about stuff you haven't got the slightest interest in.' Then he turns and smiles at me. 'How about we do that next week? You know have one of those "date nights" people bang on about?'

I don't know how to answer. Even though he's talking about going out on a Tuesday instead of a Thursday, red flags are waving madly in my brain. At the same time the smile he's giving me is so open, so hopeful, that I want to believe what he's telling me. And he's just been to church, right? Wouldn't lightning fall down out of the sky and zap him if he was lying? Or, at the very least, wouldn't he look even the tiniest bit uncomfortable about it?

I check his face for any signs of deceit and I can't find any. 'OK,' I say. 'That's sounds lovely.' Because, at the end of the day, I've decided to do things differently this time around, haven't I? And maybe I need to start trusting where once I would have been accusing, and I don't think Dan could have been quite so convincing last night *and* this morning, if he was sneaking around behind my back. At some point I have to start giving this man the benefit of the doubt.

I decide the best way to stop myself even thinking about where Dan may or may not be going tomorrow is to distract myself. I phone Becca after dinner, once Billy is down, and suggest a girls' night in.

Becca is fine during the conversation until I mention doing something on Tuesday night and then she starts to get really weird. 'Oh, I can't,' she says, all in a rush. 'I've got to … I mean I've got this thing booked …'

'Thing?' I ask, trying to ignore the plummeting sensation in my stomach.

'Yeah,' Becca says, doing her best to sound airy but I can hear the tension in her tone, and then she brightens. 'You know… Tuesday night is my belly-dancing night, isn't it?'

'I thought you stopped that ages ago, after you fell out with the teacher because she told you she didn't ever think you'd master figure eights.'

There's a moment of silence. 'Yeah, well, I did … I mean what right did that woman have to tell me I was "too tight" in my hip joints? She was practically calling me frigid! And I've never had any complaints from the guys who …'

I listen to her drone on, aware that she's very cleverly sidestepped my question, but when she pauses for breath I say, 'And this new belly-dancing class is on a Tuesday night too, is it? Still in Sidcup? What a coincidence.'

Becca had started up again, even though I'd been talking, but now her narrative rolls to a stop, like a car that has just run out of petrol. 'Yes,' she says, but I can hear the upward lilt in her tone.

'OK,' I say, my words even and cool. Reasonable. 'Maybe we can do it another night?'

Becca suggests Wednesday instead and then we say our goodbyes and then I press the button to end the call. The air is very still around me as I stare at my phone.

Dan is lying …

Becca is lying …

I try not to make the inevitable leap, but my mind goes there anyway, uninstructed and without my permission. The question is: are they both lying about the same thing?

CHAPTER FORTY-SIX

'I'm off now!' Dan calls out as he pulls his coat on. 'Have a nice time at your thing …' When I come into the hallway, he gives me an absent-minded peck on the cheek. There's a wisp of cool evening air and then it's gone again, as the door slams behind him.

I stare at the closed door, jaw tense, and then I go into the living room. Gwen, the lovely Welsh lady from next door is sitting there. She's going to be babysitting for us tonight. I told Dan if he was having a night out that maybe I deserved one too. Of course, I'm not the only one lying about where I'm going. I told him I was going to the new slimming group that's meeting in the Baptist Church hall.

'I'm going to shake a leg too, then,' I say and give Gwen a tight smile. 'I promise I won't be back too late.'

'That's fine, dear,' she says, and picks up the remote. I know she's itching to watch *Coronation Street*, so I let her get on with it.

That done, I sling my mac on and head out the door. I walk up the street in the same direction Dan has just gone. In fact, I think I can make him out farther up the road, his head bobbing as he listens along to his personal CD player.

Good. I know where he's heading, but that doesn't mean I want to lose sight of him.

Ten minutes later, we're both at Swanham station. Dan stands on the platform, whistling to himself. He seems to do that a lot these days, I've realised. I thought it was because he was happier, that 'project loose ends' was working, but now I suspect there's another explanation.

I'm skulking around inside the ticket office, hoping that when the six-forty-six arrives I'll be able to dart on board without being spotted. It should work. Dan's farther up the platform, planning to get on the first carriage, which will take him closest to the barrier at Charing Cross. I just have to hope I don't lose him once we get out.

Yes, I'm following Dan. The thing I said I'd never do.

I could confront him, I suppose, but I'm just so tired of all the lies. At least this way he won't be able to wriggle out of it. I know that for sure because he's arranged to meet someone. I saw the text messages on his phone.

Yes, I did that too. I went there.

But a little worm the shape of a question mark has burrowed in itself inside my skull, wriggling, niggling and insistent. *I have to know,* it sings, and I hum along with it. *I have to know. I have to know.* It's going to drive me mad if I don't.

The train arrives and my pulse quickens. If I don't time this right I'm going to slam face-first into a closing carriage door. Thankfully, Dan is among the first to hop on board and I have plenty of time to run and jump into the carriage that pulls up outside the ticket office before the door alarm beeps.

Once inside the train, I walk up through the carriages until I'm in the one behind Dan's. I peer through the dirty window in the door that links the two, but I can't see him. He must be sitting down, maybe farther up the carriage, or maybe just facing away from me. He's wearing his red waterproof so I'm hoping he'll be easy to keep tabs on.

I find a seat and, as the train jostles and bumps me, all I can see in my mind is the blocky message on Dan's mobile phone from an unknown number: *The Terrace restaurant, 8.30. I'll be waiting for you.*

I don't know where the Terrace is. I tried doing an Internet search, but Google is still in its early days and TripAdvisor has yet to be invented, so I came up with a big fat zero. I'm just praying it's not too far from the station, because the longer I have to follow Dan, the greater the chances of me getting caught. I'm not really good at this spy stuff. I'd have watched a few episodes of *Spooks* for tips if I could have done, but it hasn't started airing yet.

The train pulls into Charing Cross about forty minutes later. I'm there at the door, jabbing the button with my finger even before it lights up, and when it does I spring out, scanning the platform for a bright-red waterproof.

I locate it heading for the ticket barrier and give chase.

I don't run, but I do walk very fast. Dan makes his way to the exit, pauses to look around, and then makes a sharp right instead of crossing the cobbled courtyard and heading for the Strand. Oh, hell, I think. He's not going down that side road to the tube station, is he? I'm bound to get rumbled if he does.

Thankfully, though, he only walks a handful of steps before

he turns and heads into a building. My relief doesn't last long, because I notice what it is – the Charing Cross Hotel. My stomach rolls and I think I want to be sick. A hotel? That can't be good, can it? If I had any doubts, they've been shot to smithereens now.

I follow Dan into the hotel and up a large marble staircase. I hide behind a pillar when I get to the top to see where he goes next.

He walks up to the entrance of what looks like a restaurant and asks the girl standing at the host desk something. I look around and see a sign: THE TERRACE. I swallow. This is the right place. The only silver lining I can find is that at least I'm not watching him disappear into a hotel room somewhere on a higher floor.

The girl nods and smiles at Dan then gestures at him to follow her and leads him into the restaurant. Quickly and quietly, I make my way out from behind the pillar and along the carpeted corridor. Since the desk is currently empty, I take the opportunity to peer into the seating area, scanning quickly for a flash of red.

And then I see it – Dan is taking his coat off, smiling and sitting down opposite someone, but there's a waiter pouring wine at a nearby table who's blocking my view. As I wait for him to move, a thousand questions bombard my head at once: Is this real? Who is he meeting? It can't really be Becca, can it? *Can it?* The questions circle round and round unanswered, gathering speed until I feel dizzy, but then they gradually fade until just one is left: how can he do this to me?

How can he do this to *this* me?

I get why he did it the first time around, even if it was still absolutely the wrong thing to do. Things were so bad between us and then there's the seductive tug of meeting someone who thinks you're funny and exciting and wonderful, instead of boring and naggy. After all, that was why I'd got fixated on Jude in my first life, wasn't it? And who knows what might have happened if I'd gone to that reunion, if I'd had a couple too many glasses of wine?

But in this life …

I thought we were working it out, that things were going well. When I think of being together in bed at the weekend, of how Dan looked into my eyes with such tenderness and affection, I feel actually, physically sick.

I'm on the verge of turning round and walking away, unable to take any more, when the waiter who's been blocking my line of sight finally moves.

I gasp and cover my mouth with my hand. This isn't what I expected! It isn't what I expected at all!

Because it isn't Becca that Dan is about to sit down to dinner with. It isn't even another woman. The person that Dan is smiling and laughing with as they peruse their menus is a man.

CHAPTER FORTY-SEVEN

I back away. I can't stay here. I can't watch this.

But I must have walked further into the restaurant than I realised while I was staring, because now I bump into someone coming the other way. I turn and apologise to the couple who are being shown to their seats.

'Maggie?'

I turn and see Dan walking towards me, a bemused expression on his face. 'What are you doing here?'

I have no words. Literally, no words.

But then Dan's expression starts to change. Harden. 'You followed me here?'

I nod. I can hardly deny it, can I? But I don't know why he's looking so furious. I'm not the one having a secret meeting at a London hotel!

I finally hook my tongue up to my brain again. 'How long has this been going on?' I blurt out, glaring at the man Dan had been sitting with, who has now turned round to see what the commotion is. Never in a million years did I think it would be something like this.

'What do you mean, "how long"?' he begins, but then

his face screws into an expression of disgust. 'My, God! You don't – '

'I do!' I say back, trying not to shout, so it comes out more like a hiss. 'I've just seen you with my own eyes!'

Dan shakes his head, his lips clamped firmly together. I don't think I've ever seen him this furious. 'That man,' he says stiffly, 'is a literary agent! He's interested in – '

I don't wait to hear any more. I just run. I hear Dan calling after me but I keep going, my feet pounding on the wide, stone steps of the staircase. I dash through the lobby and out the door into grey drizzle of the London evening.

I'm feeling so many emotions I don't know which to pick first. Embarrassment, humiliation, disgust at myself? They're all in there. And something else too: as well as being ashamed and horrified, I'm devastated. Dan has hidden this from me in not just one life but two. Why won't he ever trust me? It doesn't seem to matter what I do, it never changes.

I'm so distraught that I manage to get on the wrong train and end up having to disembark at Orpington and wait forty minutes for another one that'll take me back to Swanham. I walk home in the rain, which has now really got its act together, and when I get home I relieve Gwen, then I get in the shower and turn the temperature up hot.

I stand there, one hand braced against the wall, and let the water run over me while I stare at the tile to the left of my splayed fingers. I take in its squareness, it whiteness. The faint discolouration in the grout surrounding it. It's much easier to do that than sort out what's going on inside my head.

After a while – I don't know how long – I turn the water

off and stand there, dripping. When I'm ready, I peel my hand from the wall and I reach for a towel, rub my hair and my face, then wrap it around me.

Oh, God. What am I going to do? Help me! I think I may have messed things up once and for all. Dan is never going to forgive me for this.

I walk across the landing and into the bedroom and let out a scream. Dan is sitting there on my side of the bed, his feet avoiding the damp clothes I hurled on the floor. He must have got the fast train back. Unsurprisingly, he's not looking much happier than the last time I saw him, around two hours ago.

He shakes his head. Eventually he looks at me and says, 'Have you lost your mind?'

I look at the floor. Maybe I have. It certainly feels a bit like that this evening. I really want to get dressed, but I also really can't face being naked in front of Dan at this moment, so I reach for my robe and put it on top of my towel, tying it tightly.

'I'm sorry,' I mumble. 'I just thought – '

'I know what you thought!' he says, his volume rising. 'God, Maggie! Why would you think that I'd do that to you?'

'Because you lied to me about where you were going,' I say. 'Because you've been lying to me about this for a very long time!'

That takes the wind out of his sails. He stops looking so appalled and rubs his hand over his face.

'Thursday nights?' I ask. 'What are they?'

He looks at his feet and then up again. 'Writing group at the library,' he mutters.

I think of all the things I imagined it would be, how far
I let myself run with it, and never in a million years would
I have guessed it right. I'd laugh if it was in any way funny.
But this isn't funny, because the fact Dan didn't even feel he
could confide in me, and the fact it was so easy for me to
believe it was so much worse than it actually was, is a sobering
indicator of just how far our marriage has sunk.

I walk over to the end of the bed and sit down. Dan joins
me. There's two feet of space between us, but it feels like the
Grand Canyon. 'Why didn't you just tell me?' I ask, and I'm
not blaming him. I just want to understand.

'I don't know … It was stupid. It's just become a habit to
keep all of this from you, I suppose. I would have told you if
something had come of the meeting.'

Oh, flip. The meeting. I look sideways at him. 'Did I ruin
it for you?'

He shakes his head. 'I don't think he really saw what
was going on, and once you'd left, we talked. He judged a
short-story competition I won, and he's interested in seeing
something longer if I can write it.'

'That's amazing,' I whisper, but all the while I'm thinking
that Dan won a competition and he didn't tell me. What
kind of bitch must I have been to him to make him behave
like that?

'I'm sorry I didn't tell you,' he says. I can see the truth of
it in his eyes. 'About my writing, about any of it. I don't even
know how it started, but when I first found out about the
writing group we weren't doing so well, and you seemed to

be so anti me doing anything like that, so I just made up an excuse that first time. I mean, I might not have gone back.'

He looks so sad that I want to put my arms around him, but I keep them carefully stapled round my middle, holding my dressing gown closed, despite the double knot. 'Why not tell me when it became a regular thing?'

He lets out a long sigh. 'I just don't think I could have faced one more fight,' he says and shrugs. 'I was a coward, I suppose. It was easier.'

I inhale then exhale, aware of how seductive 'easier' can be. It's easier to protect yourself, to blame and resent and complain than it is to build a proper relationship. We were both guilty of choosing what was 'easy'. It strikes me that marriage – a good marriage – is the reverse of those operations they do to separate conjoined twins, one lump of flesh being separated into two. On your wedding day, you start off as two distinct people, but that's the moment the process begins. Or it should. Of integrating and joining, of becoming 'one flesh'. The problem is that no one tells you it's just like the operating theatre, where you have to be naked, where you have to open yourself up and expose your most vulnerable parts, and it takes courage and guts and selflessness to do that. Why don't they mention that in the service, I wonder?

But then I think of that reading, those few short verses, and I realise it was there all along. I just didn't know it. I heard the words but I didn't really understand them. I think I might be starting to now. Just starting to.

'But things haven't always been awful,' I say. 'Recently

I thought they'd been better.' I search his face, looking for confirmation I wasn't just fooling myself.

He nods and a tear slides down my cheek. 'They have … I've been thinking about telling you, I really have.'

'But the other week … I was even trying to encourage you to write.'

He looks away. 'I know you were saying all the right words, but – '

'But what?'

He meets my eyes, goes still. 'You can be awfully dismissive of anything I suggest that you don't like the idea of,' he says. 'And this is special to me. It isn't just a suggestion of what takeaway to have or whose parents we should spend Christmas with this year.' His voice goes hoarse. 'This is my *dream*, Maggie. I had to protect it.'

Another tear falls, not because I think he's being unfair, but because I know he's right. 'From me,' I say quietly. 'You had to protect it from me. Because I'd stomped all over it too many times in the past.'

'I'm sorry,' he says again, and his face twists a little with the effort of holding all the emotion back. 'I should have told you.'

I clamp my hand to my mouth and shake my head, unable to speak. I know he couldn't have done, that I wouldn't have understood. I was too stuck in my own little spiral dissatisfaction to see.

Then Dan is reaching for me and I for him. We're holding on to each other, as if the other is the one point of stillness in a stormy sea, and if we don't cling on for all our might we might not survive. I wrap my hands around the back of his head, hold his face against my shoulder. 'I'm sorry too,' I mumble. 'I didn't mean to be so horrible. I didn't even know I was behaving that way. I was just … scared.'

Dan pulls back and looks at me. 'Of what?'

I shake my head. 'I don't know. Scared of you writing, scared of what that choice would mean. Financially, yes, but also for you … what if you tried and failed? You'd have been even unhappier than you were.'

He smiles at me. 'We can't just leave the things we want to do unexplored …. unchosen … because we're scared of what might happen if we do,' he says softly.

'I know,' I say, nodding. 'I understand that now. I didn't then, but I do now.'

I have an overwhelming urge to tell him everything in this moment. To let the truth spill out and take whatever consequences come, but this openness is so new, so fragile, I can't risk it. Maybe one day. Maybe.

Dan gives me a lopsided smile. 'We're a right pair, aren't we? Me sneaking off into the night … you tailing me.'

We meet each other's eyes. I clamp a hand over my mouth to stop myself from giggling, but it does no good. Pretty soon we're both howling with laughter. I try to stop, but every time I think about this evening it seems like a scene from a particularly bad *Carry On…* film and I just start laughing again.

It does us good, though. The endorphins wash away the last of the tension. When the hilarity finally ebbs away, and we're sighing and wiping our eyes, Dan turns to me. 'I'm sorry,' he says.

I shake my head. 'For not telling me where you were going? Don't be. I get it now.'

'No, for not trusting you,' he says. 'For blaming you for everything I wasn't happy about in my life.'

'I did that too,' I say. 'It must be contagious.'

The corner of his mouth lifts at my attempt at a joke, but then he gets serious again. 'I know I told you I hated it when you pushed me, but it's only because, deep down, I knew you were right. I knew I was just marking time, wasting my life, but it was easier to turn it back on you, to push you away, than to do anything about it.'

I nod, warmed by his words.

'I know that sometimes you were just trying to make me happy,' he adds. 'Maybe you did in a way that drove me nuts but, basically, you were coming from a good place.'

A tear slides down my face, even while I chuckle at what he just said. Yep. He pretty much hit the nail on the head. I found the most annoying way to try and help him, then launched straight in. Dan wipes the tear away with his thumb. 'It's time I started thinking about how to make you happy too,' he says.

'Thank you,' I whisper.

'And you know there isn't anyone else, don't you?' I look into his eyes. He's looking back at me, nothing hidden, and I nod. He breathes out heavily. 'Good. I would never do that. I love you.'

I find my eyes have started leaking again. My chin crumples and I nod again. 'I love you too,' I say, and we kiss. Not a steamy, let's-rip-our-clothes-off kind of kiss, but a this-is-who-I-am-and-I'm-letting-you-see-it-all kind of kiss. I feel lightness as I pull away and rest my forehead against Dan's, my ribcage rising and falling softly. It's like we've pressed the reset button on our marriage, taken it back to where it started, where it always should have been. At least, that's what I'm hoping.

'I want you to write,' I tell him. 'I want you to be happy.'

He nods. 'Thank you.'

'Will you show me something one day? Maybe something you've been working on at that group of yours?'

I know this is big for him. I know he might not be ready yet, everything is still to raw and fresh, so I'm pleased when he says, 'Wait here,' and heads off for the study. While he's gone, I turn on the bedside lamps. I feel the need for a calmer environment, not glaring light overhead. I also slip the towel out from under my dressing gown. I hear the printer going in the study and a few minutes later Dan appears and hands me a sheaf of pages, the first chapter of a sci-fi novel he's been working on for the agent. I prop my pillows up against the headboard, get comfy sitting up there, and start to read.

When I'm finished, I look up to see Dan hovering near the end of the bed. He's been full of nervous energy while I've been reading, moving around the room, tidying things he usually throws on the armchair in the corner, going backwards and forwards to the bathroom. I could be wrong, but I think he's brushed his teeth twice.

I look up to find him in dressing gown and boxers. His shoulders are tense, his face desperately trying to stay neutral but leaking a steady stream of micro-expressions: fear, hope, discomfort. Finally, he says, 'What do you think?'

I smile. 'I think it's wonderful,' I say. 'Really good. I love the fact it's a good, old-fashioned spaceship kind of story.'

I pause for a moment, considering what I should say next. In my other life he's making good progress in another genre. Maybe, if he's going to get the success he deserves in this one too, it wouldn't be a bad thing if followed the same path. I know things that Dan doesn't know, you see. I know boy wizards and hobbits are going to be big in the next few years. Spaceships and such like will have a long wait until it's their turn again.

'You've got such an amazing imagination,' I say. 'I wonder if it's going to be wasted on adults? I think maybe you should write a book aimed at children or teenagers.'

Dan's eyebrows raise. He honestly hasn't considered this, I realise, but I also remember what he accused me of before and I add, 'Just a thought. I don't want to push.'

'No,' he says, sitting down on his side of the bed. 'You might have something there. I'll think about it.'

I start to smile, but it grows into a yawn. I cover my mouth with my hand. 'Sorry,' I say. 'Must be because I'm on the bed.'

He shuffles closer. 'I'm tired too.'

I nod and lean against him. It's been utterly exhausting, all this turning myself inside out, but I feel calm and peaceful too. We lie there, not talking, not moving, until my eyelids are getting heavy.

Dan nudges me. 'You'll get cold if you fall asleep on top of the duvet,' he whispers.

I mumble my agreement and, because I'm nice and warm, I don't bother with a nightshirt; I just throw my dressing gown

off and slide underneath where the sheets are deliciously cool
and tuck the duvet around my neck. Dan reaches over and
turns his light off. He walks round the bed to do the same
to mine. I catch his hand. 'Stay,' I say with my eyes closed,
even though I have no idea if he's intending to go downstairs
or get in his side. I flap the duvet and shuffle over, making
room for him.

Usually, I'm very territorial about my half of the bed
and fiercely protective of my nocturnal space. I can tell he's
surprised because it takes a couple of seconds before he
throws off his dressing gown and climbs in. Then it's skin
against skin, warmth against warmth, and I sigh. I kiss him
softly on the shoulder, the neck, anywhere I can reach without
having to move too much, because as much as I want this
contact, I want *him*, I'm bone-tired and my brain has already
begun its shutdown procedure for the night.

We should have sex, I think hazily to myself, to cement
this new us, to put a stamp on the occasion, but I find myself
yawning more than I do kissing, touching, and Dan doesn't
seem any more energised. His arm curls around my waist.
His palm splays on my naked back. I shift and find a more
comfortable place to nestle my cheek against his shoulder. I
can't keep my lashes from meeting now.

Tomorrow, I think, as Dan's breath whispers through my
hair. Just like that first time, there's no rush.

But, as the last fragments of consciousness are drifting
away from me, I wonder if tomorrow will be too late. I know
I'm ready to let this life go now, that this Maggie and Dan
have a chance of happiness now their tide has turned, but

before I can move something – lips or hand or leg – to signal this to Dan is some way, to take this chance to know him completely one last time, I have fallen deeply asleep.

CHAPTER FORTY-EIGHT

I'm surprised when I wake the next morning to find myself on the opposite side of the bed from usual, on Dan's side. I reach for him, my eyes still closed …

And I find him. The memory of that last thought the night before rises lazily to the surface of my mind again and I open my eyes, make sure I haven't got it wrong. I could have, you know. I used to feel this way once upon a time with Dan, but nowadays, I only usually feel this way lying next to Jude.

'Hey, beautiful,' a low voice whispers and I smile, eyelids still resting lightly closed. My heart starts to skip.

I open my eyes to look at my husband, the one man who has ever felt the need to pledge himself to me body and soul, and decide I'm glad I've stayed.

There was a strange moment there, though, when it all got very muddled, when I couldn't tell what was past or present, one man or the other. It's strange. I thought the longer I did this the more my life would diverge down two separate tracks – and in some ways it has – but in other ways everything seems to be blurring together, especially when it comes to who I love and how I love them.

Besides, this gives me a chance to spend more time with

Billy. I know when I go the next time it will be the last one. I feel as if I'm in that bit at the end of a film – the big climax has come and gone, and all that is left is to show the characters taking their first steps into their happy ever after. Credits roll.

I spend a lot of time watching my son with a strange fierceness, trying to imprint every detail of him into my memory, realising I took so much for granted with Sophie. I was not a good keeper of those memories. I let some of them slide through my fingers, and now they are only vague smudges of thoughts – a colour, a word. A smile. I'm not making the same mistake again.

How did I drift through my life so unaware before? I'm actually quite cross with myself for not realising what I had when I had it.

The following night I meet up with Becca as arranged. I ask Dan if he wants to come too, not just because I realise we need to spend more time together, but because I just want him there. I was remembering how it used to be, the three of us at uni, how much fun we used to have. Dan declines, though. He says he's happy to sit in with Billy, that it'll give him a chance to start making some notes on a story idea he had years ago but never really did anything with. My mention of children's books has made him think of it in a new light. Other than that he's being very tight-lipped about it. I'm doing my best not to pepper him with questions, to back off and give him space. It's hard, though, because I'm excited for him.

Becca comes down to Swanham and we grab a bite to eat rather than going out for a drink. We end up at Pizza Express in the High Street. When I suggest sharing a bottle of wine she gives me a funny look and says she drove tonight instead of getting the train, so I end up just ordering a large glass of Pinot and hoping it'll last.

We chat about this and that, nothing of much importance at first, and I'm halfway through my Diavolo before I confront the knobbly question that's been poking at the edge of my consciousness all evening. I keep my eyes on my pizza, making sure I have a bit of jalapeño on the square I'm cutting, and keep my tone light. 'So … what did you get up to last night?'

Becca's knife and fork stop moving. I look up to find her frozen, jaw twisted halfway through a chewing motion, and then she starts again. 'I told you … I had my belly-dancing class.'

I give her a look that says, *Come on!* and it's not long before her face crumples. She puts her cutlery down. 'If you tell me what you did, I'll tell you what I did,' I say. 'And I guarantee I was the bigger fool. We're talking James Bond-type surveillance and lots of humble pie.'

There's a flicker of warmth, interest, in her eyes, but her jaw remains tense.

'Come on, Becs, you can tell me …'

Her eyes start to fill and that's when my stomach goes cold. 'You didn't see Grant, did you?'

She shakes her head violently. 'Oh, God, no! Of course not!'

'Then what?' I ask, leaning forward, lowering my voice.

She takes a glug of her Diet Coke and looks at me. 'I don't know if I'm ready to say anything yet. You don't know what it's like, Maggie, having something so huge you can't tell anyone, even if you want to. It's ... paralysing.'

Wanna bet? I think, but I just smile and nod as if I agree. This is not the time, if there ever will be a right time.

'I'm just worried about you,' I say.

Becca nods to herself then looks me in the eye. 'OK,' she says. 'The truth is ...' the pause is so long I think she's going to chicken out, but eventually, she says, '... I went to an AA meeting.'

I put my wine glass down and stare at her. 'AA? But you're not ... I mean, I know you – ' I screw up my face. 'Really?'

She begins to eat again, and in between mouthfuls she fills me in on the story. 'I know I've been known to misbehave on a night out, but I never really worried about it. I mean, loads of people do that ... But it's when I started misbehaving on nights in that it got to be a problem.'

'What do you mean?'

'I mean sitting there on my own, polishing off a bottle of wine.'

'Oh,' I say. 'Every night?'

She nods.

'And when did it start?'

'I did it sometimes when I was with Grant, when he was away for the night, but it's really since I got rid of him that it's become more of a ... thing.'

'You really think you have a problem?'

She breathes in deeply. 'I think I might have the *start* of a problem. If I'm honest with myself, it's not just having a little tipple. I've got to the point where I'm worried I need it.' Her mouth quivers. 'I'm glad Grant is out of my life, but that doesn't mean I'm not lonely … I just want to address it now before it does become something big, before it gets really out of hand.'

I feel a rush of love for my best friend. 'I think you're really brave,' I tell her. I stand up, go over to her, kneel down beside her chair and give her a hug. I feel her exhale, relax into me. 'I'm here for you. Whatever you need, whenever you need it. That's what friends are for.'

'Get up, you daft mare!' she says, pulling away and wiping the tears from under her eyes with her fingertips. 'People are starting to stare!'

I know she's not bothered, really. Not by what other people think, anyway, but I also understand this has been enough for her, that it's time to steer the conversation onto something else and save the rest for another day.

'Now,' she says, as I get up and plant my backside down on my chair. 'Your turn. So what's all this about James Bond?'

CHAPTER FORTY-NINE

To my surprise, I trundle on in this life. Days turn into weeks, but I don't mind. I'm happy. I'm just waiting for this train to finally lumber to a halt.

That's not to say that Dan and I don't have our odd tiff or that everything is butterflies and rainbows, but that's not real life, is it? *This* is real life. This is real love, I realise. Different from what I have with Jude, but real all the same. It's grown-up. It's not the first flush of romance, and it doesn't pretend to be; it's seen too much for that. Too many mistakes, too many angry moments, too many betrayals. But that hasn't stopped it.

Dan is writing. A lot. He squirrels himself away in his study like he used to, but this time I don't mind, because when he comes down again he looks alive, and this release of creative energy is doing wonders for our relationship. Now that he's finally let it off the leash, it's leaking into other areas of his life. One day I find a bunch of flowers picked from the garden waiting for me on the kitchen table, another a trail of notes – a treasure hunt – leading me to my wardrobe, where my favourite dress is hanging, along with a note that he's asked

Gwen to babysit and that I should get dressed up and meet him at the Italian in town.

It's these little things that keep us going, remind us we're on the same team, when the inevitable squabbles happen.

One night, after a particularly long writing session, Dan appears at the bedroom door. I've just tucked myself into bed with my latest paperback for company. 'Fancy reading something else?' he asks, looking more than a tad nervous and then I see the ream of printed sheets in his hands.

This is it, I think. The full stop in this life. I've had a feeling it has something to do with Dan's writing, that when he reaches a certain milestone and his future is set on a different path, it will be the trigger I need to send me leaping back home.

I hold out my hands for the manuscript and receive it eagerly.

Dan has indeed written a story aimed at younger readers, but this one is different to the one he described over the meal in my dining room back in Notting Hill. I'd guess it's aimed at slightly older kids, maybe early teens, and it's not about time travelling friends. It's about a lone boy, who has somehow fractured into three versions of himself. He has to chase himself through a dystopian world, trying to catch and eliminate the other two splinters before they get to him first and take over his life. The clever bit is that, at different times, the story is told by all three boys and it becomes harder and harder to know which one you should root for. It's gritty, exciting and gut-wrenching. When I look up again, the clock says it's past one.

Dan is dozing in the armchair on the opposite side of the room. I didn't even notice him sit down there. 'Hey,' I call softly, and he stirs. Then his brain moves into gear, realises what this signals and he sits bolt upright.

'Hey,' he says back. He doesn't ask the question that's burning on his lips.

'Oh, Dan …' I say, and I can't keep the smile off my face. 'It's brilliant! The most imaginative thing I've read in ages! I think you need to send it out to a publisher. Now.'

Dan is grinning so hard it looks as if his smile might spread farther than the reaches of his face. He tries to dampen it down, but it keeps popping back into place again. 'Well, it doesn't really work that way. I'll have to find an agent first.'

'Then start looking!' I say as I thump the pile of paper with my hand. 'This needs to be read by more people than just me.'

Dan is suddenly across the room and holding me, the pages of his beloved book have scattered across the bed. One or two drip onto the floor, but he doesn't seem to care as he looks into my face then kisses me softly. 'I'm so sorry I didn't trust you with this before,' he says. 'I should have known you would be wonderful.'

I pull back and look at him. 'No. You were right not to show me up until now,' I say. 'I'm not sure I'd have been ready before. I was too stuck in … something. But I've changed now.'

He kisses me again. 'You have changed,' he says. 'You seem …'

'What?' I ask smiling, as I can see his writer's brain struggling for the right word.

'Lighter.'

I nod. I do feel that way.

'What happened?' He's really looking at me now, as if he's trying to see past my skin to what's underneath.

I think for a moment. 'I suppose I'm like your character – Kai – I had to see different sides of myself before I knew who I really was, what I really wanted.'

He nods, as if he understands, and maybe he does. I wonder if this experience of mine affects more than just me, that it ripples out and touches those around me.

He looks a little sheepish. 'I have a favour to ask you,' he says. 'I think it's something the old you would have enjoyed, but if the new you isn't really interested, that's fine.'

'Are we talking about being naughty?' I ask laughing.

There's a sparkle in his eyes, but he says, 'Maybe later. What I was referring to was drawing. I have a feeling this book could do with some illustrations. Not loads, maybe just one at the beginning of every chapter, like a visual heading, and I was wondering if you'd be interested in doing something like that for me?'

'Oh, wow! Yes!' I say.

I can see it already. Little black-and-white silhouettes of the three boys, configured in different ways. I get up, sending more of the manuscript sliding towards the floor, and run into Dan's study, grab a sheet of paper from the printer and a biro from the desk, then I go back to join him and, resting on the dressing table, I do a quick sketch. Just the tip of a hill is visible at the bottom on the picture and there's one central silhouette of boy with his arms folded, and the others flank him, one seeming to whisper into his ear, the other poised as if to strike. I show it to Dan.

'That's it!' he almost shouts. 'Just what I was thinking, although I hadn't actually been able to visualise it. It's like you've reached into my head and pulled out what I couldn't.'

I'm ambushed by a yawn. I check the clock and realise it's almost two. I'll probably need to be up at six. I gather up the strewn paper and as I do so I smile at my husband. 'Dan, this is incredible. I'm sure you're going to be an amazing success.'

'We,' he says, stooping to help. 'You're in this now too, Maggie. *We* are going to make this a success.'

And when we've dumped the manuscript, pages all out of order, onto the armchair, we turn the light off and climb into bed. I lay my head on his chest and fling my arm across his waist and I smile into the darkness as sleep creeps over me, and as I do so I let this life go. I leave it at rest.

I jump.

CHAPTER FIFTY

A warm, salty breeze kisses the skin of my bare back. Somewhere in the distance soft waves crash on a beach. I can smell exotic flowers and coconut. I open my eyes and sit up, automatically holding the sheet to my chest.

I blink.

OK, maybe I really did die this time. Maybe a gas explosion killed us all in the night, because this surely looks like paradise to me.

There's white sand, a creamy-blue sky and sea so transparent I can see fishes swimming near the shoreline from almost thirty feet away. I stand up and walk towards it, taking the sheet with me, more because I'm mindlessly clutching it rather than by actual design. That's when I hear a grunt, someone moving beside me. I turn my head and see Jude lying face-down on a large bed, with linen so white it almost hurts my eyes to look at it.

I'm not surprised, even though I didn't expect to see him there. I seem to have slipped into a dreamlike state. I'm just absorbing the information around me rather than reacting to it. Maybe that will come later, but right now I'm happy to just walk, to pad across the cool, tiled floor. I'm in something that looks like a luxury hotel room, but one whole side is missing, leaving it open to the air.

Not really thinking about the fact I'm only wearing a sheet, I walk down a few wooden steps and onto the beach. My toes sink into the sand and I sigh. I wrap the trailing end of the cotton around myself, leaving my lower legs free, and keep walking.

While the sensible side of my head is telling me I'm probably not dead, it is being roundly contradicted by the information flooding into my brain through my senses. I keep walking until I reach the shore, let the frothy waves wash over my feet. The sea isn't chilly, but its comparative coolness sharpens my senses. After a couple of minutes I feel normal again, as if I'm back inside myself, thinking clearly.

'Well, that's a sight to behold, first thing in the morning,' I hear Jude say behind me, and I realise my bum is probably still showing, despite the sheet twisted around me. I can't tear my eye off the view – turquoise water that stretches for miles and bleeds so seamlessly into the sky I can only just tell where the horizon is. 'And you were worried about coming,' he says as he comes to join me, stands behind me and drapes his arms over my shoulders. 'I told you it would be OK.'

'Yes, you were right,' I reply, even though I have no idea what the argument was, because what about all of *this* could be wrong?

'Come on, then,' he says, taking one last look at the view. He begins to steer me in the direction of the bungalow. It's nearly eleven and we said we'd be up at the main house for pre-lunch drinks at noon.'

I nod, even though I haven't properly listened to what he's just said. It doesn't matter. All that matters is that I'm back with him and my life is absolutely and completely perfect.

CHAPTER FIFTY-ONE

I discover we're not at a resort in the Caribbean, as I had first suspected once I'd got the daft idea about heaven out of my head, but we're on a private island north of Martinique, which belongs to one of Jude's clients. It's called Flamingo Island, which is strange because there don't seem to be any flamingos here. I don't remember this man, but that's hardly surprising, since I've worked out that I've skipped almost a year forwards since I jumped away from Dan. It's like I've left that life completely behind now.

Anyway, Jason is an entrepreneur, one who's been raking in the billions. When we wander up from our private bungalow, a few minutes' walk from the much larger house that crowns the tiny island's highest hill, I discover he is one of those portly men whose faces always seem too large, too spongey, for their skulls. He wears striped shirts, even on holiday, and when I look at him carefully I can see the yuppie he must have been close to twenty years ago, red braces and all. He must have developed his laugh then, too, a resonant braying that carries far too easily on the sweet tropical air.

I learn that he was so pleased with the sixteen-bedroomed Georgian mansion Jude found him in the Buckinghamshire countryside that he insisted he join him on Flamingo Island for a couple of weeks this winter. I did not do the decoration, I discover. He hired someone with a much bigger affinity for gold leaf, velvet and glitz than I'll ever have. Still, he doesn't hold it against me. Nor I him, to be honest. I get the feeling it would have been a nightmare.

There are ten of us here: Jason's wife, Stella, who is only two years his junior, surprisingly. She's got the blonde hair and pert figure of a trophy wife, even though she's clearly in her fifties, and while her giggle is high-pitched and soft, when she thinks no one's watching, a hardness creeps into her eyes.

One of the other couples is Jason and Stella's daughter, Karin, and her husband – a German whose name I didn't catch first time around – who is Jason's right-hand man. There's a woman in her forties, Amanda, who I later discover is Stella's stylist, and Enrique is a yacht dealer based in Monte Carlo. Jos, along with partner Thomas, is the decorator who was actually let loose on Jason's country pile.

We all gather on a large terrace at one end of the large house, built in local stone and timber but, like our guest bungalow, missing a few strategic walls here and there. Every bedroom must have stunning views. Jason hands round the champagne cocktails looking very pleased with himself. He is a king and this island is definitely his kingdom. It doesn't escape me, though, that we have all worked for Jason in one capacity or another, and it makes me wonder why he hasn't invited any friends.

I don't know whether it's because I've only just jumped into this life, but as lovely as the surroundings are, I just can't seem to get the swing of the conversation as we sip our drinks and wait for an army of silent servants to deliver our lunch of fruit platters, salad and mouth-watering seafood.

Maybe it's because I've just jumped back in after being with Dan, who is a bit of a lefty and despises the sort of people who flash their cash and have no social conscience, but even though the bragging is done skilfully, elegantly, all I can hear is everyone honking on about how much stuff they've got and how wonderful they are.

I try to catch Jude's eye, to share a little moment of 'do you see it too?' with him, but he's too engrossed in one of Jason's lengthy stories, which always seems to end up with him decimating the opposition and coming out on top, to be my ally. If I didn't know any better, I'd think my partner was lapping it up.

And then something strange happens. The food is eaten and cleared away but the drinking continues, and by the time Jude is on his fourth G&T his laugh changes. It's no longer the chuckle, so deep it often comes out silently unless he finds something really, really funny. Now it's loud and obnoxious, perfectly harmonising with the others.

I know he's a bit of a chameleon, that this ability is what's helped make him as successful as he is, but I find I can't dismiss it this time. Something about it – about him – is grating on me.

By the time the women, and Jos and Thomas, start talking plastic surgery I decide I've had enough. We only flew in yesterday, so I claim jet lag and head back to our guest quarters, where I slip into the plunge pool, rest my arms along the edge, tip my head back and close my eyes.

Maybe it *is* a kind of jet lag, I muse, as I let the breeze play across my features. A kind of time-travelling jet lag. These aren't horrible people. Jason's a little abrasive, but the rest seem nice enough. Usually, I can look through the things that irritate me and find the good qualities, but today it feels as if I've lost that skill.

I relax as I lie there, feeling the cool water soothe my heated skin, and by the time Jude comes to find me – staggering a little, it has to be said – I'm feeling much more mellow. I think he has amorous intentions and I say I'll join him for a nap, but by the time I've dried off and head back to the bedroom, he's asleep on top of the sheet, shorts removed, but T-shirt still on, and he's snoring.

I watch him as he sleeps for a while, glad to be able to see, not just imagine, the jut of his cheekbones, the sharp angle of his jaw, and then I throw a loose beach dress on and take a walk in the shade of the palm trees at the beach's edge.

I haven't had a chance to talk to him about it yet, to fill in the gaps in my knowledge, but I suspect Jude agreed to this trip not just because it's the sort of thing he's always dreamed of doing but because there's an angle somewhere. A business angle.

I stop walking and stare out across the sea. A couple of dolphins are playing in the bay. I catch them doing a handful of leaps and twists before they submerge and swim off somewhere else, and then it's completely silent, just the rasp of the waves on the shore and the whisper of the wind in the palm fronds to keep me company. I let out a long breath.

I've learned something about doing things I don't think I want to do because of love recently, and often I find it's just a tweak, an attitude adjustment, and then suddenly I'm not just doing it out of sacrifice, but because I want to. Maybe that's what I need to do here? I reckon Jude must need me to be bright and sparkling and charming, his fellow ambassador for whatever scheme he's cooking up, so I resolve to try harder at dinner.

So that's what I do when we gather on the terrace, now surrounded by lit torches, later that night. I smile. I engage. I listen and try to join in their conversations as best I can. The women were a little guarded with me at lunch, still figuring me out, but I see my efforts rewarded this evening and they start to soften.

Inevitably, the conversation turns to the subject of children.

'Do you have kids?' Karin asks me. She's the nearest in age to me of the other three women and she's just been telling us all about the antics of her five-year-old, who will be here with the nanny the day after tomorrow.

I want so badly to nod, to tell them all about Sophie or about Billy. He'll have started school by now, I realise …

'Meg?' Karin prompts and I realise I've drifted off.

'No,' I say, shaking my head. 'I don't have children. Not yet, anyway.' It kills me to say this. Not just because I want to join in – I want to tell cute stories and feel my heart swell too – but because in some way I feel as if I'm disowning my children, that by my words I'm making it as if they've never existed.

'Don't wait too long!' Stella says in her Thames-estuary accent, then laughs. 'You don't want them eggs going bad on you! And it's not like you should have any trouble keeping your hands off a man like that,' she adds, a knowing look in her eye. 'I'd have had a string of little 'uns by now if I were you!' And she nudges Amanda and they both fall about laughing, not before they've leaned back to catch a glimpse of Jude and given him a long, hard up-and-down look while he drinks whisky and talks seriously with the other men.

'Don't mind Mum,' Karin says, leaning in and speaking under her voice. 'She always gets this way when she's had a few. I blame it on the HRT.'

Up until this point, I think I'd found Karin a bit intimidating, but as she rolls her eyes at her mother and mimes knocking back martinis, I chuckle and realise I've found the ally I was looking for.

However, as nice as this is, to feel I have someone to glance across the group and share a silent joke with, the rest of the evening goes steadily downhill for me. Now I've started thinking about my children I can't stop and each mental image I pull from my memory banks just makes the ache in my chest throb harder.

I miss them so much.

So much I just want to bury my face in my hands and sob. But I can't. Because tonight I need to be bright and fun. Jude needs me to be the wife …

No. Not wife.

I've spent so much time with Dan recently, used that vocabulary to describe the connection between me and the man in my life, that I keep getting the words wrong. I try again.

Jude needs me to be the woman he's chosen to spend his life with. That's right. That's the one. He needs me to be bright and fun, articulate and intelligent.

I close my eyes for a moment and concentrate, doing my best to conjure that creature up. It used to be so easy to slip into that mode with him – when he went, so did I – but now it takes more and more effort. I manage it, though. For Jude. Because I love him. Because I have the feeling that it's important not to be seen as a party pooper by this group. As a result, by the time we trudge back down the hill to our isolated little bungalow, it's not Jude who passes out with tiredness, too exhausted to take advantage of the romantic atmosphere once again, it's me.

CHAPTER FIFTY-TWO

Over the next few days, instead of lessening, the 'jump lag' seems to be getting worse. It feels like I'm wearing someone else's shoes, even though I know they're mine, and the more I walk in them, the more they rub. When Jude and I are alone, it's as good as it's ever been, but when we get together with our hosts and their other guests, that's when I feel the blisters.

And it's not as if I'm not trying. I've got quite pally with Karin, and Stella seems to have decided I need a bit of motherly advice and keeps giving it to me, whether I want it or not, and while that helps, in the general scheme of things it doesn't make a huge difference. After a while I start wondering whether, instead of jumping back into the life I left with Jude, I've landed in one that's almost identical but not quite, because this might explain this weird disconnected feeling.

I do my best, though. I laugh. I talk. I drink cocktails. I cover it well. Jude certainly doesn't seem to notice there's anything amiss, or at least I thought he didn't, but one evening, about a week into our ten-day stay, he suggests a walk along the beach just after sunset, when the air is a little cooler. The sky is pink and peach and full of massive lavender clouds as we walk hand in hand to the end of the wooden jetty where the boats come in and out and stare out back to where our real lives await us.

'Are you OK?' he asks me, turning his head to watch me as I answer.

I nod. 'What makes you ask?'

'I wondered if you were sad?'

I watch a seabird dive for a fish. 'What about?'

'About not having a baby.'

I turn to look at him, study his face in return. This is odd, I think. We've had a few strained conversations about kids over the years, but it's always me who brings it up, never Jude. I don't really understand why he's suddenly decided to mention it now, but he's hit the nail on the head. Partly, at least. 'I think that has a little to do with it.'

He nods, absorbing this, and then he pulls me into his arms and hugs me softly. 'Don't be sad, my Meg,' he whispers into my hair. 'The doctor said it might take up to a year, even if everything is normal, and we've only been trying a few months.'

I pull back, almost violently, and stare at him. Did he just say what I thought he said? Does that really mean what I think it means? That we're actually trying? Or I am just hearing it the way I want to hear it?

He reaches up and strokes my hair away from my face, even though it hadn't been blown out of place by the breeze. 'It'll be OK,' he says.

Somehow, that's enough for now. That's all I need to hear.

*

The next day we take Jason's catamaran and sail to an unin-habited island nearby. It's no more than a smudge of white sand, that stretches maybe a couple of hundred metres with a few bushes and a lone palm tree at its widest end.

It's peaceful, sitting on deck, sipping gin and tonic, dipping down into the sea when it gets too hot, then shell searching on the sand. It gives me time to think.

Jude's news about the fact we're trying for a baby has rattled free whatever it was that was bothering me, but as overjoyed as I am that it might be my reality soon, I realise that I can't hang everything on this child, all my hopes and dreams and happiness. I need to have other things that fire my passion too.

I swim back to the boat and slip a hat and a kaftan on to stop me burning, and end up sitting at the front, leaning on the wires that run between the stanchions, legs swinging over the edge, watching the waves lap against the hull. There is a tantalising glimpse of silver beneath the waves every now and then as shoals of fish swim by.

Stella and Amanda are plastered against the deck, topping up their tans, and Karin is snorkelling. Jude finally leaves Enrique, Jason and Jos in the cockpit to their conversation about golf – a sport he sees as a necessary evil – and comes to join me. 'Hey,' he says.

'Hey,' I say back.

'You've got that look again,' he tells me. 'One of the reasons we took this trip was because the doctor said it would help if we relaxed about it all. It won't work if you keep brooding over it.'

'I know,' I say. 'I'm not.'

Jude gives me sceptical look.

'But I am thinking about other things,' I tell him. 'I think I need to make some changes to my life.'

For the first time in a very long time, I see panic flit across Jude's lazily confident features. I see him swallow. 'What does that mean?'

I sigh and shrug my shoulders. 'I'm not exactly sure yet. It's just I really miss being creative …'

He gives me a confused smile. 'But you *are* creative. All the time! Look at the wonderful homes you create for people.'

I shake my head. That's not it. I'm not sure what it is – I can't quite put my finger on it at the moment. I think doing those sketches for Dan the night before I jumped back here as awakened something in me, something I need to tap into.

'It's not the same. I have this feeling – don't laugh when I say this – that I need to create something lasting. I need to stamp my creative mark on the world somehow, in a way other people can see, no matter how small.'

'But that's what you already do, Meg. Can't you see that? You turn people's houses into homes, homes they'll go on to make a thousand happy memories in. If that's not leaving a legacy, I don't know what is.'

He's right. I know he's right. I'm not explaining very well. It's just that I've been flipping between these lives for over a decade and now that I've finally landed in one to stay, I want to anchor myself to it with something a little more permanent than wallpaper and throw cushions.

I shrug again. 'That's all true,' I say, 'but I want to get more hands-on, actually *make* stuff that comes out of me. There's something inside me that can't leave that idea alone ...' I trail off, realising that, in some way I can't quite fathom, maybe this has got something to do with having babies too, creating in a very different arena. 'And as much as people gush about my designing, it won't last. In five years' time – maybe less, if they're very rich or get bored easily – they'll get fed up with it, rip it all out and have it redone.'

I stop talking, knowing I haven't finished, but not really knowing what else to say. When I turn to look at Jude he looks worried. A tiny muscle in his temple is clenching and unclenching repeatedly.

'You're one of the most sought-after interior designers in London at the moment, and you want to walk away from that? Just when we've finally got where we've always wanted to be? I don't get it.'

I shake my head. 'I don't want to walk away,' I say and reach for his hand, hoping I can magically transmit what is in my heart to his. He's just looking at the surface, the hard facts and details, and it goes deeper than that. 'I'm just ready to embrace something new.'

Jude keeps looking at me, his eyes moving from one feature of my face to another, as if it will help him process what I'm saying. I realise he's failed when he sighs and looks down. 'Without me? You want to leave Hansen and Greene?'

This is when I realise why he's behaving so strangely, why he's digging his heels in instead of working out how he can help me fly. I always knew Jude's identity was tied up with his ambitions, his work, but I hadn't realised how much.

He's taking my perceived rejection of everything we've built together personally.

'No,' I say and kiss him softly. 'That's not what I meant. I want to stay with you, you know that, in every way that counts. I just need to do something for me too. You do understand that, don't you?'

He nods, but I'm not sure he does. He wants to, though, and I have to hope that in time, I'll be able give him the reassurance he needs. He looks over to where Karin's flippers and snorkel are visible above the waves, her distorted body moving in and out of shape. 'Want to do that too?'

'Yes, please,' I say and smile at him.

When we're beneath the waves, watching fish of all colours and sizes scoot by us through the rocks, the shoals of iridescent squid that dart this way then that, I realise how quiet it is. In the silence I begin to gather my thoughts from the dusty corners of my brain. I brush them off and begin to put them in order, and while I'm sorting and cataloguing memories one thing Jude said last night floats up and glints on the surface, just like the sunlight on the underside of the waves.

When we've finally got what we've always wanted …

The problem is, even though this life is what I dreamed of, I don't know if I want it with the same heat any more. I want Jude. I want the love and the passion and, yes, part of me wants the success, but there's a part of me also that could ditch a lot of what has become our daily existence – the men like Jason, the demanding clients, the endless swatches and identikit cocktail parties.

At first I think this is very unfair of me, that I'm moving the goalposts on Jude, but then I realise that's not it at all.

A lot of this was never my dream in the first place. It was his. And I went along with it because I thought it was what I wanted too: becoming the kind of woman I knew he could admire, even doing the career he picked out for me. A career I'm good at, yes, but not one that fills my soul.

And, finally, I understand what I've been grasping for inside my head for the last few days. It all becomes clear. I thought I'd taken charge, but actually I've been guilty of using Jude's momentum to propel me though life because I had none of my own. I've been riding his coat-tails for too long, but now I'm ready to step off and fly solo. If that's not being his equal, I don't know what is.

CHAPTER FIFTY-THREE

It's our last night on Flamingo Island. Jason has arranged a big party before we all board the seaplane that will take us to the international airport on Martinique. I step down onto the largest beach of the island, the one that sits in a small bay directly below the main house.

A huge area has been decorated as if it's a Moroccan oasis. There are covered couches festooned with fairy lights and coloured cushions. Blankets and carpets piled with plump pillows in jewel-coloured satin and velvet have been laid down around a small bonfire. A table is set on the edge of the clearing, lanterns and candles illuminating the centre. The cutlery is silver, the wine glasses crystal.

We lounge around on the couches sipping cocktails. I feel decidedly decadent, but I don't seem to mind it as much. Maybe it's because I know I'm going home with Jude tomorrow, that I'll have him to myself again and I can properly start my new life.

We tuck into a Mediterranean banquet – stuffed vine leaves, lamb with figs, couscous so brightly adorned with vegetables and pomegranate seeds they rival the cushions we've left lying on the beach. When we've eaten and the plates have been cleared away, the waiters come round with champagne. Once everyone is in possession of a slender flute of golden bubbles, Jude stands up next to me, raising his glass. 'I'd like to make a toast …'

I smile to myself. I should have known this had something to do with him. He always did know how to butter people up, and he's obviously not missing the opportunity to stroke Jason's ego one last time before we leave.

I only half listen as Jude spouts on about our hosts generosity but I sip from my glass at the appropriate moment and smile at him. Jude is speaking the truth, after all. Even if I can't quite seem to 'click' with Jason, he's given us a once-in-a-lifetime experience. But Jude doesn't sit down after everyone has drunk to Jason, instead he turns to face me, keeping his glass aloft.

'I have one more toast to give,' Jude says, smiling down at me. The other guests exchange quizzical glances. I see Jason smiling magnanimously. The rest of us might not know what's going on, but he does. I look up at Jude.

'Meg,' he begins, 'you've been my loyal sidekick for all these years, always supporting, always loving me, whether I made good decisions or bad. I want you to know that I wouldn't be the man I am today, or be where I am today, without you.'

There's a little sigh from the women around the table, and Jude continues.

'So I wanted to let you know that when we get back home, I'd like to change the company name to Hansen & Hansen …'

He smiles at me, waiting for me to respond, but I don't

know how to. What does that mean? Is he going back into business with his dad? And if he is, what was all that talk about me not leaving the other day?

And then it strikes me this might be his way of supporting me and I try to tell him he's got it wrong, I don't want to leave the business, but he stops me in my tracks with a smile.

Everyone else is smiling too. I feel as if they're all in on some wonderful joke I'm just not getting. I look round the table, confused.

'Meg?'

Jude's voice pulls my gaze back to him. When he's got my full attention, he pauses for a moment, and then he begins to talk again. 'What I'm trying to say is that I want the company to change its name because I want *you* to change your name. I'm asking you to marry me.'

Everything stops then. The flickering on the bonfire ceases, the sound of the squeaking frogs in the trees. It's as if all my nerve endings have ceased transmitting and I have no sensation at all. Just for a heartbeat. And then it all starts up again, louder, brighter, more colourful.

'What?' I whisper back at him. I'm still holding my glass of champagne but my hand is shaking and tiny droplets are landing on my legs.

Jude carefully takes the glass from my hand and sets it on the table, then he pushes back his chair, gets down on one knee and takes my hand. 'I said, "Will you marry me?"'

I look into his eyes. 'Really?'

He laughs. 'Yes, really.'

I don't remember afterwards what I did first, kiss him or

answer him – yes, of course – but I know I did both at some point. There are cheers from around the table, the sound of more champagne corks popping and laughter, but I hardly notice anything. All I can look at is Jude.

I did it, I think to myself, as it all continues on around me. Whatever this whole jumping from life to life thing was supposed accomplish, I must have done the right thing, because now I'm being rewarded.

I have the man I want, the life I want, and not only has he asked me to marry him but we're going to have a baby too! I just don't see how my life could get any better.

Thank you, I whisper silently into the night sky, letting my words drift upwards along with the sparks from the bonfire. *Whoever you are and whatever you are, thank you. I won't waste this. I promise.*

CHAPTER FIFTY-FOUR

Even when we get back to London I can't stop smiling. I take a tour of my own house, grinning like a maniac, because now I know it's really mine. For keeps. I hadn't realised that up until now I'd been holding onto what I had in each life so lightly, just in case it got snatched away from me.

However, as the days go on I wonder if I jinxed my professional life by saying to Jude on the catamaran that I wasn't enjoying it as much as I used to. I can't seem to get excited about it as much any more, not even doing my favourite bit – mood boards.

I used to love pulling together the colours and swatches, scouring magazines and catalogues for the right pictures, but now it's all feeling a bit 'paint by numbers'. I'm just collecting and arranging other people's creations rather than coming up with any of my own.

And there's another strange side-effect too.

I don't realise I'm doing it until Jude asks me about it one day. We're at home. I'm watching *You've Got Mail*, Jude is going through some last-minute details for a property viewing the next day. When he finishes, he comes and sits beside me. I don't bother turning the DVD off – romcoms aren't really Jude's thing – because I know even if he sits here staring at the screen he won't really be watching. His mind will still be churning on work: how to make things bigger, brighter, more successful. I love him for his energy, but every now and then I find myself wishing he had an 'off' switch. You know, just something small at the base of his skull I could flip, and then I'll find out what he looks like when he really, truly relaxes.

He glances at Meg Ryan on screen, looking all adorable as she decides to fight back against the big bad Tom Hanks, then reaches for the newspaper, which is lying on the end of the sofa. When he picks it up, he laughs. 'You've done it again,' he says. 'It's getting to be some kind of disease!'

I pause the DVD and look across at him. 'What?'

'This!' he says, tapping the paper, and that's when I notice it, the little doodle in the margin at the bottom near the crossword. I take the paper from him and give it a good look. I do remember having a go at the crossword earlier, but I don't remember drawing this, at least, not until I see it again. It's a quick sketch in blue biro – a hilltop with three stick figure boys in various poses. Or maybe it's better described as one boy, who's splintered into three.

'You've been doing them everywhere!' Jude tells me, laughing. 'At the office, on the telephone pad in the hall. The pages of your Filofax are littered with them.'

I tear my gaze away from the drawing. 'I suppose I have,' I say. I can picture them now. I just hadn't realised there'd been so many.

'What is it?' he asks as he picks up the same biro I'd discarded earlier and carries on with the crossword.

'They're just doodles,' I say.

'I know that! I was just wondering if there was a reason you're drawing them over and over again. Is it something for a client? Because it's not the kind of thing you usually come up with – unless it's for a child's room?'

I shake my head. 'It's nothing. They're nothing.' And if there is a reason I'm drawing them over and over, I'm not sure it's anything either Jude or I want to explore. It's a bleed-over from my other life, the one I'm supposed to have firmly closed the door on.

Over the next few days, I keep discovering them. Jude was right: they're everywhere. All subtly different, some a refinement on the original I scribbled for Dan that last night before I jumped, some new ones, the boys in varying stances.

I don't like it at first. I feel as if all these tiny men are following me around, watching me. I feel as if their scratchy fingers might reach out and drag me back to where they came from, and I don't want that, but eventually I make peace with them, because I decide what they are.

They're not yearnings for a life left behind; they're my creative spirit punching through. I miss drawing, I realise. That's all it is. And isn't this what I told Jude about on the catamaran?

All I need to do now is listen to what my subconscious is trying to tell me, follow the clues and work out what I want to create. I pick up a piece of paper and a pen and I deliberately draw another one. In this one all three boys are defiant, each with their own personality and body language. I smile at the little figures when I've finished. They're under my control now. I am their god, after all.

So why do I see the tilt of challenge in the middle one's eyes as I look away? Why do I still feel he's daring me to do something I'm afraid of?

A week after we've been back home my period starts. It happens at work, in the offices we share in Mayfair. We have a smart white townhouse with black iron railings, chosen and decorated to remind clients of the types of homes we'd like to sell them. My office is up on the top floor – I like to look out over the rooftops and watch the city go about its business when I'm thinking – and I go down to Jude's office, which takes up the back of the ground floor, overlooking the courtyard garden, to break it to him.

'You must be psychic,' he says when I walk through his office door. 'I was going to ask you to come down. I've got exciting news!'

Jude always asks me to come down to him, so I'm glad the building has a lift. For some reason he prefers the clean lines and white matte walls of his office to my more bohemian space upstairs. Not only am I knee-deep in swatches and fabric samples, but I've developed a serious shopping habit on behalf of my clients. One whole room in my suite is full of gorgeous bits and pieces I've sourced from all over Europe.

'You know the film star, Tobias Thornton?' he says.

I nod. Of course I do. Everyone's seen his blockbuster action films. Back in my original life he's getting a bit past it, looking a bit like he's been living too well to really pull off being an action hero, but he's at the height of his fame now in the early noughties.

'Well, he owns Montford House in Cheshire and he's just called me because he's looking to put it on the market. I've been invited to go up there this weekend and check it out.' He grins at me. 'This is big, Meg! I reckon the asking price could be at least twenty million. Think of the commission on that!'

He looks at me, waiting for me to burst with pride, to squeal and jump and throw my arms around him. I don't jump or squeal but I do wind my arms around his neck and hug him tight. 'I'm so proud of you,' I whisper, because it's true, and then I pull back. 'This weekend?' I ask. 'As in, tomorrow?'

He nods. 'Tonight actually. He wants to meet at nine sharp in the morning and it's at least a four-hour drive. I think it's better if we go up this evening and stay over.'

'We?' I ask hoarsely.

'Of course. I told him all about your success at staging houses – there's a whole room in leopard-print you're really going to have to work your magic on – so I thought we'd make a weekend of it. He's mentioned going shooting on the Sunday too, to get a real feel for the estate.'

I can't hold it in any longer. I have to tell him my news. When I've finished he rubs my back and gives me an encouraging smile. 'It's not the end of the world,' he says. 'There's always next month.'

I know he's trying to make me feel better, but it sounded as if he was talking about a monthly raffle or something. I'm extra-gutted, because I'd half convinced myself our trip to the Caribbean had been so wonderful that I'd *have* to conceive there. It was the right time, wasn't it? I'm in this life now, fully committed. Everything's in place. So why isn't it happening?

'Maybe this Thornton thing couldn't have come at a better time?' he says. 'It'll take your mind off things.'

'Do you mind if I don't? I really don't feel up to anything this weekend. Certainly not being bright and sparkly company. I'd only be a liability.'

'But I need you, Meg. We always work best as a team, don't you think?'

I nod. He's right. We are a good team. A brilliant team, professionally. But it doesn't change the fact that all I want to do right now is curl up in a ball and hide. I still haven't come to grips with the fact I'm not pregnant yet. I know it's stupid. I know everything Jude has said is true – there *is* always next month, and the month after that and the month after that – but somehow it feels as every time I start to bleed that I'm having a miscarriage, in some way that I'm losing Billy and Sophie all over again.

'I'm sorry,' I say. 'I just can't face it.'

For a moment it looks as if he's going to try and persuade me, but then he kisses me on the forehead. 'What am I going to say?' he murmurs as he looks into my eyes.

'Whatever I want?'

He nods. 'Always.'

Not quite always I think, later that evening, when I watch him get into his car and head for the M40, because what I really wanted was to have my husband-to-be here with me tonight. I really don't want to rattle round this big old house on my own, thinking about how empty it feels with no children to fill it.

CHAPTER FIFTY-FIVE

Twenty-four hours later, I'm standing outside Dan and Becca's Victorian terrace in Swanham. I'd kind of put off calling her since I got home from Flamingo Island, unsure how she'd react to my big news, but I picked up the phone yesterday night when I was feeling in need of some company and as soon as she heard I was on my own for the weekend, she insisted I come over for dinner. I didn't need to be asked twice.

'Look at that tan!' she exclaims when she opens the door and pulls me into a hug. 'You look fantastic! I bet ten days in paradise did you the world of good.'

I promptly burst into tears. Damn those hormones, I think, and it makes me feel even worse, because I'd much rather it was pregnancy hormones making me screwy rather than just plain old period ones.

Becca's face crumples in concern. 'Maggie,' she says softly. She never has got used to calling me Meg. 'What's wrong?'

I manage to hiccup, snort and laugh at the same time. 'Actually,' I say, and pause to do a large sniff, 'I've got good news!' I wave my left hand at her, which is now adorned with the most massive diamond. 'I'm engaged,' I say. 'Jude asked me to marry him.'

She stutters a bit before she manages to congratulate me. 'And you're happy about it?'

I nod and she pulls me into a hug. 'Then why are you crying, you daft thing?' she whispers as she holds me tight, and the rest of the story comes out.

She leads me into the kitchen-diner that makes up the back end of the house. 'I'm not going to say anything trite, like 'It'll happen eventually', or 'You're still young,' she says. 'I know how much I wanted to punch people after the miscarriage when they trotted out that kind of crap.'

I almost let out a gasp, but I manage to disguise it as another sniff. Becca had a miscarriage? When? It must have happened sometime in the last year, after I left Dan but before I jumped to Flamingo Island.

As if summoned by my thoughts, I hear Dan coming down the stairs and when I catch a glimpse of him through the open kitchen door, and my stomach does a tiny flip. It catches me by surprise.

I'm just nervous, I tell myself. *It's always been a bit weird seeing him with Becca and we left each other on good terms this time. It's understandable I'm having warm feelings towards him.*

Becca opens the oven to check on the roast chicken. I smell thyme and lemon and I can see red onions sitting in the pan. It's *my* roast chicken. The one I gave Becca the recipe for. Only I haven't cooked it in years, so I suppose it's hers now.

Dan appears at that moment. 'Lovely you could make it,'

he says to me and leans in to give me a kiss on the cheek, demonstrating quite clearly that he is one hundred per cent completely over me. He wouldn't have got so close if he wasn't.

That sobers me up. Come on, Maggie. Get your two lives sorted into the right boxes. You've put the lid on that one, left it behind. I take a deep breath and do just that. It's ripples from my other life, that's all. Sooner or later they'll flatten out and disappear altogether.

After that I'm OK. We sit down and have a glass of wine before dinner.

'I'm so glad you came,' Becca says. 'It feels as if we haven't seen you for ages.'

I nod. I must have been very busy in this life before I jumped back into it again. There can't be any other reason for me staying away.

'Dan and I wanted to have you round like this, just to say thank you for dropping everything to be with me when we lost the baby.'

I look at my best friend. She is the bravest woman I know, always facing things straight on, but I hear the catch in her voice as she says the last word. Dan rubs the small of her back with his hand, a tiny attentive but almost absent-minded gesture. I can see he's got all protective over her since it happened.

'That's what best friends do,' I say, and my voice isn't entirely scratch-free.

After that I find I can look Dan in the eye properly. By showing such tenderness to Becca, he has firmly stamped himself as 'Not My Dan'. He's hers. From now on he will always be hers. The reality of that starts to seep into my soul.

Dinner is easy. We eat, we drink, we chat and laugh. I ask Dan about his books and I'm thrilled to learn he's got an agent now. Not the one he mentioned at the dinner party, or even the same one he met in Charing Cross, but another one. Not as high-profile, maybe, but she's young and hungry and he's really excited about what's going to happen next. He's completely rewritten his time-travelling story, adding more time periods and has planned the next two books in the series. The new agent is sending it out in a couple of weeks, after he's done a few last 'tweaks'.

When I think of the Dan I left behind in my other life, I know this one has already learned the lessons that one was beginning to grasp. I know he doesn't hide himself, or the truth about who he is, from his wife. He knows how to be open and supportive and, as a result, he and Becca have that weird telepathy my grandparents had. They're meshed. I'm happy to see they've succeeded where Dan and I failed, because it confirms I chose the right life, however hard it was to leave the other one behind just as it was starting to get better.

When we've finished dessert and had coffee, Dan makes Becca sit down and insists he will clear up after all the hard work she's done. I smile. I remember that. I might have moaned about his coat and shoes – which are still a trip-hazard in this new hallway, I might add – but he was always very good at sharing the housework. Jude, in comparison, seems to have forgotten he wasn't born with a housekeeper to trail around after him. Ours only comes three days a week, so the rest of the time it's me who clears up his dirty mugs or throws his pants in the washing basket.

I feel a familiar twinge of dissatisfaction and I stop myself. No. Went down that path with Dan. Not going down it with Jude. I've learned my lesson on that front. I won't let that tiny seed of resentment plant itself. However, I know that if I ignore what's bothering me, I'll water that seed anyway, so I decide to bring it up – calmly, reasonably – when I get back home. That settled in my mind, I get up and help Dan stack the dishes, then he washes while I dry.

We talk about books and drawing and music as we work, laughing about some of our contemporaries' stupid antics in college, while carefully sidestepping around any mention of our relationship. Becca sits back with a glass of red wine and throws the odd comment in from the dining table.

Dan and I remind me of how Becca and Dan used to be in my other life. Friends. I smile to myself as I put the last saucer away. I like it like this. I like it very much.

But then I go and do something stupid.

Maybe it's because of the wine. Maybe it's because with alcohol the edges of my two lives get less rigid, allowing a little bit of osmosis, but when I've finished putting the last of the crockery away, and Dan and I are having a good-natured tiff about whether *Die Hard* is the best action movie of all time, I walk up to him and slide my arm round his waist and rest my head on his shoulder, just as I might have done in the life I've left behind.

I realise the instant I've done it it's wrong. I feel Dan stiffen, and Becca gives me an odd look. I try and save myself by pretending I did it because I'm feeling a bit wobbly on my feet because I'm squiffy, and I think I just about get away with it.

We all act normal after that, but something has shifted in the atmosphere. I've ruined it, so I excuse myself and ring for a cab to take me home. I feel the need to be back in my own house, my own life, as soon as possible.

CHAPTER FIFTY-SIX

'Meg? What the hell are you doing?'

Jude finds me in the garden of our Notting Hill house. I'm dressed in a pair of overalls, my hair is tied up in a scarf and there are spots of paint across my cheeks. I look down at my handiwork. 'I'm painting a chair. What does it look like?'

He doesn't move. Just stares at me. 'I thought you didn't feel up to doing anything this weekend?'

'I perked up,' I say. 'What do you think?'

Jude stops staring at me and stares at the chair instead. 'It's a chair.'

'I know that. I was talking about the paint job.'

'It's a *white* chair.'

I thought he'd show a little more enthusiasm. I mean, I thought he'd be pleased that I haven't been moping around all weekend, that I've found something else to occupy my time. I may not be in the process of creating life at the moment, but I am in the process of creating really cute furniture. Or re-inventing it, to be more exact.

'Imagine a whole dining set like this, each with a different bold and bright seat pad.' I know it's just one chair, but I feel as if I've climbed Everest. I've done something with my own hands instead of just shopping for it, or telling other people where to install it.

Jude clearly thinks I've lost my mind. I can see it in his face.

'We did talk about this,' I remind him. 'I told you I wanted to be more hands-on, more creative …'

'Where on earth did you get it?'

'The bathroom on the second floor. I'll put it back there. There's a blue and white colour scheme, so I could use some scrap fabric to change the seat pad, rather than this old navy damask. I was just seeing if I could make the paint technique work …'

Jude's giving me that face again. 'And you abandoned me this weekend for this?'

I give him a confused smile. 'I didn't abandon you …'

'I didn't seal the deal, Meg. He's still thinking about it. And you know it's important to get a client to sign on the dotted line as soon as possible! If you'd been there you could have done that thing you do to win him over.'

'What thing?' I ask. The warm pool of feeling that has been spreading inside is now rapidly shrinking back down its own plughole.

Needed me to seal a deal. Not needed *me*.

He's standing at the top of the steps that lead down from the patio outside the orangery and onto the lower level, where I am with the dust sheet, paint cans and chair. He's towering above me a bit and he waves his hand imperiously. 'You know … you're good at smoothing things over.'

I laugh. Not a nice laugh. 'So, basically, you're saying you managed to put your foot in it with Thornton and somehow it's my fault?'

'In a way,' he says, staring back at me, completely oblivious to the fact this has not been an easy weekend for me, that he's being a total and utter plank. 'I told him the leopard-print wallpaper needed to go before he put it on the market and he had a fit. If you'd been there, you could have given him your designer spiel. So, yes, I needed you and you weren't there, which makes it partly your fault.'

My *spiel*? I feel my blood pressure start to rise.

'Well, I needed *you*,' I shoot back. 'And you weren't here, either, having put business in front of our need to have a baby!'

Jude doesn't exactly roll his eyes, but the gesture is pretty close. *Oh, that old thing*, I can almost hear him say, and I have this horrible feeling that maybe he's secretly hoping I'll never get pregnant, that he's silently relieved each time I go shopping for more Tampax. It's all I need for the tiny pilot light of anger inside me to burst into furnace mode.

'All you ever do is think about yourself, Dan!' I yell at him. 'You don't care about what I need!'

Jude's face becomes like stone. 'Who?'

There's something about the way he says it that trips me up. I stop and stare at him. He's not a happy bunny at all.

'What did you just call me?'

I put my hands on my hips. 'I think I called you selfish. Maybe not in so many words, but the gist was there.'

'What name?' His voice is getting lower and quieter with each word. A chill runs up my spine.

Oh, lord. I called him 'Dan', didn't I?

I don't know why. Maybe it was because, I'd just seen Dan last night. Or maybe it was because, in that moment, I felt just the way I had when Dan and I used to argue – misunderstood and talked down to and unappreciated. It's nothing more than that.

Jude gives me one last scathing look and then strides back inside the house, slamming the orangery door so hard behind him that the panes rattle.

The next morning I apologise for yelling at Jude, for calling him the wrong name. When he asks why I did it, I have no explanation to give him. There's nothing that makes sense when I try and stick to one life, one reality. I would have mumbled something about Freudian slips, but it's been a decade since I was with Dan in this life and it'll only make Jude crosser if he thinks I'm still carrying a torch for him after all this time. Jude is frosty for a day or so but then things go back to normal. Almost.

Month after month I'm disappointed in the baby stakes. I stop mentioning it, although Jude can hardly be ignorant. But I tell myself I mustn't give up. After all, it took a while before Sophie came along. Maybe Jude and I aren't as fertile together, maybe it'll take a few more goes. I can live with that.

To keep myself obsessing about the matter, I forge ahead with my plan for a new creative business. I abandon the idea of furniture, for now, anyway. While messing around with paint in the garden was fun, maybe I was getting a little ahead of myself. I decide I need to start with one thing and do it well, and it's after I stroll past Cath Kidston's original shop in Holland Park that I decide what my focus should be – fabrics.

Not cute little vintage-inspired florals like hers, of course, but I team up with a textile designer and we start to work on some ideas. My first project is inspired by Jude's comments about my doodles, and I draw silhouettes of boys and girls in rough strokes with bold colours. They look great as a large design on cushion covers or as a repeating pattern on bigger swathes of fabric.

My textile-designer has a friend who has a home design boutique and she takes some cushions to sell. They end up taking off in the local area. Mums even contact us asking if they can commission silhouettes that look more like their kids. We do that, but we also add a couple of different hairstyles and poses to our range and they start to sell even better. It's a blast to be making things people want to buy. I'm loving every second.

Jude, however, hates it. He doesn't say anything but I know he thinks selling a handful of cushion covers is a waste of time. 'You need to mass produce to make money,' he keeps telling me.

'Maybe it's not all about the money,' I reply. 'Maybe there's more to life.'

I honestly don't know why he doesn't understand my need to do this. After all, I can understand what drives him a little better now, why he works all the hours God sends, because I'm energised by this, thinking about how I can grow it, do it better, all the time.

I come to realise that it's not the business venture itself

that is a source of irritation for Jude, but the fact I haven't brought it under the umbrella of our company by making it an offshoot of Meg Greene Designs, which continues to run smoothly with a bit of delegation.

I've decided to create my own brand: Maggie May. Jude doesn't like that much either. He prefers Meg because it's his pet name for me, but I don't feel much like a Meg any more. I feel like me – Maggie – but the strongest and most dynamic version of her I've ever known.

It's partly my fault he's struggling with this. Jude's a take-charge kind of guy, happiest when he's in control, and for years I was happy to let him be my guiding force. It's hardly surprising he's throwing a wobbly now I've kicked him out of the driver's seat and have taken over myself.

I just need to be patient. Give him the time and love he needs to help him adjust. He'll come around. After all, he's always had a particular spark for dynamic, independent women. Now he's got his very own one with his ring on her finger.

CHAPTER FIFTY-SEVEN

The months blur into one another. Time marches on, steadily, slowly. Like it's meant to, I suppose, but then one Sunday afternoon I fall asleep in front of the TV and when I wake up three years have passed. I'm so shocked that when Jude finds me later that day all I can do is shake my head and cry. I want to believe it's a bad dream, but the missing months and years are there in a shiny new Palm Pilot.

The house is pretty much the way I remember it. There are new blinds in the bathroom, a fabulous antique lamp in the living room and different bedding and pillows. Oh, and there's an American-style fridge-freezer standing in the kitchen, but apart from that it's identical in its clinical stylishness, including the flipping bowl of lemons, which for some reason is really starting to get on my nerves.

The second bedroom is still a guest room. The third Jude's gym-slash-dumping-ground. The fourth my workroom. There are no cots or changing tables anywhere in the house. No toys in a toy box beside the sofa. No crayon pictures fixed to the front of that ridiculous huge fridge.

That night, after we go to bed, I roll over and stare at Jude. He looks blissfully innocent, his lashes dark against his cheeks, but I know something isn't right. There's no baby. Maybe we've done all we can. Maybe we've tried IVF and are taking a break. I don't know.

I try asking Jude, but this subject has obviously become a source of conflict for us. He gets that look on his face – the same one Dan used to have when I pushed about the head of department job, funnily enough – and I don't get any clear answers from him. I think we've probably argued about this too many times for us to have a conversation that isn't full of emotional pitfalls, assumptions and accusations.

I decide to hold off, to do some digging on my own, so I don't just sound as if I'm nagging on about the same old thing. I need ammunition, and that will come in the form of facts.

But that's not the worst thing about me and Jude.

More and more I want to know what happens in between these jumps of mine, when I'm conscious about who I am and how I'm living, because the other Maggie, the one who exists in the spaces, hasn't been doing a very good job of things. There's no gold band next to the diamond on my left hand. Maybe it's because the tiny distance I felt between us before I jumped is now a chasm. One of the things I found intoxicating about Jude was that he used to look at me as if I was special, as if he was lucky to have me. Now he barely looks at me at all.

Jude's spending way more time at the office or schmoozing with clients. I don't ever seem to be invited to go too. Maybe it's because we also seem to living separate business lives now. I've handed over the day-to-day management of Meg Greene Designs to Holly, who's been doing a great job as my second-in-command, and now I'm solely working on Maggie May. It seems to have grown beyond all my expectations in a really short space of time. John Lewis and a few other big chains are carrying my fabrics and home furnishings, thanks largely to some hand-drawn monochrome floral designs in rough brush strokes that seem to have become my signature look.

I'm scared. I feel as if everything is accelerating, and not in a good way.

This is not the life I envisioned. This is not the life I was working towards. It has all the outward gloss but none of the intrinsic happiness, and that has to be the most important thing, after all. The rest was supposed to be window dressing. But what do you do when your whole life is window dressing and there isn't anything else?

It's so unfair. If I was able to just live my life normally, I might be able to do something about it. I'd have a choice, but I feel powerless as I'm catapulted from one era of my life to another without warning, so fast I feel dizzy sometimes. It reminds me of that carousel my dad let me go on at the fair one year. I thought it would be fun, all those brightly painted horses with their cute names, and it was at first, but after two minutes I stopped being able to see my dad on each rotation, too disoriented by the spinning. The colours on the horses seemed to glare at me, grow louder, and instead of laughing as they circled round and round their teeth were bared and their eyes white with terror.

I want to get off! I screamed. Dad had to make the man stop the machine.

I want to get off, I now find myself whispering over and over. *I want to get off.*

But I can't. I'm stuck here. So I dive into the only things I know will keep me sane: work and finding out when and how I can hope to have a baby.

There has to be a paper trail, doesn't there? There have to be letters from doctors about test dates and results. But my search of the study, of my office, of anywhere in the house I can think of that might contain important papers, yields nothing. There's nothing. Why the hell not?

After three days of working on projects I think are good, but have no emotional connection to, because I can't remember creating them, and three nights of drifting round my big old house on my own, waiting to hear my husband's key in the lock, the drop of his briefcase on the tiled hall floor, I've had enough. I need to get out of here. I phone Becca.

It goes to answerphone and I leave a short message, but ten minutes later my mobile goes.

'Hey, you!' Becca says brightly. 'What's up?'

'Just phoning for a chat,' I say. 'Isn't it about time we went out for coffee again soon?' I don't know what's been going on in this life, but Becca's always up for a coffee and a chat, so I presume I'm pretty safe in asking.

'Absolutely! And sorry I didn't pick up earlier. I was putting Chloe down.'

I feel cold inside. I want to echo the name, but I know that will sound weird. 'You were?'

'Yeah! Someone said the terrible twos were hard, but they

didn't tell me that it could all start a few months early. It's like waging war with a tiny dictator! Of course, she has her daddy wrapped round her finger, so he's no help and I end up having to be "bad cop" all the time. *So* not fair.' I can hear the smile in her voice as she complains, though, and I suspect she wouldn't have it any other way.

I can't think of anything to say. I'm still too busy absorbing the fact Dan and Becca have a baby. Well, a child, really. My palm comes to rest on my flat stomach and I look down to the emptiness there.

'Listen, do you mind if you come over here for coffee instead of going out? Dan's worried about his deadline, so I really don't want to dump Chloe on him. I'll make a cake as penance, if you like? Coffee and walnut? I know it's your favourite.'

'Dan has a deadline?'

'Yeah, his new editor wants him to change a load of things. He's got months to do it, but you know what he's like … and when that's done they'll start the publishing process! How exciting is that?'

'Do you have a date? For the book?'

'Next year, if all things go well …' she breaks off to sigh quietly. 'I'm so proud of him. I knew he could do it.'

And so did I, I think quietly to myself, but only because you showed me first. Out of the two of us, Becca really is the one who deserves him.

'OK,' she says, snapping me back to the present. 'How about two o'clock on Saturday afternoon? I might even get Chloe to take a nap at that time, then we can really chat.'

I open my mouth to answer, but find it's harder than I expected. I didn't know Dan and Becca had a child when I suggested meeting up. I'm not sure I'm ready for that. Not when my own childless status is stinging so hard, but I also don't know how I can back out without sounding mean.

'Two sounds fine,' I finally say. What else can I do? I can't abandon Becca just because she's got the very thing I want. She's stuck by me through thick and thin. Besides, the more I think about it, the more I want to go.

It might not be my child, but it's a child. A little girl. Sophie was so cute at that age. So maybe I can get my 'baby fix' and that will keep me going for now? I imagine getting down on the floor and playing Lego or Polly Pocket. It used to drive me crazy trying to get all those rubbery little clothes onto that tiny figure but suddenly I'm really looking forward to it. In fact, I jump online and start toy shopping.

CHAPTER FIFTY-EIGHT

I arrive at Becca and Dan's with a large present bag. Becca laughs at it when she opens the door. 'I see you're planning on spoiling your goddaughter rotten. If she turns out to be brat, I'm blaming it all on you. I hope you know that!'

I laugh too, but it is more out of joy than from Becca's quip. Chloe is my goddaughter? Somehow that just makes everything even better. I am tied to her more firmly than I thought.

I hear the squawking of a recalcitrant toddler somewhere in the house and my heart lifts. The same way it used to when I heard Jude's voice, I realise, but I file that little bit of information away, too interested in meeting the creator of the squawk. The closer I've come to this moment since I spoke to Becca on the phone, the more I've realised this might be a bittersweet blessing, but a blessing all the same.

This child is Sophie and Billy's half-sister, in a strange sort of way, so I'm eager to see if I can detect any of them in her.

Becca sighs. 'These will have to save for later,' she says, taking the bag off my hands. 'I've just put her down for a nap, but it sounds as if she's fighting it all the way – as usual.'

I try not to let the disappointment show on my face as

Becca leads me through to the kitchen. I see the spot near the counter where I made my goof with Dan. It was only a short while ago for me, but for them it's been years. I'm glad we obviously moved past that awkward moment.

'Where's Dan?' I ask.

'Oh, he's upstairs, slaving over a hot keyboard,' Becca says. 'He moans about editors and deadlines constantly, but I know he secretly loves it. Just don't get him started on the subject if he comes down to grab a cup of coffee, because he can bore for Britain.'

I feel rush of warmth at the thought of seeing Dan again. I know I haven't quite managed to separate and compartmentalise the feelings from my two lives yet, but I'm on the way. Besides, Dan is an old friend in this life. Even when the process is complete, I should feel a sense of pleasure at seeing him, shouldn't I?

Ten minutes later, I hear feet on the stairs. Unmistakable, heavy feet. The warmth I feel at the sound is more than the glow of seeing an old friend, I realise too late. It spreads upwards, leaving blotches on my chest and colour in my cheeks.

Dan arrives at the kitchen door carrying a blonde-headed child. 'I don't think she's going to give in this afternoon,' he says to Becca. 'She knows someone's here.' And he shoots a smile of greeting my way that makes my cheeks burn even brighter.

I focus instead on the child in his arms. She's angling towards him, hiding her face in his shoulder. The curve at the base of her neck, the way the little cherubic ringlets collect there, reminds me completely of Sophie. I know in an instant this child will be the recipient of the fierce love I've been hoarding in readiness for so many years, that the floodgates have already opened and nothing that spills out can be called back. I know that I will spoil her rotten and maybe I will turn her into a brat, but I will adore her anyway.

'Hi, there!' I say, and smile in her direction. Surely she won't be shy for too long? She must have met me countless times before.

And then she turns, still keeping her head in contact with Dan's shoulder, burrowing into his safety, and gives me a hesitant smile.

My heart is preparing to explode with adoration, but then a weird thing happens. A flickering. It's like when you have two almost-identical images pulled up on a computer screen and you flip between then rapidly, so the some bits stay the same, but other parts alter. I feel a pulling and a pushing inside, like I'm flickering between my two lives – the original one and this one – where I see Dan holding Sophie then Dan carrying Chloe. It happens so fast I feel quivery, and then it settles onto the one image again: Dan with his daughter.

Becca's daughter.

My daughter.

Because Chloe is the spitting image of Sophie.

I don't know how that's possible, given the genetics, but that's what I see. The same brown eyes, the same determined chin. I'm filled with joy and pain in equal measures.

'Look what Aunty Maggie has brought you!' Becca says,

nodding towards the present bag. 'Why don't you go and say thank you?'

Dan puts Chloe down and she runs towards me, her shyness forgotten as her gaze is completely, one hundred per cent, focused on the toy. She pulls a Dora the Explorer doll, still in its box, out of the bag and grins at me. 'Dora!' she says, beaming, and then she remembers herself. 'Tat yoo,' she adds seriously.

I don't say anything back. How can I when the daughter I haven't seen for fifteen years is standing in front of me? And I don't just mean that because Dan is her father she looks strikingly like Sophie. I mean this *is* Sophie. Every look, every mannerism, even the sound of her voice, is exactly the same. More than that, I recognise the intangible 'Sophie-ness' of her. I know without a shadow of a doubt that this is my daughter.

'Good girl for saying thank you so nicely,' Becca says, and Sophie – Chloe – runs off with Dora in her hands, shoves it at her mum and demands to have the packaging broken apart so she can get to the doll.

'Do, Mummy!' she commands and Becca picks her up and laughs.

'What do you say? How do you ask Mummy nicely?'

'Pease, Mummy!' Chloe smiles into Becca's face and adds, 'You so pitty! Pease pitty mummy!'

'That's better!' Becca says, beaming back at her daughter. She sits her on the kitchen counter and reaches for a pair of scissors to do away with the packaging. 'Pretty Mummy is right,' she adds. 'Clever girl!'

Pretty Mummy …

Mummy.

My heart winces at the word.

This can't be real, can it? I'm just imagining this. Superimposing.

Becca hands the package to Dan. It seems to be welded together and so fiendishly tied with wire ties it would take a PhD in engineering to unravel it. Chloe, who is obviously tired, leans against Becca's shoulder, sticks her thumb in her mouth and reaches for a strand of Becca's hair, which she strokes between thumb and middle finger as she keeps her beady eyes on her father's progress.

That's exactly what Sophie used to do with me.

The adrenalin kicks in. The fight or flight response. I've never been much of a one for confrontation, so there's really only one option. 'I need to … I need to …' I mumble and then I run for the bathroom, bypassing the downstairs toilet and haring up onto the first floor. I lean against the door once I've closed it behind me and I discover I'm shaking.

I close my eyes.

This is too cruel. Some sick joke.

My hands press against my belly, as if I should find evidence that a child has been ripped from inside me and presented to someone else, but everything is as it should be. Everything is perfect and intact. Untouched. Uninhabited. Suddenly, I understand why they used to call it being 'barren'.

I can't stay up here all afternoon, though. I use the toilet, wash my hands and splash cold water on my face, before patting it gently dry with a towel so no one will guess that's what I've just done.

When I pull the latch across and emerge onto the landing, Becca is waiting for me.

'Are you OK?' she asks, frowning. 'You rushed off pretty quick there!' And then her expression changes, lights up. 'Don't tell me! It's not … you're not feeling sick, are you?'

I am, but not for the reason she thinks. I shake my head and it feels ten times its normal weight.

'Oh, honey,' Becca says and pulls me into a hug. 'I'm so sorry. I just thought … It'll happen, though. I'm sure it will.'

I nod, but I'm not very convincing.

'I know this is double-edged for you, coming here…' she adds. 'Do you, you know, need a moment before you come back down?'

'No,' I say. 'I'm fine now. Just a blip.'

Becca smiles and leads the way back down the stairs. That was a massive lie I just told, I realise, because as I order my right foot to tread on the next step down, I have no idea how I am going to survive the rest of the afternoon.

CHAPTER FIFTY-NINE

I call Jude's name when I get back home. It reverberates round my lovely three-storey house and boomerangs back to me. I thought I would burst into tears once I got home, let out the sadness I've been keeping at bay all afternoon, but instead I discover I'm really angry.

Even though, logically, I know I'm probably just using him as my scapegoat, I can't help feeling resentful. I want a baby and I don't have one, and that has to be at least partly Jude's fault. After all, I managed to have one with Dan, even if it did take a bit of trying. It's not me. Or it can't be *all* me.

I've had enough. I have to know. I have to find *something* to give me a clue as to why Sophie is sitting in Dan and Becca's kitchen, mushing her mashed potato into their tablecloth instead of mine.

I start my search in the filing cabinet in Jude's office. The bottom drawer is locked, but he always keeps that one for the ultra-important clients who are very particular about privacy, so I don't think anything of it. There's nothing in the other drawers but files on houses and clients, all business stuff. Next, I search the drawers of his desk, and when I've finished that I go and turn over my study-slash-workroom, leafing through all the paperwork until I've inspected the front and back of every last sheet of A4.

Nothing. I find nothing.

I think about Dan, about the easy way he carried Chloe about this afternoon, how he got down on the carpet and played with her for an hour, even though I could tell he was itching to get back upstairs to his book, how he didn't even moan when his daughter spilled Ribena all over his best jeans. In my mind, I try to Photoshop him out of the scene, and put Jude in his place, but Jude's face won't stick. It keeps turning back into Dan.

I make myself stand up and then I go back downstairs, start checking the kitchen drawers for bits of paperwork. Jude arrives home when I'm on drawer number three. There are batteries and old keys, rubber bands and freezer bag clips all over one end of the counter. He looks at them then looks at me. 'What on earth are you doing?'

'Hi honey,' I say sarcastically over my shoulder. 'Lovely to see you too. Yes, I did have a nice day.'

He just gives me 'we're playing this game, are we?' look.

'I'm searching for letters from the doctor,' I explain. 'Or the hospital. About the tests we had done.' We had to have tests done, didn't we? Jude always said we would.

He runs his hand through his hair. 'You know what they said.'

'Maybe I want to see it again in black and white,' I say. 'Maybe I've seen something on the Internet that'll help, and if I can just – '

'Don't do this to yourself,' he tells me. I know he's right, but I can't seem to stop. The fact he's being so reasonable just makes me even angrier. 'There's nothing wrong – with you or me! We just have to wait and – '

'But I don't want to wait anymore! I'm tired of waiting!' I turn and look at him. 'You're sure you've had all the tests? Every last one?'

'We've been through this a million times.'

Maybe the other Maggie has, but I haven't. I *need* this moment.

Jude walks over to the table. It's then I notice the nice bottle of red wine and the big bunch of flowers that's laying there. I didn't even hear him come in until he was right behind me, let alone the rustle of the cellophane as he put them down.

'What are those for?'

He looks at me. 'Don't be like that!'

I realise he thinks I'm suspicious, that maybe I think he's buttering me up because he's done something wrong. 'I'm not,' I say. 'I didn't mean to – '

But Jude isn't listening. My unreasonable mood is infectious. 'I bought them because I know I've been spending a lot of time at the office lately, trying to sell the Eaton Square house, with a total diva at the other end of the deal, and I thought that maybe I'd bring these home and we could have a nice evening in together, but clearly I was wrong!'

I'm shocked, not just about the flowers but because he wants to spend quality time with me. I haven't had much of that vibe off him since I jumped back. Have I been misjudging him? Maybe he just was really busy, maybe even hiding how stressed he was, and I was misinterpreting? I start to say I'm sorry, but Jude isn't in the mood to hear. He storms off out the room moments later I hear his study door slam.

That gives me a sense of déjà vu and it brings me up short.

Two men. Two studies. Two slamming doors. One rather shrewish wife, lashing out at them because she's unhappy and it really isn't their fault. Not completely, anyway.

I'm doing the same thing all over again. Even though I hate this merry-go-round, I have a feeling I'm the one with my hand on the crank keeping it going. Disappointment, blame, resentment. Disappointment, blame, resentment. Over and over until we all want to vomit. Do I really want to go down that road again?

This time I might actually succeed in pushing my man into the arms of another woman, and I don't want that, especially as Jasmine has re-entered our lives. Things went quiet from her for a while when she was doing a big project, travelling a lot, but she's decided to sell her house – it's too big! – and snap up a massive loft in Shoreditch, one with lots of light and space for a studio.

I know she and Jude email. I know he tells her things he doesn't tell me. Not really personal things, I don't think, but there's been a couple of times when we've met up and she's known more about some of Jude's current deals than I have. When I asked him about it, he said it was because she was neutral, not invested in the company either financially or emotionally, and just that she's got a lot of life experience and is very wise.

I pick the flowers up and begin trimming them, putting them in a vase. As I work, using my instinct to guide where the big showy flowers go and where the smaller, more delicate ones fit, I think about how I should deal with this.

The old me would have felt helpless, and all the more angry for it, but the 'now' me has hope. I turned one relationship around, and it was in a far worse state than this one. It was hard work, but not because what I did was complicated.

When it came to Dan and me, the solution was simple: all I needed to do was to be honest, kind, respectful. To see my partner as just that – my team mate – instead of my opponent. It's what we all *think* marriage is about, that we will do effortlessly when we find the right person, but actually is much, much harder than we imagine. It's so much easier to slip into bad habits, to start festering on the little things until they become big, open sores. I needed to *choose* to love, not let my fickle emotions guide me.

So, as I put the vase full of flowers in the middle of the kitchen table and clear away the tissue paper, cellophane and stalks, I choose to love Jude.

And I don't mean I drum up warm and fuzzy feelings inside. I mean I'm going to give him the time he needs to calm down, then I'm going to go and apologise for my part, and I'm going to thank him for bringing me flowers and for trying to make me happy.

And here's the big bit …

I haul in a breath while I think about this.

What if I never have a child with Jude? It makes me queasy just thinking about it, but I make myself do it anyway.

It's hard to believe that Jude's sperm are lazy and unmotivated, but maybe they are. Maybe that bit of his personality was all used up by his brain and business sense and there was nothing left for biology. Maybe we're just not a good match in this department, even if we are in every other.

Does that mean I have to take it out on him for the rest of his life? Or should I just try to find the joy in what I've got? I look around my lovely kitchen, think about my lovely life. I've got a lot.

And fate didn't deal me this hand, this life. I chose it.

So I decide to love Jude no matter what. One hundred per cent. No holds barred. Becca is right. That's what you're supposed to do.

That decided, I find two wine glasses and pour us a little of the Pinot Noir each, and then I walk along the hall to Jude's study and knock softly on the door.

CHAPTER SIXTY

The anniversary of my last jump comes and goes. There's been nothing since. Not even a five-minute skip when I've nodded off on the sofa after a long day at the office. I think I've finally stopped.

I make the trip to Swanham to see Chloe – and Becca and Dan, of course – at least two or three times a month. I have fallen in love again. Hard. That little girl has me completely wrapped around her finger. Becca and Dan tease me about it, and I laugh along, but inside I know I've got to be careful. She's not mine, even though she was once upon a time in a different life.

He's so good with her.

Dan with Chloe, I mean. And Becca, I suppose. I watch them when I visit. Dan isn't one for big, romantic gestures, like surprise trips to Paris or diamond rings, but what he lacks in expense and flair he makes up for in consistency. He brings Becca the cup of tea he always used to bring me. He always kisses her on the cheek when he comes in for the day. It's those things, and a hundred other little things they do for each other, that cement their love in place, that fill the cracks when they start to show. I soak all this information up and then I take it home to Jude. I replicate it in the hope we can gain that easy togetherness they make look so effortless.

They're coming over for lunch today. Of course they're bringing Chloe with them. It was my idea to invite them, to say thank you for all the times they've had me over to their place. Jude gave me a stony look when I suggested it, but he didn't veto. *Whatever you want ...*

He's hidden himself away in his study, even though its Sunday, but he's under strict instructions to be a charming host when our guests arrive. It's the least he can do, given that I don't drag him down to Swanham with me on a regular basis. Today is the first time he's going to meet Chloe and this makes it feel as if it's an important moment.

At noon sharp there's ring on the doorbell. As soon as the door is halfway open a small figure rushes through and attaches herself to my legs, arms clamped firmly round my knees. I laugh and reach down to pick her up.

She releases me only long enough for me to lift her up so she can attach herself just as firmly to my neck, and we walk through the house like that to the back garden, where we've set up an al fresco eating area. It's overcast and a little breezy today, but it should still be pleasant to sit outside. I've made a lot of salads, bought some really nice bread from the Italian deli down the road, and some fillet steaks are marinating in a dish on the kitchen counter. I bought a gas barbecue especially for today. Jude shook his head when he saw it, but I've assured him we'll use it again before the summer is over. A couple of burgers and sausages sit ready just for Chloe. I don't know many two-year-olds who like their meat rare. My other two certainly didn't.

Not my *other* two. My two. I must remember that.

When Chloe spots the other item I splashed out on, sitting on the lawn, a few short steps down from the deck, I'm no longer flavour of the month. She wriggles to get out of my arms and runs joyfully down the steps, Becca calling out after her to be careful, and launches herself onto the mini trampoline waiting there. Delighted squeals echo round the garden and off the high walls of the surrounding houses.

Jude comes out and greets Dan and Becca. I know he doesn't feel comfortable with them, but he does make an effort to be nice. He shakes Dan's hand, asks him how the book writing is going. Before Dan can answer, Becca jumps in, too proud of her husband to let the moment pass uncelebrated. She knows that Dan might have just mumbled something about it going OK.

'We're so excited! The book is coming out in October! The publishers want to wait to catch the Christmas market, and we're having a book launch and everything!'

I turn to look at Dan. 'What? You didn't mention this! Are you having a big swanky party filled with celebrities and everything?'

Dan just laughs. 'Hardly. We're doing something at the bookshop in Swanham, organising it all ourselves. Well, I say "ourselves" but it's Mrs Lewis here that's the driving force behind it.'

'You will come, won't you?' Becca says, looking hopefully at me, then Jude.

'Wouldn't miss it for the world!' I say. 'My best ever chance to hob nob with a famous author …'

Dan rolls his eyes and looks off down the garden. Jude nods, but is saved from responding when there's a shriek of pain from the lawn.

I start running even before I see what's happened. Chloe is lying on the grass. She begins to move, sits up, opens her mouth and wails. *She's OK*, I think as I race down the stairs to the lawn. *She's moving, she's breathing. I just need to get to her…*

But then I am overtaken by Becca as she sprints past me. It's Becca who scoops her up, Becca who shushes her and strokes her hair. My fingers itch to do the same. The fact that I can't be first in that race ever again hits me like a punch in the chest. I heave in a ragged breath and walk over to where Becca is trying to distract Chloe. I've seen enough pre-schooler tumbles to know the upset is more down to the shock of finding herself flying towards the grass than real injury.

Becca is facing away from me, swaying gently as she coos to her daughter, and I can see Chloe's head over the top of her shoulder. There are gluey tears at the corner of her eyes and she's sniffing intermittently. 'Are you OK, sweetie?' I ask, but Chloe doesn't answer. She hides her face in her mother's neck, shuts out the sight of me. I decide I have something I need to check on in the kitchen urgently.

I don't know what I say to Dan, who is heading down from the deck, as I breeze past him. Something about fillet steak, I believe. It's only when I'm standing in front of the open refrigerator, cold air blasting my face, that I manage to breathe properly again.

This isn't healthy, I think to myself. But what are the options? Never see Chloe – or Dan or Becca – again? That's ridiculous! I'm just going to have to find a way of making myself some boundaries. That's the sensible thing to do for all of us.

I pick up a pitcher of homemade lemonade that's sitting in the front of the fridge, place it on a tray and add some glasses. Time to eat, I think. That should keep us all out of trouble.

As dinner progresses I notice Jude hardly interacts with Chloe at all. He winces when she gets so excited about having her burger that she serenades it at the top of her voice, making up a special 'burger song' before she chomps into it, laughing. When a bit of carrot flies in his direction then slides under the table he looks affronted.

I take it personally. How dare he brush her off, not even make an effort? It causes me to wonder if I slid into another reality, one where Chloe was Sophie and Sophie was still mine, would Jude be as rude to her? Would he be like this with our child?

And with that last thought, my anger turns to sadness. Maybe there's a very good reason God or fate or whoever deals with these things hasn't given me a child in this life. I feel the hope I've been trying to hang onto shrivel up until it looks like the dried cranberries in the rice salad.

I stand up. They all look at me. I invent an excuse to go into the kitchen again, which is quickly becoming my place of sanctuary, and when I get there I busy myself getting the meringue roulade out of the fridge, shoving it on a plate and mounding fresh berries around it.

I hear a noise behind me and I turn. I hope it might be Jude coming to check on me, but it's Dan standing there, an empty wine glass in his hand. 'Can I get Becca a refill?' he asks and we smile at each other. We both know Becca won't fetch her own wine if she can get someone else to do it for her.

'Sure,' I say, and pull a bottle of white from the fridge and fill the glass. I expect him to go back outside, but instead he stands there, looking at me.

'Are you OK?'

I feel my eyes fill. I nod.

'You're not,' he says, and the kindness in his eyes is my undoing. 'What's wrong?'

I shrug. Where do I even begin? All the things Dan and I have been through together swirl round my head, but I can't talk about any of them. In this life all we ever were was a romantic blip, a red herring before he found Becca.

'Honestly?'

I realise I've spent too long holding it all back and that even though I can't tell Dan the whole truth, I can tell him the thing that's been buzzing round my head like a bluebottle these past few months.

'Yes, honestly,' he replies. 'We're friends, Maggie. Have been for a long time.' He reaches out and touches my bare arm, gives it a reassuring pat that should be awkward but somehow isn't. 'You can tell me anything.'

Not anything, I think, but maybe this.

I look down at the ring on my left hand. 'It's been a long time since Jude proposed to me, and we don't seem any closer to tying the knot. I suppose I'm worried he doesn't want to marry me anymore.'

'But you always said you were both so busy, that you'd prefer to wait for the time to be right rather than do it in a rush. Wasn't there a waiting list for that castle you wanted for the reception?'

I nod. 'There was. But if we'd booked in the couple of months after we got engaged, we'd married by now. I said those things because that's what you do when you're with someone, don't you? You back them up. You make the excuses, either because you really believe they're going to come through eventually, or because you've got their back.'

Dan gives me a look that tells me he understands.

'So there we have it,' I say. 'I think maybe I'm just not marriage material.' And I mean this in more than the way Dan thinks I do. I mean that even when I am married I'm not sure I'm very good at it. It's taken me almost three lifetimes to realise how selfish I can be.

'Don't be stupid,' he says, laughing my words off. 'Of course you have what it takes! You're talented and creative and kind. You're the sort of person who gives to others – I've seen the way you are with Jude. Let's be honest, I haven't always been his biggest fan, but you bring out the best in him. He'd be crazy not to want to marry you.'

'Really? You mean all of that?'

He smiles at me, that specifically 'Dan' smile, the one where he tips his head a little to the side and his eyes shine. 'Of course. I almost married you myself, didn't I? You can't be that bad!'

I know it's a joke, designed to make me laugh, but it reminds me of that day on the river when he asked me, the way his face looked when I told him I had to think about it, and then the conversation I overheard between him and Becca the night of that horrible dinner party.

I smile back at him. 'It was probably better we didn't. I don't think I was right for you.'

I realise, in the arbitrary phrasing of my words that I've hit upon the real truth. I thought it was all Dan's fault the first time around, but a lot of the blame rested with me.

Dan thinks over what I've said. He stares into his wife's wine glass for a moment, then looks up at me. 'Don't be so hard on yourself,' he says. 'In another life, I think we could have been really happy.'

My nose stings and I nod. 'In another life …'

We're looking at each other, smiling, and then something shifts. It's as if the varnish of friendship, the shell that has kept us safe from the feelings we once had for each other has dissolved. When I look at Dan I don't see my best friend's husband; I see the man I once loved, I once shared my life with. The scary thing is that I know he's looking at me the same way, and there's a sudden jolt of connection between us.

I step back before he does. I break eye contact and nod towards the glass he's holding in his hands. 'You'd better get that back out there,' I say and my smile stretches my cheeks uncomfortably. 'You know how Becca hates warm wine …'

CHAPTER SIXTY-ONE

Dan's book launch is on the Wednesday of the October half-term. I wanted Jude to come with me to be my anchor, something tangible and solid to help me remember which life I've chosen, but he says he's too busy. We planned a holiday together after that talk we had the other week, a trip to Moorea, somewhere tropical and romantic, and he says he has too many deals to close before we leave, so I go on my own.

It's raining hard when I arrive at the bookshop so I scuttle inside. I'm twenty minutes late. I planned to be. I thought it would be easier if the place was full of people already, if it wasn't just me Dan, Becca and the bookshop owner standing around, watching the door.

I know he's seen me the moment I step inside. Ever since the barbecue back in the summer it's been there, an awareness. I know he feels it too. I also know we both dance around the edges, keeping our distance. I wave and smile to Dan, but it's Becca I make eye contact with. It doesn't help the humming feeling that courses through me, though. Not one bit. If anything, it makes it worse.

It's an echo, I tell myself. That's all. And even if it isn't, that's all it can ever be.

I stand at the back when it begins. Dan's editor speaks and then Dan reads a bit from the first chapter. There are a lot of pre-teens here, dragged along by their parents. By the end of the reading, they've lost their world-weary looks and they're leaning forward. When the formal bit is over, they swarm round Dan, eager to get a signed copy. I know it's going to be a while before I can sidle up and offer my congratulations, so I wander off to find Becca. The bookshop is quite small, and when the crowd gathered for the reading it was too packed to make my way over to her.

'He's got real talent,' I say as we smile and watch him talking to a boy, aged around eleven, who gets his mum to take a picture of them both together on her mobile phone.

Becca turns to me. 'Jude couldn't make it then?'

I shake my head.

'What a shocker,' she mutters.

'You still don't like him much, do you?' I ask Becca, but I'm not angry. I think I've come round to the fact that this is as good as it's going to get between them.

Becca looks as if she doesn't want to say anything. 'He's just not my cup of tea,' she eventually replies.

I consider letting her off the hook, but we've never been able to have a calm conversation about Jude, and now I've got the chance I don't want to waste it. 'I just want to understand.'

She gives me a long, hard look and I know her brain is working. I respect the fact she's thinking her answer through instead of blurting it out, that she's tempering her words for my sake. 'I always used to think he was trying to be something he wasn't,' she says, 'with his fake accent and his posh friends. It's as if the rest of us weren't good enough for him. I dunno … Suppose I always thought he was a bit fake.'

I nod. I've always known he was like that. Not fake, really, but he dressed for the part he wanted. 'But he's not faking now,' I say carefully. 'He's a successful man, one who's worked hard to get where he is.'

Becca nods reluctantly. 'I know, he proved me wrong there.' She laughs. 'I always thought he was all mouth and no trousers.'

I laugh too. It's nice to be able to talk about this sensibly, even if we don't see eye to eye, but then I get serious again. 'You still don't like him, though. Why?'

She sends me a pleading look, but I wait.

'You don't want to know the truth,' she says.

A shiver runs through me. I have a feeling she might be right, but I also know that if we don't talk this out at some point it's always going to be a 'thing' between us, the elephant in the room. 'I think I need to,' I reply.

'I was afraid you were going to say that. Hang on.' She motions for one of the helpers – the young, toned PE teacher I'd thought he'd been having an affair with in another life, ironically – to grab another couple of glasses of wine, then hands one to me.

I look down at my glass. 'That bad, huh?' I say, sounding much more light-hearted than I actually feel.

'Always a good idea in sticky situations,' she says grimly.

I take a slug. 'OK,' I say, 'hit me with it.'

She shifts from foot to foot, fixes her gaze on a bookshelf

on the other side of the room. 'You remember you didn't go to the Christmas Ball in our second year at Oaklands and I did?'

I nod. Jude had only broken up with me a fortnight before. I really hadn't been in the mood.

'Well, I went, didn't I?' Becca takes a large, fortifying slurp of wine. 'And so did he.'

My stomach goes cold at her words and I'm sure all the blood has drained from my face.

Becca looks uncomfortable but she carries on. Now the lid is off, it's all spilling out and I don't think she can stop. 'He'd had a few beers, I know that, but I was standing on my own at one point and he came over, draped his arm around my shoulders and said something about what a pity it was we hadn't got to know each other better.'

I know what she's implying; I can see it in her eyes. 'Maybe he was just being friendly?' I suggest weakly.

She shakes her head. 'But it was such a long time ago,' she says, then carries on quickly: 'I just told him to take a hike and he laughed and went back to his friends. He's never done anything like that since – I want you to know that! It was just after that … well, it was a bit hard to warm to him. I'm not good at forgiving people when they've crossed me, and I'm even worse if they do it to someone I love.'

She looks so pained I lean in and give her a hug. 'Thank you for telling me,' I say quietly. 'That can't have been easy.'

I get it now, why Becca won't ever like Jude. Her fierce loyalty to me forbids it. I don't have it in me to be the slightest bit cross with her. In fact, knowing that 'the Queen of TMI' has kept this secret to protect me all these years only makes me love her more.

I also don't know if I can hold it against Jude. I knew he was no angel back then – he's even admitted as much to me, although he's never fessed up to this moment with Becca. Maybe he doesn't even remember it. Or maybe he's ashamed it ever happened. All I know is that when we got back together, when he asked me to run away with him, all that was behind him. I haven't had a reason to doubt him since on that front.

'You OK?' Becca says after we finish hugging.

'Yeah,' I say.

The PE teacher comes up to Becca again then, asking her something about more plastic wine glasses. She rubs my arm and gives me a wink to let me know she'll be back shortly, then scurries off to rummage through a few cardboard boxes they've got hidden under a table.

I see there's a pause in the signing frenzy and Dan is on his own. I decide to congratulate him quickly before I head home. I didn't intend to stay even this long, and I don't think it's a good idea we spend much time together at the moment, at least not until I get my head straight about him. I squeeze my way between some people and slip over the to small table he's sitting at.

He smiles at me as I approach. 'It was wonderful,' I say. 'I was spellbound.'

I see the compliment sink in. I see it means something to him. 'Thank you,' he says.

I open my mouth to take my leave, but Becca rushes over, her mobile in her hand. She brandishes it at us. 'That was the babysitter. She says Chloe woke up and is crying the house down, so I'm going to shoot off…' She glances at the PE teacher. 'I'm sure Kiera is more than capable of holding the fort.'

Dan stands up. 'Do you want me to go with you?'

Becca shakes her head. 'No. This is your night. You make the most of it.'

'OK.' He leans across and kisses her on the cheek. 'I won't be too late.'

'Sam said he was going to drag you down the Three Compasses afterwards,' Becca says, tapping a finger against his chest, 'and you're under strict instructions to let him!'

He grins at her and kisses her again, on the mouth this time. I look away.

Becca starts to head off then turns around. 'Oh, I'm taking the car,' she adds, 'Poor Melanie was beside herself, so I'd better nip back as fast as I can.'

Dan shrugs. 'It's OK. I'll walk.'

'It's tipping down out there!' Becca turns to me. 'Maggie, you'll give him a lift home, won't you? After all, he can't write his next blockbuster if he dies from the flu.' She looks at me expectantly.

'Of course,' I say, because what else can I do?

After Becca heads off, I keep busy by nominating myself Kiera's second in command. I pour drinks, collect empty plastic cups from all around the bookshop, then help box everything up again. Anything to avoid being left alone with Dan.

When Sam and his buddies drag Dan off to the pub to

keep celebrating, I have to tag along too, but I keep on the fringes of the group. We find a large table and I chat to Sam's wife, Geraldine. It's weird; she was an acquaintance in my old life, but in this one we've never talked. I know all sorts of little details about her, but she knows nothing about me.

However, when a group go off to buy another round and a gaggle of ladies head for the loos en masse, I find myself sitting at one end of the table with Dan the only person close enough to talk to.

'How are things?' he asks. 'Jude doing well?'

'We're off on holiday soon, to Tahiti' I say, thinking I sound like I'm having a conversation with my hairdresser, but maybe that's a good thing.

Dan studies me. 'You don't seem to be as excited as you should be about that. Everything OK?'

The same old excuses are on the tip of my tongue, but the look in his eyes causes me to shelve them. 'Things have been better,' I say.

'Between you and Jude?'

I nod.

'I'm sorry,' he says. 'You deserve someone wonderful, someone who would lay down his life to make you happy.'

Someone like you? I want to ask, but I keep my question to myself. It's the wrong question, the wrong man. It strikes me that the tables had been turned in my other life and I'd opened up to Jude about my marriage with Dan, he'd have seen it as an opportunity to score points, to preen his feathers and paint himself as the better man. Dan doesn't care about that. He just cares about me, how I feel. He's actually *listening*.

I have the feeling that if I wanted to pour my heart out to him for the next hour, he'd let me. He'd sit here, taking it all in, asking gentle questions when needed. He wouldn't get twitchy, wanting to check his BlackBerry after ten minutes. Dan sees the real me.

I'm not sure Jude does any more. I think he sees the gloss and sheen, the designer clothes, the good businesswoman. I have this horrible feeling that I have become just another one of his glitzy accessories.

'Long-term relationships are hard,' I say philosophically. 'But you can't give up, can you? You've got to keep trying.' I'm tired of talking about me and Jude now. I'm going to think about that on our holiday, our planned time-out to start filling the cracks and make things good as new again.

'How about you?' I ask. 'How are you doing?'

Dan frowns. 'All the writing stuff is exciting but I'm also tired. Very, very tired. Trying to hold down a job, find time to write, which I can no longer just play at – I have deadlines and everything – and having a little one in the house, it's …' he trails off, lost in thought.

'Exhausting,' I finish for him after he trails off. Somehow I knew that was the word he was going to pick.

'Exactly,' he says, nodding.

I take a sip of my mineral water. 'But Becca's wonderfully supportive,' I say. 'She's your biggest fan.'

He nods again, but this time there's less conviction in it. 'But like you say, long-term relationships can be tough.' He looks across at me, right into my eyes. 'Has Becca said anything to you?'

'About what?' I reply.

'Us. I dunno … we just seem to bicker a lot these days. I mean, we still love each other and everything, but it's not the same as it once was. Becca puts a good face on it, but I know she's thinks we're drifting apart. It's hard on her when I'm stretched in so many different directions. I thought she might have confided in you, that you'd be able to give me some advice?'

I shake my head. 'She hasn't breathed a word.' Which is odd in itself, I realise. I wonder why she hasn't confided in me? 'The early years of having kids are tough,' I tell him, and then I realise it must sound as if I'm preaching about something I have no experience of, so I add, 'Or so some of my friends say. You've just got to find a way to keep the romance alive.'

'You're right. That's it. I think we've lost some of that magic, that spark.'

Dan is looking into my eyes now. The air in this tiny corner of the pub has thickened around us. I realise that talking about magic and spark has made him remember our relationship, because that's all it was to him – magic and spark. It never had a chance to grow into anything deeper or more complex.

I'm his Jude, I realise. The one that got away. His *if only* …

And that is a very dangerous thing to be. I yawn, wide and deliberate, hoping Dan is going to catch the lifeline I'm sending him.

'I'm keeping you up,' he says, taking his cue. 'You didn't intend to be my chauffeur this evening, and you've got a long drive home. I should make a move …'

My smile of thanks is thin and weary.

Dan does the round of his pals then, saying his goodbyes, and we walk five minutes back into the town centre to where I left my car. We don't say anything on the drive back to his house, but I can smell his aftershave in the confined space of the car, I can feel the heat of his arm near mine when I reach to move the gearstick.

I pull up outside his and Becca's house but I don't make a move to get out, even though the lights are on downstairs.

'Thanks,' he says, 'for coming to support me, for being there.' Then he leans in and kisses my cheek. It's if we're two magnets stuck in each other's force field and I have to concentrate hard to pull away.

'Bye,' I say without looking at him and he slides from the car without saying another word.

I drive away, aware of the cold space where he had just been sitting and my hands are shaking. I'm scared. I know he loves Becca, that he would never do anything to hurt her, and neither would I, but I can't pretend this isn't there, that it isn't growing stronger each time I see him. I don't know what to do.

As I head off back up the A21, my beams on full, because I seem to be the only car on the road, snatches of memories from the evening play through my mind at random: Dan's smile when he first saw me, the look of pride on Becca's face while he did his reading, the iciness in my stomach after she'd delivered her bombshell about Jude.

I wish she'd told me before, because then I could have processed it, moved on, but the way things are between us now …

I decide it's better not to think about it, and I try to do that, to clear my mind and just concentrate on the road. It works for a while, but by the time I hit the London suburbs my imagination starts to wander again.

I see us all back in my garden on the afternoon of the barbecue. I play that scene in the kitchen over and over in my head. We start off with the right partners, but by the end of my private movie show the players have switched, and when the guests wave goodbye and thank the hosts for the lovely afternoon, the mother who picks a sleepy Chloe up and carries her down the path is me. It's me that Dan puts his arm around and kisses before he goes to sort the car seat out.

I know that I could do it if I wanted to. He and Becca are at a vulnerable time in their relationship, a time when it's easy to get the balance wrong and when that happens, other things – other people – can slip in under the radar. A marriage can go wrong before you even know it. I could use my 'insider info' on Dan to make that pull we're both feeling stronger.

I'd have Chloe, then. On weekends, anyway, when Dan would go and pick her up from Becca, and we'd take her to the park and be like a proper family …

I indicate swiftly and pull in to the edge of the road, almost slamming on the brakes, and then I get out of the car and walk down the pavement. It's not raining here and I need the chilly evening air to slap me out of my twisted fantasy. I'm horrified I even let myself think that.

I wander around with my cardigan clutched tight around me to keep out the cold. It's ten minutes before I'm ready to climb back in the car. Even then I'm worried the ghosts of my terrible daydream will be there waiting for me, but when I sit back in the driver's seat everything feels calm and normal. I turn on the radio and listen to some people discussing a political subject I have no knowledge of. It fills the space nicely.

As I near Notting Hill, I'm reminded of what Becca said to me all those years ago about my haircut: *one of these days you're going to have to make your mind up and decide what you really want, none of this flip-flopping between different choices.*

It's time for it to stop once and for all.

CHAPTER SIXTY-TWO

The next time I see Dan and Becca, it's Chloe's third birthday party. I could have cried off saying I needed to pack for my holiday tomorrow, but I don't. I need to see Chloe one last time.

And it will be the last time.

I can't do this anymore. Not to myself and certainly not to them. I've let myself get too close. I've started wanting things I shouldn't. Oh, I'm not a real threat to their relationship yet – I don't flatter myself that much – but I could be, and I love them both too much to do that to them.

At first I keep out of Dan's way, going into the kitchen to help myself to a drink I don't really want when he's in the living room, slipping into the hall and back into the dining room when he wanders into the kitchen, but eventually I run out of places to hide and we bump into each other just outside the kitchen door.

'Hi,' he says.

'Hi,' I say back.

We stand there for almost ages talking books and storylines, about the fact his publisher is keen to have the next book soon and that he's considering tweaking the over-arching plot.

I know I should probably make an excuse and walk away, but I'm allowing myself this little luxury, because I'm going to be easing myself out of their lives after today. It's nice to talk to a man who thinks you're talented and creative and kind, who looks at you as if you're fascinating, as if there's nowhere else he'd rather be…

'Dan!' Becca marches up.

He snaps to attention. 'Yup?'

'I've been calling you for, like, two minutes! It's time to cut the cake.' She looks down at his empty hands. 'Where's the video camera? You said you were going to get it half an hour ago.'

'Sorry,' Dan says, and shoots me a conspiratorial look. 'Got caught up talking time-travelling teenagers!' And he scurries off up the stairs. Becca watches him go. I feel a swirling inside me, the horrible stomach acid only a good dose of guilt can create.

'It was kind of my fault, I say. 'I shouldn't have got him started.'

'Yeah, whatever.' Becca frowns and keeps her eyes on the stairs until Dan comes back down them, camcorder in hand. Before she heads off back to the kitchen, I put a hand on her arm. She finally looks at me.

'Are you OK?' I ask. She seems very sombre for Becca, especially Becca at a birthday party.

She looks long and hard at me and then through the door at Dan, where he's trying to find the best spot to stand to catch the best candle action. 'Yeah… It's just been a hectic day.'

I watch her go, and then I go and stand at the fringes of

the crowd to cheer Chloe on as she blows out her candles and all her little friends squeal with delight. I try to catch her attention a couple of times, to give her a birthday hug, but she and the other kids are a hyperactive tornado, ripping through the downstairs of Dan and Becca's house and occasionally spilling into the garden and then having to be brought back in again because it's started to rain.

I wander round the party, not talking to any of other parents. What have I got in common with them that I can discuss in this life? Nothing. As I pass clusters of other women my age it's all conversations about good primary schools and potty training.

Across the room I see Dan and Becca deep in conversation. They seem be … well, not exactly arguing, but there's tension between them. Becca glances in my direction, and my stomach rolls.

I'm kidding myself that I can hang around here this afternoon and pretend it's just another day. I turn and walk back into the hallway. I see my coat on the rack near the door and before I know it I'm putting it on, then I weave through the crowd to where Becca and Dan are standing and they break off their mildly heated discussion to look at me. 'I'd better head off,' I say with a tight smile. 'Packing and all that.'

I give Becca a hug, even though I know she's not one hundred per cent in the mood for it, and as I hold her, I close my eyes and try not to cry. I want to hold her longer, because I know this has to be goodbye, and not just the affectionate gesture that says 'until I see you next time'. It's the only thing I can do.

I don't even look at Dan as I give him a lightning, split-second one-armed hug, and then I go and find Chloe. I wish I could breathe her in, hold her for at least an hour, but she gets distracted by a balloon that's been batted above our heads and she runs off laughing, trying to catch it.

Goodbye, Sophie, I whisper inside my head, and then I run out of the house and into the car. I drive round the corner, yank the handbrake on and then cry with my head against the steering wheel until the tears won't come any more.

CHAPTER SIXTY-THREE

Jude and I are due to leave for the airport at five tomorrow morning and I can't find the travel insurance documents. I hunt in the study, because I knew Jude used them for a trip to Dubai to see a prospective client, but I can't find them on his desk or in his filing.

I know I'm probably fussing about nothing but I need to keep myself busy, otherwise I will stew too much on the awful decision I've just made.

I'm still trying to work out how to do it. Becca is going to be hurt if I just cut off all contact, but I can't see any other way. I can't risk pulling back slowly, seeing them every now and then. I've considered engineering a fight, but that option seems too calculating and cruel, and even then it might not be a permanent solution. Goodness knows Becca and I have had our differences over the years, but we always find our way back to each other. One or both of us realises we've been stupid and we make up.

I can't let that happen this time.

I'm falling in love with her husband – my husband – all over again.

I pause as tears sting the backs of my eyes. I know it's true.

It's been creeping up on me for such a long time. I feel terrible that I feel this way, but I didn't choose it and this is the only way I can think of to stop it.

I swipe a tear away and carry on searching for the stupid travel insurance papers. I feel like it's a triple blow. I know Dan isn't mine to lose but I'll still miss him horribly, and then I'm also losing my best friend and my daughter, or my 'should have been' daughter, at the same time.

All I have left is Jude. I've been trying so hard to love him the best way I know how. I've been trying to turn things around but I have to admit that it's not working, not the way I want it to. That's why I'm focussing on this holiday. Maybe this is the fresh start we need to get things back on track.

I text Jude to ask him where the insurance stuff is, but he's not replying. I end up staring at his computer as I try to work out what to do next, and that's when it hits me: I'll just go online and download the policy booklet with all the phone numbers and terms and conditions in it! That's all I need, really, because I've got a note of the policy number already.

I turn Jude's computer on and when it's booted up a whole host of windows pop open. He never bothers to close all the programmes down when he turns off, usually because he's in a hurry, so they all just helpfully re-open themselves when he comes back to it. As well as various web pages and text documents, the last thing that pops open is his mail programme. I'm pushing the cursor to the corner of the screen to close it down when I notice something out of the corner of my eye.

An email. From Dr Hausfield in Harley Street.

I don't recognise that name. As far as I know the only doctor either of us has seen in the last few years is Dr Shaw, the fertility specialist, and that hasn't been for some time. Cold shoots through me. Either this is good or it's very, very bad.

Jude might have contacted another specialist … Maybe to do with the IVF treatment I so desperately wanted but he wasn't sure about. Or there is another option: Jude is ill, with something he wants to keep quiet about, which can't be good.

I have to know. I can't lose him too. Not now.

I don't actually have to click on the email to read it. All I have to do is look to the reading pane on the right.

Oh, God, I think as my eyes scan over the brief message.

Oh, Jude …

What have you done? What have you done!

I'm sitting in Jude's office chair, waiting for him, when he comes in. I know he's not going to come looking for me in the kitchen or the living room, to give me a kiss or make me a cup of tea. This is the place he always heads for first. I want to confront him at the scene of the crime. I want to see his face when he looks at the computer screen and realises I know.

Jude jumps when he sees me sitting here. I get a tiny sadistic kick of triumph, enough to bolster me for what's to come. 'Who's Doctor Hausfield?'

He tries to hide his shock. I can see his brain working away furiously, trying to guess how much I know. I'm not in the mood for a game of cat and mouse, so I press the space bar on his keyboard to wake the screen up. When he sees his email program light up, he swallows.

'Meg – '

'D'you know, I've really started to hate it when you call me that. My name's Maggie. Only that was never good enough for you, was it?' I stop myself, take a breath. I'm getting side-tracked. I need to stick to the issue at hand. Jude is staring at me. I don't think I've ever seen him so blind-sided. 'You haven't answered my question.'

'Erm … I …'

I wiggle the mouse, bring up the Internet browser. 'All I need to do is a little googling,' I say. 'You might as well tell me.'

Jude swallows again. 'He's a urologist.'

'And you were contacting him about …?'

He gives me a *Are you really going to make me do this?* look.

I stare back at him. Yes, I am.

When Jude bottles out, I push on. 'You went to see him about having a vasectomy, didn't you? This email – ' I wave in the direction of the screen ' – is asking if you're ready to book the procedure. So are you, Jude? Are you?'

He steps back, looks slightly offended, as if I'm wrong to raise my voice at him. 'I didn't do anything. I just …'

I stand up and walk towards him. 'You just talked to him about it.' My voice is low, calm.

He nods. 'Yes, that's all.' He even tries a smile, thinking he's managing to turn this around. He really should have paid more attention to me during our fifteen-year relationship. If he had, he might know that when my voice gets all soft and nice like this, it's time to get worried.

'Instead of talking to *me* about it?'

He sees too late the trap he's walked into. There is panic in his eyes. 'Listen, Meg – '

'Maggie!' I yell back at him. 'You *know* how much I want a child!'

'But I've never been sure … you know that! I've tried to be ready, but if you really want the truth, I'm not sure I'm cut out for it. I don't think I want to be a father.'

I shake my head. He doesn't get it. And the fact he doesn't has made my decision about where we go from here inevitable. He has taken my choice away. I start to cry.

'I've been patient up until now, haven't I? If you'd come to me and told me this, I would have listened,' I say, and then I pause for a moment, while I gather all the facts up in my head and test them for their truth. 'You know what? I think I might even have gone along with it if you'd been honest with me. I loved you that much. It would have broken my heart but I would have tried to do what was best for both of us.'

'I'm telling you now. Isn't that enough?'

I shake my head. 'It's too late.'

That's when he really starts to look panicked. 'Too late? What do you mean?'

'All this time you've been lying to me …'

'I didn't lie! I just didn't tell you.'

I walk up to him until our chests are only inches apart and I drop my voice to a whisper. 'And when were you going to tell me? After the op? Or were you just going to keep it your little secret? Pretend the doctor had told you you're firing blanks and hope I didn't ask too many questions?'

I see the guilt written all over his face.

That's when I leave him standing there so I can run upstairs. I make a quick phone call and then I pull a suitcase out of the wardrobe and start flinging clothes into it. Jude tries to stop me, taking things out, but I just slap his hand away and throw them back in again. The tears are coming thick and fast now. I can hardly see what I'm packing but I don't even care. 'It was the *one* thing I really wanted from you! And you couldn't even give me that? Worse than that, you went behind my back, you were ready to lie to me for the rest of our lives!'

Jude doesn't answer. He just stands there looking sombre. I think he's finally caught on to the fact there's nothing he can say to help himself. Not now. Not tonight. Or ever, really. He's crossed a line that can't be uncrossed.

I'm going to leave tonight and I'm not coming back. That's the truth. I understand now about the give and take, the 'love is patient, love is kind' stuff. I understand why it was disastrous for Becca and Grant, and why, as hard as I try, it will never work for me and Jude.

It's simple, really, when you figure it out.

It has to be equal, that's all. You *both* have to be prepared to do it, otherwise it creates an imbalance. I'm not saying it has to be perfect, mind you. I mean, even Dan and Becca still hit their speed bumps. What I'm saying is that both parties have to be willing to try.

And Jude just isn't. I'm not sure if it's me or that he doesn't have it in him, but what he wants will always come first. I think I've known that for a long time but I just haven't wanted to face it. However, tonight has given me solid and unalterable proof. That's why I can't stay. That's why I'm walking away from this life I chose. If it wasn't so sad it would be funny – the drive that drew me to him in the first place is going to be the final nail in our coffin.

I zip the case closed and then I pick it up off the bed, drop it on the floor and wheel it out of the room. 'Goodbye, Jude.'

'Maggie! Wait!'

I don't wait, though. Jude wants to make a deal. He wants to come up with a offer that will make it all go away, but he's already proved he has nothing else to give me.

The cab I called for before I started packing is waiting for me outside. I tell the driver to take me to the Hamilton Hotel. If I'm going to cry my heart out, I might as well do it on Egyptian cotton sheets. I'll be sending Jude the bill, after all …

CHAPTER SIXTY-FOUR

I can't sleep. I've taken a whole suite at the Hamilton, one that comes complete with a private terrace, so at five in the morning I put my coat on and head out there. I stand with my hands on the railing and look out over the quiet city streets. A pigeon lands on the other end of the rail and tilts its head, its beady eyes blinking at me.

The occasional cab or night bus trundles down the street outside the hotel, their engines loud and rumbly in the early morning quiet, and I wonder who those people are and where they're going, and if they understand they're lucky that they know where they're going.

Because I don't know where I'm going next. I haven't the foggiest clue.

It's strange, when this whole weird experience began it didn't even occur to me to that I might end up with neither of the men who've featured so heavily in my life – all my lives. That was probably pretty stupid of me.

Anyway, I'm here now.

I'm tempted to wish I could go back and do it all again, choose differently next time, but that's what I thought I'd already done and I still messed it up. I still didn't work it all out until it was too late.

I look up at the sky. *Are you having a good laugh?* I ask. *Because someone ought to be laughing about this, and it certainly isn't me.*

But then I calm down. I can't blame anyone else, celestial or otherwise, for the mistakes I made, for the things that were right in front of my face that I couldn't see.

I laugh out loud and it scares the pigeon away.

It's only now I've let go of all of it that I can see the truth. It was never about Jude or Dan, choosing the right man so I could be happy. It was never about *who* I loved. It was always about *how* I loved, that's what made the difference.

I sigh and turn to walk back inside. My legs are bare under my coat and it's flipping freezing out here.

My future is bare and clean, like a huge white room with nothing in it. It's up to me to decide how to decorate it. All I can do now is take what I've learned and bring it with me, because that's the only luggage I'll truly need.

CHAPTER SIXTY-FIVE

I have that weird feeling again as I start to wake up, that sense that I'm not where I'm supposed to be. I flop over onto my back, keeping my eyes closed. Of course I feel that way. I'm in a hotel room. No wonder it feels unfamiliar, not like home.

But as I lie breathing, I hear noises. The kind of noises one doesn't normally hear in a hotel. I hear banging kitchen cabinets and a letterbox clanging as someone pulls a newspaper through it, and then I hear whistling ...

I hear whistling.

I sit up, open my eyes and jump out of bed. I don't care that I'm only wearing a pyjama top and knickers, I dash out the bedroom door and across the landing.

Because it's *Dan* I can hear whistling.

I look up, imagining the sky above the concrete tiles on our roof. *Thank you, thank you, thank you! I don't know why you gave me a second chance, but you did!*

I almost want to cry. I've jumped again, and this time I'm back with the man I love, the man who loves me back, and my own little Billy ...

I run down the stairs at full pelt then skid to a halt in the kitchen, wearing a smile so huge it hardly fits on my face.

But that's when I realise my brain hasn't been firing on all cylinders, that I was so surprised and excited that I've missed some pretty vital information I should have picked up along the way.

'Maggie? Why the heck are you grinning like that?' Dan checks himself over. 'Have I got toothpaste on my face or something?'

I was going to throw myself at him, but now I can't seem to move. I shake my head, eyes wide.

'Then *what*?' He wasn't smiling along with me to start off with, and he definitely isn't smiling now. Because this isn't happy soon-to-be author Dan I recently left behind. This is *my* Dan. The original Dan. The one who hates me.

I look down and check my legs, spot the cellulite and thread veins. No longer are they smooth and regularly pampered with spa treatments; they are slightly chubby and more than a little fuzzy.

Yep. There's no doubt about it.

I'm back.

CHAPTER SIXTY-SIX

'So are we going to this reunion tonight, or what?' Dan asks as he munches on a piece of toast. 'You said you weren't but when I checked the Facebook group you were on the list of people going.'

'You checked the Facebook group?'

He nods and swallows. 'Rick contacted me and said he's up for it. I thought it might be fun.' He looks at me, waiting. I just nod. There are lots of thoughts in my head, just no sensible words.

'So we're going then?'

I nod again.

'You're sure?' He regards me suspiciously, as if my agreement has come too easily, as if he expects me to argue with him as a matter of course. 'And it's not going to be my fault somehow if you have a rubbish time and wish you hadn't gone?'

'No,' I say softly, 'of course not.'

Dan makes a grunt and the expression on his face as he goes to brush his teeth is quite clearly, *Yeah, right!*

I'm standing in the middle of the kitchen – our rather untidy kitchen, it has to be said – when he comes back down again. He mumbles something about needing to go to the library and then leans in to give me the habitual peck on the cheek. He obviously hasn't shaved for a day or two, because the pale stubble along his jaw jabs me. I don't flinch. I don't do anything.

But as he's moving away, my hand shoots out and I grab his arm. 'Wait.'

He turns, puzzled. I look him in the eyes. I mean, properly look him in the eyes, not just glance in his direction, and then I rise up on my toes and press a soft kiss to his lips. 'See you later,' I whisper.

I see the question marks in his eyes as he pulls away, the crease on his forehead, but I don't see disgust, just surprise, and for that I am grateful.

After Dan has left, I wander back upstairs and get dressed. I realise I don't like many of my clothes any more. They all seem old and washed out of shape. I wonder what on earth I've got that I could wear to the reunion tonight. Fixating on that one thing, pulling everything from my tiny wardrobe and the cases under the bed that contain the overspill, helps. It gives me time to think, time to process.

Is this real? Am I actually here?

And if I am, what the heck was the rest of it? A dream? That's far too Pam Ewing for my taste.

The honest answer is I have no idea. The one thing I do know, down in my gut, is that this is it, the end. I can feel it the same way as you can when your car slides on fresh snow and then you find salted tarmac again. I'm gripped to this life now.

I can't find anything to wear so I phone Becca. It's Saturday, after all, and there's nothing she loves more than an impromptu shopping emergency. An hour and a half later, I'm parking at Bluewater.

She's sitting outside our usual cafe, waiting for me. I was deliberately twenty-five minutes late. I hug her fiercely when I see her. She laughs and asks me what the bear hug is in aid of but I just shake my head. 'Just 'cos you're my best friend and I love you. Now, let's shop 'til we drop!'

Becca instinctively heads for M&S. She usually jokes that as well as lines called Per Una and Autograph, they should have a line called Plain, Practical and Boring, because I'd choose clothes from it all the time, but I pull her into a smaller store before we get there. I just saw a petrol-blue dress in the window that reminds me of one I had in my life with Jude.

Obviously, I have to get a bigger size, but I'm surprised how much it flatters, given how figure-hugging it is. We buy bright-red shoes for a pop of colour and I pick up some new make-up too. Becca can't stop shaking her head and looking at me. 'What's got into you?' she keeps saying but she's clearly delighted that something has.

'Only got one life to live,' I say as I throw the bags in the boot of my car. 'Might as well make the most of it.'

I find a note from Dan saying he's gone into town for something when I get back, so I go and get dressed and ready. I'm walking back down the stairs when he crashes through the front door just after six, and he's so surprised when he sees me that he actually puts his shoes in the shoe tidy.

'Wow!' he says. 'You look …' He just stares after me as I walk past him and into the kitchen.

'Thank you!' I shoot back.

'Do you need help with the zip?' he asks.

I nod. As I walked past him he must have spotted that I hadn't been able to contort myself enough to manage the last two inches. I pop my new handbag on the table and turn, lifting my hair up so he has easy access to the zip. His fingers brush accidentally, softly, across the skin there as he pulls it up. I turn round and face him.

'You never know,' I say as I look at him from under my lashes. 'I might need help getting out of it later on too.'

I never actually thought you could actually see someone's jaw drop, but Dan's does it. His mouth stays closed, but the muscles around it go slack. I smile to myself and turn away.

'You'd better get going,' I say, glancing up to our bedroom. 'We need to leave at half past.' Dan turns and sprints up the stairs. Two minutes later I hear the shower running. Fifteen minutes later he's back downstairs in his best black jeans and doing up the buttons on his chambray shirt, hair still slightly damp. That colour always did suit him.

We're just about to step out the door when my mobile rings. Dan gives me a nod indicating he'll drive, so I pluck it out of my handbag and answer.

'Mum?'

A firework goes off inside my chest.

'Mum? Are you there?'

I grin at the phone. I can't help it. 'Yes, darling. I can hear you.' I want to laugh and cry and jump around like a lunatic so the net-curtain-twitching neighbours are talking about it for weeks.

'OK, I'm going to have to be quick.'

I get into the car and close the door as I listen. 'Me too. Dad and I are going out.'

There's a bit of a stunned silence but then Sophie collects herself. 'Now, don't be cross, but the rest of the guys want to go up to the islands after we've been to Ullapool. Lewis, I think, to see some standing stones, and I know I said I'd be home in three weeks, but I'd really like to go with them.'

I imagine her chewing her lip and frowning. I can't wait to see her again. Every selfish part of me wants to tell her to forget flipping standing stones, they've been there for thousands of years and they'll probably still be there next summer, just jump on a train now and come home!

'How much longer?' I ask.

I hear the hesitation in her voice. 'Another week? Maybe two?'

I sigh. 'Then you'd better buy me an extra big bag of tablet before you come home. And I'm not joking! I want to eat my own bodyweight in sugar.'

Sophie's laugh is the best thing I've heard in three lifetimes. 'I will! You wait and see! Thank you, Mum! I love you!'

'I love you, too, sweetie,' I say, and then she's gone. I know that even though the connection has been cut, we're both still smiling.

I can see Dan looking over at me from the driver's seat. He keeps glancing my way. I know he's thinking about how I fought tooth and nail with Sophie about how long she was away, that I'd whittled her original plans from six weeks down to four. I can hear him thinking the same thing Becca did this afternoon: *What's got into you?*

Me, I think. *I've* got into me. Finally. Because, for a long time, I think I was missing in action.

CHAPTER SIXTY-SEVEN

The reunion is in the large panelled room at the front of Oaklands House. It was our common room when we were students there, but now the battered chairs and ring-marked coffee tables are gone, replaced by nice carpet and waiters with trays of wine glasses. The powers that be have obviously decided it's too nice to let the students loose in any more.

Becca, predictably, wasn't waiting for us in the car park as we'd arranged. She's running late, she said, and she's got a surprise for us and that we should go ahead without her. So that's what Dan and I do.

There's a group of people I recognise instantly as I walk through the door, art-course friends, and they squeal when they see me. Dan spots his old flatmate, Rick. We nod to each other and split up and go separate directions.

'Oh, my God!' Francesca Withers says. 'Is that Dan? You're still with him?'

I nod. 'Yes.'

I'm still with him. For richer, for poorer. For better, for worse. Although I'm hoping we've had enough of 'worse' and we can tip the scale in the other direction. I look over to where he's standing with Rick. They're laughing stupidly at something Rick has just said and they both look as goofy as they did at nineteen, except Rick has hardly any hair now.

I know it's not going to be easy. I know Dan and I are going to have tough times ahead, but I have something now that I didn't have when I was here last. Hope. We've turned it around once before. I know we've got it in us.

There's a commotion near the door and without even looking I know it's Becca making an entrance. I turn and smile, and then I smile harder, because she's not alone. She's got a rather nice-looking man in tow, and he's 'glowing' just as hard as she is.

'I want you to meet Sy,' she says as she sweeps up to the group I'm with.

I smile at Mystery Man and kiss his cheek. 'I thought you couldn't make it?'

He shrugs. 'Shuffled a few things around.' He gazes adoringly at Becca. 'She's a special lady. I wanted to be here for her because I knew she was nervous.'

'Yes, she is special,' I reply. 'And I'm glad you're taking care of her, because if you don't, I may have to track you down and hurt you.'

Sy laughs, but he nods good-naturedly. Warning received and understood. However, I have a feeling she's hit gold this time. I don't get a chance to tell her that yet, though, because she spots someone she knows across the room and screams, 'Danny Fierro! How are you, you old tart?' and rushes over to him and they air kiss loudly and begin trying to catch up on the last twenty-five years in fifteen seconds. I always did think drama students had a volume that was one notch louder than everyone else's.

I work my way round the room, saying hello to people, even making new acquaintances – people I think I will get on with now, even if we had nothing in common back when we were twenty – and I don't want to go and hide in the corner once.

That's the one legacy from my life with Jude that I will guard closely. I may not have done anything remarkable in this life. Yet. But I know I have potential, and for now that seems to be enough for me.

Eventually, I find my way back to Dan, who has been cornered by Becca and Sy as they were doing the rounds.

'So what do you do?' Sy is asking Dan.

'I'm an English teacher,' Dan says. 'Very boring, really. Lots of Shakespeare, kids sleeping through my classes …'

Everyone laughs, as they're supposed to.

'But he's a writer too,' I say, as I turn to look at my husband. 'Aren't you?'

Dan looks paralysed, as if he's trying to work out if this is just a lucky guess.

'Don't tell me you haven't been secretly working on a novel for the last year or so,' I tell him. 'Because I won't believe you.'

'A novel!' Becca squeals. 'You dark horse, you! What's it about?'

I jump in before he can answer. 'Don't disrupt the creative process by making him spill the beans yet. He'll tell us when he's ready, won't you, Dan?'

Dan is looking at me as if he can't quite believe what he's

hearing, but he nods. I hail a passing waiter and grab a couple of wine glasses. I hand one to Dan and we wait while Becca and Sy get refills too, then we all clink glasses. 'Whatever it is, it's going to be brilliant,' I say, 'and when Dan hits the bestseller lists, I'm having full body liposuction and that's that!'

We all laugh, but Dan slides his arm around my waist and leans in. 'Thank you,' he whispers into my ear. 'How did you find out?'

I smile sweetly at him. 'I have my ways and means.'

'And you don't mind?'

I shake my head. 'Not if it makes you happy.' My face crumples slightly as I discover unexpected tears springing to my eyes and I hold them back.

For the first time today, maybe even for years, my husband looks me in the eye, no barriers, no filters. 'I love you,' he says simply.

'Me too,' I say and lace my fingers with his. 'I don't know about you, but I think I'm ready to leave now.'

'Whatever you want …'

Those words, said so differently, in a different voice, don't wound as they once did, but they seem to have power to conjure up more than just bad memories, because, as we say our goodbyes, Dan stops and frowns at something on the other side of the room.

I turn my head and it seems to happen in slow motion.

Jude.

He looks just as I left him about twenty-four hours ago but at the same time he's a stranger. A slim woman is on his arm, literally hanging onto him and not just his words. Another version of me. Although she's blonde and taller, but I see the same look in her eyes, the same fear that he's not quite hers and might never be. *Good luck,* I whisper silently in her direction. *You're going to need it.*

Dan's gruff voice cuts in beside me. 'I suppose you want to go over and say hello?'

I take a long moment looking over at Jude. He lifts his head and spots me. I see recognition in his eyes, maybe even a glint of interest, but I turn away.

'No,' I say as I take my husband's hand. 'Let's go home.'

ACKNOWLEDGEMENTS

Huge thanks to my wonderful editor, Anna Baggaley, for being so enthusiastic and supportive when I wanted to try something a little different, and making it easy for me to jump outside my comfort zone. I also want to thank the whole team at HQ. I'm very excited to be one of your authors and I appreciate all the hard work you all put in on my behalf. Thanks also to my agent, Lizzy Kremer, and all at David Higham Associates.

And much love to my husband, Andy – I couldn't have written this book without you. You've stuck by my side for twenty-seven years, through the highs and the lows, and you never complain when I bore you to tears about plotting and turning points, or ramble on about the people who live inside my head as if they're real.

Writers spend a lot of time on their own, but if they're sensible, they find a crew of like-minded lunatics around to cheer them on. Many thanks to the ladies who bring me sunshine, sanity and a kick up the butt (and sometimes wine!) when I need it – Susan Wilson, Heidi Rice, Daisy Cummins, Iona Grey and Donna Alward.

HQ
One Place. Many Stories

The home of bold, innovative
and empowering publishing.

Follow us online

 @HQStories

 @HQStories

 HQStories

 HQ Stories

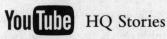 HQMusic

HQ_SM